Patrick O'Brian is the author of the acclaimed Aubrey-Maturin tales and the biographer of Joseph Banks and Picasso. He translated many works from French into English, among them the novels and memoirs of Simone de Beauvoir and the first volume of Jean Lacouture's biography of Charles de Gaulle. In 1995 he was the first recipient of the Heywood Hill Prize for a lifetime's contribution to literature. In the same year he was awarded the CBE. In 1997 he was awarded an honorary doctorate of letters by Trinity College, Dublin. He died in January 2000 at the age of 85.

The Works of Patrick O'Brian

The Aubrey/Maturin Novels
in order of publication

MASTER AND COMMANDER
POST CAPTAIN
HMS SURPRISE
THE MAURITIUS COMMAND
DESOLATION ISLAND
THE FORTUNE OF WAR
THE SURGEON'S MATE
THE IONIAN MISSION
TREASON'S HARBOUR
THE FAR SIDE OF THE WORLD
THE REVERSE OF THE MEDAL
THE LETTER OF MARQUE
THE THIRTEEN-GUN SALUTE
THE NUTMEG OF CONSOLATION
CLARISSA OAKES
THE WINE-DARK SEA
THE COMMODORE
THE YELLOW ADMIRAL
THE HUNDRED DAYS
BLUE AT THE MIZZEN
THE FINAL UNFINISHED VOYAGE OF JACK AUBREY

Novels

TESTIMONIES
THE CATALANS
THE GOLDEN OCEAN
THE UNKNOWN SHORE
RICHARD TEMPLE
CAESAR
HUSSEIN

Tales

THE LAST POOL
THE WALKER
LYING IN THE SUN
THE CHIAN WINE
COLLECTED SHORT STORIES

Biography

PICASSO
JOSEPH BANKS

Anthology

A BOOK OF VOYAGES

PATRICK O'BRIAN

The Nutmeg of Consolation

HARPER PERENNIAL
London, New York, Toronto, Sydney and New Delhi

Harper Perennial
An imprint of HarperCollins*Publishers*
77–85 Fulham Palace Road,
Hammersmith, London w6 8jb

www.harperperennial.co.uk

This edition published by Harper Perennial 2008

1

Previously published in paperback by HarperCollins 1993, 1997 (reprinted nine times),
2003 (reprinted fifteen times) and by Fontana 1992 (reprinted once)

First published in Great Britain by HarperCollins*Publishers* 1991

Map of 'Entrance of Endeavour River in New South Wales', 1773, used by
permission of David Rumsey Map Collection, www.davidrumsey.com

PS Section map © HarperCollins*Publishers*, designed by HL Studios, Oxfordshire

PS™ is a trademark of HarperCollins*Publishers* Ltd

A catalogue record for this book is available from the British Library

ISBN 978-0-00-727557-1

Set in Imprint by Rowland Phototypesetting Ltd, Bury St Edmunds, Suffolk

Printed and bound in Great Britain by Clays Ltd, St Ives plc

Mixed Sources
Product group from well-managed
forests and other controlled sources
www.fsc.org Cert no. SW-COC-1806
© 1996 Forest Stewardship Council

FSC is a non-profit international organisation established to promote the
responsible management of the world's forests. Products carrying the FSC
label are independently certified to assure consumers that they come
from forests that are managed to meet the social, economic and
ecological needs of present and future generations.

Find out more about HarperCollins and the environment at
www.harpercollins.co.uk/green

CONTENTS

MARIAE SACRUM

The sails of a square-rigged ship, hung out to dry in a calm.

1 Flying jib
2 Jib
3 Fore topmast staysail
4 Fore staysail
5 Foresail, or course
6 Fore topsail
7 Fore topgallant
8 Mainstaysail
9 Main topmast staysail
10 Middle staysail
11 Main topgallant staysail

12 Mainsail, or course
13 Maintopsail
14 Main topgallant
15 Mizzen staysail
16 Mizzen topmast staysail
17 Mizzen topgallant staysail
18 Mizzen sail
19 Spanker
20 Mizzen topsail
21 Mizzen topgallant

AUTHOR'S NOTE

Any writer whose tales are situated in the early nineteenth century and whose people are for the most part sailors must depend for a great deal of his factual information and for much of his sense of the time on the memories and letters of seamen, on Admiralty and Navy Board records, on naval historians and of course on the invaluable publications of the Navy Records Society.

All these, together with the *Naval Chronicle* and contemporary newspapers, form a wonderfully rich pasture, and one in which I have grazed with great pleasure this many a year; but occasionally, when the tale wanders to regions where even this field is somewhat bare and where first-hand experience is lacking, a providential book appears to supply the want. Some time ago, to take a small example, I wanted much more information than I could easily find about contemporary knowledge of Steller's Sea-Cow, a vast animal like a bald grey mermaid twenty feet long, defenceless, edible, that lived in the North Pacific and that was hunted to extinction within some twenty-five years of its discovery in 1741; and I had hardly formulated the wish before an elegant translation of Steller's own account appeared on my desk for review. In the case of the present tale, part of which is set in the penal colony of New South Wales, ordinarily known as Botany Bay, in the early days of Marquarie's governorship, the providential book, providential to a very much greater degree, was Robert Hughes' splendid great work *The Fatal Shore*. Although I had done a great deal of reading on the discovery and settlement of the colony when I was writing a life of Sir Joseph Banks (the first man to botanize in that notorious bay), those were early days, and there were great gaps still to be filled: yet even if I had set aside years for solid research I could not have amassed, still less arranged, the immense quantity of material in this wide-ranging, deeply-informed, humane account of all aspects of the country's history, an account which I should in any case have read with the keenest appreciation and which at this juncture I fell upon with a delight that it would be uncandid to conceal.

Chapter One

A hundred and fifty-seven castaways on a desert island in the South China Sea, the survivors of the wreck of HMS *Diane*, which had struck upon an uncharted rock and had there been shattered by a great typhoon some days later: a hundred and fifty-seven, but as they sat there round the edge of a flat bare piece of ground between high-water mark and the beginning of the forest they sounded like the full complement of a ship of the line, for this was Sunday afternoon, and the starboard watch, headed by Captain Aubrey, was engaged in a cricket-match against the Marines, under their commanding officer, Mr Welby.

It was a keenly-contested match and one that aroused the strongest passions, so that roaring, hooting, cheers and cat-calls followed almost every stroke; and to an impartial observer it was yet another example of the seaman's power of living intensely in the present, with little or no regard for futurity: a feckless attitude, but one combined with uncommon fortitude, since the atmosphere was as wet as a living sponge and from behind its clouds the sun was sending down a most oppressive heat. The only impartial observer at hand was Stephen Maturin, the ship's surgeon, who thought cricket the most tedious occupation known to man and who was now slowly climbing away from it through the forest that covered the island, with the intention first of killing a boar, or in default of a boar some of the much less popular ring-tailed apes, and then of reaching the north side where the bird's-nest-soup swallows nested. On the rounded top of a knoll, where the boar-track led inland, he paused and looked down on the southern shore. Well out to sea on his left hand the reef on which the frigate had struck, now white with the broken water of a neap at three-quarter ebb but then invisible beneath a spring-tide flood; far to his right the point where a large piece of the wreck had come ashore; left again to the scoured-out inlet to which the wreckage had been towed by the one remaining boat, carefully prised apart and reassembled in the present elegant ribbed skeleton of the schooner that was to carry them to Batavia as soon as it was planked, decked and rigged; well up the slope from this inlet the camp under the lee of the forest in which they had sheltered from the typhoon that destroyed the stranded frigate, drowned many of her people, almost all her livestock and almost all her powder; and then immediately below him the broad expanse, firm and level, where the white-clad figures flitted to and fro – white-clad not so much because this was cricket as because it was Sunday, with mustering by divisions (necessarily shaved and in a clean shirt) followed by church.

It might seem the very height of levity to be playing cricket with the schooner far from finished, with stores very low and with the little island's resources in coconuts, boars and ring-tailed apes nearly exhausted. Yet Stephen knew very well what was in Jack Aubrey's mind. The people had behaved extremely well so far, working double tides; but they were not a crew made up solely of man-of-war's men, bred to the service and serving together for years at a time; at least a third had been pressed into the Navy; there were several recent draughts; and there were some King's hard bargains, including two or three sea-lawyers. Yet even if they had all been seamen, serving in the Navy since the beginning of the war, some relaxation was essential, and they had been looking forward to this match with the liveliest anticipation. The camphor-wood or palm-rib bats lacked some of the elegance of willow, but the sailmaker had sewed a wholly professional ball, using leather that could be spared from gaff-jaws, and the players had swayed away on all top-ropes to do their service credit. Furthermore, cricket formed some small part of that penny glass of ceremony which upheld the precious spirit, not indeed to be compared to the high rituals aboard such as divisions and the solemn reading of the Articles of War, to say nothing of burials and rigging church, but by no means inconsiderable as a way of imposing order upon chaos.

What Stephen did not fully appreciate was the degree of pleasure that Jack took in this particular ceremony. As a captain Aubrey was exceedingly worried by the shortage of food and marine stores, particularly cordage, by the near absence of powder, and by the coming total absence of arrack and tobacco; but as a cricketer he knew that close concentration was necessary on any pitch, above all on one like this, which more nearly resembled a stretch of white concrete than any Christian meadow, and when he came in second wicket down, the yeoman of the sheets having been bowled by the sergeant of the Marines for a creditable sixteen, he took centre and looked about him with an eager, piercing, predatory eye, tapping the block-hole with his bat, wholly taken up with the matter in hand.

'Play,' cried the sergeant: he took two little skips and bowled a twisting lob, pitched well up. 'Never mind manoeuvres,' Nelson had said. 'Always go at them.' Jack obeyed his hero, leapt out, caught the ball before it landed and drove it straight at the bowler's head. The grim sergeant neither flinched nor ducked but seized it as it flew. 'Out,' cried Edwards, the only civilian aboard and therefore a perfect umpire. 'Out, sir, I am afraid.'

Amid the roaring of the soldiers and the universal moan of disappointment from the seamen – for the Captain was well-liked both as an officer and as a dashing bat once his eye was in – Jack said, 'Well held, sergeant,' and walked off to the three coconut-palms (long since bare of fruit) that served them as a pavilion.

'Let it not be an omen,' said Stephen, slinging his rifle and turning away. It was an exceptionally fine rifle, a breech-loading Joe Manton, and he had inherited it from Mr Fox, the British envoy they had brought out in the *Diane* to counteract the French negotiations with the Sultan of Pulo Prabang. Fox had succeeded; he had obtained a treaty of mutual assistance; but in his eagerness to carry it home he had set off to sail the two hundred miles to Batavia in the ship's stout and well-manned pinnace while the *Diane* was lying quietly on her reef, neaped, immovable until the next spring tide; and he had been destroyed by the typhoon that destroyed the frigate.

A very fine rifle; Stephen was a deadly shot; and since there was so very little powder – far too little for a general blazing away with muskets – he was the camp's chief hunter. This was a relief for everybody. During the first fortnight he had worn himself raw, pulling on ropes, helping to saw wood, beating home treenails and wedges, and he had suffered much from the inherent malignity of things – no rope, pulled over the most innocent surface, that did not succeed in twisting upon itself or catching in some minute anfractuosity or protrusion; no saw that did not deviate from its line; no mallet that did not strike his already bruised and purple-swollen hand – but his companions had suffered even more from having to re-tie all his knots and rescue him from improbable dangers, perpetually keeping one eye on the Doctor and one on their work. Even when put to dig out the choked well, the softest job in hand, he contrived to send a pick through William Gorges' foot.

Yet as a hunter for the pot he was of great value to the crew. Not only was he thoroughly at home with the weapon, but he was an experienced field-naturalist, long accustomed to following a track, to the silent, upwind approach, and to indefinite, motionless waiting. These were necessary qualifications, because although he had two kinds of swine, the bearded pig and the babirussa, they had both been hunted at some not very remote period and from the beginning they had been wary. Now the survivors were not only warier by far, but they were also very much thinner on the ground; and whereas in the first week he had been able to provide

4

all hands with twice the ship's ordinary allowance of pork in an evening's stroll, now he had to sweat over the whole island, sometimes for quite a small creature – sometimes indeed missing even that, his damaged powder fizzling in the breech.

The trail he was following at present, however, was more promising than any he had seen for some while. It was recent, so recent that when it reached the edge of a spiny rattan-patch he saw the outer rim of the deep hoof-print fall in: what is more, this animal was almost certainly a babirussa of nine or ten score, the first he had seen since Thursday week. He was glad of it, because the ship's company included several Jews and many Mahometans, united only in their hatred of swine's flesh; but a willing mind could accept the babirussa, with his extraordinary horn-like upper pair of tusks and his long legs, as the kind of deer that might be expected on so remote an island.

'I shall go round and wait for him,' said Stephen, and he fetched a long cast round the rattan-brake, walking slowly in the heat. The animal had almost certainly gone to sleep. The boars of this country, like all the other boars he had ever known, were deeply conservative, devoted to the beaten track; and by now he knew most of their paths. At the other end of this one he climbed a tree that commanded the way out of the brake, and in its broad mossy crutch he sat at his ease, embowered in orchids, of a species, a habit and colour he had never seen before. The low sun appeared through a gap in the clouds, sinking towards Sumatra? Biliton? The west in any case. And sloping under the canopy it lit the orchid, the whole spray of fifty or sixty orchid flowers, with singular brilliance, vermilion in the wet, shining green; he was still contemplating it and its attendant insects when the boar began moving again in the rattan-brake. The sound came nearer; the boar emerged, standing motionless, its square snout twitching from side to side; with a detached, clinical look on his face Stephen dropped it dead and climbed down from the tree.

He had an apron in his knapsack and he put it on to gralloch his pig, because although he had no objection to a little blood on his clothes, Killick had; and Killick's high nasal complaining righteous voice, going on and on, was so disagreeable that the inconvenience of an apron on so heavy a day was nothing to it. He also had a light tackle that allowed him to heave the beast about single-handed. This was the one piece of something like seamanship that he had studied with profit: Bonden, the captain's coxswain, had spent hours showing him how to make one end fast and how to reeve the fall through the channels; and as long as he held the top block uppermost he often succeeded at the first try. He succeeded now, and stepping back he surveyed the boar with real satisfaction: nearer eleven score than ten. And there were few dishes Jack Aubrey preferred to soused pig's face, while for his own part he was fond of a pair of cold crubeens. He hung his apron on a branch to guide those who would carry the babirussa down and wiped his hands on his jacket – on his jacket, as he realized a moment too late, gazing at the stain on the fine white linen.

'I shall try to get it off at the swallows' pool,' he said, but with no conviction. At one period in his childhood he had been under the rule of a Dominican tertiary called Sor Luisa, one of the older, more respectable branch of the Torque-madas of Valladolid (his cousin and godfather was very particular about these things), a woman for whom cleanliness *was* godliness; and his attempts at 'getting it off' had never deceived her for a moment. Now she had been replaced by a lean ageless weatherbeaten pigtailed seaman with one gold earring and a shrewish penetrating voice. It was not even that Killick was his servant, with a servant's rights; he was Jack Aubrey's steward, Stephen's man being a gentle, witless young Malay by the name of Ahmed; but Preserved Killick had known both the Captain and the Doctor so long and had acquired such a moral ascendancy in certain fields that Ahmed was no protection at all.

As Stephen had feared, the swallows' pool did nothing to

remove the stain, but with a cowardice unworthy of his age and education he concealed the blood and peritoneal fluid with a superimposed film of dirt from the water's edge, adding some algae for good measure. He called the pool the swallows' because it was near the birds' most spectacular cliff, not because they used the soft grey mud for building: far from it, indeed. The wholly sheltered nests were pearly white and translucent, with never a hint of moss or vegetable fibre, far less of mud: these were the nests deepest in the caves or rather clefts in the seaward precipice, and Stephen could see the best only from one place, where his particular cave soared up from a broad, deep stretch of shingle two hundred feet below to a narrow fissure at the top. He had an indifferent head for heights and the upper yards of even a frigate filled him with paralysing dread, scarcely to be overcome by the strongest effort of will, but here he could lie flat, with his arms and legs spread out, his body firmly pressed against the warm level rock and only his face hanging over the void, gazing at the birds below – the cloud of little grey birds that flew in at the widest part of the cave, whirled about at an extraordinary speed and then shot off from the general vortex, each to its own nest. He leant farther into the cavity, his hands spread to shade his eyes, and almost at once his wig fell off, turning and turning until it vanished among the bird-filled shadows far below. 'Hell and death,' he said, for although it was only an old scratch-wig worn almost bare, Killick had recently curled and whitened its sides (there was nothing to be done to the top): and in any case he felt naked without it. The vexation lasted little longer than the slow turning fall, however; his wild attempt at catching the wig had brought him into a much better position: certainly it meant that the sun shone right on to the back of his unprotected head, but it allowed him to lie there in the utmost comfort, his face far deeper into the cleft. His body was perfectly relaxed, and as his eyes grew even more used to the dimness of the cavern he could make out the nests themselves, stretching away and away in rows, half-cups

7

touching one another, row upon row, covering the rock-wall from sixty feet above high-water mark almost all the way up, the finest and whitest being not the top rows, which had a certain amount of wind-drifted dirt upon them, but those about twenty down, in a narrow chimney. These were the nests that were sold for their weight in silver among the Chinese; and as he had expected, the nestlings, the scrupulously clean nestlings, two to each brood, would be ready to fly any day now. Yet as he lay there, glass after glass, oblivious of the roasting sun and watching the whirl of parent-birds bringing food and carrying away faecal sacs, a frown came over his face. He concentrated all his attention upon one particularly well-lit nest, and slowly his suspicions were confirmed: again and again the incoming bird perched on its rim with all four toes pointing forward. After another half-hour he rose to his feet, shouldered his rifle, and looking back at the birds with real displeasure he walked off.

'They are not swallows at all,' he said, feeling not only indignant but deadly sick. He stepped aside into a bush: and then into a series of bushes, for the vomiting was succeeded by an imperative looseness.

Stephen Maturin was not really an ill-natured man, but his was scarcely a jovial, sunny temperament, and sometimes disturbances of this kind rendered him morose or even worse. By the time he reached the camp he was perfectly ready to savage Killick. Killick knew him very well, however, and after one glance at his filthy jacket, his indecently bare head and the dangerous look in his pale eye, silently fetched him a broad-brimmed sennit hat and said, 'Captain is just woke up, sir.'

'My indignation against those birds was quite excessive,' said Stephen inwardly. 'It was no doubt caused by a sudden flow of bile, my posture exerting pressure on the ductus choledocus communis.'

He stepped into the dispensary, mixed himself a draught, lay flat on his back for a while and then walked towards the tent, feeling somewhat better. He repeated, 'Quite excessive'; yet even so, having received Jack's congratulations on the babirussa ('I am so glad: I was getting sick of those damned apes, even made into pasties'), he said, 'As for those bird's-nest soup creatures, I am afraid I must tell you they are not true swallows at all, but only a dwarvish branch of the oriental swifts.'

'Never be so put about, brother,' said Jack. 'What's in a name? So long as they make the right well-tasting kind of nest, it would be all one if they were called ostriches.'

'Did you like them, at the Raffleses'?'

'I thought they made a capital dish. It was a very pleasant evening altogether.'

'Then perhaps we might take some in a few days' time. This is the season: the young are almost on the wing, and a little small thin midshipman like Reade or Harper could be lowered down the cleft on a rope, and collect half a dozen empty nests. And I must say I should like to net one or two of the birds, to examine their toes. But come, I have not asked you how the match went. Did we win?'

'I am happy to say we all won. It was a draw. They made more runs than we did, but they could not manage to get Fielding and the bosun out before stumps were drawn. Fortunately we had Edwards as a neutral timekeeper, so there were no wry looks, no murmurs about flogging the glass; and we all triumphed.'

'Certainly everyone looked very cheerful as I came through the camp; though the Dear knows it must have been a wearing form of sport, in this breathless heat. Even pacing slowly under the trees, I was all aswim, to say nothing of running about after a hard and wicked ball in the sultry glare, God forbid.'

'Yet I am sure all hands will turn to the better for it tomorrow; I am sure I shall. And from the look of the sky we shall have an east wind. I hope so, indeed. There is a great deal of long-sawing to be done – exhausting work even with a breeze to take away the dust and let the bottom-sawyer breathe – but once we start planking her it will encourage

9

the people amazingly, and we may be able to put to sea before St Famine's Day. Come down to the slip and I will show you what remains to be done.'

The camp, with its ditch and earthwork trim again after the typhoon, was laid out after the fashion of a man-of-war, and to avoid disturbing the foremast hands who were sitting about talking outside their tents at the farther end of the rectangle Jack stepped on to the carriage of the brass nine-pounder dominating the seaward approach and jumped over, giving Stephen a hand. It was a fine gun, one of the much-loved pair that had gone overboard with the rest when they were lightening ship in an attempt at heaving her off the reef, and the only one to be found, wedged between the rocks, at low tide, by a fishing-party: a very fine gun, but of less use than the two light carronades, even if there had been quantities of powder, because the single round-shot that was still in place when it was recovered was the only nine-pound ball they possessed.

'Sir, sir!' called Captain Aubrey's two remaining lieuten-ants, gasping up the hill towards him. 'The midshipmen have caught a turtle, out by the point.'

'Is it a true turtle, Mr Fielding?'

'Well, sir, I trust it is, I am sure. But Richardson thinks it looks a little strange; and we hoped the Doctor would tell us if it could be ate.'

They went sloping right-handed down the valley, skirting the mass of rock and earth which had slid down the hillside at the height of the typhoon – a mass in which some trees and bushes were still growing happily, others withering as they stood – across the dry bed of the watercourse the torrent had scooped out, providing them with a commodious building-slip, and out along the strand, almost to the place where the precious wreck had come ashore. The whole midshipmen's berth was there, all standing silent in the roar of the surf: two master's mates, the one midshipman proper (the other had been drowned), the two youngsters, the Captain's clerk and the assistant surgeon. Like the other officers they had changed out of their fine Sunday clothes; they were now in ragged trousers or breeches undone at the knees: some had no shirts to their nut-brown backs: no shoes of course: a poverty-stricken, hungry group, though cheerful.

'Should you like to see my turtle, sir?' cried Reade from a hundred yards or more. His voice had not yet broken and it carried high above the sea's growl and thunder.

'Your turtle, Mr Reade?' asked Jack, coming nearer.

'Oh yes, sir. I saw him first.'

In the Captain's presence Seymour and Bennett, the tall young master's mates who had turned the turtle, could do no more than exchange a look, but Reade, observing it, added, 'Of course, sir, the others helped a little.'

They gazed for a while at the pitiful flippers swimming powerfully in the air. 'What do you think is wrong with the turtle, Mr Richardson?' asked Jack again.

'I can hardly put my finger on it, sir,' said Richardson, 'but there is something about his mouth I do not quite like.'

'The Doctor will set us all right,' said Jack, raising his voice over a triple crash of breakers: the ebb was well under way, and the rip-tide, combined with the current, was cutting the steady swell off the point into a series of chaotic cross-seas.

'He is the green turtle, sure,' said Stephen equally loud in spite of his aching head but in quite a different pitch, higher, disagreeably metallic. 'And a very fine green turtle: two hundredweight, I should say. But he is a male, and of course his face is displeasing he would be rejected on the London market – he would never do for an alderman.'

'But is he edible, sir? Can he be ate? He ain't unwholesome? He is not like the soft purple fish you made us throw away?'

'Oh, he may be a little coarse, but he will do you no harm. If you have any doubts, and Heaven knows I am not infallible, you may desire Mr Reade to eat some first and then watch him for a few hours. But in any event, I do beg you will take the animal's head off directly. I hate seeing them strive and suffer. I remember one ship where they had scores made fast on deck, and the creatures' eyes were red as cherries, unwatered by the sea. A friend and I went round sponging them.'

Reade and Harper ran up to the camp for the carpenter's broad axe. Aubrey and Maturin walked back along the hard-beaten sand to the building-slip. 'That is a very horrid tide-race,' observed Jack, nodding out to sea: and then, 'Do you know, I very nearly said a good thing just now, about your cock and hen turtles. It was on the lines of sauce – sauce for the goose being sauce for the gander, you understand. But it would not quite take shape.'

'Perhaps, my dear, it was just as well. A facetious lieutenant is good company, if he happens to be endowed with wit; a facetious commander among his equals, perhaps; but may not the post-captain who sets the quarterdeck in a roar conceivably lose some of his Jovian authority? Did Nelson crack jokes, at all?'

'I never heard him, to be sure. He was nearly always cheerful, nearly always smiling – he once said to me, "May I trouble you for the salt, sir?" in such a kind way that it was far better than wit. But I do not remember him making downright jokes. Perhaps I shall save my good things, when they happen, for you and Sophie.'

They walked along in silence, Stephen regretting his unkind words, his remorse much increased by the mildness of the response: he saw an unmistakable Philippine pelican overhead, but fearing that he might be even more of a bore with his birds than Jack with his puns, clenches and set pieces he did not point it out: besides his head was about to split.

'But tell me,' he said at last, 'what did you mean by St Famine's Day? Here we have a boar of ten score and a two-hundredweight turtle.'

'Yes, it is charming: a little over a pound a head for two days, and that would be high living if there were ship's bread or even dried peas to go with it. But there ain't. I blame myself very much for not rousing out more biscuit, flour, salt beef and pork while there was yet time.'

'Dear Jack, you could not foretell the typhoon; and the boats never ceased going to and fro.'

'Yes, but it was the envoy's things that went first, and his followers'. Killick, God forgive him, privately shipped the silver in your skiff: it should have been dried peas. First things first: for, as you have said yourself, the hogs are hardly to be found now, nor even the apes. We are six upon four already. There are almost no coconuts left, and fishing produces almost nothing safe to eat, but all that to one side: it is amazing how little food you absolutely need – you can keep going and work hard on old boots, leather belts and the most unlikely things if you are in spirits. No. When I speak of St Famine's Day I mean the day when I have to tell them there is no more tobacco and no more grog. You cannot believe how they hold to those two things. And that will be in less than a fortnight.'

'Would you expect a mutiny?'

'Mutiny in the sense of outright revolt and refusal of command? No. But from some of the people I expect muttering, discontent, ill-will; and nothing makes work slower or more inefficient or more unsafe than ill-will and its perpetual quarrels. It is horrible having to drive even half a resentful, sullen crew. Then again whenever a King's ship is lost there are always a few clever fellows who tell the rest that since the officers are commissioned to a particular ship they have no authority once that particular ship is gone. They also say the seaman's pay stops on the day of the wreck, so no service or obedience is due – the Articles of War no longer apply.'

'Are these things true?'

'Lord, no. They were once upon a time, but that was knocked on the head after the loss of the *Wager* in Anson's day. Still, a good many of the hands are quite willing to believe they are going to be done in the eye again; the service has a shocking reputation where pay and pensions are concerned.' At this point the level strand was broken by the bank of debris brought down by the torrential rain: they climbed it, and there below, in the natural slip, lay the schooner, as neat an anatomy of a vessel as could be wished. 'There,' cried Jack. 'Ain't you amazed?'

'Extremely so,' said Stephen, closing his eyes.

'I thought you would be,' said Jack, nodding and smiling. 'It must be two or even three days since you saw her, and since then we have reached not only the fashion-pieces but the transoms and ribbands. There are only the counters, and then we start planking.'

'The counters, indeed?'

'Yes. Let me explain. You see the stern-post, of course. The fashion-pieces rise on either side, and then curving out from them you see the counter-timbers . . .' Jack Aubrey spoke with great animation; he and Mr Hadley the carpenter were particularly proud of this elegant stern; but his enthusiasm led him to go on rather long, and in too great detail about the rabbets and the cant-frames.

Stephen was obliged to interrupt him. 'Forgive me, Jack,' he said; and turning aside he was extremely sick.

Few things could have been more disconcerting. Dr Maturin, no mere surgeon but a physician, possessed a perfect command of health, other people's and of course his own: disease had no hold on him: he had undergone antarctic cold and equatorial heat with equal immunity, he had nursed a whole ship's company through a murderous outbreak of gaol-fever quite unscathed, he treated yellow fever, plague and smallpox as fearlessly as the common cold; and here he was as pale as an ostrich-egg.

Jack led him gently up the hill. 'It is only a passing fit,' said Stephen. And then, as they approached the earthwork, 'I believe I shall sit here and get my breath again.' This he did, in the corner of the camp where the gunner and one of his mates were turning a meagre sand-castle of gunpowder on a piece of sailcloth. 'Well, Mr White,' he said, 'how are you coming along?'

Both gunner and mate stopped their work, turned towards

him, leaning on their wooden shovels, and shook their heads. 'Well, sir,' said White in his usual shattering roar, 'I boiled out the peter from the ruined barrels, like I said, and it crystallized and mixed and ground down quite pretty with a little old piss, as we say. But will it dry in this cruel wet air? No, sir, it will not. Not even in the sun. Not even if we turn it ever so.'

'I think we shall have a wind in the east tomorrow, Master Gunner,' said Jack, so quietly that the gunner stared. 'Then you will have no trouble.' He took Stephen's elbow, heaved him up, led him to their tent, and sent a boy running for Macmillan, the assistant surgeon.

'The Doctor looked wholly pale,' said the gunner, staring still.

He was looking paler by far when Macmillan arrived. The young man was fond of his chief, but even after so long a voyage in such very close proximity he was still in great awe of him and now he was sadly at a loss. Having made the usual gestures – tongue, pulse and so on – he said very diffidently, 'May I suggest twenty drops of the alcoholic tincture of opium, sir?'

'No, sir, you may not,' cried Stephen with surprising vehemence. He had been very deeply addicted to the drug for years and years, reaching such monstrous doses that they hardly bear repetition, and suffering in due proportion when he gave it up. 'But,' he added when the pain of his own cry had died away, 'as you will have perceived there is an increasing febrility, and our best course is no doubt bark, steel, saline enemata, rest and above all quiet. True quietness, as you know very well, is not to be expected in a camp full of sailors; but balls of wax provide something not unlike it. They are behind the balm of Gilead.'

When Macmillan came back with all these things Stephen said to him, 'There will of course be no true physical effect for some time; and in the meanwhile it is possible that I shall grow light-headed. I am aware of a rapid increase in the fever and already there is a slight inclination to wandering fancies, disconnected thoughts, hallucination – the first hint of delirium. Be so good as to pass me three coca-leaves from the box in my breeches pocket and sit as comfortably as you can on the folded sail.' Having chewed the leaves for some time he went on, 'One of the miseries of medical life is that on the one hand you know what shocking things can happen to the human body and on the other you know how very little we can really do about most of them. You are therefore denied the comfort of faith. Many and many a time have we seen patients in real distress declare themselves much relieved after a draught of some nauseous but wholly neutral liquid or a sugared pill of common flour. This cannot, or should not, happen with us.'

Each retired into his memory, recalling cases where in fact it had happened; sometimes, perhaps, in his own person; and presently Stephen said, 'But I will tell you another misery that is not to be denied. In the common, natural course of events physicians, sugeons and apothecaries are faced with enormous demands for sympathy: they may come into immediate contact with half a dozen deeply distressing cases in a single day. Those who are not saints are in danger of running out of funds and becoming bankrupt; a state which deprives them of a great deal of their humanity. If the man is in private practice he is obliged to utter more or less appropriate words to preserve his connexion, his living; and the mere adoption of a compassionate face as you have no doubt observed goes some little way towards producing at least the ghost of pity. But *our* patients cannot leave us. They have no alternative. We are not required to put on a conciliating expression, for our inhumanity in no way affects our livelihood. We have a monopoly; and I believe that many of us pay a very ugly price for it in the long run. You must already have met a number of callous idle self-important self-indulgent hard-hearted pragmatic brutes wherever the patients have no free choice: and if you remain in the Navy you will meet a great many more.'

Monopoly had not yet turned Macmillan into a pragmatic

brute, however. He and Ahmed sat all that stifling humid night at Stephen's side, fanning him, giving him water from the cool depths of the well and rocking his hammock with an even motion: before sunrise the promised east wind began to steal in across the sea, bringing coolness with it, and they had the satisfaction of seeing him lapse into a quiet, untroubled sleep.

'I believe, sir, he may do very well,' said Macmillan, when Jack beckoned him out of the tent. 'The fever fell as suddenly as it rose, with a profuse laudable sudation; and if he lie quiet today, taking a little broth from time to time, he may get up tomorrow.'

Stephen was mistaken in supposing that quietness was not to be had in a camp full of sailors: while stars were still in the sky they tiptoed off in a silent body, carrying their meagre breakfast to eat at the slip, leaving only a few men whose work made almost no noise at all – the rope-making party with their junk, yarns and wheel; the gunner, ready to spread his powder as soon as the sun should give him some hope of drying it; the sailmaker, who had reached the schooner's jibs; and Killick, who intended to overhaul the Doctor's wardrobe (Ahmed was no hand with a needle), and, glorious task, to polish the entirety of the Captain's silver.

It was into a strange unnatural stillness therefore that Stephen stepped out of the tent a little before noon. Macmillan had gone to the galley to see about broth in due course; Ahmed had left much earlier in search of fresh young coconuts; and Stephen, feeling quite well though absurdly weak, had to go to the necessary house.

'I hope I see you well, sir,' said the gunner in a hoarse whisper.

'Very much better, I thank you, Mr White,' said Stephen. 'And you should be happy with this fine dry breeze.'

In a somewhat grudging tone the gunner said that in a couple of days he might be able to barrel it up, and then louder and with much more conviction, 'But you never ought to of got up – walking about in your nightshirt with an east wind blowing – if you had given me a hail I should have made that idle lobcock Killick bring a utensil.'

The gunner, like Dr Maturin himself, was a warrant-officer, and although he was not of wardroom rank he was entitled to express his opinion. The rope-makers were not, but Stephen met with so many disapproving looks and shaken heads as he went down and then up the rope-walk that he was quite glad to be back in the tent. Macmillan brought him a bowl of babirussa soup thickened with pounded biscuit (turtle being thought too rich), congratulated him on his recovery, pointed out, with a shade of reproach, that there was a close-stool in the far corner, and said that as Ahmed was sure to be back any minute – he was only going to the west point – while Killick was now within earshot, he meant to take a little sleep; and with deference he suggested that the Doctor should do the same.

This the Doctor did, in spite of a distant roar of merriment down by the slip at noon, where the babirussa turned on its spit before a noble drift-wood fire; and he did not wake until he heard first Malayan voices that he did not recognize and then Killick's saying, 'Ha, ha, mate. Tell 'em there's plenty more in the other chest. I could have spread out twice as much if I had more room.'

Ahmed translated this, adding that Captain Aubrey was very enormously rich, very enormously important, a kind of raja in his own country; and then, answering a curiously high-pitched voice – a eunuch's? a boy's? – he explained what the gunner was doing with the powder, and why. There were several other voices, English and muted, for although Ahmed had repeatedly been told, 'He is much better, mate: walked to the head like a fairy,' he had as often been told, 'But he is asleep now, so you want to talk low.'

The high-pitched voice, however, felt no need at all to talk low. It questioned Ahmed closely, insistently about the gunpowder – was that all? – was it ready? – when would it be ready? – would it be good? Eventually Stephen slipped out of his hammock, put on his shirt and breeches, and walked out. The high-pitched voice at once fell into the natural pattern of things: it belonged to a slim young woman – well, youngish – whom he took to be a Dyak from her handsome, animated face and her fine complexion. She wore a long tight skirt that gave her the swaying willowy gait of a Chinese woman with bound feet and a little jacket that did not conceal her bosom, nor was it intended to conceal her bosom. To the sailors' delight it often fluttered open in the capricious, strengthening breeze. She had an ivory-hilted kris thrust into her waistband and her second incisors (not the middle ones) were filed to a point, so that she appeared to have two pairs of dog-teeth: perhaps, reflected Stephen, it was this that made her expression so remarkably vicious. It did not deter the seamen and the few Marines remaining in the camp, however. They gathered about her, gazing like a herd of moon-calves; and the gunner, though he did not quite abandon his heap, now so powdery as to be almost ready, was particularly eager to satisfy her curiosity.

Stephen greeted the newcomers, and the young woman and her grey-headed companion replied with all the formal civility usual among those who speak Malay, but in an accent and with some variations he had never heard before. Ahmed stepped forward with his explanation: when he reached the west point in his vain search for coconuts he found them landing from a small proa with five companions; they asked him what he was about and when he explained the situation they gave him these coconuts – pointing to a little net. The tide was on the ebb, and together with the current it made such a rip that the proa could not have come up the coast even with the most favourable breeze, so he had brought these two by the middle path. 'How did she walk, in that skirt?' asked Stephen in English – a quick aside. 'She took it off,' said Ahmed, blushing.

'I admire your kris,' said Stephen to her. 'Never was a hilt made for so small and delicate a hand.'

'Give me your honoured forearm,' said the young woman,

with her startling smile, and drawing her kris, a straight-bladed damascened kris, she shaved a stretch as bare and smooth as any barber could have done.

'Tell her to do me,' cried the gunner, starting forward; and as he left the sailcloth so the east wind took it, enveloping his mate and scattering the powder far to leeward, an impalpable, irrecoverable cloud of dust. 'Look what you've made me do, Tom Evans, you infernal lobcock,' roared Mr White.

'Ahmed,' said Stephen, 'coffee in the tent, if you please. Silver pot, four cups, and a cushion for the young lady. Preserved Killick, run down as fast as ever you can and tell the Captain with my compliments that there are two sea-Dyaks here.'

'And leave my silver? And with my poor leg?' cried Killick, sweeping his arm round the improbable array all blazing in the sun. 'Oh sir, let young Achilles go. He can run faster than any man in the fleet.'

'Very well. Pray cut along, Achilles; you will never forget my compliments, sure.' And as Achilles leapt the breastwork and hared down the slope he continued, 'Do not you trust your shipmates, Killick?'

'No, sir,' said Killick. 'Nor these strangers. I do not like to say anything against a lady, but when they first came they called out, "Hey there," in their own language and looked very wishful – God love us, how they stared at the soup tureens!'

They looked wishful still as they walked past the display, but having exchanged a couple of words in a language that was not Malay they averted their eyes and passed on into the tent.

The grey-haired man was obviously the woman's inferior; he sat on the ground at a distance, and although what he said was urbane enough, in the Malayan way, it was nothing like so urbane nor nearly as copious as her conversation, a steady, lively flow, not of anything so coarse as direct enquiry but of remarks that would have elicited information if Stephen had chosen to give it. He did not choose, of course:

after so long a course of discretion his mind would scarcely agree to give the exact time without an effort. But obvious unwillingness to speak was quite as indiscreet as blabbing, and he now replied with what she must already know – replied at such length that he was still prosing away about the advantages and disadvantages of a warm climate when Jack came in, redder in the face than usual, having pounded up the hill in Achilles' wake.

Stephen made the introductions with all proper formality: Killick furtively covered the close-stool with a blue peter, upon which Jack Aubrey sat; the coffee appeared; and Stephen said, 'The Captain does not understand Malay, so you will forgive me if I speak to him in English.'

'Nothing would give us greater pleasure than to hear the English language,' said the young woman. 'I am told it is very like that of birds.'

Stephen bowed and said, 'Jack, first may I beg you not to gaze upon the young woman with such evident lubricity; it is not only uncivil but it puts you at a moral disadvantage. Secondly shall I ask these people will they carry a message to Batavia for a fee? And if so, what shall the message be?'

'It was a look of respectful admiration: and who is calling the kettle black, anyway? But I will turn my eyes elsewhere, in case it should be misunderstood.' Jack drank coffee to give himself a countenance and then went on, 'Yes, do please ask whether they will go to Batavia for us. With this leading wind set in so steady it should not take them above a couple of days. As for what the message should be, let me think while you settle the first essential point.'

Stephen raised the question and he listened attentively to the long, well-considered temporizing reply, reflecting as he did so that here was a more spirited, articulate mind than any he had met in Pulo Prabang, except when he was talking to Wan Da, whose mother was a Dyak. When she had finished he turned to Jack and said, 'In short, everything depends on the fee. Her uncle, a man of the first consequence in Pontianak and the skipper of the proa, particularly wished to be home for the Skull Festival; it would be a great sacrifice for him, for the rest of the crew, and for the lady herself, to give up the Skull Festival; and even with this prosperous wind it must take two days to reach Batavia.'

The discussion resumed, with considerations on regular feasts in various parts of the world and on the Skull Festival in particular; it approached the area of compensations and of hypothetical sums and means of payment; and while coffee was being poured out again Stephen said, 'Jack, I believe we shall come to an understanding presently, and perhaps it might save time if you were to prepare a list of things you would like Mr Raffles to send; for I presume you do not mean to abandon the schooner, and she almost ready to swim.'

'God forbid,' said Jack, 'that would be flying in the face of Providence, indeed. No: I shall just jot down a few essentials that he can send in the first fishing-boat that comes to hand, no hanging about for Indiamen or anything of that kind.' He began *1 cwt of tobacco: 20 gallons of rum (or arrack if rum is not to be had)* . . . and he had reached *100 12lb and 50 9lb round-shot; 2 half-barrels of red large-grain and one of red fine-grain* when Stephen said to him, 'We are agreed on a fee of twenty johannes.'

'Twenty joes?' cried Jack.

'It is a great deal, sure; but it is the smallest of Shao Yen's notes that I possess, and I do not wish to lead the young woman into temptation . . .' He saw a smile forming and a premonitory gleam in Captain Aubrey's eye and he said, 'Jack, at this stage I implore you not to be witty: the lady is as fine as amber, has a very penetrating mind, and must not be offended. I do not wish to lead her into temptation, I say, by giving her coin, which Satan might urge her to run away with. These johannes she can receive only when she has given Shao Yen your note and his own countersigned by me: she is perfectly acquainted with his seal. So if your list is ready pray let me have it and we will put up the two together. Furthermore, the lady, whose name is Kesegaran

– no remarks, Jack, if you please: a modest downward look, no more – states that she would be very happy to see the schooner. And since the wind, adverse for her uncle's proa, is favourable for our boat, we might gain an hour or two by wafting her down to the southern point. Besides, civility requires no less.'

They stood watching the cutter stand out to sea, gain a handsome offing, put about and skim down towards the southern point over a fine lively sea, light blue flecked with white. All hands were sitting there with naval correctness; the only incongruities were Seymour's lack of uniform and Kesegaran's way of hitching herself from the stern-sheets to the windward gunwale and perching there, riding the seas in the most natural way in the world.

'I have never seen any woman take such an intelligent interest in shipbuilding,' said Jack.

'Nor in the shipbuilder's tools,' said Stephen. 'Both she and her companion fairly groaned with desire. They may have coveted your silver – I am sure they did – but that was a mere passing velleity compared with their yearning for Mr Hadley's double-handed saws, adzes, jack-screws and many other bright steel objects I cannot name.'

'In some parts they have to sew their planks together,' observed Jack.

But Stephen, following his own thought, said, 'When I spoke of a vicious expression I did not mean vicious in any moral sense: in fact I should not have used the word at all. What I meant was fierce and savage, or rather potentially fierce and savage: certainly not to be trifled with.'

'I cannot imagine any man trifling with Kesegaran who valued his – that is to say, who did not wish to end his days as a gelding.'

'Have you ever seen a mink, brother?' asked Stephen, after some moments.

With an inward sigh Jack abandoned a play on the words mink, minx, minxes, and said he had not, but believed they were something in the line of marten-cats, though smaller. 'Yes, yes,' cried Stephen. 'The marten is a much better figure: a very handsome creature indeed, but in attacking its prey or in defending itself, of the most extreme ferocity. That was the improper sense I gave to vicious.'

A pause. 'Suppose they reach Batavia by Wednesday afternoon,' said Jack, 'do you think it would take long for them to reach your banker and for the banker to reach Raffles?'

'My dear, I have no more knowledge of their feasts and holidays than you, nor of their state of health; but Shao Yen is very well with the Governor and could send him your message in five minutes, if he is there. The Governor is wholly favourable to us, and within another five minutes he could lay his hand on some ship, boat or vessel. You have seen Batavia roads: a maritime Hyde Park Corner.'

'Then in the best of cases, providing he hits on a windward craft (and after all he was born at sea) even with this breeze we could begin hoping to see them on Sunday. New Manila cordage, fresh six-inch spikes, pots of paint! To say nothing of the essential powder and shot, rum and tobacco. Long live Sunday!'

'Long live Sunday,' said Stephen, creeping off up the hill. And 'Long live Sunday,' he repeated, swinging in his hammock and trying to find sound reasons for the feeling of extreme dissatisfaction at the back of his mind. His calling led him to be intensely suspicious and he acknowledged that he often went much too far, particularly when he was not well. Yet why had Kesegaran told Ahmed to bring them to the camp by the middle path, the quite arduous middle path rather than by the strand? It was clear that she knew the island fairly well, although she had observed in passing, and quite truly no doubt, that because of its dangerous currents it was little frequented. The middle path meant that she had seen the camp in all its nakedness and the poor simple half-wit Ahmed had made the nakedness more apparent still by telling her about the powder. The chance meeting, the circumstances in which the camp was seen, could hardly have been more unfortunate. But on the other hand, down by the slip she had seen a hundred powerful men and more, no negligible force at all; and the fact of having one's second incisors filed to a point (no doubt a tribal custom) did not necessarily argue any very great depravity of mind.

Chapter Two

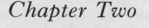

'Another misery of human life,' remarked Stephen to the morning darkness, 'is having a contubernal that snores like ten.'

'I was not snoring,' said Jack. 'I was wide awake. What is a contubernal?'

'You are a contubernal.'

'And you are another. I was wide awake; and I was thinking about Sunday. If Raffles' stores come in, we shall rig church by way of thanksgiving, eat a full ration of plum-duff, and observe the rest of the day as a holiday. Then on Monday we shall set to . . .'

'What was that noise? Not thunder, Heaven preserve?'

'It was only Chips and the bosun stealing away without a sound: they and their party mean to lay out the work early and start the tar-kettle a-going well in advance, and Joe Gower is taking his fishgig in the hope of some of those well-tasting stingrays that lie in the shallows by night. You will smell the smoke and the tar presently, if you pay attention.'

They lay there paying mild attention for several wholly relaxed, luxurious minutes, but it was not the smell of tar that brought Jack Aubrey leaping from his hammock. From down by the slip came a furious confused bellowing, the sound of blows, an immensely loud bubbling scream that died in agony.

It was still dark when he reached the breastwork, but lights were moving about down there and over the sea. The flames under the tar-kettle seemed to show the loom of a considerable vessel just offshore, but before he could be certain of it the first of the carpenter's party came scrambling up the hill. 'What has happened, Jenning?' he asked.

'They killed Hadley, sir. They killed Joe Gower. Black men are stealing our tools.'

'Beat to quarters,' cried Jack, and as the drum thundered several more hands came up the slope, the last half-carrying the bosun between them, pouring blood as he came.

Then first light in the east: false dawn: the red rim of the sun, and all at once full brilliant day. The largest double-hulled proa Jack had ever seen was lying a few yards off the mouth of the slip, close enough at low tide for dense lines of men to wade out, carrying tools, cordage, sailcloth, metal-work, while on the shore still others were gathered, some round their dead friends, some round their dead enemies.

'May I fire, sir?' asked Welby, whose Marines had lined the breastwork.

'At that distance, and with doubtful powder? No. How many charges do your men possess?'

'Most have two, sir; in moderate condition.'

Jack nodded. 'Mr Reade,' he called. 'My glass, if you please; and pass the word for the gunner.'

The telescope brought the shore startlingly close. They were carefully cutting off the carpenter's head: Gower and another man he could no longer identify had already lost theirs. There were two dead Malays or Dyaks and even at this juncture he was shocked to see that one was Kesegaran. Although she was now wearing Chinese trousers and although she had been pierced through and through she was perfectly recognizable, lying there looking fiercely up at the sky.

Jennings was still at his side, still voluble from the shock. 'It was Joe Gower that done it,' he said. 'Mr White went for to stop her taking his broad axe; she slashed his leg out of hand, and as he lay there she slit his throat quick as whistlejack – he screamed like a pig. So Joe served her out with his fishgig. It came natural to him, being a quean, as they say, and carpenter's mate.'

'Sir?' said the gunner.

27

'Mr White, let the carronades be drawn and reloaded with grape. What do you say to their charges?'

'I should not like to answer for the piece forward, sir; but the nine-pounder and the after carronade may do their duty.'

'At least change the old flannel for something dry, mix in a little priming and let them air. Those people will be busy down there for quite a while.' He turned to his first lieutenant and said, 'Mr Fielding, boarding-pikes and cutlasses have been served out, I am sure?'

'Oh yes, sir.'

'Then let the people go to breakfast watch by watch; and pray search all possible sources for powder, flasks, fowling-pieces, pistols that may have been overlooked, rockets. Ah, Doctor, there you are. You have seen what is afoot, I dare say?'

'I have a general notion. Should you like me to go down and parley, make peace if it is at all possible?'

'Do you know that Kesegaran was there, and has been killed?'

'I did not,' said Stephen, looking very grave.

'Take my glass. They have not carried her back to the proa yet. From the way they are behaving I do not think any truce is possible and you would be killed at once. In an encounter like this one side or the other has to be beaten entirely.'

'Sure, you are in the right of it.'

Killick put a tray on the earthwork and they sat either side of it, looking over the slip and the busy Dyaks below. 'How is the bosun?' asked Jack, putting down his cup.

'We have sewn him up,' said Stephen, 'and unless there is infection he will do; but he will never dance again. One of his wounds was a severed hamstring.'

'He loved a hornpipe, poor fellow, and the Irish trot. Do you see they are putting on whitish jackets?'

'The Dyak guard at Prabang wore them. Wan Da told me they would turn a bullet, being padded with kapok.'

They watched in silence for the space of two coffee-pots.

Most of the immediate looting had stopped and now the space round the slip was bright with spearheads catching the sun. Finishing his cup, Captain Aubrey called, 'Mr Welby, there: what do you make of the situation?'

'I believe they mean to attack, sir, and to attack in an intelligent way. I have been watching that old gentleman with a green headcloth who directs them. This last half-hour he has been sending off little parties into the trees on our left. Several go, but only a few come back, waving branches and calling out so that they shall be seen. And then more men have been quietly moved under the bank this side of the slip, where we cannot see them – dead ground for us. I think his plan is to send a large body straight at us – charge right uphill, engage on the earthwork, kill as many as they can and then fall back slowly, still fighting, and then turn and run so that we shall leave our lines and pursue them, whereupon the group in the forest will take us in the flank while the people in the dead ground jump up and the first attacking-party face about and between them cut us to pieces. After all, they are rather better than three hundred to our one hundred and fifty-odd.'

'You have been there before, Mr Welby, I find,' said Jack, looking sharply into the trees on the left, where the gleam of weapons could in fact be made out quite easily.

'I have seen a good deal of service, sir,' said Mr Welby. As he spoke a swivel-gun and a gingall flashed aboard the proa. The gun's half-pound ball kicked up earth on the breastwork; the gingall's bullet – probably a rounded stone – passed overhead with a wavering howl. This seemed to be the whole of the Dyaks' artillery – no muskets were to be seen – and immediately after the discharge the white-jacketed spearmen began forming below.

After a quick, low-voiced exchange with Jack, Welby called, 'Marines: one shot, one man. No one is to leave the lines. Independent fire: no one is to shoot without he is sure of killing his man. No Marine is to reload, but having fired, is to fix his bayonet. Sergeant, repeat the orders.'

The sergeant did so, adding, 'having cleaned his lock and barrel if time permits'.

Now an ululation, the beating of a small shrill drum, and the spearmen came racing up the hill in groups. A first nervous musket at a hundred yards: 'Sergeant, take that man's name.' Nearer, and their panting could be heard. The last stretch: twenty or thirty musket-shots; and in a close-packed shouting mêlée they were on the earthwork: spears, pikes, swords, bayonets clashing, dust flying, clouds of dust; and then at a huge shout from some chief man they fell back, at first slowly, still facing the camp, then faster, turning their backs and fairly running away. A dozen ardent foremast jacks ran after them, bawling like hounds; but Jack, Fielding and Richardson knew each by name and roared them back to the lines – fools, half-wits, great hulking girls.

The fleeing Dyaks stopped half way down and gathered to mock and challenge the camp with marks of scorn.

'Forward carronade,' called Jack. 'Fire into the brown.'

The flint failed at the first pull of the laniard – a frightful anticlimax – but it fired on the second and the carronade uttered a flat poop, scattering a gentle shower of grape among the Dyaks, who howled with laughter, capered and leapt into the air. Some of them waved their penises at the English, others showed their buttocks; and the powerful reinforcements from the trees came running out to join them for a charge in deadly earnest.

'After carronade,' said Jack: and his voice was instantly followed by a great solemn crash and a cloud of orange-lined smoke. While the echoes were still going to and fro the cloud swept to leeward, showing the awful swathe the grape had cut. There was a headlong flight to the slip, and although some came back, creeping low, to help their wounded friends back down the hill, they left at least a score of dead.

Now there followed a long period with no action, well on into the afternoon, but it soon became clear that the Dyaks and their Malay friends (for they were a mixed crew) had not lost heart. There was a great deal of movement down by the slip and between the slip and the proa; and from time to time they fired the swivel-gun. At noon they lit their fires for a meal: the camp did the same.

All this time Jack had been watching the enemy with the closest attention and it was clear to him and his officers that old Green Headcloth was certainly in command down there. The Dyak chief watched the English with equal care, often standing on the bank with shaded eyes; and a good hand with a rifle, having an earthwork to lean on, could certainly bring him down. Stephen could do it, he was sure; but he knew with equal certainty that Stephen never would: in any case both medicos were busy with the wounded – several men had been hurt in the fighting on the breastwork. Nor would he do it himself, not in cold blood and at a distance: although he was not displeased when a broadside cleared an enemy quarterdeck, there was still something illogically sacred about the person of the opposing commander, and some perceptible but indefinable difference between killing and murder. Query: did it apply to a man appointed as a sharpshooter? Answer: it did not. Nor did it apply in even a very humble mêlée.

Captain Aubrey, his officers and David Edwards, the envoy's secretary, ate their dinner on trestled planks laid this side of the breastwork, which had sandbags on its top to protect their heads from the not infrequent swivel-gun, whose layer made remarkably good practice, hitting the embankment or skimming just over it almost every time – such good practice that the moment they saw the flash all hands dropped to their knees, out of direct range. Their genuflexion did not always save them, however, and twice during the meal Dr Maturin was called away to deal with the more sluggish.

Dinner today was informal, so much so that Richardson might without impropriety peer between the sandbags with his telescope and say, 'It is my belief, sir, that the enemy are entirely out of water. I see three parties trying to make holes in what they take to be the watercourse; and Green Headcloth is blackguarding them like a fishfag.'

'They expected to be drinking out of our well by now,' said Welby, smiling. 'Though mark you, they may do so yet,' he added as a sop to Fate.

'The odds are more even now,' observed the purser. 'And if it goes on at this rate we shall soon have the advantage.'

'If that should come about they will surely sail away and come back three times as strong,' said the master. 'Sir, would it be foolish to suggest destroying their proa out of hand? It is frail past belief – no metal in its whole construction – and a ball in either hull or better still at the junction between 'em would knock it to pieces.'

'I dare say it would, Mr Warren,' said Jack. 'But that would leave us with better than two hundred thirsty villains eating us out of house and home. The Doctor says there are barely a score of pigs left, and only a few days' ration of ring-tailed apes. No. There is nothing I should like better than seeing them weigh and set off for reinforcements. Almost all our long-sawing is done, and very fortunately poor dear Mr Hadley had left several of his most important tools up here for sharpening and resetting; working double-tides I believe we can launch the schooner and be on our way to Batavia before they come back. Their home port is certainly in Borneo.'

'Oh,' cried the purser, as though he had been struck by a new idea: but he said no more. The swivel-gun and the gingall both hit the sandbag immediately opposite, ripping it and covering both him and the table with its contents. When they picked him up he was dead. Stephen opened his shirt, put his ear to his chest and said, 'Heart, I am afraid: God be with him.'

During the hot still hours that followed Jack, Fielding and the gunner overhauled the powder, all that had been found, scraped from barrels, withdrawn from flasks and bandoliers, signal cartridges and even rockets. 'We have a charge for each of the carronades and the nine-pounder, with just enough over to leave the Doctor half a flask for his rifle,' said Jack. 'Master gunner, it might be well to load them now, while the metal hardly bears touching: the heat will make the powder brisk. And let the nine-pounder ball be very carefully chipped – indeed, oiled and polished.'

'Aye aye, sir. Grape for the carronades, I do suppose?'

'Case is your real slaughter-house charge at close quarters, but I am afraid we have none?'

The gunner shook his head with a melancholy air. 'All on that fucking reef, sir, pardon me.'

'Then grape, Mr White.'

'Sir, sir,' cried Bennett, 'Captain Welby says they are sending men up through the forest.'

'Perhaps, sir,' said Welby when Jack joined him at his lookout point, 'it would be prudent not to direct your glass: they might think we had smoked them. But if you watch the open ground to the left of that great crimson-flowering tree at eleven o'clock from the flagstaff, you will see them slip across, their spearheads held low and wrapped in leaves or grass.'

'What do you think they are at?'

'I believe they are a forlorn hope, a storming-party sent to attack the camp from behind, where the silver is. They are to catch up a chest or two and run off into the broken country behind while their friends amuse us with a false attack in front.'

'They cannot know what the back of the camp is like. We can hold it with half a dozen men: there is a shocking great drop where the landslide swept the earth away.'

'No, sir. And as the young person came in by the west gate and left by the south, she would not have seen the drop either. No doubt it is all their general's theory; but still I am sure he thought he could rely on surprise.'

'How many men did you reckon?'

'I counted twenty-nine, sir, but I may well have missed a few.'

'Well, I think we can deal with that – Mr Reade, stop that

goddam fool pointing at the trees. Stop it at once, d'ye hear me there? You and Harper can pick up the biggest stones you can carry and take them to the north wall steps at the double. Mr Welby, I think we can afford a round apiece to your eight best marksmen. A quarter of your people down before you start your attack is discouraging. It will be uncommon brave men that go on, with such a rise in front of them.'

Almost at once the diversion began. The swivel-gun and the gingall fired as fast as they could; large bodies of men raced diagonally back and across the broad open slope between the camp and the building-slip, hallooing as they ran or howling like gibbons, and presently there was a furious discharge of crackers along the inner border of the forest. Jack had to shout to make himself heard. 'Mr Seymour, there is a forlorn hope about to make a dash for the silver by way of the north wall. Take Killick and Bonden and the eight Marines Mr Welby has told off together with whatever other men you need to line the wall and deal with the situation while we watch their attempt at amusing us and make sure it don't turn ugly.'

The feint, the diversion, did not turn ugly: the real attack did. The storming-party had been picked for strength and courage and in spite of a heavy loss the moment they left cover they ran straight on to the steps and the foot of the wall, where Killick, beside himself with pale hatred and fury, flung great stones down upon them, helped on either hand by the Marines, all the Captain's bargemen and his coxswain. Again and again a Dyak would make a back for another and up he would come, spear poised, only to be flung back at pike-point, pierced through with a cutlass or smashed with a fifty-pound stone. And presently there were no more to come. Seymour, nominally in command, had to beat on the men's backs to prevent them stoning the few dreadfully shattered cripples who were crawling off among the rocks. Even then Killick stood for a great while, livid and glaring, a boarding-axe in one hand and a jagged lump of basalt in the other.

The diversion soon lost all conviction. The diagonal running to and fro grew languid, the crackers spluttered away to one last pop. The sun too was tiring of the day – it had been extraordinarily hot – and sloped westward through a deeper blue.

'Yet even so, sir,' said Welby, 'I do not believe this is the end. Their general has lost a power of men and he has nothing to show for it. They have no water – see how they dig! – and they won't find any there. So they cannot wait. The general cannot wait. As soon as they have rested a little he will launch the whole lot at us, straight at us: he is a death or glory cove, I am sure. See how he harangues them, jumping up and down. Oh my God, they have fired the schooner.'

As the black smoke billowed up and away on the shifting breeze the whole camp burst out in a yell of desperate anger, frustration, plain grief. Jack raised his voice and hailed the gunner. 'Mr White, Mr White, there. Draw those carronades and reload with the very best round-shot we possess. Your mates have perhaps five minutes to chip them as smooth as ever they can: certainly not more. And Mr White, let there be slow-match at hand.'

This time there were no manoeuvres, no diversions. They came steadily up the hill, at first at a trot and lastly at a furious run. They came straight at the guns, with no sign of fear, but in no kind of formation either, so that they reached the earthwork in dispersed order, the fleetest first, in tens rather than fifties, and they never beat their way through the massed pikes and bayonets. Their chief arrived in the second wave, still running but scarcely able to see or fetch his breath: he leapt on to a body, slashing blindly at the seaman opposite him, and fell back, his head split down the middle with an axe.

It was cruel fighting, kill or be killed, all in a great roar of sound and the clash of swords and spears, grunting and dust, sometimes a shriek. For what seemed a great while the enemy never fell back except for another spring forward;

but the Dyaks and Malays were fighting uphill, against an enemy in close contact with strong-voiced competent naval and military commanders and sheltered by a moderate breastwork; besides, however great their courage, they were smaller, lighter men than the English, and at a given point, when there was a general withdrawal on the right and the centre, a regrouping for a fresh assault, Jack Aubrey felt the turn of the tide. He called out, 'Mr Welby, charge. Dianes follow me.'

The whole camp leapt on to the wall with a cheer. The drum beat and they hurled themselves forward. After the first frightful clash the Marines' weight and their exact order bore all before them. It was a rout, a total, disastrous rout: the Dyaks ran for their lives.

They ran faster than the English and on reaching the sea they leapt straight in and swam fast to the proa, as nimble as otters, perhaps a hundred men left.

Jack stood gasping on the shore, his sword dangling from his wrist. He wiped the blood from his eyes – blood from some unfelt blow – looked at the blazing schooner, its ribs outlined in fire, and at the Dyaks, already hauling on their cable. 'Mr Fielding,' he said in a strong, hoarse voice, 'see what can be done to put out the fire. Mr White, gun-crews, gun-crews I say, come along with me.'

They toiled up again, those that were whole; and never before had Jack so felt the burden of his weight. The bodies lay thick half way to the camp, thicker in front of the earth-work, but he hardly noticed as he picked his way through just by the brass nine-pounder. Bonden, the captain of the gun and a faster runner, gave him a hand over the parapet and said, 'They are under way, sir.' He looked round, and there indeed was the proa luffing up, coming as close to the awkward breeze as ever she could sail; the tide had been on the ebb long enough to bare the reef and she had to get all possible offing on the unhandy starboard tack to weather the west point with its shocking tide-rip and northward-setting current.

The gunner, helped by his surviving mate, arrived a moment later. 'There is more match in my tent, sir,' he called in a voice that hardly carried over the breastwork.

'Never fret about that, Mr White,' said Jack, smiling. 'The first still has half a glass to go.' And there it was in fact, untouched, unkicked in the turmoil and confusion of battle, smouldering away in its tubs, its smoke drifting away across the empty camp.

'God love us,' whispered the gunner as they crouched there laying the forward carronade, 'I had thought the set-to was much longer. Four degrees, would you say, sir?'

'Pitch it well up, master gunner.'

'Well up it is, sir,' said the gunner, giving the screw half another turn.

For a perceptible instant the match hissed on the priming: the carronade spoke out loud and sharp, screeching back along its slide; all hands peered out and under the smoke and some caught the high curving flight of the ball. Jack watched it so intently that only his heart remembered to rejoice that the powder had proved sound, beating so hard it almost stopped his breath. The line was true: the ball short by twenty yards.

Jack ran to the nine-pounder, calling to the captain of the other carronade, 'Four and a half, Willett. Fire as she rises.'

The carronade fired an instant later: a noble crash once more. This time Jack did not see the ball, but there was its white plume in the sea, just ahead of the proa, the line as true as the last. He heaved on his handspike, shifting the lay of the gun a trifle to the right, called, 'Stand by, there,' and clapped the match to the touch-hole. At the same moment the proa's helmsman put his tiller hard over to avoid the shot and sailed straight into the point of its fall. There was no splash. For an instant all hands looked blank: then the two hulls fell apart, the great sail collapsed, the entire vessel disintegrated, and the whole, already spread over twenty or thirty yards of sea, drifted fast towards the west point and its terrible overfall.

'What is the cheering?' asked Stephen, coming bloody-handed from the hospital-tent and peering molelike through spectacles he now wore for the fine-work of surgery.

'We have sunk the proa,' said Jack. 'You can see the wreckage sweeping past the cape. They will be in the tide-rip directly – Lord, how it cuts up! – and no man living can swim through that. But at least we do not have to fear any reinforcements.'

'You take your pleasures rather sadly, brother, do you not?'

'They fired the schooner, do you see; and from what little I saw there is no hope of saving a single frame.'

Fielding heaved himself wearily over the corpses and the parapet, took off his battered hat, and said, 'Well, sir, I give you joy of your glorious shot: never was there such a genuine smasher. But I am very sorry to have to report that although several hands got burnt in their zeal, there is nothing, nothing we could do to save the schooner. There is not a single frame left entire – left at all. Even the keelson is gone; and of course all the planking. As well as the cutter.'

'I am heartily sorry for it, Mr Fielding,' said Jack in a voice intended as a public communication – a score of men were within earshot. 'I am sure you and all hands did their best, but it was a hopeless blaze by the time we reached it: they had certainly spread tar fore and aft. However, here we are alive, and most of us fit for duty. We have many of poor Mr Hadley's tools; there is timber all around us; and I have no doubt we shall find a solution.'

He hoped the words sounded cheerful and that they carried conviction, but he could not be sure. As it usually happened after an engagement, a heavy sadness was coming down over his spirits. To some degree it was the prodigious contrast between two modes of life: in violent hand-to-hand fighting there was no room for time, reflexion, enmity or even pain unless it was disabling; everything moved with extreme speed, cut and parry with a reflex as fast as a sword-thrust, eyes automatically keeping watch on three or four men within reach, arm lunging at the first hint of a lowered guard, a cry to warn a friend, a roar to put an enemy off his stroke; and all this in an extraordinarily vivid state of mind, a kind of fierce exaltation, an intense living in the most immediate present. Whereas now time came back with all its deadening weight – a living in relation to tomorrow, to next year, a flag promotion, children's future – so did responsibility, the innumerable responsibilities belonging to the captain of a man-of-war. And decision: in battle, eye and sword-arm made the decisions with inconceivable rapidity; there was no leisure to brood over them, no leisure at all.

Then again there were all the ugly things to be done after a victory; and the sad ones too. He looked round for a midshipman, for by now most of the people had come up the hill again; but seeing none he called Bonden, the invulnerable Bonden, and told him to ask the Doctor whether a visit would be convenient. 'Aye aye, sir,' said Bonden, and hesitated. 'Which you have a nasty trough up there' – tapping his scalp – 'that did ought to be looked to at the same time.'

'So I have,' said Jack, feeling his head, 'but it don't signify. Cut along now.'

Before Bonden could come back Richardson limped up to say that the Dyaks had taken the heads not only of the carpenter and his mate but of all those killed on the lower or middle ground. Some could not be identified: should the bodies be brought up? Were our own dead by the camp to be separated by religion? What was to be done with the dead natives?

'Sir,' said Bonden, with a queer look on his face, 'Doctor's compliments and in five minutes, if you please.'

Every man has his own five minutes: Jack's was shorter than Stephen's and he came into the tent too early. Stephen was carrying a slender arm to a heap of amputated limbs and the bodies of patients who had already died; he put it down on a shattered foot and said, 'Show me your scalp, will you now? Sit on this barrel.'

'Whose was that arm?' asked Jack.

'Reade's,' said Stephen. 'I have just taken it off at the shoulder.'

'How is he? May I speak to him? Will he be all right?'

'With the blessing, he may do well,' said Stephen. 'With the blessing. That swivel-gun flung him down with his head against a rock and he is still stunned entirely. Sit on the barrel. Mr Macmillan, hot water and the coarse shears, if you please.' As he mopped and snipped he said, 'Of course I have not a full list for you since not all the dead have been counted and there are still some wounded to be brought up the hill; but I am afraid it will be a long one. The midshipmen's berth has suffered very heavily. Your clerk was killed in the charge; so was little Harper; Bennett was virtually disembowelled and though we have sewn him up I doubt he sees tomorrow.'

Butcher, Harper, Bennett, Reade: dead or maimed. As Jack sat there with his head bowed to the swab, the shears and the probe, tears fell steadily on his folded hands.

The first sad, weary days of mass burial – more dead men, both sides taken together, than living – and the visiting of the wounded, seeing faces he had known all this commission, good, decent faces almost all of them, yellow and thin with pain, sometimes with fatal infection, lying there in the heat and the dreadful familiar smell. Then the later funerals as the worst cases dropped off, one, two and even three a day. And all this with extremely little food. Stephen had shot only one small babirussa; the apes were no longer worth his remaining charges; and of the few fishes caught by casting from the rocks or hauling the seine most were scaleless lead-coloured things that even the gulls would not eat.

On the morning after the last patient on the danger-list died – a young Dyak who had borne resection after resection of his gangrenous leg with admirable fortitude – Stephen was late in obeying the pipe of *All hands on deck – all hands aft* that preceded the Captain's address to the ship's company. By the time he slipped into his place Jack was still

dealing with naval law, the perennity of commissions, the
Articles of War and so on: all hands listened attentively,
with grave, judicial expressions as he repeated his main
points once again, particularly that which had to do with
the continuance of their pay, each according to his rating,
and the compensation in lieu of spirits not served out. They
stood there close-packed, confined between imaginary rails,
exactly as though they were still aboard the *Diane*, and they
weighed every word. Stephen, who had heard the essence
before, paid little attention; in any case his mind was elsewhere. He had been attached to the Dyak, who showed
unlimited trust in his skill and benevolent intent, who would
take food only from him, and whom he really thought he
had saved as he had in fact saved young Reade, now sitting
there wraith-like on a carronade-slide, his empty sleeve
pinned across his chest, and as he had saved Edwards, who
stood alone, there where the envoy and his suite had always
had their place.

'But now, shipmates,' said Jack in his strong deep voice,
'I come to another point. You have all heard of the widow's
cruse.' No single officer, seaman or Marine showed the least
sign of having heard of the widow's cruse, nor any sign whatsoever of intelligence. 'Well,' continued Captain Aubrey,
'*Diane* shipped no widow's cruse. And by that I mean
tomorrow is St Famine's Day.' Comprehension, alarm,
despondency, extreme displeasure showed in the faces of all
the old man-of-war's men present; and the hum of whispered
explanation kept Jack silent for a long moment. 'But it is not
the worst St Famine I have ever known,' he went on.
'Although it is true that today's is the last issue of grog and
the last cheese-paring scrap of tobacco, we still have a little
biscuit and a cask of Dublin horse not very badly spoilt
and there is always the chance the Doctor may knock down
another of the island gazelles. And there is this point too.
The officers and I are not going to sit on silk cushions swilling wine and brandy. The gun-room steward and Killick
are going to put all our stores into a general pool, under

double guard, and as long as it lasts each mess will draw its share by lot. That is what the gun-room steward and Killick are going to do, whether they like it or not.' This was very well received. Killick's extreme jealousy of the Captain's stores, even the oldest heel-taps of his wine, had always been notorious, and the gun-room steward's hardly less so. Both looked pinched and intensely disapproving, but the ship's company in general laughed as they had not laughed since before the battle. 'Then again,' said Jack, 'God helps those that help themselves. We still have Ned Walker and two others who were rated carpenter's crew. We still have plenty of sailcloth and a fair amount of cordage. We can save many of the nails and spikes from the schooner's ashes, and my plan is to run up a six-oared cutter to replace the one they burnt, pick a crew of our best seamen with an officer to navigate and send them off to Batavia for help. I shall stay here, of course.'

All these things coming at once confused his audience. Upon the whole there was a hum of agreement, even of very strong approval, but one man called out, 'Two hundred mile in an open boat, with the monsoon like to change?'

'Bligh sailed four thousand in a twenty-three-foot launch crammed with people. Besides, the monsoon does not change for close on a fortnight, and even a parcel of grass-combing lubbers can put a seaworthy cutter together in that length of time. In any case, what is the alternative? Sit here and watch the sun go down on the last of the ring-tailed apes? No, no. Better a dead dog than a lead lion. That is to say . . .'

'Three cheers for Captain Aubrey's plan,' cried a perfectly unexpected voice, a taciturn, highly-respected, middle-aged forecastleman named Nicholl. 'Hip, hip, hip . . .'

The cheering was still going on when Stephen, with his rifle in the crook of his arm, walked down past the blackened wreckage in the slip; the skeleton with its elegant curves was still recognizable, and as heavy rain had fallen in the night the whole gave off something of the desolate acrid smell he had caught the first day.

He walked out along the strand westwards, meaning to climb by his usual path behind the cricket-pitch, but after he had been going for some time he saw a moving object in the sea. At this point he was well above the ordinary high-tide mark, in a region where the most uncommon storms, like that which had destroyed the *Diane*, cast up massive debris, among which there grew interesting plants, sometimes with surprising speed. He sat, pleasantly shaded by ferns, on the trunk of a medang and drew out his pocket-glass. As soon as it was focused his first opinion was confirmed: he was gazing into the large insipid kindly square-nosed face of a dugong. It was not the first he had seen, but it was the first in these waters, and certainly he had never had a finer view at any time. A young female dugong, about eight feet long, with her child. Sometimes she held it to her bosom with her flipper, both of them poised upright in the sea, staring straight before them in a very vacant manner; and sometimes she browsed on the seaweed that grew on the rocks out there; but at all times she showed the utmost solicitude for her child, occasionally going so far as to wash its face, which seemed a pointless task in so limpid a sea. Was her presence, and that of some fellow-mermaidens much farther out, a sign of the coming change of season? 'How glad I am that the boat is still only a hypothesis,' he said, having pondered on the question. 'Otherwise it would have been my duty to pursue the innocent dugong. They are said to be excellent eating, like poor Steller's Sea-Cow: or rather Steller's poor Sea-Cow, the creature.'

Presently the dugong dived and swam away to join her friends browsing on the far side of the reef and Stephen was thinking of getting up when a strangely familiar sound caught his ear. 'You would swear it was a pig rooting,' he said, moving his head slowly to the right. It was in fact a pig rooting, as fine a babirussa as he had ever seen: the animal was snorting and grunting at a great rate, wholly intent upon a wealth of tubers. It presented a perfect target

43

and Stephen very gently brought up his gun. The babirussa was as innocent as the dugong; he shot it dead without the least compunction.

When at last he had hoisted the boar into a tree with his tackle he said, 'Twenty-two score if he weighs an ounce. Mother of God, how happy they will be. I shall follow the back-track as far as I can – never was such a day for tracks – to see where he came from, and then I believe I shall indulge myself with a view of the swifts. I feel no resentment against them now, I find, none at all, and I wish to see the state of the vacated nests. Poor little Reade, alas, will never climb down to take them for me. But Heavens, what youth and stamina and a cheerful mind will do in the face of a shocking injury! He will be running about in a fortnight, whereas the bosun, middle-aged and sunk in gloom, will take a great while to recover from a far less serious wound.' His mind ran on in this way as he followed the clear track as far as a much-favoured wallow in the upper part of the island. In earlier days he would have seen a dozen tracks or more, new or old, converging upon this shallow pool of mud; now there was but this single line, coming from the north-east.

'I shall branch off here,' he said by the tree from which he had shot an earlier boar, and he walked uphill to the edge of the northern cliffs. But he was still quite far from the precipice when he skirted what had been a puddle in the night and was now a broad patch of mud, soft mud. On its farther edge, as clear as well could be, he saw a child's footprint: nothing leading to it, nothing leading from it. 'Either that child is preternaturally agile and leapt a clear eight feet, or it was an angel setting one foot on earth,' he said, his search in the low scrub on either side having revealed nothing. 'We have no ship's boy anything like so small.'

Another hundred yards resolved the puzzle. Near the edge of the precipice, where he had lain with his head down the narrow cleft, the same cleft down which Reade was to have been lowered, stood seven baskets, filled with the finest nests and carefully wedged with stones. And if that was not clear enough there was a junk lying offshore, with boats going to and from the little sandy cove.

When he had sat there for some minutes, his mind turning over the various possibilities, he heard children's voices down among the trees. They were raised in anger, mockery, challenge and defiance, in Malay or Chinese indifferently; they rose in a shrill crescendo that ended with a distinct thump, a scream of pain, and a concerted wail.

Stephen walked down and found four children under a tall medang, three little girls howling with woe, one little boy groaning with pain and grasping his bloody leg. They were all Chinese, all dressed in much the same way, with pads on their knees and elbows for cave-climbing.

They turned to him and stopped howling. 'Li Po said we could go and play when we had gathered seven baskets,' said one girl in Malay.

'We never meant him to go right up to the top,' said another. 'It is not our fault.'

'Li Po will whip us past all bearing,' said the third. 'We are only girls.' And she began grizzling again.

Stephen's appearance did not astonish or alarm them – he too was dressed in wide short trousers, an open jacket and a broad hat, while his face, so long exposed to the sun, was now a disagreeable yellow – and the little boy, who in any case was partly stunned, let him examine the leg without resistance.

Having more or less staunched the blood with his handkerchief and made his diagnosis Stephen said, 'Lie quite still, and I will cut you seven splints.' This he did with his hunting knife, and although time pressed with very great urgency, professional conscience obliged him to trim them before cutting his thin cloth jacket into strips for pads and bandages. He worked as fast as ever he could, but the little girls, calmed by his grown-up, competent presence, talked faster still. The eldest, Mai-mai, was the boy's sister and their father was Li Po, the owner of the junk. They had come from Batavia to fetch a cargo of ore from Ketapan in Borneo, and as they did every season when the wind was favourable and the sea calm, they had deviated from their course for the bird's-nest island. When they were very young they had had ropes lowered from above, but now they did not need them. They came right up from the bottom, using pegs driven in here and there in the bad places; but generally it was quite easy to creep along the ledges and slopes, carrying a small basket in one's teeth and filling the large ones at the top. Only thin people could get through in some places. Li Po's brother, the one who was killed by Dyak pirates, had grown too fat by the time he was fifteen.

'There,' said Stephen, gently tying a final knot, 'I believe that will answer. Now, Mai-mai, my dear, you must go down at once and tell your father what has happened. Tell him I am a medical man, that I have treated the wound, and that I am going to carry your brother to our camp on the south side. He cannot possibly be lowered to the junk in this state. Tell Li Po there are a hundred Englishmen in a fortified camp nearly opposite the reef, and that we shall be happy to see him as soon as he can bring the junk round. Now run along like a good child and tell him all will be well. The others may go with you or come with me, just as they choose.'

They chose coming with him out of a desire for novelty, an unwillingness to see Li Po just at present, and the glory of carrying the rifle. The path was narrow, their legs short, and they had either to run in front of him and talk over their shoulders or else behind and call out to the back of his head as he carried the boy; for there was no question of their not talking, with so much to communicate and so many important things to learn. The slimmer of the two, whose eyes had that extraordinary purity of curve only to be seen in Chinese children, wished Stephen to know that her best friend in Batavia, whose name could be interpreted as Golden Flower of Day, possessed a striped Dutch cat. No doubt the old gentleman had already seen a striped Dutch cat? Would the old gentleman like to hear an account of the plants in their garden, and of the betrothal ceremonies of their aunt Wang? This and a catalogue of the varieties of edible bird's nests, with their prices, lasted almost to the edge of the forest, and they could be heard from the camp well before their forms could be seen.

'Lord, Jack,' said Stephen when the boy had been put into a cot with a basket over his leg and Ahmed at hand to comfort him, and when the little girls had been turned loose to admire the wonders of the camp, 'there is a great deal to be said for the Confucian tradition.'

'So my old nurse always used to tell me,' said Jack. 'Just let me send for your blessed gazelle, and then tell me where you found them and why you are looking so pleased.'

'The tradition or shall I say doctrine of infinite respect for age. As soon as I told that worthy child to run along like a good girl now, she stood up, bowed with her hands clasped before her, and ran off. It was the turning-point, the crisis: either all was wrecked or all succeeded. Had she proved froward, or stubborn, or disobedient I was lost . . . The animal is behind and rather beyond the cricket-field, in a tree one half blackened by lightning, one half green. That is how I shall bring up my daughter.'

'Don't you wish you may succeed? Ha, ha, ha! Bonden, there. Bonden, the Doctor has saved our bacon again – has *saved our bacon* – so take three more hands and a stout spar to the lightning-struck tree by the cricket-pitch as quick as ever you like. Now, sir?' – turning to Stephen.

'Now, sir, prepare to be amazed. There is a vast junk with empty holds lying off the north side of the island: the children had come ashore to collect edible bird's nests. I believe the vessel will come round as soon as the wind serves, and I think it likely that its owner and captain will carry us back to Batavia. That boy in splints is his son. And I have draughts on Shao Yen, a Batavia banker he must necessarily know, draughts that will certainly pay our passage; and if his demands are not exorbitant they will leave enough over for some modest vessel that may still enable us to keep our rendezvous in New South Wales or even before.'

'Oh Stephen,' cried Jack, 'what a glorious thought!' He beat his hands together, as he did when he was very deeply moved, and then said, 'He had better not be exorbitant . . . By God, to keep our rendezvous . . . With this wind we should be in Batavia in three days at the most; and if Raffles can help us to something that will swim at something better than five knots we have time in hand for a much earlier rendezvous. Time and to spare. Lord, how providential that you happened to be by when the poor boy broke his leg.'

'Perhaps hurt it would be more exact. I will not absolutely certify the fracture.'

'But he has splints on.'

'In such cases one cannot be too careful. How pleasantly the breeze is freshening.'

'If your junk is at all weatherly – and I am sure she is a wonderfully weatherly craft – it should bring her round by the afternoon. Just how big is she? I mean,' he added, seeing the look of deep stupidity in Stephen's face, 'what does she displace? What is her tonnage? What does she weigh?'

'Oh, I cannot tell. Shall we say ten thousand tons?'

'What a fellow you are, Stephen,' cried Jack. 'The *Surprise* don't gauge six hundred. How does your blessed junk compare with her?'

'Dear *Surprise*,' said Stephen, and then recollecting himself, 'I do not let on to be an expert in nautical affairs, you know; but I think the junk, though not so long as the *Surprise*, is distinctly fatter, and swims higher in the sea. I am fully persuaded that there is room for everybody, sitting close, and for what possessions we may have left.'

'If you please, sir,' said Killick, 'dinner is on table.'

'Killick,' said Jack, smiling on him in a way that Killick would have found incomprehensible if he had not been listening attentively, 'we have not put all our wine into the common pool yet, have we?'

48

'Oh no, sir. Which there is grog for all hands today.'

'Then rouse out a couple of bottles of the Haut Brion with the long cork, the eighty-nine: and tell my cook to knock up something to stay the little girls' hunger till the gazelle comes in.' To Stephen he said, 'The *Haut Brion* should go well with the *Dublin* horse, ha, ha, ha! Ain't I a rattle? You smoked it, Stephen, did you not? No reflexion upon your country of course, God bless it – mere lightness of heart.' Chuckling he drew the cork, passed Stephen a glass, raised his own and said, 'Here is to your glorious, glorious junk, the timeliest junk that ever yet was seen.'

The glorious junk appeared round the point before the end of the second bottle and began beating up for the anchorage. 'Before we drink our coffee I shall just look at that dressing,' said Stephen. 'Mr Macmillan,' he called in the hospital-tent, 'be so good as to give me two elegant splints and white bandage galore.'

They unwound the strips of jacket and swabbed the scratch quite clean. 'Something of a sprain do I see, sir,' said Macmillan, 'and a considerable tumescence about the external malleolus; but where is the break? Why the splint?'

'It may exist only in the form of an imperceptible crack,' said Stephen, 'but we must bind it up with as much care and attention as if it were a compound fracture of the most untoward kind; and we shall anoint it with hog's lard mixed with Cambodian bole.'

Returning to his coffee he observed that Jack Aubrey, light-hearted though he was, had not overlooked the necessity for a show of strength: the earthwork was bristling with armed men, all clearly visible from the junk.

Li Po came up the hill therefore with a submissive, deprecating air, accompanied only by a youth carrying a contemptible box of dried litchis and a canister of discreditable green tea: Li Po begged the learned physician's acceptance of these worthless articles – mere shadowy tokens of his respectful gratitude – and might he see his son?

The little boy could not have played his part better. He

moaned, groaned, rolled his eyes with anguish, spoke in a faint and dying voice, and shrunk petulantly from his father's caressing hand.

'Never mind,' said Stephen. 'His suffering will be less once we are afloat; I shall attend him every day and when I remove these bandages in Batavia you will find his leg perfectly whole.'

Chapter Three

When the *Diane* ran on to her uncharted reef she was carrying the British envoy to the Sultan of Pulo Prabang back to
Batavia, the first stage in his journey home: Mr Fox had
been successful in negotiating a treaty of friendship with the
Sultan in spite of active French competition, and since he
was extremely eager to carry it to London he and most of
his suite set out in the frigate's pinnace with an officer and
crew to sail the remaining two hundred miles in what
appeared to be favourable weather. At the same time he left
a fully authenticated, signed and sealed duplicate with his
private secretary, David Edwards, both as a reasonable precaution and as a means of getting rid of him: Mr Fox had
taken against the young man and did not wish for his company during the long voyage from Batavia to England.

But the pinnace had been overtaken by the same typhoon
that shattered the grounded *Diane*; and with the envoy and
the original lost this duplicate took on an entirely different
importance, and the penniless cheerful sanguine young man,
much in need of some settled employment, built great hopes
upon it. If he were to appear in Whitehall and say to the
minister, 'Here, sir, is the treaty with the Sultan of Prabang',
or, 'Sir, I have the honour of bringing you the treaty concluded between His Majesty and the Sultan of Prabang,'
surely it must lead to something? Not indeed to the knight-
hood or baronetcy that Fox had expected, but surely to
some little place under Government – attaché in one of the
smaller, more remote legations, or Deputy Harbinger to the
Board of Green Cloth? He was an honourable creature and
he had no knowledge of the poisonous letter that Fox had

enclosed with the duplicate, a letter that spoke ill of practically everyone aboard the *Diane*, particularly his secretary; but Stephen, who as an intelligence-agent was obliged to live by a different code, was well acquainted with its contents.

Edwards, bound by duty, a lingering affection for his chief, decent interest and everything that was proper had enveloped the treaty in linen, waxed silk and an outer case: he always carried it in his bosom, and now as he and Stephen stood side by side on the lofty poop of Li Po's junk, gazing astern, he tapped his chest, which gave out an answering hollow, cardboardy sound, and said, 'Sometimes it appears to me that this document is under a curse. It has been wrecked and very nearly sunk; it has been attacked by Dyaks and very nearly burnt; and now it is in grave danger of being seized by pirates, to the utter annihilation of all our efforts.'

'Sure, this is a sight calculated to freeze a man's blood in his veins,' replied Stephen, looking at the wicked proa tearing along in their wake, close-hauled to the south-west breeze, both its outriggers skimming white on the sea: wicked, in that it was certainly a pirate and much faster than the junk, but not very dangerous, in that it was small, containing no more than fifty men squeezed tight and possessing not a single gun. 'Yet even so, I think they will *sheer away*, as Captain Aubrey would put it, as soon as he and Mr Welby have ranged the Marines along the side. In any event, Mai-mai, who has more experience of sea-Dyaks and of pirates in general than any twelve of us, assures me that this is only a low Karimata proa. She wonders at its assurance, since this is Wan Da's territory. When he is neither hunting nor on duty at the palace he sails up and down the strait and to and fro in it, levying tribute on all those who have accepted his protection and sinking or burning the rest.'

At last the Marines came clumping up, red coats, white cross-belts, bright muskets and all, fit for any parade-ground. They lined the rail, all the rails, and Captain Aubrey called up to Stephen, 'Pray tell him to port his helm.'

A series of barking falsetto orders in Chinese and the

junk began a smooth curve that displayed her overwhelming armament, which included the two carronades. The pirates, having contemplated this for a while, turned and went racing away to the northwards in search of an easier prey.

'Mr Welby,' said Jack, 'it might save many valuable lives, was you to dismiss your jollies at once, and let them take off their stocks.' With Li Po he exchanged smiles and bows, and to Stephen and Edwards he said, 'I am so sorry to have kept you in fear and trembling all this while, but the construction of the junk is so very unlike anything we are used to that the poor fellows could not come at their things – boots in one hold, accoutrements in another, bayonets far from cross-belts, and pipeclay in the after-magazine with the gunpowder. Would you believe me, gentlemen, if I were to tell you that this vessel has no less than six separate holds? And when I say separate I mean divided from one another by a watertight bulkhead.' His officers came swarming up a ladder to a curious little deck or platform without a name in the Royal Navy vocabulary, looking about them with the lost amazement usual in landsmen aboard a man-of-war. 'Ain't I right, Mr Fielding,' he called, 'when I tell the Doctor here there are no less than six separate holds?'

'It is an understatement, sir,' replied Fielding. 'Richardson and I make seven and the master reckons eight: we are going to make another tour. The midshipmen say they have reached double figures.'

'Mai-mai, sweetheart,' said Stephen down through a grating beneath which the little girls could be seen playing an elaborate form of hopscotch, 'would you be a kind child and show these gentlemen each several compartment of the junk in turn? I am sure they will give you a whole ship's biscuit for yourself.' Ship's biscuit: they were passionately attached to it, old though it might be, and could not be brought to believe that in ordinary times the seamen were given a pound every single ordinary working day.

'It is a strange way of building a ship,' said Jack, 'but Lord, it has its advantages! If the *Diane* had had those bulkheads she would be swimming yet.' And he went on about the wonderful economy of knees, the flexible strength far surpassing even what Seppings could provide, until the vacant expressions before him quenched his flow.

'I must dress that boy's leg,' said Stephen. 'On the right there is still another pelican.'

He had not only the splints to attend to under the anxious parent's eye and the startling purple balm to renew, but also his serious rounds in company with Macmillan who, he found to his surprise, was drunk. Some degree of drunkenness was a common state aboard a man-of-war after dinner and here the degree was more pronounced than usual, the grog having been mixed with Li Po's arrack, a spirit almost twice as strong as that saved from the *Diane* after the purser had stretched it with pure rain water and a little vitriol; and Macmillan had of course dined in the midshipmen's berth at noon. For all that Stephen was surprised, Macmillan being ordinarily a most exact, abstemious man. Even now he was perfectly steady and his dressings were perfectly neat, but his more or less neutral English was invaded by his native Scotch, with its curious glottal stops, strong aspirates and rolling r's, and his general attitude was more assured and loquacious than usual. 'I lay awake the nicht,' he observed, 'and on a sudden it came to me why you had crackit yon wee bairn's leg. Heuch, heuch, you must have thocht me a puir slow-witted gowk.'

'Not at all, at all,' said Stephen. 'There is a naevus on his shank that we might do well to cauterize against future trouble. Did you remark it?'

'Aye, that I did. My wife had the very same, but abune the knee.'

They were in the relative privacy of the space that served both as captain's store-room and as dispensary, and Stephen, who had a real esteem and even affection for his assistant, felt required to say, 'I was not aware you were a married man, Mr Macmillan.'

For some while Macmillan did not reply, being occupied

with putting their pills, plaster, draughts and bandages away with his usual obsessive neatness, but when he did speak it was as though he had already made a comprehensive answer, his present words being a continuation. 'I had thocht a wife was a pairson a mon could tell his dreams to; but then one day she flung the collops in my face straight from the skillet, cried, "The Hell with your faukit dreamings," whipped out of the door and locked it fast behind her.' He closed the medicine-chest, making the same movement with the key, and said, 'I never saw her more.' They lived at the very top of a lofty house in Canongate, he added in parenthesis before going on in a different voice, 'But I never was a good husband to a canty young woman like her. Even as a boy I had dreams of tall candles bending over in the sun, right down to touch the shelf; and when I was a man it was much the same – I would be there pointing a pistol with a certain triumph, you understand; and the barrel would droop, droop.'

Some decks away, some holds away, Stephen heard the drum beat *Roast Beef of Old England* for the officers' dinner. 'You must forgive me, Mr Macmillan,' he said. 'The Captain is so particular about punctuality.'

The Roast Beef that day consisted of the remains of the babirussa, some cooked in the English, some in the Chinese way, a variety of little Javanese dishes and then the best bird's-nest soup that any man much under the rank of emperor was ever likely to see before him.

'I think, gentlemen,' said the Captain, two minutes after they had drunk the King's health, 'that we are coming up into the wind. Doctor, would you let your Ahmed jump up on deck and see what is afoot?'

Ahmed came back in a moment, and bowing he said in a conciliatory, deprecating tone 'that they were stopping, loosening the sails to let a pirate come up, a pirate twice the size of the junk: Li Po had told him that flight was neither possible nor desirable – nothing more fatal.'

'This is out of the frying-pan into the fire,' said Edwards to Stephen as they stood on coils of rope immediately behind

Jack and his officers, gazing at the uncommonly large war-proa immediately to windward and the canoe that was paddling towards them.

'If you please, sir,' said Reade in a low voice, 'may I share your coil?'

'Of course you may, Mr Reade,' said Stephen. 'Take my hand; and for God's sake take care of your stump against the wooden thing here. To see so perfect a union damaged would break my heart.' And returning to the secretary he went on, 'A very striking figure, Mr Edwards; but not, if you will forgive me, quite accurate: gridiron would be nearer the mark, since Malays always grill their Christian prisoners. Those, that is to say, whom they do not crucify. You may read of this at length in the Père du Halde.'

'I should not feel nearly so strong an inclination to apostatize if it were not for this treaty,' said Edwards.

The canoe came alongside: its chief and two lieutenants were handed in at the junk's version of an entering-port, where Li Po and his mates received them with deep, reverential bows. At Li Po's first words the chief stared about with astonishment at the English seamen, the Marines (now in old shirts and trousers), the officers, and finally Stephen. At this his face changed to candid delight and he hurried over, his hand held out in the European fashion. 'Wan Da, my dear, how do you do?' asked Stephen. 'You recognize Captain Aubrey, I am sure, and his valuable officers? And Mr Edwards, who bears the precious treaty?'

Certainly he did, and would be delighted to drink coffee in his own vessel with Dr Maturin and the Captain as soon as his lieutenants had done their business. This consisted of taking a hundred and twenty-five silver dollars and three baskets of bird's nests by way of toll; and since Li Po had been telling out the coins with a morose deliberation ever since that well-known proa had been seen, picking the lightest and most dubious in his store, the transaction did not take long. Yet even in that short time Stephen had heard enough of Wan Da's description of the French frigate *Cor-*

nélie, now ready for sea in Pulo Prabang, and her frantic attempts at obtaining a minimum of stores for the voyage, to refuse the invitation on Jack's behalf – 'Listen, brother,' said he in an aside, 'we are asked across to the other ship; but it will only mean your listening to an immense amount of talk or making it longer still by translation: I will tell you the gist when I come back' – and to go across alone.

'Yes,' said Wan Da, leading Stephen to a range of cushions, 'she herself is ready for sea; she lies in the fairway; and all the most experienced navigators have advised them, given the season of the year, to sail by the Salibabu Passage. So they will, they swear, if only they can lay in supplies enough to take them there. And indeed they are doing fairly well. They have no money or credit of course, but they have traded six nine-pounders, with a quantity of round-shot and grape, twenty-seven muskets, two cables, one bower anchor and a kedge, for food, mostly sago. How sick of sago they will become, long before the Salibabu Passage, ha, ha, ha!'

'Do you really believe that an armed and desperate ship will confine itself to sago, Wan Da?'

'Not if it can possibly meet a weaker ship in some far corner of the sea. A tiger must be served. But then as I was telling you aboard the junk, there is the question of powder. Their gunner was a careless man, and even when they first came many barrels had been spoilt: then there was the immeasurable rain in the typhoon – your typhoon: it really grieved my heart to hear your news,' said Wan Da, laying his hand on Stephen's knee. 'And all they had ashore was flooded. Now the French envoy, the captain and all the officers have given up their rings, their watches and ornaments, what table silver they have, their silver fittings – shoe-buckles, locks and hinges – to make up a sum to buy as many barrels or even half-barrels as the Sultan will let them have.'

'It is of course a royal monopoly?'

'Oh yes. Except for the Chinese and their fireworks. What quantities the French may privately have had from them, I cannot tell. Not much, I should think, and that little of no great force.'

'What is the Sultan's view?'

'He is indifferent. Now that Hafsa is so great with child, she has brought him a new concubine from Bali, an enchanting long-legged creature like a boy, said to be remarkably perverse.' Wan Da reflected for some moments, with an inward smile, and went on, 'He is quite besotted, and he leaves everything to the Vizier.'

Stephen knew Wan Da intimately. They had hunted together and Wan Da had acted as the intermediary in Stephen's purchasing the Council's good-will by means of draughts on Shao Yen. After some thought he brought out yet another of these papers with the Chinese banker's well-known red seal and said, 'Wan Da, pray do me the very great kindness of seeing whether this will persuade the Vizier to set his face against powder for the French. Point out to him that they may use it to bombard Prabang in revenge for having been given no treaty: they might confiscate the English subsidy, strip the royal treasury, violate the concubines. You owe the French nothing. You have protected them according to your word. What happens to them far away, in the remote Salibabu Passage for example, is no concern of yours. In any event, as you know very well, whatever is to happen has already been decided: what is written is written.'

'Very true,' said Wan Da. 'What is written is certainly written: it would be folly to deny it.' But he did not seem wholly decided or convinced and when he turned to the coffee-pot once more he did so with a constrained, embarrassed smile.

'Do you remember Mr Fox's rifled gun, the one he called the Manton?' asked Stephen after another cup or so and some words about the honey-bear.

Wan Da's expression changed to one of the most pleasurable recollection, retrospective joy, appreciation. 'The one with the swan's head on the lock?'

Stephen nodded and said, 'It is now mine. Would you do me the honour of accepting it as a keepsake? I will give it to your boat's crew when they take me back; for now, dear Wan Da, I am obliged to leave you.'

'Your Excellency,' said a secretary, 'one of the big local junks has come in, loaded to the gunwales with distressed British seamen.'

'From one of the Company's ships?'

'Oh no, sir: they are mostly white or whitish as far as one can see through the dirt. Jackson looked at them through his telescope, and he thought they belonged to the Mauritius privateer that put in last month.'

'Well, damn them all. Do the necessary, Mr Warner: the cavalry barracks is reasonably healthy; and you can indent upon Major Bentinck.'

The Governor returned to his orchid, an epiphyte poised high on a stand, so that its spray of about fifty white flowers – white of a singular purity with golden centres – hung down to his drawing-board, almost touching the particular clock by which he timed his moments of leisure. He was too deeply concerned with exact structure to be a fast worker and he had only added nineteen before the secretary returned and said, 'I do beg your pardon, Excellency, but there is a fellow from the junk who insists on seeing you – has papers he will give only into your hands. He says he is a medical man, but he has no wig, and he has not shaved for a week.'

'Is his name Maturin?'

'I am ashamed to say I did not catch it, sir: he was in quite a passion by the time I reached the hall. A small slight pale ill-looking man.'

'Desire him to walk in, and cancel my engagements with the Dato Selim and Mr Pierson.' He put his drawing-board, watercolours and orchid carefully to one side and pressed the well-worn knob on his clock; as the door opened he hurried forward crying, 'My dear Maturin, how very happy I am to see you! We had given you up for lost. I trust you are well?'

'Perfectly well, I thank you, Governor; only a little ruffled,' said Stephen, whose face was indeed somewhat less sallow than usual. 'The sergeant offered me fourpence to go away.'

'I am so sorry: almost all the people have been changed. But do please sit down. Drink some orangeado – here is an ice-cold jug – and tell me what has happened all this time.'

'Fox successfully negotiated his treaty. The *Diane* then sailed to keep a rendezvous off the False Natunas. The other ship did not appear and at the end of the stipulated time Aubrey steered for Batavia. In the night the frigate struck on an uncharted reef at the height of a spring tide. The sea was reasonably placid, the stranding far from disastrous – in no way a wreck – but it proved impossible to get her off, in spite of the most extreme exertions, and we had to resign ourselves to waiting for the next very high water at the change of the moon. Mr Fox thought it his duty to lose no time and he sailed for Batavia together with his suite in the stoutest of the ship's boats, carrying the treaty. He was overtaken by the typhoon that destroyed the *Diane* on her reef, and I fear he must necessarily have been lost. You have had no word?'

'No word at all; nor could there be any word, I am afraid. That typhoon was horribly destructive: two Indiamen were dismasted and many, many country ships foundered. There was no conceivable hope for an open boat.'

After a pause Maturin said, 'He left an authenticated duplicate with his secretary, Mr Edwards, as a formal precaution. I have it here' – holding up a folder. 'It was of course Edwards's office and privilege to bring it to you, but the poor young man is prostrated with dysentery and he begged me to take it, with his duty and respectful compliments, in order that no time should be lost.'

'Very proper in him.' Raffles took the envelope from the folder. 'You will forgive me?'

'Of course.'

'No envoy ever obtained better terms,' said Raffles at last.

'They might have been dictated by the ministry.' His satisfaction was not quite whole-hearted however and having looked questioningly at Stephen he went on, 'But there is an accompanying letter.'

'There is, I am afraid,' said Stephen. 'I read it to see whether my part in the transaction was given away – revealed – I will not say betrayed. A certain strangeness had led me to suppose that this might possibly be the case.'

'That at least he did not do,' said Raffles. 'But it is a shockingly discreditable piece of invective. Poor Fox. I have seen this coming for some years: but to such a degree . . . You may not think so, Maturin, but as a young man he was excellent company. Terribly discreditable,' he said again, looking at the neat, deliberate writing with distress.

'So discreditable that I was tempted to suppress it.'

'Does Mr Edwards know the contents of the letter?'

'He does not, poor young man. Indeed, he builds all his hopes on delivering the treaty and whatever goes with it in Whitehall.'

'I see. I see. You can absolutely assert that, Maturin?'

'I can, too.'

'It would blast Fox's reputation if it were made public. All his friends would regret it extremely . . . Olivia, my dear,' he cried as his wife passed the french window, wearing gardening-gloves, 'here is Dr Maturin back from his travels, and most of his companions with him.'

'I beg your pardon most humbly, ma'am, for appearing in this state, in pantaloons, unpowdered hair and what might almost be taken for a beard,' said Stephen. 'Captain Aubrey declared that I should not go, that I should bring disgrace on the service; but I evaded him. He himself will not set foot on shore nor will any of his men until they are fit for an admiral's inspection. For you are to understand, ma'am, that we travelled in an unwashed junk ordinarily employed in carrying ore, a potent source of filth, and our garments were stowed in a bewildering multiplicity of compartments; so it will be an hour or so before he can do himself the honour of waiting on you. In the meantime, however, he desires his best compliments.'

Mrs Raffles smiled, said that she was very happy to see Dr Maturin again, that she would at once send to ask Captain Aubrey and his officers to dine that afternoon, and that she would now leave them.

'Now,' said Raffles, as the men sat down again, 'do you choose to tell me how the treaty was obtained?'

'There were of course many factors – the subsidy, Fox's arguments and so on – but one was the fact that your banker and that dear man van Buren brought me acquainted with the proper intermediaries, and I was able to conciliate the good-will of a majority in the Council.'

'I hope you do not suppose that Government will ever refund more than a tenth part of your expenditure, and that only after seven years of impertinent repetitious questioning?'

'I do not. It was an indulgence I allowed myself: mostly for the good cause but also I must admit from a restless desire to undermine Ledward and his friend.'

'Oh, what happened to them?'

'It appears that having lost all credit at court they were killed in an affray.'

'I beg pardon.'

'And since the French had virtually no money at all, Ledward having gambled it away, there was no competition, so the indulgence was not a costly one. I mean to offer myself another: the purchase of a tolerable merchantman, approved for swift sailing.'

'So you do not intend to go home in an Indiaman?'

'Never in life. Did I not tell you of our rendezvous with – with another vessel in these waters or farther afield, and our return by way of New South Wales?'

'Yes, you did, but I had imagined the time was past.'

'Not at all; several possibilities were foreseen. Besides, in your private ear, it is not inconceivable that we may meet the *Cornélie*.'

'Would not that call for a very considerable ship – a very considerable outlay?'

'Very considerable indeed, no doubt. But then I have a not inconsiderable surplus in Shao Yen's hands; my gifts were pitifully small. And if that is not enough I can always draw on London.' A pause, an unnatural pause. 'You look down, sir: you have, if I may so express myself, an uneasy, embarrassed air.'

'Why, to tell you the truth, Maturin, I must confess that I feel both uneasy and embarrassed. There is no personal mail for you or Aubrey – I presume it is gone to New South Wales – but I have what may be very wretched news for you. Did you not tell me that you had changed your unsatisfactory bank?'

'So I did too. As sullen, unobliging a set of illiterate dogs as ever you could wish to see.'

'And that in their place you had chosen Smith and Clowes?'

'Just so.'

'Then with very much regret I am obliged to tell you that Smith and Clowes have suspended payment. They are broke. There may eventually be some small dividend for the creditors, but at present there is not the least possibility of your drawing on them.'

Stephen had an instant, brilliantly clear vision of the attorney's office in Portsmouth in which the document requiring his bank to transfer all he possessed to Smith and Clowes was written, together with a power of attorney addressed to Sir Joseph Blaine, who was also the executor of his will – a document framed by an able lawyer, a man of business thoroughly accustomed to dealing with shifts, evasions and bad faith, an aged dusty man who took real pleasure in his task, his toothless jaws munching as his pen scratched on and on. The dusty room was lined with books, for reference rather than delight, and the dusty window looked out on to a blank wall: a reflector hanging at an angle sent a certain hint of day to the dim ceiling, and the reflexion

63

of a passing gull moved across as a darker shadow among the cobwebs.

'There, sir,' said the lawyer, 'if you will copy that, for in such matters holograph is always best, I defy the most contentious cavilling prig in the kingdom to get round it. You will not forget to sign both documents and send them off to Sir Joseph by the evening post. The bag is not sealed until half past five o'clock, which gives you plenty of time to copy two sheets wrote small and to go aboard before the turn of the tide.'

The recollection and even the attorney's creaking little speech could scarcely have taken a heartbeat of time, for here was Raffles' voice going on almost without the loss of a word, 'But on the other hand, I do have some less dismal tidings, I am happy to say, some trifling set-off. We have recently weighed a Dutch twenty-gun ship – she had been sunk on purpose several months ago because of infection – and now she is as trim and tight as the day she was launched. If we were on the terrace you could see her with a glass; she lies just inside the island by the Dutch Company's yard. As I say, she is only a twenty-gun ship, so she can hardly set about the *Cornélie*, but at least she may enable you to keep your appointment.'

'You astonish me, Governor. I am amazed, happily amazed,' said Stephen.

'I am glad of that,' said Raffles, looking at him doubtfully.

'May I go and tell Aubrey of our good fortune? I left him in a sombre mood, conning over the innumerable ship's books and papers belonging to the late *Diane* that he must present to the senior naval officer here: he is sadly puzzled, because when the Dyaks attacked our island he lost both his purser and his clerk.'

'Lord, Maturin,' cried Raffles, 'you never told me about that.'

'I am a very poor reporter of battles. I do not see them nor in general do I take part. In this one I was in the hospital-tent almost all the time; I did not even join in the final charge.

It was a severe engagement. They killed and wounded many of our people: we destroyed them entirely. But Captain Aubrey will give you an exact account. He leapt about the field of blood as though it were his native heath. You know a tiger's coughing roar, of course?'

'Of course.'

'That is the noise he makes when in battle. Will I go and fetch him now, and shift my clothes into something more worthy of dear Mrs Raffles' table?'

'Certainly: my barge will carry you over at once, and bring our guests back. Pray, how many officers survived?'

'All but the purser, the clerk and one midshipman, though Fielding will limp the days of his life, and Bennett, a master's mate, is still in a very precarious state, while little Reade lost an arm.'

'That little curly-headed boy?'

'No. The little curly-headed boy was killed.'

Raffles shook his head; but there was no decent comment, and he only said, 'I will send for the barge.' Having done so he said, 'As for Aubrey, ship's books and senior naval officer, there is none here, none nearer than Colombo: that is why I have such a free hand with this Dutch ship. I may observe that I have known cases where all a ship's books and papers were lost in a wreck or by enemy action, and the authorities remained totally unmoved, giving a quietus out of hand; whereas a missing docket or receipt or signature in one of the many, many volumes has meant interminable wrangling correspondence and accounts unsettled for seven years, or even ten. I throw this out quite unofficially, of course.'

On his way down to the water's edge Stephen asked the Governor's coxswain to lead him to a toy-shop. 'I wish to buy dolls suitable for three little Chinese girls,' he said; for it had been arranged that he and Jack should stay at the Residence, and as Li Po was urgent to sail for his cargo of ore on the next tide, this was probably the last time he would see them.

'Dolls, sir?' said the coxswain in a wondering voice; and he considered for some time before going on, 'I don't know any but a Dutch shop, and what a Chinese girl would make of a Dutch doll I cannot tell. You will know best, sir, in view of the parties concerned. In view of the parties concerned,' he repeated, with some satisfaction.

He led Stephen to a shop by a canal, a shop with two bow windows on either side of an open door in which there sat a fat Batavian sloven.

'The gentleman wants to buy a doll,' said the coxswain. 'Doll,' he said much louder, jerking his arm and head in a wooden manner.

The sloven looked at them with pale narrowed suspicious eyes, but at length recognizing the Governor's livery she heaved herself up and let them into the shop. The choice was limited to half a dozen figures showing the clothes fashionable in Paris several years ago. She turned up their skirts and petticoats to show their frilly and above all removable drawers: 'Real lace, yis, yis,' she said. Having gazed at them for some minutes Stephen, in despair, picked the three less offensive images.

The sloven wrote the price on a card, large and plain, and gave it to the coxswain, repeating, 'Real lace, yis, yis.'

'She says half a joe apiece, sir,' said the coxswain, deeply shocked, for half a joe was close on two pounds.

Stephen laid down the money and with a leering smile the sloven added three complimentary chamber-pots to the parcel.

'Well, I don't know, I'm sure,' said the coxswain. 'I never seen a Chinese girl with anything like this. Nor yet a little Moor.'

As the Governor's barge pulled out to the junk Stephen reflected on his new poverty, but superficially; he did not enquire into the nature of his feelings or rather of the feeling that was taking shape at some depth. For the present he was scarcely aware of anything but a general sense of loss and a certain dismay. Often in battle he had had men brought to him, shockingly hurt but hardly conscious of it, particularly if the wound could not be seen.

'I shall dismiss it for a week or so,' he said. He had done this with various misfortunes, losses and infidelities in the past, and although dreams sometimes undid him by night and although there were other disadvantages it still seemed to him the best way of dealing with a situation where distress and emotion were likely to get out of hand. Relative importance often proved less than he had supposed in the first confusion of mind.

Aboard the junk he called Mai-mai, Lou-mêng and Pen T'sao and gave them his presents. They thanked him politely, bowed again and again, and cherished the carefully folded wrapping paper; but it was clear from their wondering look at the figures and their shocked, even indignant recognition of the garnished chamber-pots that Stephen had not given the pleasure he had hoped for: though with a certain lack of confidence, it is true.

He had better luck in the den he shared with Jack Aubrey. Making his way through the labyrinthine bowels of the big junk and along its broad short decks he saw that Mrs Raffles' invitation had been received. Elegant broadcloth coats, calculated to resist an arctic gale, were hanging, brushed and trim, in shady places, and their owners, wearing white breeches, stood close to them, keeping as cool and dust-free as possible.

'There you are, Stephen,' cried Jack, an involuntary smile ruining the severity of his tone, 'and much credit have you spread on the service, no doubt: I wonder the dogs did not set upon you. Ahmed and Killick took your clothes in hand the moment the invitation came, and there they are laid out on the chest. I will pass the word for the ship's barber.'

'Before he comes,' said Stephen, 'let me tell you two things or three. The first is that Raffles has a ship for you, a Dutch twenty-gun ship that was wholly immersed for some months on purpose and that has now been raised.'

'Oh, oh!' cried Jack, his face lighting with joy – that is to say glowing bright red, his teeth gleaming in the redness and his eyes a brighter blue – and he shook Stephen's hand with paralysing force.

'The second is that when we met Wan Da he told me, as you know, that the *Cornélie* would be sailing soon. What I did not tell you was that she would be following much the same course that we should have taken in the *Diane* and must take in this dredged-up Dutchman, by the more or less obligatory Salibabu Passage, that she was extremely short of powder, and that as it is a state monopoly I asked him to persuade the Vizier to allow her none.' The plum-coloured happiness disappeared from Jack's face: he looked down. 'At that time,' went on Stephen, 'I had our possible merchant-man in mind, and I did not choose to have her captured or blown out of the water if I could avoid it. In any case, the *Cornélie* probably has *some* powder, salved or purchased from the Chinese merchants; and of course I cannot tell how successful Wan Da may have been.' He thought it better not to say anything about the ship's books at present; there was something of a pause, and in that pause began the drumming of the monsoon rain, louder and louder.

'Well,' said Jack, something of the first glow returning. 'I cannot tell you how delighted I am about the Governor's ship' – raising his voice – 'Killick. Killick, there. Pass the word for the barber.'

'Gentlemen,' said the Governor, 'I cannot tell you how delighted we are, Mrs Raffles and I, to see you at this table. We would indeed wish there were more of you, and that you were all whole; though to be sure' – bowing to his bandaged guests and smiling particularly at Reade, who blushed and looked at his plate – 'there are many glorious precedents . . .' It was a well-turned, sincere speech of welcome, delivered with that felicity which had often carried the day in committees; but it did not quite hit the naval tone, and Raffles' hearers, ordinarily fed much earlier in the day, were hungry, clammily hot and thirsty in spite of the rain that had pierced their boat-cloaks, and any speech would have been too long for them; they displayed no sullenness but no very eager attention either, and when Reade turned pale the Governor came to an abrupt close, skipping five paragraphs and drinking to their happy return in ice-cold claret-cup, considered more healthy in this climate for invalids and the young.

Dish after dish, and cheerfulness returned, helped by Mrs Raffles' natural kindness, natural gifts as a hostess, and by the cool breeze that followed the rain; it was wonderful to see how much the invalids and the young contrived to eat and how pleasantly they were persuaded to take an informal leave as soon as any lassitude appeared.

It was a diminished company that reached the port; a still smaller one that joined Mrs Raffles and the two other ladies for coffee and tea; and only Jack, Stephen and Fielding survived to walk into the library with the Governor. Jack had already made his acknowledgments, his most heartfelt acknowledgments, for Raffles' kindness in offering him the Dutch ship, the *Gelijkheid*, and now the Governor gave him a portfolio of her plans, sheer draught, deck draught, profile and everything else capable of exact measurement and representation, and over these the sailors pored with close professional attention while Ahmed brought the surviving botanical specimens from the voyage. Before opening the packet Stephen gave Raffles a succinct account of Kumai, that other Eden, its orang-utangs, its tarsiers, its tree-shrews. 'If I could foresee a fortnight's peace, I should go there tomorrow,' said Raffles. 'A visit of courtesy to the Sultan, confirming the alliance, would be a perfect excuse; and the sloop *Plover*, due from Colombo at the end of the month, would give me pomp enough. But you can have no idea of how uneasy rests a head with even a hemi-demi-semi crown upon it. Java and its dependencies have a vast population of rajas and sultans and great feudatories, and they are all given to parricide, fratricide and coups d'état; and then there is the enmity between the Javanese, Madurese, ordinary Malays of course, Kalangs,

Baduwis, Amboynese, Bugis, Hindus, Armenians and the rest; they all hate one another but they are all ready to combine against the Chinese, and quite a small riot can spread with extraordinary speed.' He looked attentively at the packet. 'Should you like a knife?' he asked.

'I believe I can manage the knot,' said Stephen, seizing it with his canine teeth. 'Sailors do so hate to see one cut cords, ropes or even string,' he added in a muffled voice. 'There: I have it. Now this first packet is a more or less promiscuous collection of what was growing in the boreen behind van Buren's house. I make no doubt that most are familiar to you.'

'By no means all,' said Raffles: and as he sorted them into two heaps he observed, 'There is a man coming this evening who knows a great deal about these epiphytic plants. Jacob Sowerby. He has published in the *Transactions*, and he has been recommended to me for the post of government naturalist. I have seen one or two others, but ... Now this' – holding up a limp object that could have appealed only to a devoted botanist – 'is something I have never seen, nor anything remotely like it.'

'Your Excellency,' said a secretary, 'Major Bushel sends to beg you to come to the Chinese market: your presence would deal with the trouble at once. Captain West has already turned out the guard in case you see fit to go. And Mr Sowerby is here.'

'I am so sorry,' said the Governor to Stephen, and to the secretary, 'Very well, Mr Akers; I shall go by the Lion Court. Pray make my excuses to Mr Sowerby: I hope to be back in half an hour. You may as well show him up,' he called back from the farther door.

Mr Sowerby walked in, a tall thin man of perhaps forty: from his tense expression it was clear that he was nervous, and from his first words it was clear that his uneasiness had made him aggressive.

Stephen bowed and said, 'Mr Sowerby, I believe? My name is Maturin.'

'You are a botanist, I suppose?' said Sowerby, glancing at the specimens.

'I should scarcely call myself a botanist,' said Stephen, 'though I did publish a little work on the phanerogams of Upper Ossory.'

'A naturalist, then?'

'I think I might fairly describe myself as a naturalist,' said Stephen.

Sowerby made no reply for some time but sat there biting his nails; it was clear to Stephen that the man regarded him as a rival, but his manner was so disobliging that Stephen did not undeceive him. Eventually Sowerby, looking at his bitten nails, said, 'A very small book would deal with the phanerogams of Ossory. Ossory is in Ireland; and no great work would be required to deal with the whole country, except perhaps for the very low forms of life in the bogs. I have been there. I have been there, and although I had been told of its poverty I was astonished to find how very poor it was in fact, flora, fauna and populace.'

'Oh, come; it is not every island that can boast the arbutus and the phalarope.'

'It is not every island that can boast the Iceland moss, or such hordes of barefoot savage children in the capital city itself. Extreme poverty . . .'

Although the poverty of which Sowerby was speaking in the present instance referred to birds – no woodpeckers, no shrikes, no nightingale – the word suddenly brought Stephen's realization of Smith and Clowes's bankruptcy to life, and this added a fresh dimension to his already complex feelings. He was determined not to show how Sowerby's reflexions wounded and angered him, but it was difficult to support the comparison of Trinity College in Dublin 'and its pinched brick lodgings for the students with the splendid courts of my own Trinity at Cambridge, itself but part of a far greater university: but the entire difference between the two islands is on the same scale,' and almost impossible to listen with any appearance of equanimity to the long tirade about

71

'the disgraceful events of 1798, when a numerous band of traitors rose against their natural sovereign, burnt my uncle's rectory and stole three of his cows' or the statement that this poverty and this ignorance had always been and would always be the lot of that unfortunate priestridden community as long as they persisted in the Romish superstition.

'Oh Governor,' said Stephen, turning as the far door opened and Raffles came in with a mission accomplished look on his face, 'I am so glad you are come just at this moment, to hear me crush my – I will not say opponent but rather interlocutor – with a singularly apt quotation that has just floated into my mind. Mr Sowerby here maintains that the Irish have always been poor and ignorant. I maintain that this has not always been the case and I support my statement not out of any annals such as those of the Four Masters which might be looked upon as biased but out of a purely English authority, that of your own Venerable Bede himself, God be with him. "In the year 664," he says in his *Ecclesiastical History*, "a sudden pestilence" – which in Irish we call the Buidhe Connail, the Yellow Plague – "depopulated the southern coasts of England, and soon afterwards, extending into the province of the Northumbrians, ravaged the country far and near, and destroyed a great multitude of men . . . It did no less harm in the island of Ireland, where many of the nobility and of the lower ranks of the English nation . . ."' He coughed and went on, ' "Where many of the nobility and of the lower ranks of the English nation were, at the time, studying theology or leading monastic lives, the Irishmen supplying them with food, and furnishing them with books and their teaching gratis pro Deo."'

Jack had been watching him closely, and with great anxiety; he knew that Stephen was furiously angry and he knew what Stephen was capable of. Now as his friend sat down, his hands no longer trembling, Jack cried, 'Well quoted, Doctor! Well quoted upon my honour. I could not have done half so well, without it had been the Articles of War.'

'It was indeed a knock-down blow, my dear Maturin,'

72

said Raffles. 'One of those replies one usually makes the day after the event. What have you to say, Mr Sowerby?'

Mr Sowerby had only to say that he meant no national reflexion, was unaware that the gentleman came from Ireland, begged his pardon for any involuntary offence, and took advantage of the sailors' departure to make his bow.

'I hope all went well?' said Stephen.

'Oh yes,' said Raffles. 'It is almost the end of Ramadan, you know, and the stricter Muslims grow fractious by the end of the day, particularly such a burning day as this: tomorrow they will be their usual amiable selves, greasy with mutton-fat. But I am sorry you had to endure that fellow. It must have seemed very long.'

'The gentleman's second name is Prolixity,' said Stephen.

They sorted their orchids in silence for a while and then in a hesitant voice Raffles said, 'You are no doubt usually surrounded with gentlemen and fellow-officers – people who know your origin and your worth. I wonder whether you are aware how widespread these illiberal opinions are? Poverty, illiteracy, Popery and so on? And the very strong dislike of those in any way connected with the rising? If you have not mixed with the kind of people who are in authority in New South Wales, I am afraid you may be deeply shocked, should you stay any length of time.'

'I did have a passing glimpse of them in the time of that unfortunate man William Bligh; we touched at Sydney Cove for some essential stores in the *Leopard*. The people were in a state of insurrection, but from what little I saw of the officers they seemed to me, with some exceptions, a parcel of beggars on horseback, with all the froward arrogance and vanity the term implies.'

'Alas, there has been no improvement since then.'

'It is an odd thing,' said Stephen, after a pause, 'that when the American colonists broke away from England, a great many English supported them; even James Boswell did so, to my astonishment, in opposition to Dr Johnson. Yet when the Irish tried to do the same, no voice, as far as I know,

73

was heard in their favour. It is true that Johnson, speaking of the infamous union with Kevin FitzGerald, said, "Do not make an union with us, sir. We should unite with you, only to rob you;" but that was long before the rising.'

'It is a standing wonder to me that Johnson should have borne with that scrub Boswell, and that the scrub should have written such a capital book. I remember a passage where the Doctor grew outrageous about the revolting colonials and called them "a race of convicts, that ought to be thankful for anything we allow them short of hanging", and another where he said, "I am willing to love all mankind, *except an American*," and called them "Rascals – robbers – pirates", exclaiming he'd "burn and destroy them". But then the intrepid Miss Seward said, "Sir, this is an instance that we are always the most violent against those whom we have injured." Perhaps the same violence is now in action against the Irish. Will you join me in a bowl of punch?'

'I believe not, Raffles; though I am very sensible of your kindness. Indeed, as soon as we have sorted through this heap I shall bid you good night. It has been a somewhat wearing day.'

As he passed through the corridor where the secretaries lived he caught the heavy scent of opium, a drug he had used for many years in the more convenient form of laudanum, taking it sometimes for pleasure and relaxation, sometimes for the relief of pain, but above all for dealing with emotional distress. He had abandoned it on his reconciliation with Diana, doing so for many reasons, one of them being his belief that a man ought to manage without bottled fortitude. Plain fortitude from within, that was the cry; but as he caught that familiar smell it occurred to him that he might well have been tempted to break his resolution if he had happened to have a pint bottle at hand: tonight was going to call for an uncommon constancy of mind. For one thing he had been exceedingly angry, which was no help to sleep at all. For another it was likely that his more loquacious self, in spite of all the discipline he could impose upon it, would, in moments of distraction or near sleep, certainly torment him with observations on his new poverty – his inability to oblige Diana, to endow a chair of osteology, to do the handsome thing on occasion, to maintain some of the annuities he had promised, to undertake remote voyages in the *Surprise* when peace should come at last. And if he slept at all, the waking would be worse, with all these aspects invading his mind afresh; accompanied, no doubt, by others he had not yet perceived.

The event proved him totally wrong in both instances. Sleep came at once, jumbling the last words of his paternoster, a deep sleep in which he lay totally relaxed until in the first hint of light he became aware of the luxury of lying there in a state of almost disembodied ease and well-being; then of the delighted recollection that they had a ship; and then of a massive form between him and the faint source of light and of Jack's rumbling whisper asking him if he were awake.

'What if I am, brother?' he replied.

'Why, then,' said Jack, his deep voice filling the room as usual, 'Bonden has as it were found a little green skiff, and I thought you might like to come with me and look at the raised Dutch sloop whose name I never can recall.'

'By all means,' said Stephen, getting out of bed and flinging on his clothes.

'Of course, I suppose you could wash and shave later,' said Jack. 'We are to breakfast with the Governor, you recall.'

'Aye? Well, I dare say we are, but a wig covers a multitude of sins.'

At this time the citadel of Batavia, which contained the Governor's residence, was in a somewhat chaotic state, the last Dutch administration having tried to deal with the appalling mortality from fever by doing away with many of the moats, canals and water-defences, and by temporarily diverting others, with the result that Stephen had but to step from his window into the green skiff, and with Bonden's helping hand to settle himself on a borrowed cushion in the stern, where Jack joined him. They pulled gently along this narrow winding domestic waterway for a hundred yards or so, once looking straight into an astonished kitchen, once into a room from which they averted their blushing faces, then out through the ruined watergate, along the canal through the shallows, running gently with the tide, and so into the open bay. The growing day was perfectly calm, and the few large fishing-proas that were in motion paddled through the mist, singing gently.

Stephen went to sleep again. When he woke, Bonden was still pulling with the same steady rhythm, but the sun rising behind them had burnt off all the hazy vapours, the smooth sea was a most delicate united blue and Jack Aubrey was staring right ahead through the brilliance with extreme concentration.

'There she lays,' he observed, noticing Stephen's movement; and Stephen, following his gaze, saw an island with a wharf, and alongside the wharf the hull or body of a dull brown ship, rather small.

'Oh,' he cried, before his wits were quite returned, 'it has no masts.'

'What sweet, sweet lines,' said Jack, and in a parenthesis to Stephen, 'She will be towed to the sheer-hulk in a day or so – masts in God's plenty. Did you ever see sweeter, Bonden?'

'Never, sir: barring *Surprise*, in course.'

'The boat ahoy,' came the hail.

'*Diane*,' replied Bonden in a voice of brass.

The acting deputy-assistant-master-attendant received the Captain of the *Diane* with what formality his working-party of four would allow, but the ceremony was wrecked by a vehement and indeed shrewish yell from below: 'John, if you don't come this directly minute your eggs will be hard and your bacon all burnt.'

'Pray go along and take your breakfast, sir,' said Jack. 'I can find my way about perfectly well. His Excellency gave me her plans last night.'

She was in fact perfectly familiar from his last night's

studies, yet as he led Stephen up and down the ladders, along the decks and into the holds he kept exclaiming, 'Oh what a sweet little ship! What a sweet little ship!' And when they were on the forecastle again, looking back towards Batavia, he said, 'Never mind the paintwork, Stephen; never mind the masts; a few weeks' work in the yard will provide all that. But only a brilliant hand with noble wood at his command – you saw those perfect hanging knees? – could produce such a little masterpiece as this.' He considered for a while, smiling, and then said, 'Tell me, what was the title poor Fox tripped over during our first audience of the Sultan?'

'*Kesegaran mawar, bunga budi bahasa, hiburan buah pala.*'

'I dare say. But it was your translation of it that I meant. What was the last piece?'

'Nutmeg of consolation.'

'That's it: those were the very words hanging there in the back of my mind. Oh what a glorious name for a tight, sweet, newly-coppered, broad-buttocked little ship, a solace to any man's heart. The *Nutmeg* for daily use: *of Consolation* for official papers. Dear *Nutmeg*! What joy.'

Chapter Four

Little that happened in Batavia remained unknown for long in Pulo Prabang, and shortly after the *Nutmeg* had been brought into service as a post-ship with all the formality that circumstances allowed, a message came from van Buren, congratulating Stephen on his survival, giving news about a young, highly gifted and affectionate orang-utang that had been presented to him by the Sultan, and ending, 'I am particularly desired to tell you that the ship sails on the seventeenth; quite how well provided my informant could not undertake to say, but he hopes that your wishes have been at least in part fulfilled.'

The seventeenth, and the *Nutmeg* barely had her lower masts in: her beautifully dry, clean, sweet-smelling holds, scraped to the fresh wood by innumerable coolies and dried, all hatches off, all gun-ports open, in the last fiery parching blasts of the previous monsoon (not a cockroach, not a flea, not a louse, let alone rats, mice or ancient ballast soaked in filth), were so empty that she rode absurdly high, her bright copper showing broad from stem to stern.

The Dutch dockyard officials and above all the Dutch dockyard mateys were highly skilled and conscientious, even by Royal Naval standards; but they formed a close corporation and they could not abide interlopers. They were willing to work as fast as their limited numbers allowed, and even (for a consideration) to work for some hours beyond the allotted time; but no outside artificers were to be taken on, however able (except for the really vile task of scraping, which was confined to a particular caste of Bugis) and no helping hand was required from any Nutmeg whatsoever.

In the yard the ship was the mateys' preserve. If Mr Crown the bosun, dancing with impatience, laid a finger upon a becket that strictly speaking belonged to the riggers there would be a cry of 'All out' and all the guilds in all branches would down tools and walk off, symbolically washing their hands as they crossed the brow, to be recalled only after prolonged negotiations and payment for the hours lost. They might in theory be part of a conquered nation and their yard, timber, cordage and sailcloth might belong to King George, but the impartial observer would hardly have guessed it, and the wholly partial chief victim, old, lined and grey with frustration, roared out, 'Treason – mutiny – hell and death – flog every man-jack of them round the fleet,' twice or even three times a day.

'I suppose you gentlemen of the Navy are wholly opposed to corruption,' observed Raffles.

'Corruption, sir?' cried Jack. 'I love the word. Ever since my very first command I have corrupted any dockyard or ordnance or victualling board officer who had the shadowiest claim to a traditional present and who could help get my ship to sea a little quicker and in slightly better fighting-trim. I corrupted as far as ever my means allowed me to, sometimes borrowing for the purpose; I do not think I seriously damaged any man's character, and I believe it paid hands down, for the service, for my ship's company and for me. If only I knew the ropes here, or if I had my purser or clerk, both experts in the matter at a lower level, I should do the same in Batavia, saving your respect, sir, and do it on a far larger scale, being far better provided now than I was then.'

'It is a pity none of our Indiamen are due for a couple of months. Their captains understand the matter perfectly well. Yet even so, I think that if my clerk of the works had a word with the superintendent something might come of it. Of course neither you nor I can appear, and I certainly cannot use official funds; but unofficially I will do anything in my power to help you get away as soon as possible. I deplore the necessity for oiling wheels that should run of themselves, but I recognize its existence, especially in this part of the world; and in the case of the *Nutmeg* I am willing to give all the support I can.'

'I am exceedingly obliged to you, sir; and if by means of your worthy clerk I can learn roughly the cost of the solution, I shall do my best to raise it with what I have here. And if I cannot, there may be some commercial house that will accept a draught on London.'

'Who do you bank with, Aubrey?'

'With Hoare's, sir.'

'You did not change, like poor Maturin?'

'No. No, by God,' said Jack, striking his fist into his palm. 'That was the worst day's work I ever did in my life, and I curse the day I ever told him about Smith and Clowes. For my part I had a few thousand with them for convenience; but all the rest I left with Hoare's.'

'In that case Maturin's friend and mine, Shao Yen, will accommodate you.'

Shao Yen did so accommodate Captain Aubrey, and the various guilds concerned were so thoroughly persuaded to abandon their ancient practices for a while that within thirty-six hours the ship swarmed with eager workers, including all the Nutmegs who could find standing-space: Jack and his officers had often, very often had to drive a crew – Fielding was uncommonly good at it, and Crown was no laggard – but never before had they to urge such restraint, to beg their men not to over-exert themselves in this damp, unhealthy weather, or to run such risks up there. Those Nutmegs, the afterguard and their like, who had no highly technical duties to perform, painted ship, supervised from a distance by Bennett, that most unlikely survivor from the battle, who hovered in a skiff, calling, 'Half an inch more below the gun-sill' as the *Nutmeg* assumed the Nelson chequer, in Jack Aubrey's opinion the only pattern for a man-of-war, and one whose exact paint he found in plenty at Batavia; for although the Royal Naval presence was now

reduced to a single lieutenant and a score of clerks and ratings, a very considerable squadron had been in the port and
might well come back again. A wealth of supplies, most of
them captured, had therefore been left; and from this wealth
Jack Aubrey fitted out the *Nutmeg*, wandering at large in
Ali Baba's cave, or rather caves, for the vast selection of new
cables was kept well away from the gunpowder in its vaulted
stores: everything in its place, everything a sailor's professional heart could long for.

He had long since decided that if he met the *Cornélie*, his
only chance (unless Stephen's unsavoury plot had succeeded) was flight or battle at close quarters. With her twenty
nine-pounders, the *Nutmeg* could not play at long bowls
with the French thirty-two-gun eighteen-pounder frigate,
particularly if the French guns were as well pointed as
French guns usually were; but if he could engage yardarm
to yardarm, and if he were armed with thirty-two-pounder
carronades, he could throw in a broadside of three hundred
and twenty pounds as opposed to ninety pounds and board
her in the smoke.

Carronades, then, and he and the gunner and his mates
walked up and down in the dim storehouse behind the ordnance wharf, amazed at the wealth before them, amazed at
their liberty of choice (for the Governor had given Captain
Aubrey a free hand), and almost unable to make up their
minds as they hurried from piece to piece, testing them
for smooth perfection of bore. There was a sort of hurried
anguished joy in the final choosing of the twenty smashers;
and then there was also the frightful question of the round-
shot, since carronades, as opposed to long guns, allowed
very little windage and required an almost perfect sphere
for anything like accuracy, even at their short range. Each
ball weighed thirty-two pounds; each carronade called for a
very great many (there had to be quantities for practice, all
hands being so much more used to the poor *Diane*'s great
guns); and between them they must have rolled many, many
tons along the dusty floors and through the testing hoops.

But with all their virtues – light weight, light charge, small crew, great murdering-power – carronades were awkward bitches. They were so short that even when they were fully run out their flash would sometimes fire the rigging, above all if they were traversed; and then again they heated easily, jumped and broke free. So since Jack designed the *Nutmeg* primarily as a carronade-vessel (though he retained his old brass nine-pounder and another long gun very like it as chasers), he spent hours with all those concerned making the ports exactly suitable for the short, stocky, rebellious creatures and ensuring that no rigging led close by their mouths however far they were traversed. Furthermore, at shocking cost in douceurs to the Dutch, he set a band of brilliant Chinese carpenters to work, changing the ordinary carronade-slides to those with an inclined plane to absorb much of the recoil.

And this was not his only extravagance. 'What is the use of being almost rich,' he asked Raffles – Stephen being elsewhere – 'if you cannot dash away on occasion?'

On this particular occasion he dashed away to a most surprising extent in sails – sails for every weather from wanton zephyrs to what might be expected off the Horn – and in cordage: best Manila almost everywhere, above all in the standing rigging, for which he maintained that nothing could exceed that costly rope in its three-strand shroud-laid form.

All this, and his search for a carpenter, purser, clerk and two or three capable young men for his midshipmen's berth (Reade and Bennett, though full of good-will, could not go aloft, nor were they up to a night-watch in heavy weather), meant that he saw little of Stephen, who, with his surviving patients well on the mend, spent much of his time with Raffles, either in the citadel or at Buitenzorg, the Governor's country retreat, where his gardens and most of his collections were to be found, pored over, commented upon.

Shortly after the Chinese carpenters came aboard Stephen was on his way to Buitenzorg on a hot rain-threatening morning, and he stood pondering by his horse, a pretty little

Maduran mare, while Ahmed patiently held her head. Was it worth carrying a large, heavy, imperfectly waterproof cloak rolled behind the saddle, with the possibility of being both wet and stifled if the weather broke, or was the wiser course to risk a thorough soaking – wet through and through but comparatively cool? Perhaps it might not rain at all. While he was weighing these considerations he saw Sowerby approaching with an oddly hesitant step, sometimes stopping altogether. Eventually he came within hail, took off his hat and called, 'Good morning, sir.'

'Good morning to you, sir,' replied Stephen, putting his foot in the stirrup. In spite of the gesture Sowerby came on and said, 'I was about to leave this letter for you, sir. But now that I have the happiness of the meeting, I hope I may be allowed to acknowledge your magnanimity by word of mouth: His Excellency tells me that I owe your recommendation to my appointment – my appointment to your recommendation.'

'Faith,' said Stephen, 'you owe me little thanks: I was shown papers put forward by the various candidates – I thought yours by far the best, and said so: no more.'

'Even so, sir, I am profoundly grateful; and as an esteem of my token I trust you will permit me to name a nondescript plant after you. But I must not detain you – you are on your way. Pray accept this letter: it contains a specimen and a full description. Good day to you, sir, and a pleasant journey.'

By this time Sowerby was almost blind with nervous tension; his colour came and went, his words tumbled over one another; but by some miracle he handed the letter over without dropping it, stepped safely past Ahmed's restive horse, put on his hat, avoided a stone pillar at the roadside by half an inch, and walked rapidly off.

Steadily they rode, steadily it rained. From time to time freshwater turtles crossed the road, partly walking, partly swimming, always directing their course to the south-west. More frequently, after the first hour, and in far greater numbers, troops of massive fire-bellied toads also made the passage; they too pressed on earnestly to the south-west. But by this time the horses, which had capered at the sight of turtles, were too depressed to shy at even a very numerous body of toads; they plodded on and on, their ears drooping and the warm water streaming off their backs.

It streamed off Stephen's back too, between his coat and his skin, for he had decided against the cloak; and it would have streamed off Sowerby's specimen too but for the fact that one of Stephen's meannesses had to do with wigs. His comfort, his status as a physician, and his sense of what was right required him to have a wig; but he was very reluctant to pay for it. He was now reduced to one alone, a physical bob; and as he considered the Batavian wig-makers' prices exorbitant, this survivor was to serve for all occasions. At present it was protected by a round hat, itself kept from the downpour by a neat removable tarpaulin sheath, and tied under his chin by two lengths of white marline, while a stout pin ran through it all, making the valuable wig as fast to its wearer's head as his scalp itself, and in the crown of this round hat lay Sowerby's letter.

As he sat in the blue morning-room at Buitenzorg, wearing one of the Governor's powdering-gowns while his own clothes were being dried elsewhere, he held up the crisp dry envelope and said, 'I am about to achieve immortality. Mr Sowerby intends to name a nondescript plant after me.'

'There's glory for you!' cried Raffles. 'May we look at it?'

Stephen broke the seal, and from several layers of specimen-paper inside the letter he drew a flower and two leaves.

'I have never seen it before,' said Raffles, gazing at the dirty brown and purple disc. 'It has a superficial resemblance to a stapelia, but of course it must belong to an entirely different family.'

'Sure it smells like some of the more fetid stapelias too,' said Stephen. 'Perhaps I should move it to the window-sill. He found it growing as a parasite on the glabrous bugwort.

These viscid tumescent leaves with inward-curling margins incline me to think that it is also insectivorous.' They considered the plant in silence, breathing as it were sideways, and then Stephen said, 'Do you think the gentleman may have had some satirical intent?'

'No, no, never in life,' said Raffles. 'Such a thing would never occur to him: he is wholly methodical, utterly humourless; a classifier who has nothing to say to values.'

'Lord, Raffles,' cried his wife, coming in, 'what is this very ill smell? Has something died behind the wainscot?'

'My dear,' said the Governor, 'it is this new plant, which is to be named after Dr Maturin.'

'Well,' said Mrs Raffles, 'it is much better to have a flower named after one than a disease or a fracture, I am sure. Think of poor Dr Ward and his dropsy. And certainly this is a prodigious curious plant: but perhaps I might ask Abdul to take it to the potting-shed. Dear Doctor, they tell me your clothes will be quite dry in half an hour; so we shall have an early dinner. You must be starving.'

'The naming of creatures after one's friends or colleagues is a very pretty custom,' observed the Governor, when she had gone. 'And no one ever did it more handsomely than you with *Testudo aubreii*, that glorious reptile. And speaking of Aubrey reminds me that I have not seen him for days. How does he do?'

'He does very well, I thank you, running about day and night to get his ship to sea with even more than the usual mad naval haste – running about with such zeal that he has scarcely time for meals and none for over-eating, I am happy to say.'

'Does he need any more hands?'

'I think not. There are about one hundred and thirty of us left, and seeing the *Nutmeg* will need only small gun-crews – no more than three or four to a carronade, if I do not mistake – he feels that she is quite well-manned. And he is happy with the notion of promoting his carpenter's mate to poor Mr Hadley's place. But as you know he is still short of a

85

purser, a clerk and two or three young gentlemen.'

'As for the purser, my enquiries have not led me to any man I could recommend, but I have an excellent clerk – he was wounded in the leg when we took this place, but he is recovered now and he gets about quite nimbly – and two young gentlemen, who may or may not suit. Do you think Aubrey could dine on Thursday? I could produce my candidates before or after, just as he chooses. And I could ask him, in a general way, about his immediate plans. I think I could do so without indiscretion, because quite apart from my intense curiosity about whether he means to risk an encounter with the *Cornélie* or to outrun her, I could, by stretching my authority a little, detach a sloop, the *Kestrel*, to accompany him as far as the Passage, if he wishes. She should be in by the end of the week.'

Stephen said, 'Speaking without the least authority – what is that at the window?'

'A tangalung, a Java civet,' said Raffles, opening the casement. 'Come, Tabitha.' And after a pause the pretty creature, striped and spotted, came and sat in his lap, looking at Stephen with a frown.

Stephen lowered his voice respectfully and went on, 'Without the least authority, I think I may assert that no offer could be more unwelcome.'

'Oh, indeed?'

'My impression – and this is only my impression: I betray no confidence, still less any consultation – is that Aubrey means to attempt the *Cornélie* if he can find her. The presence of the *Kestrel* could make no difference to the physical outcome of the engagement, since she carries only fourteen pop-guns and is no more capable of setting about a frigate than a frigate is capable of setting about a ship of the line; but it would have a disastrous effect upon the metaphysical result. If Aubrey's attempt should fail, then the *Kestrel* must be sunk or taken too: the *Cornélie* would beat two opponents and cover herself with laurels. But if Aubrey's attempt is successful, as God send, then the *Cornélie* is defeated by the overwhelming odds of two to one; she suffers no disgrace and Aubrey wins no glory. For you are to consider that newspapers and the public take very little notice of the relative strength of opposing ships.'

'Aubrey is much attached to glory?'

'Certainly: he fairly worships Nelson. But I do not think there is any taint of vanity about him, as perhaps there was in his hero. Aubrey's personal triumph however, is a matter of no importance in this hypothetical encounter: the essential aim, which he recognizes with perfect clarity, is to lower French self-esteem, particularly French naval self-esteem. It is, I do assure you, a matter of such importance that I should go to – have been to – surprising lengths . . .'

The nature of these lengths was never revealed: the door opened and the English butler, once a fine plump rosy specimen of his kind but now yellowed and shrunken with Javan ague, announced that His Excellency was served.

'Heavens, Mr Richardson, my dear, what a hullaballoo!' cried Stephen, going aboard the *Nutmeg*. 'What are all these people about?'

'Good morning, sir,' said Richardson. 'They are rattling down the shrouds.'

'Well, God be between them and evil,' said Stephen. 'It looks horribly dangerous to me. Would himself be in the ship?'

He was in the cabin, taking his ease with a pot of coffee after an exceedingly hard morning that had begun in the darkness: he looked pale, worn, but contented.

'I should never have believed that so much could be done in three days,' said Stephen, looking around, 'for it is absolutely no more since I was here. The cabin is almost the same as our old one – clean, trim, comfortable; and these neat little carronades leave one so much more room, what joy. Raffles asks us to dine on Thursday, here in Batavia: he has a clerk for you whom he guarantees and two midshipmen whom he does not. No honest purser, I am afraid.'

'Thursday?' said Jack, his face falling. 'I had reckoned on warping out for the powder-hoy tomorrow forenoon, getting our livestock in during slack water, and sailing on the evening tide.'

'I know that tomorrow he has a council-meeting and then a great dinner for a score of potentates at Buitenzorg.'

'Of course he is very much taken up,' said Jack; and having reflected he went on, 'Thursday means the loss of a couple of days. Yet it would make me most uneasy not to do the civil thing by the Governor; he has been so uncommon obliging. But I tell you what it is, Stephen: was you to see him before Thursday and beg him not to trouble with his clerk and the reefers, but just tell a secretary to give them a note for me, how very much better that would be. He and Mrs Raffles would not have a couple of awkward louts on their hands and I could get a much better notion of their capabilities. Do you know why they were discharged?'

'Drunkenness, fornication and sloth were their undoing; and they were not so much discharged as abandoned. They left their disorderly house at about noon, made their staggering, crapulous way to the strand, and found that the squadron had sailed at dawn. They have been living in squalor ever since; for although the Governor has taken some little indirect notice of them, it does not appear that their friends have relieved them in any way, possibly for want of time rather than of inclination. It does after all take an eternity for an Indiaman to come and go.'

Jack gazed at the South China Sea for a while – brilliant sun and countless small craft moving busily under it, but a greenish tinge to the water, with a rain-charged cloudbank rising a hand's breadth from the horizon in the south – and then pouring Stephen another cup he said, 'As for the purser, I can do without. Poor Bligh had an intelligent, reasonably honest steward and a knowing Jack-in-the-dust: and in any case Captain Cook was his own purser. I should most cordially welcome a good clerk however; it would wound my heart to lose all our records as you suggested – my observations for

Humboldt were to some extent combined with them – and a clever man used to ship's books could perhaps disentangle the confusion. Besides, there was the awful case of Macintosh – you remember Macintosh: took the *Sibylle*, thirty-six, in a running fight right down the Channel – who tried the same solution when he went ashore in the Cyclades and lost half his papers. He took the remaining half, wrapped it up in a sheet of lead on which he wrote "S – the Navy Board, f – the Admiralty, b – the Sick and hurt" and dropped it overboard. A week later a Greek sponge-diver brought it to the flagship in perfect condition and asked for a reward.'

'He counted his chickens without reckoning with his host,' said Stephen.

'Yes. As for the reefers, I shall look at them of course; but an unrecommended reefer, and an oldster at that . . . I had been thinking of young Conway of the foretop; but it is an awkward thing coming through the hawse-hole in your own ship giving orders to men who were your messmates yesterday, quite apart from joining a midshipmen's berth full of people who were your superiors. And then again my promotions have often been unlucky. The quarterdeck is a damned unhealthy place in action, you know.'

'Little do I know of battle,' said Stephen, 'but I had imagined that the midshipmen were with their gun-crews or in the tops with the small-arms men.'

'So they are, most of them; but there are always some on the quarterdeck with the captain and first lieutenant – aides de camp, as you might say.'

On Wednesday the *Nutmeg* sailed out into the bay, picked up the Dutch moorings the *Diane* had used, and underwent a very severe examination by her captain, her master and her mate of the hold. Neither in the yard nor alongside the powder-hoy had they been able to get far away enough to judge her trim as they could wish, but now they had all the room in the world, and all three were agreed that she was a little by the stern. The laying of the ballast and the stowing of the hold was an exceedingly laborious, highly-skilled process; it had been completed even to the installation of the livestock, so that the familiar smell of swine now rose from the fore hatchway and wafted along the decks; and to undo it all would have led not perhaps to mutiny but quite certainly to muttering. Fortunately Mr Warren, who was well acquainted with the Captain's devotion to trim and to sailing his ship as fast as ever she could go, had so arranged the hoses that he was able to shift some tons of water to and fro along the ground-tier. 'I think half a strake will do it, sir,' he said.

Jack nodded, and filling his lungs he called, 'Mr Fielding: pray start pumping forward.'

'What a voice our Captain has,' said Stephen, walking to the boat with Welby. 'It carries a vast distance; yet you are to remark that it has none of the hoarseness or metallic quality we find in auctioneers, politicians, shrews.'

'There is a bird in my part of England we call a mire-drum or bull of the bog that is almost as good. You can hear him a good three miles off on a calm evening. But I dare say you know all about that, Doctor.'

'Oh sir. Sir, if you please,' called a voice from behind – a youth running along the quay and panting as he called. 'If you are going to *Nutmeg*, please would you take us with you? We have a note for the Captain.'

'How do you mean, *we*?' asked Welby, frowning.

'There is my friend too, sir, just the other side of the bridge. The heel of his shoe came away again.'

'Then let him take off the other shoe and carry them both in his hand,' said Welby. 'And at the double. We cannot wait here all night.'

'Come on, Miller, come on,' cried the youth in a shout that cracked in the middle. 'Carry your shoes in your hand. The gentlemen cannot wait here all night.'

Stephen considered them as the boat pulled out across the calm water. They were pale, sallow youths, all elbows and knees (What is the English for *âge ingrat*? he wondered); they were thin and underfed, and although they had obviously taken great pains with their appearance and their remaining shabby outgrown clothes they were barely presentable. Indeed, their very care had done them disservice, for they were neither of them practised, expert shavers and both were at the pimply stage: the gashes and excoriations had turned ordinarily plain adolescent faces into something quite repulsive. They were pitiful as the lost and anxious young are pitiful but they did not seem to Stephen particularly interesting youths until one of them, catching his piercing gaze just before the boat touched, said in a low voice, 'I am afraid we must seem rather squalid, sir.' He said it shyly but with a direct look and an evident confidence in Stephen's good-will that touched him. 'Not at all, at all,' he said; and as he went up the side, 'I wonder what Jack will make of them. I hope he will find they are seamen. Otherwise they must take to the loom or the plough.'

A friendly hand pulled him up the last step and he saw Fielding smiling down upon him. 'There you are, Doctor,' he said. 'The Captain desired me to let you know that he is in the cabin with a surprise.'

Smiles again in the cabin, perfectly easy on Jack's fine red face, diffident on that of his neighbour, a small man, standing behind a great array of papers. 'There you are, Doctor,' cried Jack, 'and here is an old shipmate of ours.'

'Mr Adams,' said Stephen, shaking his hand, 'it gives me great pleasure to see you again; and I wish you joy of your recovery.'

'Mr Adams swears he can sort out all this chaos, deal with the necessary replacements and provide us with a full set – we shall preserve everything, and we shall be able to pass our accounts!'

'I have every confidence in Mr Adams' thaumaturgical powers,' said Stephen, speaking with the utmost sincerity, for Adams had been captain's clerk and secretary in the *Lively* when Jack was her temporary commander and he was renowned throughout the Mediterranean for his ability: troubled pursers from other ships came privately aboard for his advice, and many a captain's dispatch owed its clear, accurate account of a complex action to his pen. He could have been a purser himself long ago, but he disliked the candle-counting side; and in any case it was easier for a captain's clerk to take part in cutting-out expeditions, which were his particular delight.

'I should have waited on you as you came in,' said Adams, 'but I was drinking the waters at Barbarlang and never knew you were here till Tuesday, when the Governor sent to let me know, bless him.'

When three bells struck and there was a slight pause Stephen cried, 'But I have quite forgot those unhappy youths. Our boat carried them out, bearing the Governor's or rather a secretary's note, and they are still waiting on the – waiting outside.'

'I shall see them presently,' said Jack.

'You may see them at once, for me, sir,' said Adams, gathering up his papers. 'I am away to the purser's steward. If he has anything of a headpiece, he and I can fill in all these gaps.'

Five minutes later the youths were brought in, pale with waiting and apprehension. Jack received them in a detached, non-committal manner: his present happiness did not cloud his judgment as far as the ship was concerned and his first impression was scarcely favourable: these might very well be the kind of midshipman that any captain would leave behind without any rigorous search.

He quickly learnt their service history – undistinguished – and their natural abilities – moderate. After some thought he said, 'I know nothing about you. I know none of the captains you have served under: I have no note from them and the secretary's chit merely names you, without any recommendation. And of course there is an R against your names on the *Clio*'s books: you are technically deserters. I cannot take you on my quarterdeck. But if you wish I will enter you on the books, rating you able.'

'Thank you, sir,' they said, very faintly.

'The notion of the lower deck don't please you?' said Jack. 'Very well. I am not short-handed and I shall not press you. Nor shall I take you up as deserters. You may go ashore in the next boat.'

'We had much rather stay, sir, if you please,' they said.

'Very well,' said Jack. 'Of course life on the lower deck is hard and rough, as you know very well, but the *Nutmeg* has a decent set of people, and if you keep quiet, do your duty and do not top it the knob – above all do not top it the knob – you will have quite a good time: what is more, you will come to understand the service through and through. Many a good man has started his career as a rating or has been turned before the mast when he was a midshipman and has ended by hoisting his flag. Killick! Killick, there. Pass the word for Mr Fielding. Mr Fielding, Oakes and Miller here will be entered on the ship's books, rated as able. They will belong to the starboard watch and be stationed in the foretop. Purser's steward will issue slops, beds, hammocks, under Mr Adams' supervision.'

'Aye aye, sir,' said Fielding.

'Thank you very much, sir,' said Oakes and Miller, their distress concealed, or rather attempted to be concealed, by a decent appearance of gratitude.

On Thursday Ahmed came into Stephen's cabin with a conscious expression and a prepared speech in his mouth; he knelt, struck his forehead on the deck, and begged leave to depart. He was languishing for his family and his village; it had always been understood that he should return to Java with the tuan; and now the ship was about to leave for an unknown world, a worse England. As a farewell present he had brought the tuan a trilobate betel box in which he might carry his coca-leaves, and a wig, a poor thing, but the best the island could produce.

Stephen had expected this, particularly as Ahmed had been seen leading out a Sumatran beauty; having given him leave to go he added a small purse of johannes, those broad

Portuguese gold pieces, and wrote him a handsome testimonial in case he should wish to be employed again. They parted on excellent terms, and Stephen wore the wig, adequately powdered, to the Governor's dinner.

The meal ran its pleasant course, and although Jack and Stephen were the only men invited, Mrs Raffles had asked no fewer than four Dutch ladies to keep them company, Dutch ladies moderately fluent in English who had contrived to keep their delicate complexions in the climate of Batavia, and whose bulk had not diminished either, nor their merriment. For the first time in his life Stephen found that he and Rubens were of one mind, particularly as their generous décolletés and their diaphanous gowns showed expanses of that nacreous Rubens flesh that had so puzzled him before. The nacreous flesh did in fact exist: and it excited desire. The notion of being in bed with one of these cheerful exuberant creatures quite troubled him for a moment, and he regretted Mrs Raffles' signal, at which they all departed, while the men gathered at the end of the table.

'Aubrey,' said the Governor, 'I dare say Maturin has told you how he received my suggestion of detaching the *Kestrel* as far as the Passage when she comes in?'

'Yes, sir, he did,' said Jack, smiling.

'I am sure he was right; but he was speaking as a man primarily concerned with the political aspect, and I should like to hear the opinion of a sailor, a fighting captain.'

'Well, sir, from the purely tactical view I should much regret having the sloop in company. Her presence might well mean that there would be no engagement at all. The *Cornélie*, seeing us hull-down, in poor light, might easily over-estimate the *Kestrel*'s strength – she is after all shiprigged – and sheer off, never to be seen again. But above all the sloop is not due for several days and even then she would surely have to refit and water and take in stores; and every day means the loss of one hundred and fifty or two hundred miles of easting with the present breeze. As for the rest, the political or what I might even call the spiritual side, I thoroughly agree with Maturin: the more the French navy can be persuaded that they are always to be beat, the less likely they are ever to win. So with your permission, sir, I mean to slip my moorings within five minutes of taking leave of Mrs Raffles, and once I have sunk the land, to stand eastwards under all the sail she can carry.'

'My dear,' said the Governor in the drawing-room, 'we must not keep Captain Aubrey for more than the ritual cup of coffee. He is fairly pawing the ground – he is all eagerness to stand eastwards and persuade the French that they are always to be beat.'

'Before he goes,' said Mrs Raffles, 'he must tell me what he has done with those poor unfortunate young men. It quite used to make my heart bleed when I saw them hanging about the Chinese market, looking so wan and shabby and sad: it would have grieved their mothers past expression.'

'I took them aboard, ma'am, but not on my quarterdeck: before the mast.'

'Among the common sailors? Oh Captain Aubrey, how barbarous! They are gentlemen's sons.'

'So was I, ma'am, when I was turned before the mast. It was rough and hard and in the graveyard watch when no one could see me I wept like a girl. But it did me a power of good: and I do assure you, ma'am, that upon the whole your common sailor is a very decent sort of man. My messmates on the lower deck were as kind as could be, except for one. Gross of course, on occasion; but I have known midshipmen's berths, aye and wardrooms, grosser by far.'

'It would I am sure be indiscreet to ask why you were turned before the mast,' said the Dutch lady most at home in English.

'Well, ma'am,' said Jack with an engaging leer, 'it was partly because of my devotion to the sex, but even more because I stole the captain's tripe.'

'Sex?' cried the Dutch ladies. 'Tripe?' They whispered among themselves, blushed, looked very grave, and fell silent.

In the silence Jack said to Mrs Raffles, 'To return to

your unfortunate young men. They seem to me to have the makings of seamen, but I mean to try them out on the lower deck for a few weeks. If my impression is right, I shall bring them aft, which will fall in well with my notion of promoting a valuable young foremast-jack. He would come aft with them, feeling neither lost nor a stranger in the midshipmen's berth. I have seen to it that they are in the same watch; and they are messmates.'

The *Nutmeg of Consolation* received her Captain without ceremony, instantly hoisted in his gig, slipped her moorings, and as her little band (a tromba marina, two fiddles, an oboe, two Jew's harps and of course the drum) played *Loath to Depart* she made her way out through the shipping with the last of the tide and a fair but very faint breeze. Although the Nutmegs had been kept very, very busy they had still found time to make friends ashore, and a little group of young women, Javanese, Sumatran, Maduran, Dutch and mingled, waved until handkerchiefs could no longer be seen and the ship was little more than a whiteness in the haze towards Cape Krawang.

She was still there on Friday, Saturday and Sunday, for the monsoon, which had been blowing so true and steady all the time they were in Batavia, now gave way to breezes so contrary she was never able to weather that wretched headland. Jack tried everything a sailor could try: anchoring with three cables end to end to stem the flood and take advantage of the ebb; going to sea in search of a favourable wind among the Thousand Islands; beating up tack upon tack, with the *Nutmeg* running as fast through the sea as the utmost attention and consummate seamanship could drive her, but with no gain, because the entire body of water upon which she skimmed with such breathless care was moving westwards at an equal or even greater pace. Sometimes, when it fell calm, he tried sweeping, for the *Nutmeg*, though much bigger than most vessels that resorted to these massive great oars, was not too proud to win a mile or two towards the cape at the cost of sore and somewhat ignominious labour. And sometimes he towed, with all the ship's boats pulling their hearts out ahead. But most of the time the air was in motion of some kind and he sailed: this gained him no easting, but he did learn a great deal about his ship. She was neither brisk nor lively with the wind much abaft the beam, but on a bowline she was as fast and weatherly as a man could desire, almost as fast and weatherly as the *Surprise*, and without her tendency to gripe and steer wild if an expert hand were not at the wheel. During the frequent and oh so unwelcome calms he and the master changed her trim until they hit upon the improbable lay that suited her best – the half-strake by the stern they had begun with – and then the *Nutmeg* steered herself.

Yet even with a perfect trim she could not fly in the face of nature and sail against both wind and tide; and at breakfast on Sunday Jack said, 'I have very rarely acted on principle, and on the few occasions when I have done so, it has always ended unhappy. There was a girl that said, "Upon your word of honour now, Mr Aubrey, do you think Caroline handsomer than me?" and on the principle that honour was sacred I said well yes, perhaps, a little; which angered her amazingly and quite broke off our commerce, do you see. And now, out of mere principle again, I stayed until Thursday for the Governor's dinner – I am not blaming you, Stephen, not for a moment: though it is true that you can never be brought to understand that time and tide wait for no man – but when I think of all that double-reef topsail south-wester wasted, a wind that might have carried us as far as 112°East, why then I say be damned to principle.'

'Is there any more marmalade?' asked Stephen.

Jack passed it and went on, 'But religion is another thing, if you understand me. I mean to rig church this morning, and I wonder whether it would be improper to pray for a fair wind.'

'It is certainly allowable to pray for rain, and I know that it is quite often done. But as to wind ... might not that have a most offensive resemblance to your present heathen practices? Might it not look like a mere reinforcement of your scratching backstays and whistling till you are black in the face? Or even, God forbid, to Popery? Martin would tell us the Anglican usage. We Papists would of course beg for the intercession of our patron or some perhaps more appropriate saint: I shall certainly do so in my private devotions. Yet even without Martin, I believe you would be safe in forming, if not in uttering, a vehement wish.'

'How I wish Martin were here: or rather that we were there, east of the Passage. How are they doing? How have they done? Will they be true to their time? Lord, how I wonder.'

'Who is this Martin they are talking about in the cabin?' asked Killick's new mate, a man-of-war's man from Wapping, left behind with six others from the *Thunderer* to recover from Batavia fever. He alone had survived; and as he had not only his proper discharge, smart-ticket and a commendation from his captain but had also sailed with Jack and Killick at various times in the last twenty years he had been taken on board at once. It was not that he was a particularly well-trained or genteel servant – indeed he was if anything even rougher than Killick – nor that he was an uncommonly expert seaman, being rated able only by courtesy; but he was a cheerful obliging fellow; and above all he was an old shipmate.

'You ain't heard of Mr Martin?' asked Killick, stopping short in his polishing of a silver plate.

'No, mate: never a word,' said the mate, whose name was William Grimshaw.

'Never heard of the *Reverend* Mr Martin?'

'Not even of the *Reverend* Mr Martin.'

'Which he had only one eye,' said Killick; and then, reflecting, 'No. Of course it was after your time. He was chaplain of *Surprise* in the South Sea, being a great friend of the Doctor's. They went collecting wild beasts and butterflies on the Spanish Main – serpents, shrunken heads, dried

98

babies – curiosities, you might say – which they put up in spirits of wine.'

'I saw a lamb with five legs, once,' said William Grimshaw.

'Then when the Captain had his misfortune and took to privateering, Reverend Martin came along too, having had a misfortune likewise. Something to do with his bishop's wife, they said.'

'Bishops don't have wives, mate,' said Grimshaw.

'Well, his miss, his sweetheart, then. But he came along as surgeon's mate, not as parson, no parsons being wanted in a letter of marque.'

'Nor in a man-of-war neither.'

'And there he is as surgeon of *Surprise* at this wery moment, cutting up his shipmates – a fearless hand with a knife by now, having stuffed so many crocodiles and baboons and the like – and waiting for us, God willing, off of some islands beyond this Passage, a quiet, good-natured gent, not too proud to write a letter for a man or a petition for the ship's company: and your petitioners will always pray. They went west about and we went east about, to meet on the far side of the world, do you see; and the skipper wishes the Reverend was here this minute to ask whether it is lawful to pray for a wind, or would it be Popery.'

'Poor unfortunate buggers,' said Grimshaw, dismissing the questions of prayer.

'How do you make that out?' asked Killick, narrowing his eyes.

'Because why, if you sail steady westwards and you come to the line where the date changes, say if you cross it of a Monday, why, tomorrow is Monday too – and you have lost a day's pay.'

Killick pondered, looking shrewish, discontented, suspicious: then his face lightened and he cried, 'But we been sailing steady eastwards, so if we cross it of a Monday, tomorrow is Wednesday and we have Tuesday's pay for nothing, ha, ha, ha! Ain't that right, mate?'

'Right as dried peas, mate.'

'God love you, William Grimshaw.'

This charming news spread round the ship, bringing about an effervescence of cheerfulness that lasted until the next day, so that when church was rigged Jack noticed a lack of the usual placid steady, even bovine attention, and after a few hymns and a psalm he closed his book, made a significant dismissive pause, and said, 'And those that see fit may form an humble, earnest wish, though not a presumptuous request, for a fair wind.' He was answered by a surprising volume of sound: the humming and buzzing usual in chapels (many of the West Country hands were Nonconformists), a general 'Aye', something not unlike 'Hear him' – a confused surge of agreement, but so loud that he was displeased.

So loud that many of the *Nutmeg*'s people were even more displeased, and they freely blamed their shipmates' want of discretion for the truly shocking weather she had to endure for a period that seemed to go on and on, past all reason, with both watches on deck much of the night and the warm, phosphorescent, tumultuous seas swirling deep in the waist of the ship and lifelines stretched fore and aft.

Jack had learnt the *Nutmeg*'s ways in light airs, calms and contrary breezes; now he found how she behaved in squalls, fresh gales, stiff gales, hard gales and gales so strong that she either scudded under a close-reefed foresail, if she had sea-room, her people keeping the most zealous watch for uncharted rocks; or if she had not, as she had not among the frightful reefs and scattered islands of the Macassar Strait, she lay to, doing so as neat and dry as a duck, under her main staysail. Not only did she lie to admirably, but even in a very strong blow she retained her weatherly virtues, coming up to within six points of the wind or even slightly more and making very little leeway; and this as she quite often had to do, when an unexpected island loomed up and they put the helm hard over to claw off the unwelcome shore.

It is true that apart from three or four unnatural squalls that took her aback off Celebes, the gales were all nominally favourable, in that they came roaring over the white-crested sea from the south or south-west; and it was true that all the Nutmegs had known even stronger winds and far higher seas, with the added disadvantage of frostbitten hands, ice-covered decks and rigging, and the danger of cathedral-sized icebergs in the night, when they were sailing the late *Diane* east through the high southern latitudes; but now they took the foul weather as unfair, being so wholly unexpected – it was unnatural to be obliged to change the entire suit of sails three times, ending up with the coarse, terribly heavy stuff ordinarily used for a rough passage south of the Horn. Furthermore all this toil advanced them little: although winds came from the right quarter, the *Nutmeg* could scarcely make any use of them in these dangerous, largely unknown waters.

It was only when they had almost reached the equator again that the monsoon recovered some sense of what was fitting and the ship was able to send up her topgallantmasts once more. This was on a Friday. That day and most of the next were taken up with changing, drying and restoring sails while the *Nutmeg* glided smoothly over the innocent sea at four knots with lookouts posted on every eminence she possessed, and while the evening peace was shattered by the roar of the carronade exercise and the deeper single note of the chasers.

During the earlier calms all hands had had a great deal of practice with the neat little weapons, a mere seventeen hundredweight apiece, and their crews had even come to love them: Jack could say with perfect truth, 'A good exercise, Mr Fielding.' Adding, 'But it would have been even better with more midshipmen. We need at least two more forward and another on the quarterdeck.'

'I quite agree, sir,' said Fielding; and then seeing that Captain Aubrey did not intend to be more specific he asked, 'Do you mean to rig church tomorrow, sir?'

'I think not,' said Jack. 'It may be that things are best left to themselves; so let us content ourselves with divisions and the Articles for this bout. At least until we are in open water. And I do not think we will beat to quarters either. The hands could do with something of a rest.' Then after a pause, 'Let us take a glass below as soon as the cabin exists again.'

The cabin bulkheads, the cabin furniture, the Captain's fiddle, the miniature of Sophie and everything that could interfere with the action of the guns – with the clean sweep fore and aft that ships under Jack Aubrey's command adopted almost every evening of their lives – had been struck down below at the first beat of quarters. Now they were being restored with extraordinary speed by the young carpenter and his crew – practised hands indeed – and within five minutes there was a Christian room again, with sherry and biscuits set out on a tray.

Jack said, 'I think of promoting Conway, Oakes and Miller. Have you any observations?'

'Conway has always been an outstanding young fellow, of course,' said Fielding. 'And Oakes and Miller behaved well in the recent heavy weather.'

'So I noticed. I know very well they are far from perfect, but we do need reefers. Can you suggest any other foremast hands that would do better?'

'No, sir,' said Fielding after some consideration. 'Honestly speaking, I cannot.'

The naval idea of rest might have dismayed many a landsman. Hammocks were piped up half an hour earlier than usual and during breakfast the bosun roared down the main hatchway, 'D'ye hear there, fore and aft? Clean for muster at five bells: duck frocks and white trousers,' while his mates farther forward cried, 'D'ye here, there? Clean shirt and shave for muster at five bells,' calls almost as familiar in a man-of-war as a cock-crow in a farmyard.

From the end of breakfast the ship was in a state of strong, directed and habitual activity: all hands, apart from the few still-beardless boys, shaved, using either their own razors or

submitting to the *Nutmeg*'s barber, while all those with pig-
tails sought out their tie-mates for a mutual combing and
replaiting. There was a great deal of dry holystoning of the
deck, a great deal of washing hands and faces in basins by
the scuttle-butt, and the spotless frocks and trousers, washed
last Thursday in a close-reefed topsail gale, made their
appearance, often adorned with ribbons along the seams,
together with broad-brimmed sennit hats with the ship's
name already embroidered on their bands. At the same time
the Marines polished, pipeclayed and brushed what they
had not polished, pipeclayed and brushed on Saturday
evening; and of course all bags were brought up and arranged
in pyramids on the booms. Those officers who could had
waited until the last moment before changing into their best
uniforms, yet even so they were coming to a slow boil before
Richardson said to Bennett, the mate of the watch, 'Beat to
divisions,' and Bennett, turning to the drummer, said, 'Beat
to divisions.' At the first stroke of the generale the Marines
filed aft, right aft, clump clump, and to the sound of martial
cries they formed in ranks across the ship with Welby at
their head, attended by his non-commissioned officers and
the drummer, while the seamen ran to their appointed
stations, in single rows along the rest of the quarterdeck, the
gangways and the forecastle, their officers and midshipmen
calling out, 'Toe the line, there. Oh you wicked lubbers, toe
the line.' When they had been reduced to some sort of order,
the officer of each division reported to Fielding that his
men were present, properly dressed and clean, sir. Fielding
stepped across the deck to Jack, took off his hat and said,
'All the officers have reported, sir.'

'Very well, Mr Fielding,' said Jack. 'Then we will go
round the ship, if you please.'

This they did, starting as usual with the Marines; then
came the afterguard and waisters – one division in the *Nutmeg* – under Mr Warren and Bennett; the gunners, under
Mr White, for want of a quarterdeck officer, and Fleming;
and the foretopmen, under Richardson and Reade. These

were the youngest, most agile and most highly decorated members of the ship's company; they took a harmless delight in being fine and many were thickly tattooed as well as being ribboned and embroidered fore and aft. Conway was among them, a cheerful young man with bright blue seams to his trousers; so were Oakes and Miller, less cheerful but obviously bearing up quite well – they had even ventured upon a little pink piping round the edges of their frocks. They had been growing steadily less cadaverous at each muster; their pimples had diminished. Then came the forecastlemen, older, experienced hands under Seymour; yet even among these men, who in some cases had been at sea for forty years, there was not one who had made the circumnavigation, not one who had foreseen the gained day; and they too retained some of that unusual elation of spirits.

At each division the officer saluted, the men whipped off their hats, smoothed their hair and stood fairly straight; Jack walked along the line, looking attentively at each man, each well-known face. This was something of a feat when there was a sea running, for there was a strongly-held conviction that since the *Nutmeg*, though small, was ship-rigged and commanded by a post-captain, she should be considered a frigate, and that the hands should line the gangways regardless of the fact that this left precious little room for a portly captain to pass, still less to inspect, a portly foremast hand.

Presently this stage was over, and having inspected the spotless galley with its shining coppers Jack and his first lieutenant passed aft along the empty berth-deck, each berth ornamented with pictures, gleaming pots, Javan peacock-feathers, and a candle on the largest chest; they looked at the cable-tiers, the store-rooms, and eventually they came to the sick-berth, where Stephen, Macmillan and a newly-acquired loblolly-boy received them, reported on the five obstinate cases of Batavia pox and the one broken collarbone – a sheet-anchor man who was so pleased by his gained day that he undertook to show his mates how to dance the Irish trot poised on the fore-jeer bitts.

The Captain returned to the quarterdeck and the brilliant sunshine. The Marines carried arms with a fine clash and stamp, all officers saluted, all the seamen's hats came off. 'Very well, Mr Fielding,' he said. 'We will content ourselves with the Articles, and then contemplate dinner.'

The sword-rack lectern and the boards containing the Articles were at hand: Jack ran through the familiar text at a canter, and ending with ' "All other crimes not capital, committed by any person or persons in the fleet, which are not mentioned in this act or for which no punishment is hereby directed to be inflicted, shall be punished according to the laws and customs in such cases used at sea," ' he carried on, 'Mr Fielding, as there is some little time before eight bells, you may take in the royals and haul down the flying jib.'

For his own part he had a couple of hours and more in which to contemplate dinner: but the pause was worse for his guests, Richardson and Seymour, because the gun-room ordinarily dined well before the cabin and the midshipmen's mess even earlier, at noon itself.

However, it was a meal worth waiting for. Jack's cook Wilson had excelled himself with a fish soup, made mostly of prawns bought from a passing proa, and a roast saddle of mutton, followed by a variety of puddings; and the pale sherry they drank throughout had not suffered at all from at least three crossings of the equator. How they got it all down in a temperature of eighty degrees in an almost saturated atmosphere, and they wearing stout broadcloth, was a wonder to Stephen: all three were now lashing into the baked rice pudding, he observed, the treacle tart, the boiled sago God preserve them, the Shrewsbury cakes, with every appearance of cheerful appetite. Though a discerning eye, very well accustomed to Jack Aubrey's face, could make out that quite another mood underlay the Captain's jovial manner.

'It is a very odd thing,' said Jack, 'that all the people should be so very much surprised and delighted by the gained day. After all, ships have been carrying convicts to Botany Bay and coming home by the Horn these twenty years and more, and you would expect it to be a part of general knowledge. But I am glad there should be a feeling of holiday aboard; it chimes in with what I mean to do this afternoon.'

'By your leave, sir,' cried Killick, hurrying in with a great silver dish all ablaze – a flaming sugared omelette that he set down in front of Jack, the crowning glory of the feast and Wilson's pride and joy.

It was not until they had eaten it all and had drunk the loyal toast and several others that Jack continued, 'You will forgive me if I turn to service matters for a moment. I intend to rate Conway, Oakes and Miller midshipmen before the last dog. May I look to you to ease them into the berth, Mr Seymour? It can be an awkward business, coming aft.'

'I should be very happy to do so, sir,' said Seymour. 'And Bennett and I could lend a hand with uniforms, until they can reach a proper tailor. We bought poor Clerke's things when they were sold at the mast, and he was very well provided – three of everything.'

'Well, sir,' said Richardson, rising to his feet, 'I am very glad indeed to hear your news; and though I must not presume to congratulate you on your choice, I believe I may say that it will very much ease the work of the ship. And I may certainly thank you most heartily for my splendid dinner.'

The day declined, and the breeze with it; by the time the watch was mustered the *Nutmeg* was wafting along over a smooth, soup-warm sea with little more than steerage-way. Nearly all hands were taking the somewhat fresher air on deck, and although it was too hot and clammy for dancing, there was singing on the forecastle. There was singing between decks too, in the midshipmen's berth, where the three new young gentlemen were plying scissors, needle and thread to make their infinitely coveted uniforms fit.

'What do you say to some music, Jack?' said Stephen, coming in with a partition in his hand. 'It is long since we played, and I have just turned up the Clementi piece we used to enjoy in the Mediterranean.'

'To tell you the truth, Stephen,' said Jack, 'I have not the heart for it. I should turn it into a God-damned dirge: I should turn anything into a God-damned dirge. I have been checking my calculations with the master and our figures agree very close. I have made a wrong decision. I should have waited at the mouth of the Sibutu Passage, lying to off the island at its eastern end, so as to engage him at musket-shot and then yardarm to yardarm.' He showed Stephen the great chart spread out over the table. 'With the south-west monsoon he had to go north about Borneo, into the Sulu Sea and then steer south for the Sibutu Passage into the Celebes Sea, for no one in his senses would venture upon the Sulu Archipelago; and having passed through he would bear away for Salibabu. And there, if my plans had gone right, I should have been waiting for him. But my plans have not gone right: they were based on the regularity of the monsoon, and the monsoon has not been regular. The days of heavy weather that made us so slow and cautious in the Macassar Strait would have hurried him through the open Celebes Sea: but if I had steered straight for Sibutu instead of slanting eastwards in this miserable breeze under the lee of the high land, I believe I should have got there first. Whereas now I am convinced that he is through and running fast for Salibabu. I might just possibly catch him before he gets there if the *Cornélie* is ill-found and a heavy sailor; but it would not do me much good if I did. The kind of engagement I look for is not a stern chase but a surprise attack at close quarters, boarding her in the smoke. Though it is a thousand, ten thousand to one I never see him at all. I am afraid these last few days of calm have wrecked me.'

'But if the *Cornélie* sails through the Salibabu Passage, will she not run into Tom Pullings and the *Surprise*?'

'In the first place Tom Pullings would have to be there.'

'Is that unlikely?'

'The odds against it are very long. Half a world between us and God knows what seas. And then in the second place the *Cornélie* would have to keep right over on the north side of the channel, quite out of her way, to be seen even hull-down from Kabruang, where I hope Tom will be lying at anchor until the twentieth. And not only to be seen but to be recognized from a distance. For who would ever expect a Frenchman in these waters? And even if these three improbabilities were overcome, would Tom leave his place of rendezvous for a chase that might lead him over two or three hundred miles of sea? Each one is unlikely, and for all four to coincide . . . No, as far as I can see, our only hope is to crack on like smoke and oakum, to make all sneer again, and try to make up for those infernal days of lying to. We have, after all, a beautifully clean bottom.'

'When you speak of a surprise attack and boarding in the smoke, are you not forgetting the possibility of her having no powder?'

'I had not forgotten it,' said Jack coldly. 'No, I had certainly not forgotten it; though taking a ship in those circumstances would be about as creditable as . . . To be sure, the possibility exists, but I cannot base any plan of attack upon it. The only thing that is clear is that I must try to come up with him and then act accordingly – act in a seamanlike manner,' he added, smiling affectionately, for his tone could not but have been wounding. He was very much on edge, as Stephen was perfectly aware.

The morning watch found this cracking on in progress; and with all hands on deck after breakfast it was carried farther. Royal masts were sent up and their sails were set upon them, very fine and delicate canvas too; and since the wind, a good steady topgallant breeze, was now abaft the beam, studdingsails too made their charming appearance, four on the weather side of the foremast and two on the main, with a crowd of staysails; spritsail and spritsail topsail, of course, with all the jibs that would stand, a noble array.

Presently skysails flashed out above the royals, and all hands watched the water rise high at the bows, sink to the copper abaft the forechains and then race hissing along her side, leaving a broad wake behind, stretching straight and true to the west by south.

Chapter Five

Miller, the uglier of the two resurrected midshipmen, had been commended for his piercing eyesight and his diligence as a lookout not only by Mr Richardson, his divisional officer, but by the Captain himself, and now he could scarcely be prised from the masthead. He had an immense respect for Captain Aubrey: Jack's natural authority, his reputation as a fighting captain, and his power of lifting up or casting down played their part of course, but it was his cracking on that raised Miller's respect to an enthusiastic veneration. In his five years at sea he had never seen anything like it; and his shipmates, some of whom had been afloat ten times as long, assured him he never would. And to be sure, Jack Aubrey, with a very sound, new-masted, new-rigged, clean-bottomed ship, drove the *Nutmeg* extremely hard now that he was in the deep waters of the Celebes Sea. He had good officers, a fairly good set of hands – they were not Surprises yet, but they were already far better than the common run – and a strong sense of frustration and guilt about his wrong decision. Day after day the *Nutmeg* ran eastwards under towering pyramids of canvas, Jack rooted to the quarterdeck and Miller to the masthead; Miller longed beyond anything to delight and astonish Captain Aubrey with the first report of the *Cornélie*'s topgallantsails just nicking the horizon.

Day after day the degrees of longitude went by, with Jack and the master checking and double-checking them by chronometer and by lunar observation, and with Miller spending his watches below high above them; sometimes he took his meals up there in a handkerchief and always the telescope Reade had given him, saying, 'It is no use to a one-armed cove, you know; but you shall treat Harper and me to a bowl of punch when we reach Botany Bay.' Many a proa did he see, particularly west of 123°E, and the occasional junk coming down from the Philippines; those he reported in a non-committal howl, often angering the official lookouts and rarely earning much thanks from the quarterdeck. For the last few days, however, he had been mute; not only were there no vessels to be seen, but there was no horizon either. A soft warm haze filled the air, making it difficult to breathe and impossible to distinguish sea from sky – there was no edge to the world – and only a providential clearing of the mist to the north-north-west allowed him to discern a ship some two miles away, a ship steering south-east under topsails, no more. In a confident roar he hailed the quarterdeck: 'On deck, there. A ship hull-up on the larboard quarter, steering south-east.'

A moment later, transmitted by one taut set of rigging after another, he felt the vibration of a heavy powerful body racing aloft, and then he heard the Captain's voice from the maintop telling him to clear the way. They passed in the shrouds on either side of the topmast and Jack said, 'Where away, Mr Miller?'

'Perhaps half a point on the quarter, sir; but she comes and goes.'

Jack settled himself on the crosstrees, staring over the soft blue sea to the north-north-west: hope, which had almost given way to resignation, flared up again, making his heart beat so that he felt its pounding in his throat. The haze cleared once more, showing the sail quite close; and hope fell to a reasonable pitch. Of course a ship steering south-east could not have been the *Cornélie*: nevertheless he gave the order that ran up the colours and brought the *Nutmeg* round in an elegant curve to close the stranger, a quite remarkably shabby Dutch merchantman, fat and deep-waisted. She made no attempt to escape, but lay there with a backed topsail until the *Nutmeg* ranged up on her windward side. Her crew, mostly black or greyish brown, lined the rail, looking pleased. Not one of her little range of guns – six-pounders, in all likelihood – had been run out.

'What ship is that?' hailed Jack.

'*Alkmaar*, sir, from Manila to Menardo.'

'Let the master come across with her papers.'

The boat splashed down, the master came across: his papers included a licence to trade from Raffles' secretariat in Batavia and they were perfectly in order. Jack handed them back and offered the Dutchman a glass of madeira.

'To tell you the truth, sir,' said he, 'I had much rather have a keg of water, however old.' And in answer to Jack's questioning eye he went on, 'Two or three barrels would be more welcome still, if you can spare them. We have been down to half-pipkins these last days, but even so I doubt we can fetch Menardo without a recruit. The hands are mortal dry, sir.'

'I think we can manage that, Captain,' said Jack. 'But drink up your wine and tell me first how you come to speak English so well, and then how you come to be so short of water.'

'Why, as for the English, sir, I was in and out of herring-busses, Dutch or English, no matter which, when I was a little chap and a young man – in and out of Yarmouth all the time. And it was there I was pressed and sent aboard the *Billy Ruffian*, Captain Hammond, for close on two years, until the peace. And as for the water, we started the top two tiers over the side, running from a couple of pirate junks off the Cagayanes; but when we were free of them, I found that some fool had started almost all the ground tier too, dead against my orders. Oh, it has been a damned unfortunate voyage, sir. Next thing a French frigate – a *French* frigate in these here waters, sir, would you believe it? – brought us to.'

'How many guns?'

'Thirty-two, sir. Far too many for me to argue with. She was short of water likewise, but when I showed them we had barely enough to get home with, if that, whereas she had a good watering-place under her lee, since she was bound for the Passage and beyond, she let it alone. I must say they behaved quite pretty, considering – no pillaging, and left our cargo be – nothing wanton – and though they did take all our powder and all our sails bar what you see, sir, the officer spoke civil and gave us a draught on Paris that may be honoured some day, I hope.'

'How much powder?'

'Four barrels, sir.'

'Halves, I suppose?'

'No, sir, whole barrels. And best Manila large-grain cylinder-powder at that.'

'Where is the watering-place?'

'The island called Nil Desperandum, sir; not the one down in the Banda Sea, but the northern one. It is a slow business watering there because of the winding passage and the smallness of the stream – no basin – but it is the best water in these parts, and I should have gone along with them, only I could never have beat back again against the monsoon. My ship ain't the *Gelijkheid*. What do you call her now, sir?'

'*Nutmeg*,' said Jack; and after a little more conversation about the French frigate, the *Cornélie* of course, her crew and her qualities, and about the watering-place at Nil Desperandum, he stood up, saying, 'Forgive me, Captain, but I am pressed for time. I shall have to send the water over by the fire-engine: I shall come alongside as close as I can and pass a line for the hose. You had better get back to your ship at once and lay everything along.'

The ships parted after perhaps the most unpleasant quarter of an hour in Fielding's life as a first lieutenant. There was a considerable swell; the fire-engine's hose was criminally short; the Alkmaars were criminally negligent in booming-off and the Nutmegs were not much better; they had no respect for his paintwork. And if he had heard Captain Aubrey call out that there was not a moment to be lost once he had heard him a score of times; and even after the lane of water between the ships had widened to a quarter of a mile and the Dutchmen's grateful hooting was faint on the breeze, his spirits were so ruffled that he kicked a ship's boy for pulling off loose ribbons of paint on the blackstrake.

Immediately afterwards he was summoned to the cabin, and he hobbled aft with an uneasy heart, straightening his clothes as he went. He knew very well that Captain Aubrey disliked starting with a rope's end or a cane, kicking, cobbing, and even reproachful words such as 'lubber' or 'damn your infernal limbs' unless they were uttered by himself; and the first lieutenant did not relish the prospect of reproof.

When he opened the door however he found the Captain leaning over a chart with the Doctor on one side and Mr Warren on the other. 'Mr Fielding,' said Jack, looking up with a smile, 'do you know what Nil Desperandum means?'

'No, sir,' said Fielding.

'It means Never say die, or Luck may turn yet,' said Jack, 'and it is the name of an island about three hundred miles to leeward, just before the Passage.'

'Indeed, sir? I had imagined it was somewhere east of Timor.'

'No, no; that is another one. It is the same with Desolation. There are plenty of Desolation Islands, and there are plenty of Nil Desperandums too, ha, ha! With any luck we shall find the *Cornélie* watering there. My aim is to run in and get as close as possible to her. And for that we must look as much like a merchantman as ever we can. How I wish I had thought to exchange the *Alkmaar*'s thin, patched, shabby sails for a suit of ours! But zeal will do wonders.'

'Yes, sir,' said Fielding.

'Never mind your paintwork, Mr Fielding,' said Jack, 'never mind your prettily blacked yards, square by lifts and braces; take your pattern from the *Alkmaar*, and be damned to cleanliness.'

'Yes, sir,' said Fielding, who minded very much indeed about his paintwork and who had turned the *Nutmeg* out with exceptional care, the trimmest twenty-gun ship in the service, fit for any admiral's inspection.

'Ha, ha,' said Maturin suddenly. 'I remember what a vile mud-scow we made of the dear *Surprise*, to deceive the *Spartan*. Turds everywhere.'

'Oh sir,' cried the master in protest.

'Mind you, Mr Fielding,' said Jack, 'the filth does not have to be fundamental. It does not have to bear very close scrutiny. We only have to look so like a merchantman that we can come within range; for once we start firing we must of course do so under our own colours.'

Stephen left them discussing the details of this horrid change and went to make his rounds. Macmillan greeted him with an anxious face and said, 'I am very sorry to tell you, sir, that two dental cases have reported; and I must confess that I am at a loss, wholly at a loss.'

Macmillan uttered these words in Latin, as well he might, the patients being just at hand, their anguished eyes fixed upon the surgeons. In any case the Latin comforted them, being the tongue of the learned, not of some cow-leach who had taken the bounty and who topped it the physician on the forecastle.

'So am I,' said Stephen, having examined the teeth, awkwardly-placed, deeply carious molars in both cases. 'So indeed am I. However, we must do our best. Let me see what instruments we possess . . .' Looking them over he shook his head and said, 'Well, at least let us apply oil of cloves and then stuff the hollows with lead in the hope they will not crumble under our forceps.'

A vain hope; and when at last he left the seamen to the care of their messmates and the ship's butcher, who had held their heads, he was paler than they.

'It is an odd thing,' he said, returning to the cabin, where Jack was settled on the rudder-casing, plucking the strings of his fiddle and watching the broad wake tear away, 'It is an odd thing, yet although I can take off a shattered limb, open a man's skull, cut him for the stone, or if he is a woman deliver him of an uneasy breech-presentation in a seamanlike manner and without a qualm – not indeed with indifference to the suffering and the danger but with what may perhaps be called a professional constancy of mind – I cannot extract a tooth without real agitation. It is the same with Macmillan, though he is an excellent young man in every other respect. I shall never go to sea again without an experienced tooth-drawer, however illiterate he may be.'

'I am sorry you had such a disagreeable time,' said Jack. 'Let us both take a cup of coffee.' Coffee was as much his universal remedy as the alcoholic tincture of opium had once been for Stephen, and he now called for it loud and clear.

Killick looked sourer than usual: coffee was not customary at this time of day. 'It will have to be black, then,' he said. 'I can't go on milking Nanny watch and watch. Do, and she will go dry. A goat ain't a cistern, sir.'

'Strong black coffee,' said Stephen some minutes later. 'How well it goes down: and how glad I am that I did not indulge myself in my coca-leaves on finishing with the sick-berth as I had intended. They calm the mind, sure, but they do away with one's sense of taste. I shall chew three when the pot is out, however.' These leaves, which he had first encountered in South America, were his present, purely personal, catholicon, and although he travelled with enough, packed in soft leather bags, to last him twice round the world, he was remarkably abstemious: these three leaves, now to be chewed so late in the afternoon, were an unusual treat. 'Surely,' he said, gazing about, 'the ship is going at a most uncommon speed? See how the water flings wide; see how the turbulence sweeps away into the past; and there is a general sound all about us – you are to observe that we both raise our voices – that cannot be located but whose predominant note is almost exactly that G your thumb is plucking.'

Hardly were these words out than Reade came bouncing in. His wound had healed wonderfully, but Stephen still made him wear a kind of padded bandolier to protect the socket in case of falls and lurches, and his empty sleeve was pinned to it. He was treated with extraordinary tenderness by all hands; he had entirely recovered his spirits and he had already developed an agility that almost compensated for his loss. 'Mr Richardson's duty, sir,' he said, 'and he thought you would like to know that we are doing twelve knots and one fathom almost exactly. I chalked it up myself.'

Jack laughed aloud. 'Twelve knots one fathom, and that with the wind so far abaft. Thank you, Mr Reade. Pray tell Mr Richardson that he may set a skyscraper on the foremast if he sees fit: and that there will be no quarters this evening.'

'Aye aye, sir. And if you please he said that was I to see the Doctor I should tell him there is a prodigious curious bird keeping company, very like an albatross, with somewhat in its beak.'

Stephen ran up on deck in time to watch the bird's long struggle to disengage the cuttle-fish bone it had transfixed. Once the bone was free the albatross wheeled away, racing southward across the wind and vanishing almost at once among the white horses. 'I thank you heartily for showing me the bird,' he said to Richardson, who replied, 'Not at all, sir,' and then, taking him by the elbow, 'If you will stand just here and bend a little, looking at the top of the foremast, I will show you a skyscraper in a minute. We set them flying, you know.'

Stephen bent and gazed, and amidst a series of orders, pipes and the cry of 'Belay!' he saw a triangular scrap of white appear high above all the other whitenesses, clear in the sun, to the evident satisfaction of the many hands along the immaculate deck – it had just been swept for the second time since dinner.

'One of the smaller albatrosses,' he said, coming back, 'and it was in the act of detaching a cuttle bone from its upper mandible. The bird may have carried it for a thousand miles and more.'

'I wish it had been a letter from home,' said Jack. They were both silent for a moment, and then Jack went on, 'I had always connected albatrosses with the high southern latitudes. What kind was this one?'

'I cannot tell. I only know that it was not Linnaeus' exulans, though he has it wandering in the tropics. There is one species from Japan that has been described and another from the Sandwich Islands. This may have been either or some quite unknown bird; but I should have had to shoot it to make sure, and I have grown rather tired of killing . . . You have noticed, I make no doubt, that the horizon is now quite clear.'

'Yes. The haze vanished in the night, and we had an excellent observation of Rasalhague and the moon which confirmed our position not only by chronometer but even by our dead reckoning almost to the very minute of longitude, which was tolerably gratifying, I believe.' Then, seeing that this splendid news aroused no particular emotion nor indeed anything but a civil inclination of the head, he said, 'What do you say to taking up our game where we left off? I was winning, you will recall.'

'Winning, for all love: how your ageing memory does betray you, my poor friend,' said Stephen, fetching his 'cello. They tuned, and at no great distance Killick said to his mate, 'There they are, at it again. Squeak, squeak; boom, boom. And when they do start a-playing, it's no better. You can't tell t'other from one. Never nothing a man could sing to, even as drunk as Davy's sow.'

'I remember them in the *Lively*: but it is not as chronic as a wardroom full of gents with German flutes, bellyaching night and day, like we had in *Thunderer*. No. Live and let live, I say.'

'Fuck you, William Grimshaw.'

The game they played was that one should improvise in the manner of some eminent composer (or as nearly as indifferent skill and a want of inspiration allowed), that the other, having detected the composer, should then join in, accompanying him with a suitable continuo until some given point understood by both, when the second should take over, either with the same composer or with another. They, at least, took great pleasure in this exercise, and now they played on into the darkness with only a pause at the end of the first dog-watch, when Jack went on deck to take his readings of temperature and salinity with Adams and to reduce sail for the night.

They were still playing when the watch was set, and Killick, laying the table in the dining-cabin said, 'This will stop their gob for a while, thank God. Keep your great greasy thumbs off of the plates, Bill, do: put your white gloves on. Snuff the candles close, and don't get any wax or soot on the goddam snuffers – no, no, give it here.' Killick loved to see his silver set out, gleaming and splendid; but he hated seeing it used, except in so far as use allowed him to polish it again: moderate, very moderate use.

He opened the door into the moonlit, music-filled great cabin and stood there severely until the very first pause, when he said, 'Supper's on table, sir, if you please.'

It was a good supper, consisting, through Mrs Raffles' kindness, of spaghetti, mutton chops, and toasted cheese followed, again through Mrs Raffles' kindness, by plum cake. During the meal they drank their usual toasts, and with the last of the wine Jack said, 'To the dear *Surprise*, and may we meet her soon.'

'With all my heart,' said Stephen, and drained his glass.

They sat reflecting in silence while the current sang past the hull and after some minutes Jack said, 'I wonder whether you would not be well advised to sleep below for this bout. I am going to take the middle watch and I shall be in and out at all hours. I mean to let her run all night and to start disguising her tomorrow; and at first light we shall gut the cabin and trundle the chasers aft.'

In most of Jack Aubrey's commands Stephen, as the ship's surgeon, had an alternative cabin opening off the gun-room: he lay there now, gently swaying with the *Nutmeg*'s pitch and roll as she ran through the darkness. He lay there on his back, with his hands behind his head, perfectly at his ease. He did not sleep. The coffee and even more the coca-leaves quite outweighed the port, but he did not care. His mind ran along as smooth and easy as the *Nutmeg*, one ear hearing the general deep voice of a taut-rigged ship with a fine spread of canvas abroad, the unchanging naval sounds, the faint, faint bells in due succession, the cry of 'All's well' right round the ship, the muffled trampling of bare feet at the changing of the watch. It ran with no particular guidance, drifting agreeably from one set of ideas to another connected by some tenuous association until they came to the possibility however remote of finding the *Surprise* at the far end of the Salibabu Passage. As he evoked her name so he had a clear-cut mental image of her; he smiled in the darkness; and then quite suddenly the loss of his fortune came back to him, his present relative poverty. The *Surprise* might belong to him, but there would be none of those splendid cruises he had promised himself when peace came back again – cruises in which no imperious voice should ever say, 'There is not a moment to be lost,' and in which he and Martin could wander at large on unknown shores and on remote islands never seen by any man, still less any naturalist, where birds could be taken up by hand, examined, and put back on their nests.

Relative poverty. He would not be able to cruise; he would not be able to endow his chairs of comparative osteology; they would have to sell the house in Half Moon Street. But although he had committed himself to a certain number of annuities his calculations (such as they were) seemed to show that a modest competence might remain if he continued in the service; and perhaps they might be able to keep Diana's new place in Hampshire, for her Arabian horses.

In any event he was perfectly certain that she would take it well, even if they had to retire to his half-ruined castle in the mountains of Catalonia. His only fear was that on hearing the news she would sell her famous great diamond, the Blue Peter, the joy of her life: for not only would doing so take away that joy but it would also give her an immense moral advantage, and Stephen was convinced that moral advantage was a great enemy to marriage. Few happy marriages did he know among his friends and acquaintance, and in those few the balance seemed to him equal. Then again he found it more blessed to give than to receive; he had a strong disinclination to being obliged; and sometimes, when he was low-spirited, he put this down to an odious incapacity for gratitude.

Moral advantage. After his parents' death he had spent much of his childhood and youth in Spain, housed by various members of his mother's family before finding a true home with his godfather and cousin Don Ramón: two of these relations, Cosí Francesc and Cosí Eulália, he knew well at three distinct periods of his life, as a small child, as an adolescent and as a grown man. At the time of his first visit they were a newly-married pair and they seemed quite fond of one another, though they were already tolerably strict and severe – early-morning Mass every day in the icy cathedral of Teruel. During his next stay the fondness was by no means apparent in anything but forms of unselfishness and deference to the other's will; and at his third it was quite clear to him that what fondness there may have been had been eaten away by a struggle for moral superiority. Their life had become a competitive martyrdom: competitive fasting, competitive holiness, competitive fortitude and self-denial, a dreadful uncomplaining cheerfulness in that ancient cold damp stony house, an intensely watchful competition that could only be won by the cousin that died first; though Cosí Eulália told him as a secret never to be divulged that she had spent all Don Ramón's presents and all her dress allowance for the last three years in prayers and Masses for her husband's spiritual welfare.

It was not that he thought Diana would profit from her advantage in any way or even be aware that she had one – that was not her style at all. It was rather that he, with his fundamentally rather inferior character, should be oppressed by her generosity.

Six bells, quite distinctly. What watch were they in now, for the love of God? And surely the ship was moving faster still: the fundamental note had risen half a tone. What more tiresome life than a sailor's, perpetually obliged to leap out of bed and run about in the noxious damps? His mind turned to his probable, almost certain daughter, now little more than a larva with virtually no conversation, but with such potentialities! A Mozart string quartet began singing in his head.

'If you please, sir,' said a voice that had been going on for some time and that he connected with the irregular motion of his cot. 'If you please, sir.'

'Were you jerking the strings or lifts of my cot, Mr Conway?' asked Stephen, giving him a malevolent look.

'Yes, sir. Beg pardon, sir,' said Conway. 'Captain's compliments, and it is all over now: hopes you have not been too much disturbed and that you will join him at breakfast.'

'My compliments to the Captain, if you please, and I shall be happy to wait on him.'

'There you are, Stephen,' cried Captain Aubrey. 'Good morning to you. I thought you would be amazed.'

Amazed he was, and for once it showed in his face; for although the forward bulkhead had been replaced, so that he walked into the dining-cabin through the usual door, past the Marine sentry, the rest of the space aft was bare – no wall dividing the dining-cabin from the great cabin – a great bare space with nothing in it but the two chairs, the breakfast-table and far away the nine-pounder chase-guns hard up against the ordinarily imperceptible stern-portlids. The chequered canvas deck-covering was gone; the room was strangely vast and empty – not a chest, not a book-case, not an elbow-chair, nothing but these guns on the bald planking, with their shot-garlands, wads, rammers, worms and the rest. There was almost nothing familiar in the cabin but the table, the far-off stern-windows, the carronades on either side, and the delightful smell of coffee and frying bacon brought aft by who knows what complex eddies and counter-currents.

Jack rang the bell, observing, 'I have not invited any officers or mids. They are all too filthy; and in any case it is far too late in the day. You will be even more amazed when you go on deck. We started ruining the poor *Nutmeg*'s looks when we ordinarily clean the decks, and I do assure you the forecastle is already a hissing and an abomination.'

Breakfast came in, breakfast on the heroic scale, calculated for a large, heavy, powerful man who had been up before first light and who had so far eaten no more than a piece of biscuit. The clash of knives and forks, of china upon china, the sound of pouring coffee, a conversation reduced to such words as 'Will I pass you another egg, so?'

'That cannot have been four bells,' said Stephen, looking up from his plate with an attentive ear.

'I believe it was, though,' said Jack, who had now reached marmalade and his second pot of coffee.

'It was benevolent in you to wait, brother,' said Stephen. 'I take it kindly.'

'I hope you got *some* sleep, at all events,' said Jack.

'Sleep? And why should I not sleep, at all?'

'As soon as the idlers were called we made enough din to raise the dead, getting the chasers aft and opening the port-lids. I doubt they had been opened when she was weighed from the bottom of the sea, they were so cruelly tight. Painted in too, of course, right across the upper counter for pretty, so they could not be seen. I thought it would have broken Fielding's heart as we beat and thumped them into some sense of their duty; but he looked a little less wretched when we had the guns in place. The breeching and the tackles hide some of the scars. And so you slept through it all: well, well.'

Stephen frowned and said, 'I cannot conceive what you hope to gain by placing them there, and ruining our parlour, our music-room, our one solace on the ocean's bosom. But then I am no great sailor.'

'Oh, I should never say that: oh not at all, not really,' said Jack. 'But if you like I will explain them by telling you about my plan of attack, if anything that depends upon one probable surmise but countless unknowns can be called a plan.'

'I should be very happy to hear it.'

'As you know, we hope to catch the *Cornélie* watering at Nil Desperandum, in the cove on the southern side: a not unreasonable hope, since watering there is a very slow business and she needs a great deal for the next leg of her voyage. In the best of cases I should run in, looking like a Dutch merchantman in need of water too and of course wearing Dutch colours: I should run in under shabby topsails, and with luck I should come close alongside, whip up the ensign, give her a broadside and board her in the smoke. It should not be a very difficult boarding: if she had even a small party ashore our numbers would be about equal, and then there is the immense advantage of surprise. But that is the best of cases, and I must provide for others. Suppose for example she lies awkwardly or suppose I miss the channel – in short, suppose I cannot run close alongside, then I must turn about, since I cannot engage her broadside to broadside at any distance, not with carronades against her long eighteen-pounders. Turn and entice her out, for I have no fear of her not chasing: I know she is short of stores – in fact she is probably very, very short. Her being out of water so soon makes it seem likely that she left Pulo Prabang in a great hurry.'

'Nothing could be more probable than a quarrel in those circumstances. The Frenchmen had lost all credit.'

'So, do you see, I am sure of her chasing us: and I am sure of being able to outsail her both by and large. The Dutchman assured me she could not come within seven points close-hauled; and she is wretchedly equipped for a breeze abaft the beam. She was so short of sailcloth that they took mere rags from the *Alkmaar* as better than what they had. My plan is to make her think we are trying to escape – the usual lame-duck tactics – and so lead her through the Salibabu Passage by night, disappear behind the second island at the far end, sending a well-lit boat ahead, and come out as she passes by. Once she is past we have the weather-gage, and it would be strange if we did not lay her alongside in a matter of a glass or two.'

'Would she indeed chase all night in these dangerous parts?'

'Oh, I think so. Salibabu is a deep-water passage, much better known than the South China Sea; and in any case her captain is a bold enterprising man – he heaved his ship down at Pulo Prabang, which I should scarcely have dared to do – and as I say, he is desperately short of stores. He has an enormous tract of ocean to sail across: and would risk anything to seize a well-found ship, man-of-war or not. Furthermore his course lies through the Passage: it does not take him an inch out of his way. I am so sure of his attempting us that I have shifted the chasers aft, as you see. He will certainly pepper us as we run and I should like to be able to reply. You will say that a nine-pounder' – looking affectionately at *Beelzebub*, his own brass chaser – 'will not carry away a frigate's foreyard or even foretopsailyard at the distance I intend to keep, which is profoundly true; but there is always the lucky shot that severs a lift or a backstay, causing sad confusion. I remember when I was a boy in the West Indies a six-pounder fired from the forecastle that cut the chase's peak-halliards, a valuable schooner that was going from us like smoke and oakum – down came her mainmast, and of course we snapped her up. To be sure, that works both ways; and the French are sometimes devilish clever at pointing their guns.'

'On the perhaps rather wild supposition that the *Cornélie* is limited to the four barrels she took from the *Alkmaar*, how long would the peppering last?'

He regretted his question as soon as he had asked it; and indeed Jack answered rather coldly. 'Four barrels would allow one hundred and twenty shots from a nine-pound chaser, or four eighteen-pounder broadsides if the bow gun were left out, which it often is.' But at this point a somewhat haggard Fielding came in to report progress.

'How are the hands taking it?' asked Jack.

'There was a certain amount of reluctance here and there, as you noticed yourself, sir,' said Fielding, 'but now they all seem won over to the idea, and some of the younger topmen have to be restrained rather than encouraged. A proper rag-fair she looks forward: Irish pennants, slush over the side, the heads enough to make a mad-house blush.'

'I will come as soon as the Doctor has finished his cup,' said Jack. 'I promised him he should be amazed.'

'I am with you now,' said Stephen, starting up. 'Pray lead on.'

'There,' said Jack as they all three stood at the quarterdeck barricade, facing forward. There were several other officers on the leeward side and they too watched Stephen's face attentively.

'Where am I to look?' he asked.

'Why, everywhere,' cried both Jack and Fielding.

'It seems much the same to me,' said Stephen.

'Oh for shame,' cried Jack amidst a general sound of disapproval. 'Do not you see the loathsome deck?'

'The rope-yarns hanging about in the rigging?' asked Fielding.

'The loose reef-points?' asked the master, moved beyond discretion.

'The fag-ends of rope everywhere?'

'There is a blue patch on this near topsail that may not have been there yesterday,' said Stephen, anxious to please. 'And perhaps the sail itself is less bright than usual.' This had no success however: pursed lips, shaken heads, mutual looks of intelligence; while behind him an involuntary growl burst from the quartermaster at the con. 'Perhaps I had better occupy myself with what I am more competent to judge,' he said. 'I shall take my morning rounds. Do you choose to accompany me, sir?'

Jack ordinarily visited the sick-berth with the surgeon, to ask the invalids how they did – an attention that was much appreciated – but this morning he excused himself, adding, 'You were no doubt misled by our not having shifted the other sails; but it will be clearer after dinner.'

Even before dinner the change was somewhat more evident. Stephen came on deck in time to see the taking of the sun's altitude as it crossed the meridian. He had been present at this ceremony times without number, but he had rarely seen it carried out so earnestly – every sextant and quadrant the *Nutmeg* possessed was in action and all the midshipmen stood elbow to elbow along her starboard gangway – and never with the ship in such a condition. The tide of squalor had flowed aft, almost reaching the holy quarterdeck, and even the most unobservant eye could not fail to notice the grimy, patched topsails (the most striking contrast to the brilliant sunlit white of the courses, topgallants and royals, and their own spotless studdingsails), the carefully dulled brass, the uneven ratlines, the dirty buckets hung here and there in defiance of all decency, the general air of advanced seediness. Many of the hands had spent their time on line-of-battle ships, which called for sweepers almost every glass and which never, never resorted to practices of this kind; and at first they looked upon the deliberate profanation with horror. But gradually they had been won over, and now, with the enthusiasm of converts, they daubed her sides with filth, almost to excess.

The ceremony came to its invariable end with the first lieutenant stepping across the deck, taking off the hat that he had put on for the purpose, reporting noon to Captain Aubrey and receiving the reply, 'Make it so, Mr Fielding,' which gave the new naval day its legal existence. And immediately after this, as eight bells was struck and the hands were piped to dinner with the usual roaring and trampling, he noticed Jack and the master exchange a nod of satisfaction, from which he concluded without much difficulty that the *Nutmeg*, racing along in this spirited way, her bow-wave flung white and wide, was doing so on the right parallel.

Their own dinner, which again they took by themselves in the austere, echoing great cabin, was barely edible, Wilson having lost his head in the excitement, but apart from observing, 'Well, at least the wine goes down well; and I believe there is rice pudding to come,' Jack took little notice. After a glass or two he said, 'You do understand, Stephen, do you not, that all this is merely provisional, just in the event that the *Cornélie* has done exactly what I want her to have done?' Stephen smiled and nodded, reflecting, 'And I do understand how the evil eye can be attempted to be averted.' Jack went on, 'This morning I did not tell you about my sequence of events, though it is of the very first importance. To begin with, I must raise the island at first light to make sure whether the *Cornélie* is there or not: it would be absurd to carry out some of the more extravagant capers I have in mind until that is decided. I am reasonably confident that we can do so, and with most of the night to spare: the master and I and Dick Richardson all agree very closely in our reckoning, and we should have a very good lunar observation tonight with this clear sky. If it tells us that we are where I think we are, I shall reduce sail and draw in gently until dawn, when I hope Nil Desperandum will be in sight, away to leeward.'

'Ha, ha,' said Stephen, fired for once with a kind of martial fervour. 'I shall desire Welby to give me a call at – at four bells, would it be? He sleeps next door: sleeps, that is to say, when he is not trying to learn French, poor soul.'

'I shall send the mate of the watch,' said Jack. 'Then suppose she is there, we strike topgallantmasts down on deck, dip below the horizon, carry out my other capers, and stand in under topsails, quite leisurely, you understand, because if circumstances are not right – and everything depends on circumstances – or if my direct attack fails, I must entice her out a little after noon, so that we may run through the Passage in the night; and after moonset I can draw ahead, put the helm hard over, nip behind my island, showing neither a glim nor a scrap of canvas and lying to a drift-anchor till she passes, chasing the lights of the boat we have sent on. And once she is, once she is to leeward – why, there we are. We have the weather-gage!'

'Ah? Very good. Will I pour you some wine?'

'If you please. Capital port: have rarely drunk better. Stephen, you are aware of the importance of the weather-gage, are you not? I do not have to explain that a better sailer who has the weather-gage can force an action as and when she chooses? The *Nutmeg* cannot play at long bowls with the *Cornélie*, cannot keep up a broadside battle at long range; but coming up fast in her wake she can range alongside, hammer her and board her. Though of course I do not have to tell you that.'

'It would be strange if the weather-gage had to be explained to so old a sea-dog; though I must confess that there was a time when I confused it with that thing which creaks on the roof, showing which way the wind is blowing. Yet could you not obtain this valuable gage by some less arduous means than running a hundred miles and hiding behind a more or less mythical island which no one has ever seen, and that in the dark, a perilous proceeding if ever there was one?'

'Why, no. I cannot work to windward of him without exposing myself to his broadside at a distance, which our ship cannot stand: and if I reduce sail to let him come up he will very naturally decline, put his helm down and batter me from beyond the effective range of carronades. For I cannot go on the assumption that the *Cornélie* has no more powder than the *Alkmaar*'s four barrels. And as for the island, it is not mythical at all. There are two of them, rising steep-to from fifty fathom and well surveyed. The Dutch used the Passage a great deal, and Raffles gave me an excellent chart. But even so, let us hope that the first plan of running in and boarding her straight away comes to root. That is to say . . .' He paused, frowning.

'Rules the roost?'

'No . . . no.'

'Takes fruit?'

'Oh be damned to it. The trouble with you, Stephen, if you do not mind my saying so, is that although you are the best linguist I was ever shipmates with, like the Pope of Rome that spoke a hundred languages – Pentecost come again . . .'

'Would it be Magliabechi you have in mind?'

'I dare say: a foreigner, in any case. And I am sure you speak quite as many, and like a native, or better; but English is not one of them. You do not get figures quite right, and now you have put the word clean out of my head.'

The old sea-dog appeared on deck next day at dawn, looking as some other old dogs do when they are roused untimely from their pad: uncombed, unbrushed, matted. He was not exceptional. Nearly all the officers were in their oldest working clothes and some had been up much longer. Yet even if Dr Maturin had been tarred and feathered he would have excited no remark. All eyes were fixed on the lookout at the jack-crosstrees, and the lookout's eyes were fixed on an island sharp on that pure horizon to the east-north-east. The sun was up, quite clear of the sea, an incandescent ball already, and its rays lit almost all the island's upper part: those on deck could see no more; only the telescope high above could make out that distant shore. The breeze was now right aft; it had diminished, and there was little sound from the rigging. They stood there in silence, the whole ship's company, as the sunlight travelled down the south-west side of Nil Desperandum.

Warren the master uttered a thundering fart. No one smiled, frowned or took his eyes from the masthead. At long, regular intervals the ship passed through the peaks of the south-west swell, her cutwater making a sound like *shshsh*.

The cry came down, shaky with emotion: 'On deck there.' A pause for two waves. 'She's there, sir. I mean I see a ship, yards across, lying perhaps half a mile offshore: topsails loosed to dry.'

'Hard over,' said Jack to the man at the wheel; and raising his voice, 'Very good, Mr Miller: jump down on deck now. Mr Fielding, we will strike topgallantmasts directly, if you please.'

With the topgallantmasts on the booms and the *Nutmeg* safely out of sight of the land, Jack said, 'When we have furled everything but topsails and forestaysail, we may proceed with our painted strips. But furled in the loose bunt, swagging horribly, with gaskets all ahoo, d'ye hear me there, Mr Seymour,' – directing his voice nominally to Seymour on the forecastle but in fact to the ship's company, who had hitherto been encouraged to furl with exact precision, as taut and trim as in a royal yacht, and who now gazed at one another with wondering grins; for in spite of all that had gone before this was a degree of impropriety that even the boldest minds had not conceived.

The strips of which Captain Aubrey had spoken were lengths of sailcloth with gun-ports painted on them, strips of the kind that many merchantmen with few or no actual cannon wore along their sides in the hope of deterring pirates. They took up a great deal of space on deck while they were being prepared, as Stephen knew very well, having seen Jack use them before; but this time, with a crew not used to Captain Aubrey's ways, they took even more and he retreated farther and farther. On reaching the taffrail he decided that he was really too much in the way and that he should retire, in spite of the extraordinary beauty of the sea and sky and the champagne quality of the air, uncommon between the tropics and almost unknown to Dr Maturin, never an early riser.

'Bonden,' he called to his old friend the Captain's coxswain, 'pray desire your mates to pause for a moment. I wish to go downstairs, and I would not tread on their work for the world.'

'Aye aye, sir,' said Bonden. 'Make a lane, there: make a lane for the Doctor.' He led him by hand through the pots and brushes to the companion-ladder, for the *Nutmeg* was lying to across the swell and Dr Maturin had never had much sense of balance except on a horse; and leaving him firmly attached to the hand-rail he said, 'I believe we may have some fun after dinner, sir,' with a conspiratorial smile. Stephen found Macmillan by the medicine-chest, trying to get paint off his trousers, and after some conversation about spirits of wine as a solvent and the extraordinary zeal of seamen in any faintly illegitimate and deceptive ploy he said, 'And yet as I am sure you have noticed, the ordinary work of the ship carries on as it were by its own momentum: the glass is turned, the bell is struck, the watch is relieved; when a brace is required to be adjusted, or rounded-in, as we say, the hands are there; the salt pork is already in its steep-tubs, growing a little more nearly edible; and I have no doubt that at eight bells it will be eaten. Let us walk into the sick-berth.'

Here they changed into Latin, and having looked at one hernia and the two obstinate remaining Batavia poxes he asked, 'How is our fourth man?', meaning Abse, a member of the afterguard, whose complaint was known as the marthambles at sea and griping of the guts by land, a disease whose cause Stephen did not know and whose symptoms he could only render more nearly bearable by opiates: he could not cure it. 'He will go in an hour or so, I believe,' said Macmillan, opening the screen. Stephen looked at the comatose face, listened to the shallow breathing, felt the almost imperceptible pulse. 'You are right,' he said. 'A release, if ever there was one. I should like to open him: I should like it of all things.'

'So should I,' said Macmillan eagerly.

'But it does so upset their friends, their messmates.'

'This man had none. He was a galley-ranger and had to mess by himself. Nobody came to see him but the Captain and his divisional officer and mid.'

'Then perhaps we have a chance,' said Stephen. And pushing back the screen, 'God rest his soul.'

*   *   *

132

Dr Maturin was mistaken about the salt pork. The breeze, against the promise of the sky and against the evidence of the barometer, so declined in the course of the forenoon watch that Captain Aubrey advanced his plan by an hour; and the pork was eaten, raw inside, at six bells.

The hands did not complain. By this time the *Nutmeg* had been made to look as shabby as the *Alkmaar* and they were standing in with the prospect of an uncommonly brisk action within an hour or so; there was not so much a high degree of tension as of enhancement of all feelings; and when their grog came below this did not seem so much increased as infused with a great share of mirth − witty remarks exchanged between those who were to be allowed on deck, looking like Dutch sailors during the approach, and those who were not. 'There are some slab-sided Dutch-built buggers that are allowed to show themselves. Because why? Because they look so harmless no one would be frightened of them. A maid would not be frightened of them, ha, ha; nor a wife, ha, ha, ha!'

'I have rarely heard the people so cheerful,' said Stephen in the Captain's store-room. They arranged Abse's body neatly between two chests and he went on, 'I believe I shall go up and ask the Captain whether we shall have leisure before the engagement: it is so tedious, struggling with the rigor mortis.'

But when he had climbed the successive ladders he saw to his surprise and regret that the *Nutmeg* was already well in with the land and that although her pace was sober, moderate, mercantile, there would be no time for the autopsy he had in mind. Jack was eating a ham sandwich and talking to Richardson, but he looked across as Stephen appeared and smiled: Dr Maturin had slipped on the old black coat he usually operated in and he could easily pass for a down-at-heel merchant's supercargo. Jack himself was in loose trousers and shirtsleeves and on his head he wore a Monmouth cap, a villainous flat worsted affair, still to be seen among old-fashioned seamen, which had the advantage of containing his long yellow hair, no longer so bright as it was in the days when he was familiarly known as Goldilocks, but still conspicuous.

'There she lies,' he said, turning to Stephen; and there indeed she lay under the blue sky, a trim and elegant ship with her red gun-ports open to air the deck. She was two-thirds of the way down the bay the *Nutmeg* was now entering, framed by the shore with its white rim and by the rising forest-land behind, bright green in places. There was quite a surf running, and white water could be seen beyond the *Cornélie*'s starboard bow and here and there in other parts of the bay.

'The tide is at the full,' said Jack. 'Slack water this last half-hour. Have you been busy? There are sandwiches in the quarter-gallery, and a pot of coffee, if you feel so inclined. Dinner may be rather late: the galley fires have been out this age.'

'We have been as active as ants, carrying our sick to their bay and making all ready in the berth: lint galore, swabs, pledgets, chains, saws, gags. When do you suppose the action will begin?'

'Not for an hour or so, unless she smokes us first. As you see, there is no plain ring of coral enclosing a lagoon: it is more a question of independent reefs with a winding passage between them and a surprising great bar off the mouth of the stream. That is why she is lying so far out, no doubt. It is awkward for her boats, and when one of her cutters went in just now I think she touched on the tail of the bank. Do you see the watering-party?'

'I believe so.'

'At the foot of the black cliffs two points on the starboard bow: take my glass.'

The black cliff, the stream leaping down it, and the seamen gathered round their casks came startlingly close in the brilliant light. 'There may be some extremely interesting plants on that damp rock-face,' said Stephen. 'May I look at the *Cornélie*?'

'It might be indiscreet from the quarterdeck: the sash-light in the quarter-gallery would be better. Do you see Dick on the foretopsail yard? He is going to con the ship from there. It ought to be the master, but his bowels are upset. We have to head almost for the watering-place, then there are two dog-legs half a mile apart before we can luff up and run under her lee.'

'I shall go and peer at them from the lavatory, eating a sandwich as I do so.'

'Stephen,' said Jack in a low tone, 'look for Pierrot, Christy-Pallière's boy, will you? I hope you do not see him, because that would confirm my idea he is ashore. I fairly dread killing him.'

'You mean the young French officer you met in Pulo Prabang, our friend's nephew? But you forget I never saw him, either as a boy or as a man.'

'Very true,' said Jack. 'Forgive me.'

The *Nutmeg* stood on, with her captain alone on his quarterdeck, apart from a single man at the wheel and Hooper by the lee rail, looking like a ship's boy. Richardson stood high on the yard, looking down into the clear water ahead, dark blue for the deep water of the channel, light for the shoals on either side. A score of seamen stood about on the forecastle, their hands in their pockets, or lounged on the gangway, even leaning on the rail. All the rest of the ship's company were out of sight under the forecastle, under the gangways, on the half-deck and in the cabin. All the gun-crews were at their stations, and those who could make out anything through the cracks of their portlids or through holes in the canvas strips, told their friends what they saw in a low voice, with striking accuracy. The boarders had their weapons at hand, cutlasses, pistols, boarding-axes, pikes; slow-match smoked in tubs beside the carronades – Jack would never trust to the flint-lock alone; and now the atmosphere was grave.

Behind its sliding door the quarter-gallery was quite cut

off from the close-packed attentive crowd and its rumble of voices: it was the Captain's washing, shaving and powdering closet, and together with its companion on the other side (his privy) it was one of the few upper parts of the ship left undisturbed when she was cleared for action. With its wash-basin removed it made a pleasant little place from which to view proceedings; and Stephen was luckier with his sash-light than any of the hundred-odd below decks, except for those who could command a scuttle.

Like them he saw the *Cornélie* come closer as the *Nutmeg* glided diagonally across the bay, disappear from his field of vision as she took the first dog-leg in the channel and reappear ten minutes later on the second, remarkably closer, still firmly moored; and as the *Nutmeg* continued her turn the motionless *Cornélie* and the sea around her moved steadily forward almost as far as his eyes could follow. It was now that he saw a signal break out at her masthead, just two imperative flags reinforced by a quarterdeck gun: the jet of smoke and then the crack, loud in this waiting silence. A strong voice from the deck above him: 'Stand by. Stand by, there. Man the lee-braces,' and the ship vanished beyond the edge of the sash-light.

For Jack she was still very clearly in sight, and he did not need his glass to see her open ports fill with eighteen-pounders run out.

The *Nutmeg* was tracing the long curve that was to carry her alongside the frigate, now almost right ahead and broadside on. The French colours ran up to the *Cornélie*'s mizen-peak: Jack waited for the warning shot.

There was no warning shot. Instead the three aftermost eighteen-pounders fired to kill almost simultaneously.

'All hands,' called Jack as the balls raced overhead at topsail height a few yards to starboard. It was clear that his disguise had been pierced, but although he might be raked fore and aft he still hoped to sail the *Nutmeg* close enough to engage with real effect. Below him in the waist the bosun sprung his call: the officers came running up to the quarterdeck. 'Courses and staysails,' said Jack. 'Bear a hand, bear a hand, bear a hand, there. Mr Crown, cast off the painted strips. Mr Fielding, ensign and pennant.'

Stephen heard the crash of a ball somewhere forward, and then in a turmoil more apparent than real his door slid open and Seymour called in his ear, 'They have smoked us, sir. Captain desires you will go below.'

The *Cornélie*'s remaining eighteen-pounders fired in a long rippling sequence, her side vanishing behind the smoke. Holes appeared in the topsails and courses; the tack of the mainsail, just belayed, sprang free; the balls sent water splashing from the forecastle aft; several shot up white fountains close at hand; the last shattered the larboard cathead.

'Good practice for such a distance,' observed Jack.

'Very creditable, sir,' said Fielding. 'I wish it may not improve, however.'

A pause during which the *Nutmeg*, in spite of her wild maincourse, advanced two hundred yards, and then in a deliberate fashion all the *Cornélie*'s larboard guns fired, one after another. Six balls hit the hull, masts or yards; one carried away half the larboard quarter-gallery; and the six-teenth came the length of the ship at chest height, killing two men on the forecastle and three on the quarterdeck: Miller, just next to Jack Aubrey, a hand at the wheel, and the master.

'Man the lee braces,' called Jack, wiping Miller's blood from his face: and to the men who had instantly taken over the wheel, 'Port your helm.'

The *Nutmeg* turned fast to starboard, and in a voice that reached the orlop he gave the infinitely welcome order, 'Fire as they bear.'

Now the sick-berth echoed not only with the sledge-hammer blows of the enemy's shot but the much louder cracking roar of the *Nutmeg*'s thirty-two-pounder carron-ades and the shriek of their slides as they recoiled. Stephen, Macmillan and Suleiman the loblolly-boy were already busy – splinter-wounds, contusions, a forearm broken by a falling block – but as they stitched and bandaged and splinted they nodded to one another with satisfaction. Bonden, carrying young Harper down in his arms, said, 'We are slogging it out, sir; a pleasure to see.'

So they were, and the sky echoed and re-echoed with their thunder, a continuous roar beneath the separate explosions. The *Nutmeg*, like most Dutch twenty-gun ships, carried all her armament on a single deck: she was firing into the wind, so that her smoke was instantly swept away: it was therefore easy for the quarterdeck to see the pitch of her thirty-two-pound balls. She was firing remarkably fast, at least twice the speed of the *Cornélie*, and her teams were working perfectly together, ammunition coming up from the magazines with clockwork regularity: but at high elevation their shot was wild, and at low, though their line was true, the balls fell short. The *Cornélie* was slow by any standard, partly because she was firing to leeward and the eddying smoke obscured her view; but even at three-quarters of a mile she was shockingly accurate. Furthermore, although she was clearly husbanding her powder, never wasting a shot, she quite certainly was not limited to four barrels nor anything like it.

'Stand by the chasers,' called Jack. 'Mr Fielding, we will wear ship.'

The *Nutmeg* turned, bringing the wind right aft, came up again on the starboard tack and sailed off as she had come. As she turned the stern-chasers managed to get in three shots each, two of which certainly went home; but the *Cornélie* fired two broadsides, the first of which might have dismasted the *Nutmeg* if she had not put her helm hard over at the right moment. The second fell short.

'If they had fired as quick as they fired straight,' reflected Jack, 'we should have been hard up in a clinch, and no knife to cut the seizing.' He did not confide this thought to his first lieutenant however but said, 'She is finding it hard to win her anchor.' Even without his telescope he could make out that the short-handed *Cornélie* was having a wretched time at the capstan; and with it he could see the straining red-faced men, sometimes only three to a bar, trying to force the drum to turn: then shifting over to the other cable, heaving on that, veering the first and so trying again, rather than leave anchor and cables so many thousand miles from any replacement.

'And they are having no better luck with their longboat,' said Fielding. Jack turned, and there on a small reef not a quarter of a mile from the shore, was the *Cornélie*'s massive longboat, firmly wedged on a falling tide. From the white water on either side it was clear that in his haste to join the ship the coxswain had steered for a narrow passage through the coral, the nearest way, and had misjudged the breeze or his draught or the leeway, if not all three. With real pleasure Jack saw that the active officer in a skiff directing their urgent attempts at unloading the casks and refloating the boat was Pierrot Dumesnil, that amiable young man, now in a frenzy of exasperation.

'They have their work cut out for some little while. But not for too long, I hope,' said Jack, looking up at the sun. 'There is not a world of time to spare. Now, Mr Walker?'

'A foot in the well, if you please, sir,' said the carpenter, 'but me and my mates have three comfortable plugs in the holes – there was only three hit us near or under the water-line. But the launch and the spars either side have suffered something cruel, and your larboard stern-gallery is well-nigh wrecked.'

Jack also heard the bosun's report, which had few surprises – he could see cut rigging and damaged sails on every hand – and then he said to Fielding, 'Let us heave to in the fairway with a stage over the side, as though we were in danger of foundering. Half a dozen hands can make the proper show while the rest are knotting and splicing: and we should pump, but on the far side. Mr Conway, pray ask the Doctor whether it would be convenient for me to come below. Mr Adams,' he said to his clerk, 'did you take notes?'

'Well, sir,' said Adams, 'I hardly knew what to do. Seeing

we had not beat to quarters, officially we were not in action; so I made what I may call unofficial remarks. And seeing our people were not killed in regular action, I told the sailmaker I thought they should be sewn up in their hammocks, not disposed of in the usual way. I hope I did right, sir.'

'Quite right, Mr Adams.'

Down to the orlop, and by the time he reached it his eyes were sufficiently used to the gloom between decks for them to see Stephen's hands bright red under the hanging lamp. 'How much have we suffered?' he asked.

'Three splinter-wounds died of loss of blood as soon as they were brought down or before,' said Stephen. 'Apart from that I have six in a very good way, with the blessing; a broken arm and some contusions; no more. For the dead you know better than I.'

'The master, I grieve to say; young Miller; Gray, a good man, at the wheel; and two more on the forecastle – a single raking shot.'

He sat between Harper and Semple, one of his bargemen, both of them splinter-wounds, and told them how the day was doing. 'She could hit us very hard and we could scarcely hit her at all . . .'

'Our *Agag* hulled her twice, just abaft the cutwater,' said Harper, light-headed with loss of blood. 'I saw them go home with my own eyes. How we cheered!'

'I am sure you did. But now we mean to lead her on, lie in wait at the end of the Passage, and engage her at close quarters. She has fouled her anchor and her longboat is aground at present; but I dare say everything will be in order within an hour, and we can wait an hour.'

Chapter Six

Captain Aubrey did not have to wait so long. In forty-seven minutes the *Cornélie* had plucked both herself and her long-boat free, had stowed it on the booms in a seamanlike manner and had begun her pursuit of the *Nutmeg*. By the time they had threaded the channel from Nil Desperandum to the open sea and had settled down to the long chase that would lead them to the Salibabu Passage it was clear that the Frenchman had no intention of catching his quarry, no intention of overtaking the *Nutmeg* and closing with her. He had seen some of her thirty-two-pound balls come aboard and he had no desire to see any more; a distant action was his aim, and every time Jack offered him the chance of drawing closer he declined it. His plan was so to reduce her speed by damaging her sails and rigging that he could yaw and reduce her with raking broadsides from half a mile or more.

It was clear too that Jack had over-estimated the *Cornélie*'s powers. He had not supposed that a clean-bottomed frigate in tolerable trim could make less than eight or nine knots with this steady south-west monsoon on her quarter, even though the breeze had diminished somewhat during the day; but he was mistaken; with her whole pitiful spread of thin, patched sailcloth abroad the *Cornélie* could do no better than seven and a half: and although the *Nutmeg* was towing a heavy unseen buoy it was difficult to keep up a convincing appearance of flying with all possible speed – of really trying to escape. However, with sheets a little less taut than they should have been, some rather rough steering (Bonden was a master at this and he had several tricks at the wheel) and a slightly defective bracing of the yards it could be done;

and so they ran eastwards, firing with a steady deliberation at something near the extreme range of their chasers.

Jack remained on the quarterdeck until he had the *Nutmeg*'s pace as exactly adjusted to the *Cornélie*'s as possible, and then he called Seymour. 'Mr Seymour,' he said, 'I am giving you an acting order as third lieutenant: I have mentioned it to Mr Fielding. You will arrange matters with him after the ceremony.'

It was expected. Someone had to keep the master's watch, however young. Nevertheless Seymour flushed and said, 'Thank you, sir. Thank you very much,' in a tone that showed how moved he was. As he spoke the starboard stern-chaser fired below them: Jack nodded and ran down the smoking companion-ladder to the smoke-filled cabin – the quartering breeze filled the whole space for a minute after each shot – and he found the two gun-crews glaring through the murk, the more fortunate with their heads right out of the port.

The argument faded as he came in, and the gunner said, 'We may have hulled her that time, sir.'

'I believe it passed right over,' said Reade, very shrill.

'Mr Reade, pipe down,' said Jack.

'Aye aye, sir. Beg pardon, sir.'

Jack took a telescope and bending he trained it over the great expanse of sea, a long swell with small waves crossing it diagonally, some white horses making the main a deeper blue. The *Nutmeg*'s wake ran out and out, wider than usual because of the turbulence of the hidden buoy; and in a direct prolongation of the line came the *Cornélie*, throwing a fair bow-wave in the very water the *Nutmeg* had passed through eight minutes before. She had everything she possessed set and drawing and in all likelihood she had very little in the way of spare canvas: perhaps none at all.

It was a difficult position. If he wounded her slightly, reducing her speed by a knot or two, she would probably give up the chase as hopeless: if he did not fire with reasonable accuracy the Frenchman would not believe in his flight.

On the other hand, if an unlucky shot slowed the *Nutmeg* for even a few minutes the *Cornélie* could put her helm hard over and give her a broadside from those horribly well-pointed eighteen-pounders. And an unlucky shot from the *Cornélie* was more probable than the other way about: her bow-chasers were firing from the forecastle, some eight feet higher than the *Nutmeg*'s upper deck; furthermore they were firing at the *Nutmeg*'s exposed stern, her vulnerable rudder. While these thoughts were racing through his mind he noticed that the frigate was pumping ship, sending a fine spout of water to leeward. 'When she has got rid of all that, perhaps she will come on a little more briskly,' he reflected. Then aloud, 'Mr White, what elevation are you using?'

'Rather better nor six, sir,' said the gunner, who laid the starboard gun while Bonden did the same for *Beelzebub*.

At this the *Cornélie* fired at the top of the rise. The ball pitched short but came ranging along the *Nutmeg*'s side in a series of great bounds, the last near enough to send spray aboard.

Jack leant over *Beelzebub*, his hand on the warm bronze, and as Bonden freed the quoin – the wedge that raised or lowered the barrel – with his handspike, Jack drew it back and back: they understood one another with no more than a grunt and a nod, for the Captain loved to point a gun and they had been through these motions some thousands of times; and when the elevation brought the middle of the *Cornélie*'s foretopmast yard into the sights he called through the open companion, 'Mr Fielding. Mr Fielding, there. Pray see if you can catch the flight of the ball. I am pitching it well up.'

'Aye aye, sir,' replied Fielding, and now Jack laid the gun: 'Muzzle to the right . . . a trifle more . . .' the men with the crows heaving it with the utmost delicacy. 'Back a hair's breadth.' With his eyes fixed along the sights he felt for the match. The *Nutmeg* rose on the swell, and just before the gun was on its mark he stabbed the glowing end down on the priming. A hiss lasting a barely measurable instant of time and then the gun went off, shooting back under him with frightful force and filling the air astern with smoke and shattered wad. His head was already out of the port by the time the breeching checked the gun's recoil with its usual deep satisfying twang and a lucky shift of air allowed him to see the ball for more than a second of its path, a black diminishing blur.

'A little wide of her starboard mizen-chains, sir,' called Fielding.

Jack nodded. Other manoeuvres were possible, such as cracking on and eventually fetching to windward of her, but they were all time-consuming, they all jeopardized his ship and his rendezvous. To be sure, this was a perilous caper, but all things weighed he thought it the best solution. 'Let us keep it up, Mr White,' he said, 'but discreetly: no Guy Fawkes' night blazing away.'

They fired on steadily. Once a ricochet from the *Cornélie* spoilt the gingerbread-work below the *Nutmeg*'s taffrail, and twice holes appeared in her fore and main courses. *Beelzebub* was growing hot when Jack noticed Reade standing there with the look of one who has a message to deliver. It was in fact an invitation: since the Captain had missed his dinner, did he choose to take a cold collation in the gun-room?

Jack found that he was exceedingly hungry. At the thought of eating, his mouth watered painfully and his stomach gave a twinge. He said, 'Yes, with pleasure,' extricated himself from the tight-knit gun-crew, Bonden taking his place, and stepped over to the quarter-gallery to wash his hands. Opening the door with his eyes still fixed on the chaser he very nearly fell headlong into the sea, saving himself only by a violent leaping writhe. 'Make this handle fast to the quarter-piece cleat,' he said. 'The Doctor might come to grief, else.'

The Doctor was already in the gun-room, and he and the other officers welcomed Jack with potted meat, anchovies, hard-boiled eggs and ham, pickled gherkins, onions, mangoes; they were as hospitable as could be, and Welby mixed a bowl of cold arrack punch. Yet with Warren's chair standing there empty it was but a low-spirited meal, and towards the end of it Adams came in with a prayer-book: speaking over the crack and thunder of a stern-chaser's shot and recoil he said in Jack's ear, 'I have marked the page with a piece of marline, sir.'

'Thank you, Mr Adams,' said Jack; and having considered for a minute, 'I believe, gentlemen, that our old shipmates will forgive us if we bid them farewell in the simplest way, and in our working clothes.' There was a murmur of agreement, a shifting of chairs, a certain uneasiness about finishing the punch.

Five minutes later, as eight bells struck and then continued with a half-second tolling, Jack took up his station by the drift of the quarterdeck. The chasers were housed and silent; all hands were present. Jack read the grave, beautiful words; the weighted hammocks slid over the side one after another with scarcely a splash, meeting the rise that answered the hollow after the bow-wave.

The *Nutmeg* had put her helm down a couple of points for this ceremony; and after one unanswered shot the *Cornélie*, seeing what she was at, fired no more.

When he had closed his book and the people had returned to their duty and the *Nutmeg* to her course, Jack said to Fielding, 'We must give them a leeward gun in acknowledgment.' He told Oakes to see to it, adding, 'Aftermost leeward carronade,' so that there should be no mistake: Oakes was still very much shocked by the loss of his friend. He had never seen action before, and it was much better to keep him running about. The Captain and first lieutenant walked aft to the taffrail, and as the gun fired Jack took off his hat. He was reasonably sure that the Frenchman was there on his forecastle; they had seen one another often enough through their telescopes.

'She is still pumping,' observed Fielding.

'So she is,' said Jack absently. 'But by God how the sun has raced across the sky; and there is that goddam moon already.' There she was indeed, discernible in the brilliant sky, pale, lopsided, stupider than usual, twenty degrees above the dark loom of the land in the east, visible this last hour and more. 'At this pace we shall never get her through the Passage before morning. I hope to God she makes more headway when she has cleared her bilges at last.'

'Sir,' said Fielding, 'I believe she is sending something aloft. A skysail.'

They both fixed it with their telescopes. 'It is a pair of sheets,' said Jack. 'A pair of sheets sewn athwartships and folded at the top. Well, damn my eyes: he does not lack good will.' Leaning to the companion he called down, 'Avast firing, there.'

'Out,' cried the Marine sentry next to the space ordinarily occupied by the cabin door. He turned the glass and stepped forward to strike two bells.

Like figures on an ancient clock the midshipman of the watch and the quartermaster came from their respective stations to meet at the lee rail, the one carrying log and reel, the other a small sand-glass. The quartermaster heaved the log: the stray line ran out: 'Turn,' he said. The knotted line span off the reel, the midshipman holding the glass to his eye. 'Stop,' said he and the quartermaster checked the line.

'What do you find, Mr Conway?' asked Jack.

'Seven knots and a little better than three fathom, sir, if you please.'

Jack shook his head, went below and said, 'Mr White, you may encourage her with a steady fire, shot for shot. But let your balls be a little short. If we are to get her through the Passage before dawn we must not hurt a hair of her head; and it will be nip and tuck even then. Short, but lifelike, do you understand?'

'Aye aye, sir. Short but lifelike it is,' replied the gunner. It was clear that he was not at all pleased.

'Mr Fielding,' said Jack, returning to the quarterdeck, 'when I have had a word with Chips I am going aloft. If that skysail should bring the *Cornélie* up a trifle, and if her shot should come aboard, you may draw away.'

The carpenter and his crew were busy in the waist, making a framework very like the outline of the *Nutmeg*'s stern-windows, an essential part of Jack's plan to deceive the *Cornélie* when the moon had set. 'How are you coming along, Mr Walker?' he asked.

'Pretty well, sir, I thank you; but I doubt the boat may be horrid unhandy.'

'Never fret for that, Chips,' said Jack. 'If all goes well she will not have to swim above half an hour.'

'If all goes well,' he repeated inwardly, mounting to the foretop and so on without a pause to the crosstrees and a little way out on the yard. Sitting there he had a perfect view of the eastern half of the sky, clear and perfect and evidently domed, with a clear and perfect sea stretching half way to the horizon, where, on a line as straight as a meridian, it changed from a light-hearted, white-flecked blue to that troubled shade seen in the autumn Mediterranean that Stephen used to call wine-dark. Beyond this line, on either side, rose high land, dark, stretching away out of sight to the south-east and tending to converge: the mouth of the Salibabu Passage. It was still a great way off at this gentle rate of sailing; and from the position of the damn-fool moon he could tell that the sun, hidden by the main topsail, was already far down in the west.

'No doubt we shall have a stronger breeze in the Passage,' he said, 'it being funnel-shaped. But even so there is the tide to reckon with. It will be a damned near-run thing.' He called an order down to the deck that altered the *Nutmeg*'s course half a point, so that she should keep to the southern shore. This would be necessary for the eventual turn, but for the time being his aim was to avoid the full force of the tide, which would start flowing westwards in a few hours' time.

When he was at sea, when the present and the immediate future were so much with him, and above all in even so slight an action as this, Jack Aubrey spent little time dwelling on the past; but now his spirit was oppressed. Quite against his own intellectual judgment he was, like so many seamen, a superstitious creature: he did not like the dark land, the ill-coloured sea ahead, with its hard bar; and as well as grieving him, young Miller's death had confirmed many an irrational notion.

He sat there some considerable time: twice he felt the yard move under him as it was braced a little more truly to the wind; and throughout his meditation the guns continued, though with less zeal on the *Nutmeg*'s side, the intervals growing longer.

Time passed: orders, hammering in the waist, the noises of a ship running with no great urgency: the steady pitch and roll, magnified up here, but not so much as to break in upon his thoughts.

Three bells below him. Some more or less autonomous part of his mind said, 'Three bells in the first dog-watch,' and at the words a sort of moderate cheerfulness returned. They reminded him of Stephen Maturin's reply to the question 'Why is it called a dog-watch': his instant 'Because it is curtailed,' which Jack thought the wittiest thing he had ever heard in his life. He valued it extremely and he often, perhaps too often, told the story, though the heavier gentlemen in company and even sometimes naval wives had to be reminded that dog-watches were made considerably shorter than the rest. Curtailed. Cur-tailed.

The reply had been made many years ago, but it had improved with age, and now it made him smile as he swung off the yard, seized a shifting backstay, slid easily down it and dropped on to the forecastle. Walking along the gangway to the quarterdeck he noticed two new holes in the main studdingsail, and he saw Fielding and the bosun busy with tackles to hoist out the decoy-boat in the fullness of time.

'How are we doing, Mr Richardson?' he asked, looking beyond him at the distant *Cornélie*.

'Just eight knots at two bells, sir: she was gaining on us, and she hit the larboard stern-gallery again; so I hauled the sheets aft.'

'Damn that stern-gallery. I had fitted a new basin. A new *china* basin, most uncommon genteel.'

'Yes, sir. Should you like another heave, sir?'

'No. It is almost the end of the watch.' What little haze there was in the western sky was beginning to flush – a very delicate gold and pink – and the sun was scarcely his own width from the sea. Jack looked keenly over the side and at the wake: he was almost certain of another fathom, but the wish could so easily be farther than the thought, and he said, 'Well, perhaps. It is so much easier to be sure of the glass when there is light.'

'Eight knots and just one fathom, sir, if you please,' said Reade, the midshipman of the watch, some moments later. The *Cornélie* fired as he spoke and the ball sent up its plume no more than fifty yards astern: she was keeping pace. 'Come, this is encouraging,' said Jack. He stayed to see the sun go down, outlining the Frenchman in a brief blaze of glory, and when he went below five minutes later the dusk was already creeping over the sea from the east, while the moon had gained in substance.

'Sir,' said Killick at the foot of the companion-ladder, 'I have moved your night-gear into poor Mr Warren's cabin. Which Mr Seymour is overjoyed to stay in the midshipmen's berth until your sleeping-place is set to rights.' Killick's face had the wooden expression it always wore when he was either suppressing that which was true or suggesting that which was false and Jack knew perfectly well that his steward had quite unnecessarily forced the arrangement on Seymour and the gun-room – unnecessarily, because it would certainly have been offered.

'I see: then rouse out a case of the eighty-seven port,' he said and carried on to the gun-room, where he found all the officers apart from Richardson gathered round a chart on their long table. 'Gentlemen,' he said, 'I must trespass upon your hospitality for tonight, if I may. The cabin is to remain lit, and if the *Cornélie* goes on pelting us we must reply, to keep up her spirits.' The gun-room said they should be very happy; and Jack went on, 'Mr Fielding, you will forgive me speaking of service matters here, but I will just observe that once we are in the Passage, it would be as well to heave the log every bell: then again hammocks may be piped down for the watches below to get some sleep against tomorrow; and the galley fires may be lit again. And lastly, I shall take the middle watch, turning in after we have had supper – I am obliged to you for your kindness, Mr Seymour.' Seymour hung his head and searched for an elegant reply, but before he found one Jack said, 'Doctor, may we look at your sick-berth while the fires are lighting?'

'I tell you what, Stephen,' he said as they walked along, 'I know the constraint of having your captain in your bosom – all sitting straight, no belching, no filthy stories – so I have ordered up a case of our eighty-seven port. I hope you do not mind it?'

'I mind it very much indeed. Pouring that irreplaceable liquid into my messmates is impious.'

'But they will appreciate the gesture: it will take some of the stiffness away. I cannot tell you how disagreeable it is, feeling like a killjoy whose going will be a relief. You are luckier than I am in that way. They do not look upon you with any respect. That is to say, not with any *undue* respect. I mean they have an amazing respect for you, of course; but they do not look upon you as a superior being.'

'Do they not? They certainly looked upon me as a very disagreeable one this afternoon. I was cursed sullen, snappish and dogged with them all.'

'You astonish me. Had something put you out?'

'I had set aside a corpse for opening, an interesting case of the marthambles; I was going to ask your good word as in duty bound, but before I could do so some criminal or at least some busy hand had sewn it up and placed it among those you buried.'

'What a ghoul you are, Stephen, upon my word.'

*   *   *

Supper was a grave but extraordinarily copious meal; and although they had not served together very long they had experienced so many vicissitudes that this might have been a five-year commission, which lessened the no doubt inevitable formality. Seymour, of course, on his first day as a member of the gun-room mess, said nothing, and Stephen was as usual lost in thought; but Fielding and even more Welby felt free to tell quite long anecdotes, and in spite of the Ghoul's predictions all hands seemed thoroughly to enjoy the 1787 port, possibly to some degree because Killick said, 'I have decanted the eighty-seven, sir: which it was very crusty, *being so uncommon old*,' the last words being uncommon loud. A third decanter was passing round when Stephen, raising his voice above the stern-chaser overhead, suddenly asked, 'Would this be a sloop, at all?'

They had heard some pretty strange things from the Doctor, but none so far beyond all probability, so very far, that for a while there was a complete silence.

'Do you mean the *Nutmeg*, Doctor?' asked Jack at last.

'Certainly. The *Nutmeg*, God bless her.'

'Bless her by all means. But she could not conceivably be a sloop while I have her, you know. Was she under a commander she would be a sloop; but I have the honour to be on the post-captain's list, and that makes her as much a ship as any three-decker in the service. What put such a wild fancy into your head?'

'I was contemplating on sloops. A friend of mine wrote a novel and showed it to me for my opinion, as a naval man.' The gun-room looked down at their plates with a certain fixity of expression. 'I thought it a very pretty tale, but I did take exception to the hero's commanding a sloop and taking a French frigate: yet just now it occurred to me that the *Cornélie* is undoubtedly a frigate; that we, though small, aspire to take her; that perhaps my objection was unfounded, and that sloops do in fact capture frigates.'

'Oh no,' they cried, the Doctor was wholly in the right – never in the history of the Royal Navy has any sloop taken any frigate – it would have been flying in the face of nature.

'But on the other hand,' said Jack, 'a post-ship of much the same displacement and broadside weight of metal as a sloop has been known to do it. It is the presence of a post-captain aboard, and his moral superiority, that turns the scale. A glass of wine with you, my dear sir. Now, gentlemen, in a few minutes' time we shall be mustering the watch, so I shall thank you for a splendid supper, take a look at the sky, and then turn in.'

'And we must thank you for some splendid wine, sir,' said Fielding. 'It will be my standard of excellence whenever I drink port again.'

'Hear him, hear him,' said Welby.

On deck the breeze had freshened perceptibly, coming in warm over the rail, one point on the quarter. By the light of the binnacle the log-board showed that their speed had increased to eight knots and three fathoms: and the *Cornélie* was keeping up. The moon showed her clear, but it was not so brilliant that it hid the light of the battle-lanterns on her forecastle or the suffused glow from the open ports along her side, still less the stab of flame as she let fly with her starboard chaser. Both ships were now well into the Passage. To the south he could see the lights of a fishing-village, just where his chart had set it. The other side was too far off to see clearly, but it heaved up there, silvery in the moonlight with great black shadows.

Eight bells. Seymour relieved Richardson: the watch was mustered and the starbowlines went below to get what sleep they could with the guns banging and growling on the deck above. Fielding had come up to ease Seymour into his first independent watch and he was now in the waist, going through the motions of shipping the frame and its lanterns on the decoy-boat, now poised so that it could be lowered down in a moment – motions that the chosen band, made up of Bonden, two bosun's mates and a very powerful black sheet-anchor man called Darkie had already performed again and again.

Jack watched them for a while and then walked into the bows with Fielding. 'I shall be very surprised if the *Cornélie* don't pipe down now,' he said. 'But in any case I mean to draw ahead another couple of cable's lengths, to prevent any stray ball doing real harm; though of course she must have our stern-windows clear in sight. I shall give the orders to brace up and ease off the buoy and then turn in. Good night to you.'

'Good night, sir.'

As Jack was going below the gunfire died away, the *Nutmeg* having the last word; and as he turned in he saw that he was not to sleep in the dead man's cot. His own, an unusually long one, had been brought down and slung fore and aft. Killick was in many ways a wretched servant, fractious, mean, overbearing to guests of inferior rank, hopelessly coarse; but in others he was a pearl without a thorn. For a moment Jack passed some other expressions in review, and having reached bricks without price he went to sleep.

The familiar waking to a faint lantern in the darkness and the words 'Close on eight bells, sir.' He woke at once, as he had woken so very often since his boyhood, said, 'Thank you, Mr Conway,' and swung out of his cot. Some unsleeping recorder had taken notice of the ship's progress during this time and he was not at all surprised to learn from the run of the water along her side that the *Nutmeg* had lost speed.

Shirt, trousers and canvas shoes, and he walked quietly out of the dim gun-room. In the moonlit waist he cupped his hands in the scuttle-butt, dashed water into his face and came aft as the sentry went forward to strike eight bells.

'You are a good relief, sir,' said Seymour. 'But I am very sorry to say the breeze has dropped.'

'Nip,' cried Conway, and coming across from the lee rail he reported, 'Seven, sir, seven on the knot.'

'Good night to you both,' said Jack; and as the wheel, the con, the lookout posts and the guns changed hands he retired to the taffrail. Away on the larboard quarter now, well out in the channel, there lay the *Cornélie*, a little farther, a little dimmer. The moon, passing through a veil of cloud, was near her height: high water would come well after her southing and in any case the *Alkmaar* had stated as a known fact that it was three hours later here than at Nil Desperandum; yet even so the flood would have been setting west for some time now. With the log-board by a stern-lantern he added up the figures for the last four hours' progress. Thirty-one sea-miles. It was not what he could have wished, but it was not very bad: the issue was still open. This present watch, the graveyard watch, was the decisive period, for it was now that the tide would have its say. He had of course asked about the Passage as soon as he heard that the *Cornélie* was likely to take it, and he had learnt that unlike some parts of the Pacific it had two high tides in a lunar day, the first no great matter, the second, that which the *Nutmeg* was to stem throughout his watch, stronger. But just how much stronger no one in Batavia could tell him. Of course it depended on the age of the moon, and in her present gibbous state she would not be exerting her full influence nor anything like it. From all their calculations and from what little they had in the way of observations from Dalrymple, Horsburgh and others, he and the master (an excellent navigator) had decided that at this point in the lunar month they could expect a westward current of two and a half knots; and in his plan he had allowed for rather more than three.

Few things are harder than judging relative movement by night on an unknown coast with little in the way of marked features. By now most of the few scattered villages had put out their lights, and the difficulty of locating them was increased by the glowing remains of fires lit to clear scrub and forest earlier in the day.

Bell after bell the midshipman of the watch reported seven knots, seven and two fathoms, seven and one fathom, while every hour the carpenter or one of his mates stated the depth of water in the well: never more than six inches. And throughout this time Jack Aubrey examined the shore with his night-glass, trying to find a bearing that would give him some notion of the current's speed. A vain attempt: for this some near, clear, fixed point was required.

At just after three bells the fixed point appeared; and not one fixed point but four: four anchored fishing-boats strung out in a line two cable's lengths away on the starboard bow, all with flaring lights to attract the fish. 'Mr Oakes,' he called, 'bring log-board, chalk, half-minute glass and a lantern.'

He hurried along the gangway and as the first boat came abeam he called, 'Turn,' followed it with his azimuth compass until Oakes cried, 'Out,' and so read off the difference. The same with the second, third and fourth boats, all far enough apart for his mind to reach an approximate, shocking solution of the triangles.

He went below and worked them out carefully. They were even worse than he had supposed: the tide was flowing at five and a half knots and when the moon was farther west it would flow faster still. The ship's speed with regard to the land was two miles an hour less than he had counted on. The tide would flow six hours in all, setting the far end of the Passage twelve miles farther off, and by the time they reached it the sun would be well up in the sky.

No, it would not do. For conscience' sake he ran through his calculations again, but they only confirmed the first and second workings and his feeling of extreme disappointment.

Back on deck he reduced speed for the second time. The *Cornélie*, out there in the stronger current, was falling behind; and although he was no longer sure of what he should do he did not wish to lose touch with her. He leant over the taffrail, watching the moonlit and slightly phosphorescent wake stream away: clearly there was now no hope whatsoever of carrying out his plan, and for some time he was lost in melancholy, even very bitter, reflexions. For some considerable time, while the muted life of a man-of-war by night went on behind him: the quiet voice of the quartermaster at the con, the replies of the helmsman, the murmur of the watch under the break of the forecastle and of the gun-crews below him, the striking of the bell, followed by, 'All's well, forecastle lookout,' 'All's well' from all the stations right round the ship.

But his naturally sanguine temperament had recovered somewhat before five bells, the dead hour of the night, and he greeted Stephen cheerfully enough: 'There you are, Stephen. How happy I am to see you.'

'I am sorry to be so late. Sleep overcame me, luxurious sleep.'

'I suppose you wished to see the occultation of Menkar.'

'Not at all. I had intended to come and sit with you: for as I understand it there is to be no battle until after the moon has set.'

'Come, I take that very kindly in you, brother. But I am deeply sorry and indeed ashamed to tell you that there is to be no battle at all, at least not for a great while and not in the form I had hoped for. The *Cornélie* is such a very dull sailer, such an infernal slug, and I made such a stupid mistake about the flow of the tide that it is quite impossible we should be through the Passage before daylight.'

Five bells and the ritual heaving of the log. 'Seven knots, sir, if you please,' said Oakes, his young blubbered face even paler, even more pitiful, in the moonlight.

'It sounds quite well, don't it?' said Jack when he had gone. 'But the whole body of water in which she is making her seven knots is moving westwards at five or better, so that the mouth of the Passage is only two miles nearer every hour, instead of the four I had relied upon. It made me quite low in my spirits, I assure you – absolutely hipped – blue devils for a while. But then it occurred to me that it was not the end of the world if we missed our rendezvous with Tom, and that the right thing to do was to keep the *Cornélie* in sight, lead her well beyond the strait, fetch a wide cast and work to windward of her in the open sea. With this breeze we can make twelve knots to her seven.'

'Could you not both keep your rendezvous with Tom Pullings *and* pursue the *Cornélie*?'

'Oh no. Tom is, or should be, lying well to the north. I should have to spread everything we possess to reach him in time, and the *Cornélie* would instantly see what we were about. Her captain is no fool – see how he smoked us at Nil Desperandum. No. I should hare off to find Tom, perhaps miss him and quite certainly miss the *Cornélie*. You have no idea how a ship can slip off and vanish in an island-studded sea, given a few hours.'

'I am sure you are right. And then there is the much surer, more genteel, more comfortable rendezvous at Botany Bay, or Sydney Cove to be more exact. Jack, I cannot tell you how I long to see a platypus.'

'I remember you spoke of it last time we were there.'

'A damnable, a hellish last time it was too, upon my soul. Frowned upon by the soldiers, scarcely allowed to set a foot on land, hurried away with almost no stores and nothing but a well-known and commonplace little small green parakeet – oh, it was shameful. New Holland is gravely in my debt.'

'Never mind. It will be much better this time. You shall watch great flights of platypuses at your leisure.'

'My dear, they are mammals, furry animals.'

'I thought you said they laid eggs.'

'So they do. That is what is so delightful. They also have bills like a duck.'

'No wonder you long to see one.'

The night was even warmer than usual and they sat there very easy and relaxed on two paunch mats, talking at random about that voyage in the *Leopard*, about the scent that was now coming off the land, distinct wood-smoke on some occasions, green things, sometimes separable, on others, and about the acuity of one's nose after only a short time at sea and the wonderful cleanliness and lack of stench aboard the *Nutmeg*, even in her hold.

The moon set: the stars glowed brighter still, and Jack harked back to his observatory at Ashgrove Cottage. An intelligent Dutchman in Batavia had shown him a better way of turning the dome, based on the practice of millers in his own country – of wind-millers, of course.

Eight bells. Fielding took over, but Jack remained on deck, and when Bonden came aft in the darkness some time later he said, 'Bonden, you will have to tell your mates it will not do. The tide is too strong, the Frenchman too slow.'

'Oh yes, sir,' said Bonden. 'Which I only came aft to say Killick has a pot on the hob and a dish of burgoo, and should you like it on deck or below?'

'What do you say, Doctor? Upstairs or down?'

'Oh, down, if you please. I must look at my patients quite soon.'

'Do you mind if we wait five minutes? I should like to see the crescent Venus.'

'Venus? Ah, God love us,' said Stephen, oddly disconcerted. 'By all means. I am sure you have remarked the sea is much less agitated?'

'Yes. It often happens before the turn of tide, you will recall. Presently we shall have the ebb, and the whole mass of water will pour back eastwards, millions and millions of tons of it. And I dare say it will flow faster with the wind pushing it: there is promise of a close-reefed topsail breeze, as well as squalls.'

Stephen could see no promise of any kind, apart from a profounder darkness in the west, but knowing that salamanders, cats, sea-monsters had senses he did not possess he agreed; he also looked at the risen Venus, a vacillating form so near the horizon, but extraordinarily brilliant and sometimes, in the telescope, distinctly horned.

They went below and took their infinitely welcome burgoo and coffee in the gun-room, still talking very quietly, although by this time the idlers had been called and the grind of holystones cleaning the deck in the darkness rumbled through the ship. Their talk ran back and back to that voyage in the *Leopard*, to the wholly relative delights of Desolation Island, and to Mrs Wogan. 'She was a fine woman,' said Jack, 'and a rare plucked un: as I recall she was being transported for pistolling the runners that came to arrest her, and I do like a woman with spirit. But it will not do, you know: it will not do, having women aboard. There –' pointing at Stephen's second bowl of burgoo, which had slopped on to the table '– and that is what I meant by the changing tide. It is on the ebb now, and with the rising breeze behind it we shall have seas of quite a different kind. Do you hear the rain? That is one of my squalls: cats and dogs for twenty minutes and then a clear sky. The sun will be up presently.'

'I must go and see my patients. I am not altogether happy about young Harper.'

Splinter-wounds occupied them for some time: instances of healing at first intent, instances of malignant impostumes; and when Stephen stood up Jack said, 'I will come with you.'

Down the ladder and away aft. 'You observe the sweetness even here?' asked Stephen. 'Well may she be called the *Nutmeg*.'

Before Jack could reply there was a tremendous triple crash overhead and the simultaneous discharge of both stern-chasers. He raced up the various ladders, reached the quarter-deck in the last veil of rain and the first light of dawn and instantly grasped the position: the *Cornélie*, bringing up the wind, bringing up the tide, spreading a little more makeshift canvas and moving faster out there in the channel, had come up hidden by the squall to well within range of her long guns, had yawed and fired a full broadside. One of her balls had struck the *Nutmeg*'s maintopsail yard in the slings and though the halliards had already been let go the great sail was billowing away to leeward, making a noise like thunder.

'Port the helm,' he cried, partly to ease the sail but much more to change the *Nutmeg*'s course, which was now carrying her diagonally across the *Cornélie*'s path.

'She don't steer, sir,' shouted Fielding over the roar of the chasers. 'Tiller-rope shot away and a ball between rudder and stern-post.'

Jack hailed the forecastle. 'Spritsail course and topsail. Cast off the buoy.' Then turning, 'Mr Crown, relieving-tackles directly. Mr Seymour, clew up to windward: cut the leeward robands: bundle all you can into the top.' He ran into the cabin and as the starboard-chaser fired and recoiled said, 'Check her inboard.' He leant far out and there was Richardson in his nightshirt, slung over the stern, up to his chin every time a sea overtook her, prising furiously at the ball with a handspike. 'Dick,' he called, 'has it pierced or is it wedged?'

'Mostly wedged, sir, between the upper pintle-strap and . . .' a rising smother of foam cut him short.

Withdrawing, Jack said, 'Bonden, give me a bight of rope fast to the munnion. Tell bosun to haul the helm hard a-starboard the moment the tackles are shipped. Pass me a crow. Mr White, carry on.'

A moment later he was in the white boil of the wake. The massive crowbar sank him but with a hearty kick he rose to what surface there was and seized the pendant-chain hook as the *Cornélie* began a rolling broadside. Swinging himself under the overhang Jack heard one ball strike the *Nutmeg*'s hull and then Mr White's stern-chaser deafened him. With one foot on the ring-plate and his left arm round the rudder he stabbed his crow into the space beneath the half-buried ball and tried to force it out while Richardson levered it from the other side. Wave after wave drowned them in foam for the *Nutmeg* was gathering way, and it seemed hopeless: Jack's strength was going fast. He was near losing his grip on the iron when the whole rudder to which they were so intimately attached gave a groan and moved slightly to larboard. A last wrench and the ball fell free.

They exchanged a nod, mouths shut tight against the flying sea, and Jack, dropping his bar, tried to climb aboard. His arms refused their duty and he hailed his coxswain. They hauled him up, cruelly scraped against the counter; and then came Richardson, his leg streaming red from an unnoticed wound. They both sat, sodden and gasping, and

Jack said, 'Run her up, Bonden.' The gun slammed against the port and almost instantly fired.

As the smoke cleared Jack saw Fleming race in bawling, 'Mr Fielding says she steers, sir.' At the same moment he saw the *Cornélie* begin her turn to close the growing distance and he said, 'Thank you, Mr Fleming. Desire him to put her before the wind and to send me one of the waisters.' Then to Richardson, 'Dick, how do you find yourself?'

'Perfectly well, sir, I thank you; I never felt it at the time. I think the pendant-hook must have caught me.'

The waister came in: touched his forehead. 'Jevons, give Mr Richardson a hand below. Dick, get yourself bound up: tell the Doctor we are before the wind: and if he says you are to stay below, then you stay below.'

Richardson's answer as the waister heaved him up was lost in the crash of guns and a savage cheering. 'Hulled her amidships, sir,' called Mr White. 'I saw the splinters fly.'

Staring through what gap there was Jack saw the frigate plain, lit by the sun through a gap in the clouded east, and now three-quarters on; the light caught the stream jetting from her starboard chain-pump.

He stood up, flexed his hands and arms and swarmed up the ladder to the quarterdeck: a scene of apparent confusion under the troubled sky. 'We have cleared away a spare yard, sir,' said Fielding, 'and the topsail is passing down as you see, but Seymour says the mast is too much injured.'

'Cut half way through a foot from the crosstrees, sir.'

The bosun reappeared. 'New tiller-ropes shipped, sir,' he said.

'Very good, Mr Crown: stand by to bend a sail to the crossjack yard.'

The *Cornélie* opened with her bow-chasers again, the plume of one ball drenching them. 'Aye aye, sir,' said the bosun at last, more amazed by the order than the splash, hearty though it was. He had never bent a crossjack in his life.

'Mr Fielding, sway up fore and mizzen topgallant

masts . . .' The orders came fast, with no emphasis but with great authority: as soon as this strange sail was set and drawing and hammocks piped up, hands were to go to breakfast by half-watches: four picked hands at the wheel with Fielding himself at the con.

All this while the chasers had been barking at one another with no greater effect than pierced sails and some cut rigging, but by the time the crossjack was giving its almost unknown and potentially very dangerous thrust the *Cornélie* had made up the distance lost during her broadsides and she was gaining fast. Jack altered course to bring the wind from right aft to near enough her quarter for the crossjack not to becalm the maincourse: she gathered way at once. After ten minutes of very close attention and the setting of two more jibs he decided that their speeds were as nearly equal as he could expect without a maintopsail, and he told Seymour, in charge of the aftermost larboard carronades, and his two midshipmen to stand by. The *Nutmeg* had fine round buttocks and these carronades, trained as far aft as possible, could be brought to bear by a turn of no more than two points from the *Nutmeg*'s present course.

He called down through the companion, now a shattered remnant of wood with splinters of glass in parts of the frame, 'Mr White, run out your gun, make all fast and give the larboard smashers play: Mr Seymour, we are about to put the helm a-lee. Fire as they bear; fire high; fire quick.' Crouching under the foot of the crossjack, that anomalous, inconvenient sail, he took the wheel himself.

Round she came, easy, moving faster, the hands too anxious about the strange sail's sheet and tack to worry about the *Cornélie*'s chasers: round: and the first carronade went off, followed by two simultaneously. As Jack had expected the *Cornélie* put her helm hard over and answered with a full broadside; and as he expected it was not nearly so accurate as her first deadly shooting. How many times Seymour's division fired he could not tell, so confused was the sequence, but at one time he heard them roaring like maniacs for round-shot, their racks and garlands running low. 'I think it was six apiece, sir,' said Adams, standing there with an inkhorn in his buttonhole and a watch in his hand, taking notes.

The *Cornélie* did not fire again but resumed the chase, with the loss of two cable's lengths; but still she was bringing up the wind and still she had the advantage of the faster ebb.

And so they ran, mile after mile, the *Cornélie* perfectly aware that the *Nutmeg* had but to sway up a new maintopmast to outpace her, and perfectly determined that she should not do so. Again and again she yawed, fired a broadside and came on; and whenever she had a little advantage, as when the *Nutmeg*'s damaged mizen topsail split and carried away, she fired first from starboard and then from larboard, with all the guns she possessed, making a terrible noise. Indeed, their whole progress along the Passage was marked by great flights of sea-birds startled from their ledges on the cliffs.

The *Nutmeg* usually answered with a jig and an almost equally noisy discharge of carronades, run out in astonishingly rapid succession – almost as many balls on the one side as the other. Upon the whole the *Cornélie*'s gunnery was far less accurate – 'and it is scarcely surprising,' observed Jack to Fielding as he stood peeling an orange over the taffrail, 'for if they have been pumping like this all night I wonder they can run up their guns at all, let alone point them straight' – but five minutes after this stupid remark (for which he cursed himself), at the moment when at last they were about to sway up the new topmast – all laid along – and when the far end of the Passage was opening, the *Cornélie*, well within range, yawed and fired two careful, slow, deliberate broadsides that did much damage, above all by cutting the toprope itself and its attendant tackle so that the half-hoisted mast plunged straight down, piercing the deck and wrecking its carefully worked heel and fid-hole.

Yet the *Cornélie* had lost distance by her double turn and

she did not even fire her chasers before the debris was cleared away, before the carpenter and his crew were busy on the heel, and before the opening by which Jack had hoped to elude the Frenchman lay broad on the starboard beam. It was then that the cry came down from the foretopgallant yard: 'Sail ho.'

'Where away?'

'On the larboard bow, sir. I see her royals just behind the headland, sir. Another. Two sail of ships, sir. Three. Four. God love us. You will see 'em presently, sir.'

'Topmast ready, sir,' said Fielding to Jack.

'Sway it up, Mr Fielding, if you please,' said Jack. 'The topgallant after it, and cross the yards as soon as possible.'

He walked with a composed step to the forecastle and fixed the headland with his glass. Minutes passed; one of the stern-chasers fired a ranging shot and the duel began again – his prohibition against hurting a hair of the *Cornélie*'s head had lapsed long since, and the *Nutmeg*'s one desire was to cripple her before she knocked away a mast. 'You'll see 'em directly this minute, sir,' said the lookout in a conversational tone.

The first ship glided out from behind the cover of the high ground. She was not much more than a mile away, and with the breeze on her beam and a press of sail she was steering south-east at perhaps ten knots – a fine bow-wave. Against the young sun he could not make out her armament, but her American colours were plain enough. Two followed her, both steering the same urgent course, both of about the same size, heavy sloops-of-war or small frigates, both wearing American colours. Signals were exchanging at a great pace. A fourth ship and his stony heart broke into flower. He walked back fast, not running, to the quarterdeck: 'Mr Richardson and the yeoman of signals,' he called, and Richardson, the signal lieutenant, came hobbling from the waist, his leg thick with bandages. Titus the yeoman followed him, racing aft from the heads. 'Colours, jack at the jack-staff, private signal, *Diane*'s number, and *Chase to the north-west*. Then telegraph *Well met Tom*. All from topgallant and stay; and a couple more jacks on the yard.'

Richardson repeated this; Adams wrote it down; the yeoman ran to his colour-chest; Jack called, 'Mr Reade, pray jump down to the sick-berth and tell the Doctor with my congratulations that the *Surprise* is in sight.' He looked into the waist, where the hawser to the lower capstan was tautening to sway the topmast up to the trestle-trees, and he was about to tell Fielding to send up the pennant as soon as the topgallant was in place when a thought froze his heart once more: had the *Surprise* been captured by an American squadron?

He walked forward. Colours, private signal and direction to chase were already flying; he watched the *Surprise* with rigid attention. She had hauled her wind and she was running past the other three with her familiar greyhound ease. Behind him the firing had stopped. He heard the orders for swaying up the topmast and the cry 'Launch ho' when it was home and fidded; but all this came from a great way off. Titus composed the message to be sent by telegraph, muttering 'T,O,M'; and at last the *Surprise*'s colours gave a twitch and raced down. They were replaced by her own to the cheering of far more of the *Nutmeg*'s hands than had any business to be looking about them; and glancing aft Jack saw that the *Cornélie* had worn and was heading for the heavy rain-squalls in the north-west.

'The Doctor's compliments, sir,' said Reade. 'He gives you joy of the meeting and will come on deck as soon as he is free.'

Dr Maturin was free by the time the *Nutmeg*, with her maintopsail, maintopgallant and man-of-war's pennant restored, had turned in pursuit of the *Cornélie*; she was close-hauled to the wind and she was tearing along at a splendid pace, throwing the water white and wide, but the *Surprise*, coming up to leeward, had had to ease off her sheets not to pass too fast. Stephen came running up in the black coat and apron he wore in action, and the contrast between the drying blood on the dusty blackness and his shining face was particularly striking.

'There she is!' he cried. 'I should have recognized her anywhere. What joy!'

'Yes, indeed,' said Jack. 'And I am so glad you came before we had to clew up the crossjack. You may never see another.'

'Pray point it out,' said Stephen.

'Why, it is this sail just above our heads, set on the crossjack yard,' said Jack.

'A very handsome sail too, upon my word: ornamental to the last degree. How she comes along, the brave boat! Huzzay, huzzay! There is Martin in front of the thing – I forget its name. I shall wave my handkerchief.'

The *Surprise* ranged up within pistol-shot, and shivering her foretopsail she paused abreast of the *Nutmeg*, travelling at much the same pace. Her rail was lined with happy, grinning faces, all well known to Jack and Stephen; but there was an etiquette in these matters at sea, and not a word did they utter until the two captains were opposite one another, Jack Aubrey still in his vile Monmouth cap, Tom Pullings in working clothes with a uniform hat clapped on for the ceremony: beneath it his dreadfully wounded face was ablaze with joy.

'Tom, how do you do?' called Jack in his powerful voice.

'Blooming, sir, blooming,' replied Pullings, pulling off the hat. 'I hope I see you well, and all our friends?'

Jack returned the salute and his long yellow hair streamed away to leeward. 'Never better, I thank you. Go ahead now and get into her wake; it will not take you long – she turned very heavy. But do not close till I come up. She will strike to the two of us: no powder wasted; nobody knocked about. What are your consorts?'

'*Triton*, sir, an English letter of marque, Captain Goffin, twenty-eight twelve-pounders and two long nines; and the others are American prizes.'

'So much the better. Carry on, then, Tom. You are in for a ducking,' he added, still in the same steady roar, as the first drops came sweeping across the deck.

The *Surprise* filled her foretopsail, forging ahead directly, and now that the official words were done greetings flew to and fro in spite of the rain. 'Captain Pullings, my dear, how do you do? Pray take care of the damp. — Mr Martin, how do you do? I have seen the orang-utang!' 'What cheer, Joe? What cheer, shipmates? What cheer, Methusalem?' And from some facetious hands far forward, 'What ho, the crossjack, ha, ha, ha!' with antic gestures.

The Nutmegs stared in amazement at this familiarity, for although Killick and Bonden — Killick particularly — had regaled them with accounts of Captain Aubrey's importance and wealth (a glass coach with gilded wheels and two puddings a day in the servants' hall) and Dr Maturin's supernatural skill and fashionable life (calls the Duke of Clarence Bill and takes tea with Mrs Jordan), they had never spoken of the *Surprise*.

Yet there was little time for amazement, since as soon as the *Surprise* was beyond the range of a moderate call, they were required to furl and unbend the hated crossjack and set the valuable driver, which gave the *Nutmeg* an additional knot; and even before it was cracking full the *Surprise* had vanished into the squall, a grey blur of tearing water.

The next half-hour was exceptionally anxious, and its minutes stretched out beyond all reason. It was not merely the decks all awash, water shooting from the lee scuppers, nor even fear of the ironbound coast, since Jack had his bearings clear; it was his dread that the *Surprise*, misled by the *Cornélie*'s slowness, might suddenly find herself alongside, facing her heavier guns at close range. In the middle of this unhappy time thunder cracked and rolled with enormous force at masthead height, continuous thunder shutting out any possible gunfire; and of course lightning to and fro in the even stronger deluge.

At his side Adams looked like a drowned rat — they all

looked like drowned rats: there was no point in putting on so much as a sou'wester in this milk-warm flood. 'Sir,' said Adams into his inclined ear, 'I beg pardon, but Mr Fielding said I might speak to you, seeing it was a special case. The gunner is to make up his books, and he is sadly troubled about the crow lost overboard: does not like to ask, but would esteem it a favour, was you to give him a certificate, countersigned by yourself as purser and master, and then by Mr F.'

A wholly extravagant triple peal with a reek of sulphur intervened, but when it was over Jack said quite mildly, 'Put me in mind of it when I am signing papers.'

This prodigious clap was the end of the squall. The thunder passed away to leeward, a distant rumble; the rain thinned, cleared, and there, five hundred yards ahead, was the *Surprise* lying to, bright in the clean-washed air. But she lay to alone. In the broad sunlit Passage there was no other ship at all: the coast to larboard, the horizon ahead and to starboard, and no other ship on the sea.

His astonishment lasted hardly long enough to name it. All those boats around the *Surprise*, more than any one frigate could carry, and the fact that she was taking men in by the score on either side and by the stern-ladder meant that the *Cornélie* had foundered. The telescope showed him men being slung up, almost inanimate – uniformed men.

'Mr Seymour, lower down a boat, any boat that will swim,' he said and hurried below, calling out for some kind of a decent coat, hat, breeches. And recalling that the *Surprise* was after all Stephen's private property, he sent to ask whether he chose to go across, adding that 'at present the sea was rather rough'. The midshipman came back with Dr Maturin's compliments, but at the moment he and Mr Macmillan were engaged on an urgent task. 'They were going at it with a saw, sir,' said Bennett, still pale and queasy.

The only boat undamaged after the long cannonade was the small cutter: it carried him across the sea to the side and the steps he knew so well. The *Surprise* had already shipped man-ropes and white-gloved side-boys; she received him in style, and there was a spontaneous, disorganized but hearty cheer as he ran up to the gangway, where Tom Pullings greeted him with an iron grip. 'She foundered, sir,' he said. 'We saw her getting her boats over the side as we came out of the squall: she was up to her port-sills, and as they pulled away she put her bows under a head-sea and slid down like she was sailing. We picked up a rare lot swimming about and clinging to hen-coops. But here is her commanding officer, sir: succeeded his captain in the action. He speaks English and I told him he was to surrender to you.'

He turned with a gesture of introduction and there among the group of officers, British and French, over to leeward, was Jean-Pierre Dumesnil; he came forward pale and almost dead with fatigue, offering his sword.

'Jean-Pierre!' cried Jack, advancing to meet him, 'By God, I am so happy to see you. I was afraid that . . . No, no. Keep your sword and give me your hand.'

Chapter Seven

' "No, no. Keep your sword and give me your hand," I said; and perhaps that may sound rather like Drury Lane, when the fellow in pink breeches and a plumed helmet raises his fallen enemy and the still-room maid is found to be the Duke's daughter, but at the time I do assure you it came quite natural. I was so very glad to see him. If you have had the long letter that Raffles promised to put aboard the next Indiaman you will know who I mean, Jean-Pierre Dumesnil, the nephew of that Captain Christy-Pallière who captured me when I had the *Sophie* and who treated me so well – the nephew I met in Pulo Prabang, changed from a little fat midshipman to a tall thin young officer, second of the *Cornélie*. I thought him a fine young fellow then, and I think him an even finer fellow now. (I beg you will look in the bottom right-hand drawer of the black scrutoire and find the direction of his Christy cousins: I think they live in Milsom Street. He went to Dr Hall's school in Bath during the peace and he often stayed with them – desires his duty and most affectionate greetings; and you will tell them he is quite unhurt.) During the engagement one of our thirty-two-pounders played Old Harry on the *Cornélie*'s quarterdeck, leaving Jean-Pierre in command, and another caused her to spring a butt low down in her bows. She made so much water that pumping day and night they could only just keep her free, even with a following wind. Yet for all that, and in spite of being short-handed, he fought his ship nobly. He might even have had us, if we had not met the *Surprise* in the mouth of the Passage with four ships in company – Tom Pullings had heard the sound of gunfire long before daylight and had come tearing down from his station well to the north. The four came into sight round a headland first, wearing American colours, and I said, "Why, Jack, you are between the Devil and the deep blue sea," meaning the *Cornélie*'s devilish eighteen-pounders behind me and the concentrated fire of an American squadron in front and no sea-room to manoeuvre. But then I saw the dear *Surprise* appear – Lord, what joy! – and I threw out the signal to chase to the north-west.

'Clearly, five against one was not fair odds, so Jean-Pierre hauled his wind in the hope of getting away behind one of the islands to the south under cover of a squall. But his people had scarcely been able to keep pace with the leak even when they had the wind well abaft the beam, and now with a head-sea and all hands utterly exhausted she could no longer swim. He just had time to get his boats clear before she settled. The *Surprise* recovered them – some could barely stand, and had to be hauled aboard in slings – and when the *Nutmeg* came up and I went across he surrendered to me.

"Then, the Passage being but an uneasy place to lie in, we proceeded eastwards to this sheltered road, anchored in sixty-fathom water and made acquaintance with the other ships. The *Triton* is a heavy letter of marque, almost as large as the *Surprise*; she is commanded by Horse-Flesh Goffin, whose court-martial for a false muster you will probably remember, and they had been cruising together for some time. The others were splendid American prizes they had taken, all the more splendid because they contained the cargoes of several other vessels too small to be worth a prize-crew. One of them is crammed with furs, sea-otter and the like, much demanded in China, where both ships were bound. Upon the whole the *Surprise* seems to have had an unusually successful cruise even before these two big merchantmen, capturing Nantucket and New Bedford whalers and sending them into South American ports, but I do not know exactly – we have so much to say to one another and there was so much to do in the poor battered *Nutmeg* that I do not know half what there is to know.' He was sitting at the starboard extremity of the line of sash-lights that filled the great cabin with sunshine reflected from a dappled sea, a window that was more familiar to him than any he had known on land, and looking out he saw the *Nutmeg*, trim again after a surprisingly short stay in this road, with the carpenter and his crew over the side, putting the last touches to the stern-gallery. He glanced along the table to the other end of the range; but seeing that Stephen was writing busily, with a contentious look on his face, he let his gaze wander over the table itself, which had been set, quite exceptionally, in the great cabin, to seat fourteen men in comfort; and he saw not without a certain complacency that it was set with uncommon magnificence. This was the sort of occasion that Killick loved more than his soul, and Jack's silver, preserved through all the vicissitudes of the voyage, blazed and twinkled in the shifting light. Stephen scratched steadily on, though now his look was more benign as he wrote, '. . . and so, having demolished Baker on the economy of the solitary bee, I shall only add that I am heartily tired of being a solitary bee myself. I have no words to express my longing to hear from you again, to learn that you, and perhaps our daughter, are recovered, well and happy. And so far as material things affect happiness, it may increase yours as it has increased mine, to know that if these prizes reach port, *our* economy may be somewhat less sparse, pinched, anxious, grey.'

Jack returned to his letter: 'Yet *Surprise*'s share of these two merchantmen alone should be something of a relief to poor Stephen, as owner and fitter-out he has the largest share, of course. Something of a relief, I say; but I am afraid it can go only a very little way towards recovering his fortunes. I am not sure how they stand, because although as soon as I heard of the bank being broke I hurried to his room and said that I had never regretted anything in my life so much as my advice to move to Smith and Clowes, that I hoped and prayed he had not followed it to a disastrous extent, and I had meant to go on to say that we had shared purses before and must certainly do so again. But I stumbled over my words – I had already put it badly – and he pulled me up – "No, no. Not at all. It was no great matter. I am infinitely obliged to you." Since then he has said nothing and although from time to time I have thrown out what I hope were delicate hints and suggestions he has not seemed to notice them; and with a man Lucifer could not hold a book, bell or candle to for pride I cannot raise the subject directly. But, however, when this voyage is over I shall beg him, as a favour, to sell me the *Surprise*: not only would it give me extraordinary pleasure, but it would at least serve to keep him afloat.

'To go back to the other ships: the Americans are rather thinly manned, many of their people having been set ashore in Peru, it being so much wiser to put it out of their power to rise upon you and recapture the ship; but there is little risk of that, since they will be escorted not only by the *Triton*, which is a powerful ship for these waters and full of hands, but by the *Nutmeg* too. It will be quicker for her to return to Batavia by way of Canton, there waiting for the north-east monsoon – quicker than beating back into the teeth of this one. I offered Tom the command, but he said he had rather stay with us; so Fielding has her, and very highly delighted he is.'

Killick came in and stood breathing heavily in the doorway and looking disagreeable. They took no notice, intent upon their letters; he came forward to the table and moved some knives and forks, quite unnecessarily, and with unnecessary noise.

'Get out, Killick,' said Jack, without looking round.

'Killick, you break in upon my thoughts,' said Stephen.

'Which I only came to say the cook has burnt the soup, the Doctor ain't shaved yet, and your honour has spilt ink on your breeches, your only decent breeches.'

'God's blood – hell and death, so I have,' cried Jack. 'Go

and rouse out my second-best – Stephen, we may poach upon your comforts, may we not? Killick, go and ask Mr Martin, with the Doctor's compliments, for three slabs of portable soup.'

'Three slabs of portable soup it is, sir,' said Killick, adding, 'It won't be nearly enough, though; not nearly enough,' as it were to himself.

Jack returned to his letter. 'My dear, we are to have a farewell dinner in half an hour. There is plenty of time, but I know that all hands concerned are anxious for its success, the more so in that *Nutmeg* is a regular man-of-war with a pennant, and led by Killick they will come in on one pretext or another, or peer through the companion, glooming and coughing at us until we are up there, square-rigged and spotless, to welcome our guests.'

He had finished the letter, with love and kisses all round when the door opened for Tom Pullings, now acting as the frigate's first lieutenant again, in spite of which he was wearing the uniform of his rank as commander, a splendid uniform, though somewhat creased and smelling of tropical mould, not having been put on for the last nine thousand miles. 'Forgive me, sir,' he said, 'but you did not hear me knock; and I believe a boat is putting off from *Triton*.'

'Thank you, Tom,' said Jack. 'I shall just seal this letter and then I am with you.'

'And sir, I am very much ashamed to say that when you first came aboard I quite forgot to give you a letter handed to me at Callao. It was in the pocket of this here coat and it flew clean out of my mind till I heard it crinkle.' Jack instantly perceived that the letter was from his natural son, begotten when he was on the Cape Station in his youth, and he scarcely heard Pullings' confused account of a clergyman that had visited the *Surprise* when she put in, had been deeply disappointed at finding that Captain Aubrey was not aboard, nor Dr Maturin; spoke perfect English, only with a sort of brogue; you would have said he was an Irishman, only he was black, coal-black. Tom had met him again at the Governor's,

174

where he stood next to the Bishop, dressed in a purple frock and treated with great respect. It was there that he had given Tom this letter. Renewed apologies: retreat.

'A letter from Sam,' said Jack, passing the first sheet. 'How well he expresses himself – a very happy turn of phrase, upon my word. There is a message for you,' – passing the second – 'And something in Greek. Pray read it all.'

'How he is coming on, to be sure: he will soon be Vicar-General, at this rate. It is not Greek but Irish, and referring to my intervention with the Patriarch it says *May God set a flower upon your head*.'

'Come, that is civil. I could hardly have put it better myself. So the Irish have a writing of their own? I had no idea.'

'Certainly they have a writing of their own. They had it long before your ancestors left their dim Teutonic wood; and indeed it was the Irish first taught the English the ABC, though with indifferent success, I freely admit. Yet this is a very handsome letter, so it is.'

'Now, sir,' said Killick, a razor in his hand, a towel over his arm, 'the water is getting cold.'

'He is the dearest fellow,' said Jack to himself, reading Sam's letter through once more, 'but how glad I am it came when mine was done.' Sam's existence was perfectly well known and accepted in Ashgrove Cottage; it was perfectly well known and a source of much amusement aboard the *Surprise*, many of whose older hands had seen the young man first come aboard, his father's image, though shining black. But Jack Aubrey's mind, though logical in mathematics and celestial navigation (he had read several papers to the Royal Society, with great applause on the part of those Fellows who understood them: gloomy fortitude on the part of the rest) was less so where laws were concerned: some, and almost all of those to do with the service, he obeyed without question; others he transgressed at times and then suffered in his conscience; others again he laughed at. Sam's place in this shifting landscape was obscure. Jack could not feel any easily defined guilt at that remote fornication, and he heartily loved his black popish priest of a boy; but a contradiction still remained, and it would have made him profoundly uneasy to read a letter from Sam while he was himself writing to Sophie.

The letter itself was perfect. Between the *My dear Sir* and the *Your most humble obedient and affectionate servant* it spoke of Sam's pleasure at seeing the ship, his disappointment at not being able to pay his respects to Captain Aubrey and Dr Maturin; of his journey across the Andes; of the great kindness of the Bishop, an ancient gentleman from Old Castile. Everything was entirely discreet; anyone could have read it; yet the whole breathed affection; and Jack had returned to the beginning still again when Killick wiped the smile off his face with the news that the *Nutmeg* too had lowered down a boat.

In point of fact neither this nor the *Triton*'s was coming to the *Surprise*; they had quite different tasks, and the foolish anxiety on the part of the frigate's people meant that Jack stood on the quarterdeck, hot in his best clothes in spite of the awning, for what seemed a very long and hungry waste of time. The group to leeward, Pullings, Davidge, West and Martin, the first, second, third lieutenants and the assistant surgeon, found the waiting equally hot and even hungrier. Hot, because although only Pullings was in uniform (West and Davidge, dismissed from the Navy, had no right to it; nor had Martin, though for different reasons) the others were dressed in formal clothes; and they too regretted their coats, waistcoats, high tight neckcloths, leather shoes. Hungrier, because they had reverted to the old-fashioned dinner at two bells (Pullings messing with the gun-room rather than in solitary state), and that was now an hour and a half ago. Presently Martin's lot improved, for Stephen came up, severely buttoned, shaved and brushed, and they fell into a most animated conversation in a neutral zone abaft the capstan, just not encroaching on the Captain's holy windward solitude; and the immense amount of information each had

176

to convey abolished all thought of food. This was a comfort denied the lieutenants: their minds ran on their dinner; their stomachs rumbled, they swallowed from time to time, but they said little, so little that Mr Bulkeley the bosun could be heard in the waist quietly reproving one of his mates for being barefoot: 'What will the gentlemen think of us when they come up the side?'

This would be in the very near future, for now the real boats had shoved off, and Killick and his mates were on their way with trays of glasses, bottles, fritoons and what other delicacies the *Surprise* could afford.

'Killick!' they called, not very loud; but Killick affected not to hear, and pursing his lips he posed the trays on the gleaming capstan-head, everything arranged just so, the pieces of bacon-rind neatly crossed, nothing to be touched until the feast began.

'Stand by,' cried the bosun, and poised his call. 'Side-men away,' called West, the officer of the watch, as the first boat hooked on and the guests were piped aboard.

The first was Goffin, a tall burly black-haired man with a red face, a post-captain who had been cashiered (though he still wore the naval uniform, with trifling changes). He saluted the quarterdeck; all the officers returned the salute: he said, 'How do you do, Aubrey?' without a smile and turned straight to Killick and the capstan; his nephew followed him, somewhat more gracious; then came the people from the *Nutmeg*, with the two surviving French officers, and finally Adams, accompanied by Reade and Oakes, for whom Jack felt a particular responsibility and who were to remain in the frigate; though they, having dined at noon, could not reasonably hope to dine again.

When all the officers had taken their whet, which was limited to gin, Hollands and Plymouth, and madeira, Jack led them below; as they trooped in, crowding the great cabin, Goffin called out, 'By God, Aubrey, you do yourself proud,' and he moved towards the head of the table with its splendid array.

'Here, sir, if you please, opposite your young gentleman,' said white-gloved Killick, showing him a place at the other end, next to Pullings.

He swelled, his face went a darker red, and he sat down. It was impossible to fault the arrangement: by immemorial convention the captured French officers sat on Jack's right and left and the King's officers took place of those who were not or who were no longer King's officers. If this had been a small informal gathering and if Goffin had been a friend Jack might have ordered things differently: but then again he might not – when he had been struck off the list himself, when he had been in Goffin's uncomfortable position, well-meaning but thick-headed friends had sometimes given him the precedence due to his former rank; and he could feel the misery yet. Goffin however saw the matter in another light; he felt that his condemnation for the trifling offence of false muster was so merely technical (he had entered the name of a friend's son on his ship's books to win the wholly absent boy some years of service-time when he should in fact go to sea; a common practice, but illegal; and his clerk, repeatedly kicked and cuffed, betrayed him) that he deserved better treatment. He sat for some time, trying to work out some remark that, though offensive, should not be too gross.

He had a perfectly good opportunity with the soup, which smelt so like a glue-factory that the two Frenchmen put down their spoons before exchanging a haggard look and submitting to the horrors of war, while Pullings, for the honour of the ship, called to Stephen, 'Very good soup, Doctor,' and Jack said quietly to his neighbour, 'I am so sorry, Jean-Pierre: it was a desperate measure. Please tell your friend not to finish it.' But Goffin missed his chance; soups were all one to him; he ate it mechanically and passed his plate for more; and only when the plate was empty did he say to his nephew on the other side of the table, an elderly young gentleman who had failed to pass for lieutenant, 'Was you ever at a Lord Mayor's banquet, Art?' 'No, sir.' 'Or any of the City halls, Grocers', Fishmongers' and the like? This is the sort of show you see among the commercial gents.'

The shaft missed its mark, because Jack was laughing in his deeply amused, full-throated way at one of his own jokes, but this and various other jets of malignance were perceived by those at the lower end of the table and it did not take long for Jack to become aware of their uneasiness. He guessed its source when he saw that dark face down there at Pullings' right and he was certain of it a moment later.

In a pause Fielding had just said, 'Speaking of bears, sir, did I ever tell you that my father was a midshipman in the *Racehorse* under Lord Mulgrave, or Captain Phipps as he was then, in his voyage towards the North Pole? He was not exactly shipmates with Nelson, who was in the *Carcass*, but they saw a great deal of one another ashore, and they got along together famously. Nelson . . .'

'You must not talk about Nelson with two French officers in company,' cried Horse-Flesh. 'It ain't civil.'

'Oh, never mind us, sir,' replied Jean-Pierre with a laugh. 'Our withers are unwrung. We have Duguay-Trouin, to name but one.'

'Duguay-Trouin? I never heard of him.'

'Then you have a treat in store,' said Jean-Pierre. 'A glass of wine with you, sir.'

'A glass of wine all round,' said Jack. 'Bumpers now, gentlemen, and no heel-taps. To Duguay-Trouin, and may we never meet his like.'

After this, at Stephen's suggestion, they drank to Jean Bart too. Killick and his mates ran in and out; the heap of empty bottles rose high in the steerage; an array of far more creditable dishes covered the table and Jack said, 'Pray, Mr Fielding, go on with your account. It was not Nelson's famous attempt at a bear's skin, I collect?'

'Oh no, sir: in fact it is not much of a story at all, except when my father tells it, but I will just give the bare bones to show there is another side to the creature.'

'*Bare bones* is very good,' said Welby, chuckling into his wineglass.

'The ships were coming back from about eighty-one north; they had very nearly been frozen in, and after prodigious exertions they were lying in Smeerenburg Bay in Spitzbergen. Most of the people were allowed ashore; some played leapfrog or football with a bladder, and some ran about the country in hope of game. Those who kept to the shore killed a walrus, an enormous creature as I am sure you know, sir: they stripped off the blubber, ate what a whaler in the company told them was the best part, cooking it over the blubber, which burns pretty well, once the fire has a hold. Then some time later, a day or so later I think my father said, three white bears were seen coming over the ice, a she-bear and her cubs. The blubber was still burning, but the she-bear plucked out some pieces that were not alight and that had some flesh on them; they ate voraciously, and some of the seamen threw lumps from the carcass they still had towards her. She fetched them one by one, carried them back to the cubs and divided them. As she was fetching away the last piece the men shot the cubs dead and wounded her severely as she ran. She crawled as far as the cubs, still carrying the piece, tore it apart and laid some before each; and when she saw they could not eat she laid her paws first upon one, then upon the other and tried to raise them up. When she found she could not stir them, she went off; and when she had got at some distance, looked back and moaned; and since that did not induce them to come away, she returned, and smelling round them, began to lick their wounds. She went off a second time as before, and having crawled a few paces, looked again behind her, and for some time stood there moaning. But her cubs still not rising to follow her, she returned to them again, and with signs of inexpressible fondness went round one, and round the other, pawing them, and moaning. Finding at last that they were cold and lifeless, she lifted her head towards the men and growled; and several firing together they killed her too.'

A decent silence; and Stephen said in a low voice, 'Lord Mulgrave was the most amiable of commanders. He it was that first described the ivory gull; and he took particular notice of the northern jellyfish, or blubbers.'

One bell in the first dog-watch; the conversation had grown more general again, a steady hum of talk at the upper end, and Welby, his face now matching his scarlet coat, had engaged the *Cornélie*'s monoglot third lieutenant in a far more confident and comprehensible French than any of his shipmates had expected, when from the glum far end came Goffin's voice, loud, somewhat out of control: 'Well, seeing that many of us are out of favour in Whitehall, I'll give you a toast: here's to the Navy's black sheep, and may they all soon be whitewashed with the same brush.'

They took it remarkably well: both West and Davidge contrived a smile, and they all drank their wine and drew on every reserve of anecdote or remark about tide, weather, current – anything to prevent a silence, Welby coming out unusually strong with an account of the Pentland Firth, and Martin and Macmillan keeping up a fine flow on the subject of scurvy, its cure and prevention. But it was a relief when after pudding – a noble great spotted dog and the best dish of the meal – they heard Jack say, 'Doctor, please would you explain to your neighbour that we are just about to drink His Majesty's health; that it will be perfectly in order for him not to join us; but if he should choose to do so, we are privileged to drink it seated.'

The *Cornélie*'s third lieutenant did so choose; so did Jean-Pierre, who even added the words 'God bless him'; and shortly after this Jack suggested that they should take their coffee on the quarterdeck.

Coffee, no great amount of brandy, and then farewells, obscurely righteous and indignant on Goffin's part, most affectionate upon that of the Nutmegs, who were to carry a whole sheaf of letters to Canton, and loving upon Jean-Pierre's.

'I am afraid that was a most unsuccessful dinner,' said

Jack, as they stood watching the boats pull away, Horse-Flesh being sick over the side. 'They are delicate things: I have noticed again and again that in parties of this kind one man can wreck it all.'

'He is a gross fellow,' said Stephen. 'He cannot hold his wine.'

'He is losing it now, by God,' said Jack. 'Tell me, do our invalids really have to eat that dreadful soup?'

'It was mixed four times too strong, and then was attempted to be disguised with some of the original broth, itself made of decayed swinesflesh in the first place and then burnt. But it is not the soup that is making him vomit so; it is the black choler.'

'Ah? I am sure you are right. Perhaps I should have made the invitation easier to refuse. When I was in his case I dare say I wrecked many a party with my gloom, before I learnt to have previous engagements. It is hardly to be believed, how important a man's rank becomes to him – I mean his place in our world, our wooden world – after he has served twenty years or so, and its order, laws, customs and God help us even clothes have grown second nature. And poor Horse-Flesh – Lord how he pukes – must have served nearer thirty. He was second of the *Bellerophon* in ninety-three, when I took passage in her; and he stood five places above me on the post-captains' list.'

'Yet he broke one of its laws.'

'Oh yes – false muster. But I meant its important laws: instant obedience, high discipline, exact punctuality, cleanliness and so on. I always thought them of the first importance and now that I am back – I thank God for it every day – I have still more respect for them, and even for the lesser rules too. Discipline is all of a piece, said St Vincent, and I do not think I could bring myself to put anyone's name on the books; unless indeed your daughter should prove a son with a taste for the sea. Captain Pullings, I believe you have something to say.'

'Yes, sir, if I may be so bold. When we have won our

anchor and parted company, the people would take it kindly, was you to go round the ship . . .'

'That is exactly what I have in mind, Tom. Quarters, though without a clear run fore and aft, as soon as we are under way; and then I go round.'

'Yes, sir. Just so, sir. But what I mean is, in square rig. They have not seen a gold-laced coat except for mine, and that only twice since Lisbon, which don't really signify, me being only a volunteer.'

Jack was much attached to the crew of the *Surprise*, a difficult but highly seamanlike body made up of man-of-war's men and privateers, with a sprinkling of merchant seamen; and they were much attached to him. Not only had he done them exceedingly proud in the article of prizes when the *Surprise* sailed as a letter of marque, but he had won them protection from impressment; and although in the course of the present voyage he had been snatched away at Lisbon to command another ship, he had also been very publicly restored to the Navy List; so now he returned in the gold-laced splendour of a post-captain, conferring a delightful respectability on the frigate and her people. Privateering ships had a shocking reputation upon the whole – in fact some were hardly to be distinguished from pirates – and the privateersmen aboard rejoiced in their new status, their freedom from criticism; and they loved to see the massive symbol of it, with the Nile medal in his buttonhole and his number one scraper on his head. The general feeling aboard was that the Surprises now had the best of both worlds, the relative freedom and equality of a letter of marque on the one hand, and on the other the honour and glory of the King's service: a charming state of affairs, particularly when it was coupled with the possibility of very great rewards. But so far their Captain had scarcely made his official entrance.

From far over the water came the sound of bosun's calls as the prizes and their guardians prepared to ship capstan bars.

'Very well, Tom,' said Jack. 'But this coat is killing me. I shall go below, take it off, and see whether I can grow a little cooler. When you and the other officers have shifted into nankeens, let us get under way; then I will ask the people how they do. Doctor, will you come with me? Do not you feel the heat?'

'I do not,' said Stephen. 'Sobriety and moderation preserve me from plethory; they preserve me from discomfort in what is after all but a modest warmth.'

'Sobriety and moderation are capital virtues and I have practised them from my earliest youth,' said Jack, 'but they are sadly out of place in a host, who must encourage his guests to eat and drink by example; so there is a Roland for your . . .'

In his shirtsleeves and stretched out on the locker by the open stern-windows, Jack loosened his waist-band and reflected for a while. The name Oliver floated up out of a score of others and he called, 'Killick. Killick, there.'

'What now?' cried Killick, also in his shirtsleeves; he had worked exceedingly hard to clear the table and he was not pleased at being torn from his enormous washing-up, far too delicate to be trusted to seamen who would use brick-dust on plate the minute they were left unwatched.

'Roland and Oliver: have you ever heard of them?'

'There is a Roland, sir, gunsmith off of the Haymarket; and there are Oliver's Warranted Leadenhall Sausages. Many an Oliver's Warranted Leadenhall Sausage have I ate at the Grapes when we was ashore.'

'Well,' said Jack, unconvinced. 'I may drop off. If I do, give me a call when we are under way.'

He heard the pipe *All hands unmoor ship* followed by its invariable sequence: the muffled thunder of running feet, orders, pipes, the steady click of pawls, the stamp and go of those manning the bars and the shrill fife on the capstanhead; and his mind tried to recapture the exact state of the ship's company, her complete-book, as it stood when he left her in Portugal, but so much had happened since then, and he had eaten and drunk so heartily at dinner, that his mind refused its duty, and at the distant cry of thick and dry for weighing he went to sleep. During the extraordinarily active period that had followed dropping anchor in this road, with the repairing of the *Nutmeg*, the disposal of the French prisoners, the inspection of the prizes, the transfer of his and Stephen's possessions to the *Surprise*, and his farewell to his former shipmates, who cheered him in the kindest way when he went down the side for the last time – in these hours of continual running about he had of course seen the Surprises, but only in a fleeting way, exchanging very few words except with his bargemen, who pulled him from ship to ship in the warm calm sea. He slept; but his sleep was pervaded by an anxiety: few things wounded a foremast jack more than having his name forgotten and it was an officer's duty to remember it.

In fact it was not Killick who woke him but Reade: 'Mr West's duty, sir, and *Nutmeg* has hoisted *permission to part company*.'

'Reply with affirmative and add *Merry Christmas*: you will have to telegraph that. Where are we?'

'We have just catted the best bower, sir, and we were just about to fish it when a man called Davis fell overboard. Mr West passed him a line, and they hauled him aboard not a minute ago, much scraped.'

Jack was on the point of saying, 'Then they can heave him back again,' but Reade was much caressed by everyone aboard – in the *Nutmeg* grim old forecastle hands would run the length of the gangway to hand him up a ladder, and it promised to be much the same in the *Surprise* – and he had a certain tendency to be above himself: this was not to be encouraged and the remark changed to a dismissive 'Thank you, Mr Reade.' But the feeling behind it remained. Davis was a very large dark hairy man, dangerously savage, clumsy – his shipboard name of Awkward Davis arose from both these qualities – and so devoid of nautical skill that he was always quartered in the waist, where his enormous strength was of some use in hoisting. Jack had once saved him from drowning, as he had saved many a man, being a capital hand at swimming; and the grateful Davis had persecuted him ever since, following him from ship to ship, impossible to shake off, though he had been offered every opportunity of deserting in ports where merchantmen were offering wages far above the Navy's £1 5s 6d a month.

A disaster of a man, violent and quite capable of maiming or even killing a valuable hand out of jealousy or an imagined slight; but half a glass later Jack found himself shaking Davis' hand with real pleasure – a terrible grip followed by others almost equally powerful, for though the Surprises were pleased to see their Captain in his full naval glory once more, his white silk stockings, his hundred guinea presentation sword and the Turkish chelengk in his hat intimidated them a little; and although his progress was remarkably talkative for a King's ship, it was restrained for a privateer, so the seamen put nearly all their welcome into their handshake. Fortunately Jack too had enormous hands, quite as strong if not quite as horny; and fortunately the *Surprise*, having left England ostensibly as a private ship of war, was much less heavily manned than a King's ship – apart from anything else she carried no Marines – and there were not many more than a hundred hands to shake. As for the names, which had so worried him, they came without the slightest difficulty. Of course it was easy enough with very old shipmates like Joe Plaice, who had sailed with him in many a commission – 'Well, Joe, how are you coming along, and how is the headpiece?' 'Prime, sir, I thank you kindly,' said Joe, tapping the silver dome that Dr Maturin had screwed on to his damaged skull in 49 degrees south a great while ago, 'And I give you all the joy in the world of them two swabs' – winking at the crowned epaulettes that Jack had never worn until his reinstatement appeared in the *London Gazette*. But it was much the same with the other hands he had taken on at Shelmerston, privateers or smugglers to a man: 'Harvey,

Wall, Curtis, Fisher, Waites, Halkett,' he said to the next gun-crew, standing about their charge, old *Wilful Murder*, in easy, informal attitudes, 'how do you do?' and shook hands all round. And so it went until he reached *Sudden Death*, and there he was very nearly brought up all standing by six profoundly bearded faces, each showing a broad, pleased, expectant smile beneath the mat. 'Slade, Auden, Hinckley, Mould, Vaggers, Brampton, I trust I see you well.' The position of the gun, its name and something about their stance had brought the names of the ship's Sethians darting into his mind.

'Very well, sir,' said Slade. 'Which we thank you for your kindness. Only Auden here' – both his neighbours pointed at him – 'lost two toes in Tierra del Fuego; and John Brampton sinned with a woman in Tahiti, and is in the sick-berth yet.'

'I grieve to hear it. I shall visit John by and by. But prosperous otherwise, I hope?'

'Oh dear me yes, sir,' said Slade. 'Not quite up to your Nebuchadnezzar pitch, but Seth has been very good to us.' He and all his mates jerked their thumbs at what in their sect was both a holy and a lucky name.

'Ha, ha,' said Jack, his mind running back to the glorious prizes they had taken in their first cruise together, 'I am glad the barky has done well.' They all looked affectionately over the side to where the *Nutmeg*, the *Triton* and the two merchantmen stuffed with wealth were standing away to the north-west with the wind two points free, now more than half hull-down. 'But you must not expect the Nebuchadnezzar touch again, not in these waters.'

'Oh no, sir,' said Slade, and all his friends went tut, tut, tut. 'All we hope for to do now is to go quietly home with what we have, and if we get there' – the same simultaneous movement of six thumbs – 'we mean to build a tabernacle of shittim-wood for our chapel – you know our chapel, sir?'

'Oh yes, indeed I do.' So did anyone else coming in to Shelmerston from the sea; for although the chapel was not large it was built of white marble ornamented with gilt brass esses, and it made a striking contrast with the rest of the town, mostly thatched, homely, vague in outline.

'And in this here tabernacle we mean to deposit our beards, as what we call a thank-offering.'

'Very right and proper,' said Jack, and having shaken hands he moved on to *Belcher*, whose captain had almost certainly been both a pirate and a cannibal and whose hand was without any doubt the roughest and most vice-like in the ship. 'Well, Johnson, Penderecki, John Smith and Peter Smith . . .' said Jack, and so along the starboard side, where only the second captains and a boarder stood by each gun, and down into the entrails of the ship. This tour resembled an inspection at divisions, but Jack was not accompanied by his first lieutenant nor any of the divisional officers; it was a wholly personal affair, and although his dinner had not been a success, and although the soup was still with him, his face was set in pleasure as he walked through the hot and smelly gloom towards the sick-berth. The ship was in high man-of-war order; she had lost only five hands – three Lascars of pneumonia in the cold, wet, tedious passage of the Strait, one washed out of the head by night in the heavy weather that met them as they emerged into the Pacific, and one killed when they boarded the first merchantman – and there was no doubt that under Tom Pullings she was a happy ship. Yet surely the stench was a little much, even for the orlop?

Light showed under the sill of the sick-berth door and there were voices within; as he opened it he heard with satisfaction that the two medical men were talking in Latin. The only other inhabitants were Wilkins, who had a broken arm that would not knit and who could not therefore shake hands, though grateful for the visit, and the simpler Brampton brother, the Tahiti pox, who was too ashamed to move or speak.

'Mr Martin,' said Jack, after he had seen the invalids, 'this is in no way a personal reflexion on you or Captain Pullings, but is not the atmosphere down here uncommon thick, not to say unwholesome? Dr Maturin, do you not find the atmosphere uncommon thick?'

'I do too. But I am of opinion that this is no more than the ordinary atmosphere, the ordinary fetor of an aged man-of-war; for you are to consider, that in foul weather, hands in the grip of peristalsis or micturition will seek some secluded corner within the ship rather than be washed off the seat of ease out there in the open prow. So after some generations we live above a floating cess-pit, the offence being aggravated by many other factors, such as the tons and tons and advisedly do I say tons of the vile slime that comes aboard on the cables when we have lain in a port like Batavia or Mahon, a slime made up of the filth of slaughter-houses and human habitations, to say nothing of putrid debris brought down by streams – mud and slime that drips from the cables in their tiers into the space below, which is never, never cleaned. The *Nutmeg*, dear colleague' – turning towards Martin, who looked somewhat out of countenance – 'was as sweet as her name implies, with never a cockroach, never a mouse, still less a rat, she having lain on the sea-bed for months together. All her wooden members had swollen tight together, like those of a wine-barrel when at last you get it tight, so that once she was pumped dry and aired within, dry she remained, with no foul bilges swilling to and fro; and this we have been used to long enough for our noses to grow delicate.'

'Wilkins is to be hung in an airy space upstairs tomorrow,' said Martin. 'And Brampton must finish his salivation in peace and quiet.'

'I shall see that another windsail is shipped,' said Jack; and before he went he leant over Brampton's cot and said, rather loud, 'Cheer up, Brampton; many a man has been far worse than you, and you are in very good hands.'

'The woman tempted me,' said Brampton; and after a short silence, 'I shall go to Hell.' He turned his head away, his body heaving with sobs.

With the Captain gone they reverted to their Latin and

Martin said, 'Do you think I can decently offer him comfort?'

'I cannot tell,' said Stephen. 'For the moment I should exhibit a slime-draught with two scruples of asafoetida.' He turned to the medicine-chest. 'I see you have changed nothing,' he said.

'Oh no, indeed,' said Martin; and then, 'I am afraid the Captain was not quite pleased.'

'It was only that I thoughtlessly said the ship was old,' said Stephen. 'He cannot bear it.' Having smelt the mixture he added a little more asafoetida and said, 'What induced you to say that the patient must finish his salivation in the sick-berth?'

'Because anywhere else he would be exposed to his shipmates' playfulness, their facetious enquiries after his membrum virile and often-repeated witticisms: the Sethians are an austere set of men and this lapse has amused the ordinary dissolute mariners. They mean no harm, but they will play off their humours, and until he has his health their mirth may kill him. The mind is not very strong, and I am afraid his friends are ill-advised to dwell so much on sin and its wages.'

By the time they had dosed Brampton and summoned the loblolly-boy to sit with the patients – no visitors to be allowed until further notice – a somewhat fresher air was wafting down the new windsail into the depths, and as they reached the quarterdeck Jack said to Pullings, 'If it is kept carefully trimmed to the wind it will do a great deal, but' – raising his voice – 'remarks have been passed about the charnel-house, cess-pit stink between decks, so perhaps we had better open the sweetening-cock.'

'I am very sorry about the stench, sir: I had not noticed any. But then it is a little close and hot, with the wind so far abaft the beam.'

'Mr Oakes, Mr Reade,' called Jack.

'Sir?' they said, pulling off their hats.

'Do you know where the sweetening-cock is?'

They looked a little blank, and Oakes said hesitantly, 'In the hold, sir.'

'Then go to the carpenter and tell him from me that you are to be shown how to turn it on; and it is to be left on until there is eighteen inches of water in the well.' When they had gone he turned back to Pullings and said in the same carrying tone, 'Of course we shall have to pump ship an hour or so longer, which is very hard in this heat; but at least it will clean the bilges. Clean the bilges like a milk-maid's pail.'

This was heard by all on the quarterdeck except the medical men, who were very slowly climbing the shrouds of the mizen mast, concentrating too hard on their anxious task for any satirical fling to reach them. Privacy was the rarest of all the ship's amenities: each had a cabin, but it was for solitary reading, writing, contemplation or sleep, being as small (all proportions guarded) as a fattening-coop for a single bird; and although Stephen had the run of the great cabin, the dining-cabin and the sleeping-cabin (which was but fair, he being the owner of the ship), none of these places was suitable for the long, detailed and even passionate discussion of birds, beasts and flowers, the rooms belonging equally to the Captain; nor was the gun-room, with its many other inhabitants. Both would do for the occasional display of skins, bones, feathers, botanical specimens; and indeed their long tables might have been made for the purpose; but in earlier voyages they had found that the only place for long, comfortable, uninterrupted conversation was the miz-zentop, a reasonably spacious platform embracing the head of the lower mast and the foot of the one above it, poised some forty feet above the deck, walled on either side by the topmast shrouds and their dead-eyes, and aft by a little wall of canvas extended by a rail, while the front was open, giving them a good view of all the ocean that the maincourse and maintopsail did not shut out, when the mizzen topsail was not set. The maintop would have been higher; the foretop would have given a better view (unbeatable with the foretopsail furled); but in either case getting there was more public: kind hands from below would place their feet on the ratlines, strong and sometimes facetious voices would call out advice; for although they made light of the peril and would even take a hand from the shroud and wave it to show how little they regarded the height, there was something about their attitude and their rate of progress which persuaded watchers that even after all these thousands of sea-miles they were not seamen, nor anything even remotely resembling seamen. But the quarterdeck (from which the mizzentop was reached) was out of bounds for three-quarters of the ship's company; furthermore, whereas the main and fore tops were often filled with busy hands, the mizzentop was much more rarely used, particularly with the wind so far abaft the beam.

Less used, but even so the relevant studdingsails were kept there, folded into long soft parcels; and upon these they reclined, gasping, with their backs against the firm canvas, as they had so often sat before. 'Well, there you are again,' said Martin, looking at him with affectionate satisfaction. 'I cannot tell you with what regret I saw you leave the ship half the world away. Apart from all other considerations, there I was with no mentor and a sick-berth potentially full of diseases that I could not even name, far less treat.'

'Come, you have done pretty well. No more than three men in a hundred degrees of latitude: that is pretty well. And when all is said and done, there is little we can do in the physical line apart from bleeding, purging, sweating and administering blue pill and even bluer ointment. Surgery is another matter. You have made the neatest job of poor West's nose.'

'It was simplicity itself. A snip – I used scissors – a few painless stitches, and as it recovered its feeling so it healed.'

'Without even laudable pus?'

'Without anything at all. It was frostbite, you know, not syphilis.'

'So he told me: he told Captain Aubrey and me at once.

I am afraid people are tactful: avert their eyes without any questions and look no more.'

'I am afraid they do. But tell me, tell me, what have you been doing all this time, and what have you seen, apart from the orang-utang?'

Stephen smiled at him, and as he smiled so the events of these past months presented themselves scarcely as a sequence but more nearly as a whole. From them he picked what was proper to tell, together with the inward reflexion 'What are the three things that cannot be concealed? Love, sorrow, and wealth are the three things that cannot be concealed: and intelligence-work comes a very close fourth,' and the realization that these mental processes had occupied no more than two rolls of the ship, magnified in space up here but clearly not in time. 'You must know,' said he, 'that Captain Aubrey was called back to England to be fully reinstated and to take command of the *Diane*. She was to carry an envoy to the Sultan of Pulo Prabang, who was contemplating an alliance with the French; and since this island – oh such orchids and coleoptera, Martin, apart from my celestial ape and the unimaginably huge rhinoceros! – lies in the South China Sea, almost across the path of our Indiamen coming from Canton, and where should we be without our rhubarb and tea, God preserve us, the envoy's mission was to induce the Sultan to change his mind. It was thought useful that I should go too, speaking French and having some knowledge of Malay as well as medicine. And so we went, sailing as fast as ever we could, making only one stop, at Tristan da Cunha; but that was very nearly our last, the ship being heaved nearer and nearer and nearer a sheer wall of rock by rollers topmast high and never a breath of wind to give us motion. I assure you, however, we survived it, and I even set foot on Tristan, flattering myself I should see wonders while they were watering and taking in greenstuff. It will not surprise you to learn that I was snatched away within hours, *within hours*, on the plea that they must not lose some favourable conjuncture of wind, tide or the like. Then the far southern ocean, and there at last I had albatrosses, giant petrels, stink-pots, pintadoes: but at such a cost! Monstrous billows, an incessant shrieking wind that allowed human thought and speech only when we were in the vast deep hollow of the wave; and then ice; ice on the deck, ice on the ropes, ice-mountains in the sea of most prodigious size and I must confess prodigious beauty that threatened to *do us in* as the seamen say; so Captain Aubrey directed our course to more Christian seas and I was in great hopes of seeing Amsterdam Island, a remote and uninhabited speck untouched by any naturalist, its flora, fauna and geology wholly undescribed. I saw it indeed, but only far to windward, and the ship carried on under a press of sail for Java Head.'

The sun had set in its usual abrupt tropical manner soon after they had made themselves comfortable: night had swept over the sky, showing the eastern stars after the few minutes of twilight, and now on the larboard beam a glowing planet heaved up on the horizon, lying there for a moment like the stern-lantern of some important ship. Martin was a man of peace; Maturin, with certain qualifications, was in principle opposed to violence; yet both had absorbed so much of the man-of-war's and even more the letter of marque's predatory values that they fell silent, staring like tigers at the planet until it rose clear of the sea and betrayed its merely celestial character.

'I must ask Captain Aubrey the name of that prodigious star,' said Stephen. 'He is sure to know,' and as it were in answer to these words they heard Jack tuning his violin far below. 'I shall pass over Java and the great kindness of Governor Raffles, a most distinguished naturalist, for the now, though I shall show you some of my specimens when we can find a table free – did you know there was a Java peacock? God help me, I never did: a famous proud bird he is too – and shall only observe that we reached Pulo Prabang; that our envoy outwitted the French, although they were there before us; and that he induced the Sultan to sign a treaty of alliance with Great Britain. Happily all this took some time – would that it had been longer by far! – in which I had the inestimable good fortune of becoming acquainted with Dr van Buren, of whom you may have heard.'

'The great Dutch authority on the spleen?'

'The same. But his interests spread far beyond.'

'To the pancreas, the thyroid?'

'Even farther. There is nothing in the animal or vegetable kingdoms that does not arouse his eager deeply-informed curiosity. It was to him that I owed my introduction to an inconceivably remote Paradise inhabited by Buddhist monks where the birds and beasts have no fear of men – have never been harmed – and where I walked hand in hand with an amiable aged female orang-utang.'

'Oh, oh, Maturin!'

'And other wonders that I have noted down; but if I should tell you a half of them, and show you the half of my specimens, with remarks, we should still be talking when we reach New South Wales; and I have not yet heard a word from you. Let me just close my summary by telling you that we sailed off in triumph with our treaty, that we cruised at one of the points of rendezvous without success, and that in the course of our return to Batavia the *Diane* struck an uncharted reef – there are many in that uncomfortable sea, it appears – ran on to it by night and at the very height of flood. We could not pull her off; but there being an island fairly close at hand we carried most of our possessions to it in rowing-boats, formed a military camp and sat down, tolerably easy in our minds, to wait for the next spring tide, which, as you probably know, depends on the moon. We were tolerably easy, because our well supplied us with water and the woods with boar; while the island was not without interest, being inhabited by ring-tailed apes, two sorts of pig, *sus babirussa* and *barbatus*, and numerous colonies of the so-called bird's-nest-soup swallow, which I am sorry to say is not a swallow at all but only a dwarvish species of oriental swift. The envoy, however, did not wait for us to settle: he was eager to return with his treaty, and Captain Aubrey gave him the new launch with adequate stores and crew for the voyage to Batavia, a voyage of no more than two hundred miles that would have been no great matter but for a typhoon that destroyed our ship on its reef and certainly overwhelmed the open boat. We were building a schooner from the wreckage when a horde of ill-favoured raparees attacked us – Dyaks and Malays led by a nasty confident quean, a bloody-minded covetous froward strumpet. They killed many of our people, but we killed more of theirs: they burnt our schooner, the thieves, as they left, but we destroyed their proa entirely with one brilliant ball from the Captain's long nine. Then it was the anxious time, with the boar so thin on the ground and barely a ring-tailed ape at all; but, however, a junk that put in for bird's-nests carried us back to Batavia, where Governor Raffles gave us that charming ship the *Nutmeg* in which you found us. There. Those are the essentials, which I hope to fill with notes and specimens as we sail along. Now pray tell me what you have done and what you have seen.'

'Well,' said Martin, 'although I have not seen an orang-utang, my journey has not been without its interesting moments. You may recall that last time we had the happiness of walking in the Brazilian forest I was bitten by an owl-faced night-ape.'

'Certainly I do. How you bled!'

'This time I was bitten by a tapir, and bled even more.'

'A tapir, for all love?'

'A young striped and spotted tapir, *Tapirus americanus*. I saw his huge dark-brown distracted mother at the turn of a little sort of track or path by the river. She rushed wildly into the water below and was seen no more. I found that he was caught in a pitfall, and when with infinite pains I had seized him and hoisted him to the edge, he bit me. If there were any light I should show you the scar. And before I could get out of the pit a band of Indians came up, no doubt those that had dug it; and they reproached me very bitterly, stabbing the air with their spears. I was exceedingly uneasy, so uneasy that I hardly felt the pain; but happily a party from the ship appeared, and one of the seamen who spoke Portuguese gave them a piece of tobacco and desired them to go about their business. But it comes to me that one of the party was Wilkins, whose broken arm you saw in the sick-berth: may I break off for a moment and ask what you thought of him?'

'It seemed to me an ordinary distal radius-ulna transverse fracture with some lateral displacement effectively reduced: the kind of break you would expect from a fall. But as it was dressed according to the Basra method I did not see much of the arm. When did it take place?'

'Three weeks ago; and it is not yet knit, nor beginning to knit. The ends are closely approximated – there is crepitus – but there is no union.'

'You suspect scurvy, I collect? Sure, that is a usual sign, though by no means infallible. And incipient scurvy would in part account for John Brampton's extreme lowness of spirits. Are we out of juice?'

'No. But I opened a new keg no great while ago, and I doubt its quality. We bought it in Buenos Aires.'

'I have a net of fresh lemons and an elegant private keg, wholly reliable, which will do for some months. But as Captain Aubrey does not intend to touch at New Guinea, and as the voyage is long, we may ask him to steer in time for a convenient, well-charted, well-stocked island.'

Eight bells below them and the watch was mustered – loud, unmistakable calls, hoots and pipes.

'Lord,' cried Stephen, 'I shall be late again. Will you sup with us?'

'Thank you: you are very good, but I must beg to be excused this time,' said Martin, looking through the lubber's hole with some anxiety. 'We shall have to climb down in the dark.'

'So we must,' said Stephen. 'If it were not for my engagement I should as soon have stayed up here, so soft and gentle a night, with no fear of the moonpall or of falling damps.'

'If we had a little dark lantern we could see better,' said Martin.

'Truer word was never spoke,' said Stephen. 'I do not like to call for one however; it might seem unseamanlike.'

'It was this very top Wilkins fell from when he broke his arm. It is true he was drunk at the time, but the height is much the same.'

'Come, let us show more than Roman fortitude,' said Stephen. 'Gravity will help us, and perhaps St Brendan.' He let himself down through the hole, his feet groping for the ratlines, very narrow up here, where the shrouds were crowded in so close. His toe found one, far, far down, and he let go the rim; but he did so without considering that he should have waited for the roll to swing him in towards the mast. For a moment as disagreeable as any his hands clawed the empty darkness: they did in fact seize a shroud, the aftermost of all, for he had not waited for the pitch either. He clung there long enough to be able to answer with an even voice when Martin, who being on the other side had profited by the roll, asked him how he did: 'Perfectly well, I thank you.'

'Forgive me if I am a little late,' he said, walking into the smell of toasted cheese. 'I am just come from the mizzentop.'

'Not at all,' said Jack. 'As you see, I have not waited for you.'

'I was in the mizzentop from before sunset until a couple of minutes ago.'

'Yes,' said Jack. 'Should you like some wine, or shall you wait for the punch?'

'Considering my excesses at dinner and the state of the wine in this climate, I believe I shall confine myself to punch, to a very moderate dose of punch. What an elegant toasted-cheese dish. Have I seen it before?'

'No. This is the first time it has been out of its box. I had ordered it from the man in Dublin you recommended, and

I picked it up when we were last at the cottage. Then I forgot all about it.'

Stephen lifted the lid and there were six several dishes, sizzling gently over a spirit-lamp under the outer shell, the whole gleaming from Killick's devoted hand. He turned it this way and that, admiring the workmanship, and said, 'It is the long road you have come, Jack, that you can forget a hundred guineas or so.'

'Lord, yes,' said Jack. 'Lord, we were so miserably poor! I remember how you came back to that house in Hampstead with a fine beef-steak wrapped in a cabbage-leaf, and how happy we were.'

They talked of their poverty – bailiffs – arrest for debt – sponging-houses – fears of more arrests – various expedients – but presently, when these considerations of wealth and poverty, the wheel of fortune and so on had been dealt with, the zest and cheerfulness went out of the conversation; and after his second dish of cheese Stephen became aware of a certain constraint in his friend. The frank hearty laugh was heard no more; Jack's eyes were directed more at the massive gun that shared the cabin with them than at Stephen's face. Silence fell, as much silence as could fall in a ship making eight knots, with the water singing along her hull, her troubled wake streaming, and all her standing and running rigging together with its countless blocks uttering their particular notes in a general volume of sound.

Out of this silence Jack said, 'I went round the ship this afternoon to ask our shipmates how they did, and I noticed that they were many of them older than when I saw them last. That made me think perhaps I was older too; and when you spoke of the barky as an *aged man-of-war* it quite put me about. And yet it was absurd in me to toss all these together in one gloomy pot; for although the Sethians may have grown beards a yard long, and although no doubt I ought to wear lean and slippery pantaloons, a ship and a man are different things.'

'Is that right, brother?'

'Yes, it is: you may not think so, but they are quite different. The *Surprise* is not old. Look at *Victory*. She is tolerably spry, I believe. Nobody would call her old, I believe. But she was built years before the *Surprise*. Look at the *Royal William*. You know the *William*, Stephen? I have pointed her out many and many a time among the hulks at Pompey. A first-rate of one hundred and ten guns.'

'Sure I remember. A dreadful-looking object.'

'That is only because of the uses she has been put to. It is her heart and life I am talking about: her timbers are as sound as the day she was built, or sounder: you run your knife into one of her knees and it will bend or break in your goddam hand; and I saw a length of one of her shrouds, when the worming and service were taken off, perfectly sound too. White untarred cordage, and perfectly sound. And the *Royal William* was laid down in 1676. Sixteen seventy-six. No, no; perhaps the *Surprise* is not one of your gimcrack modern craft, flung together with unseasoned timber by contract in some hole-in-the-corner yard: she may have been built some time ago, but she is not *old*. And you know – who better? – the improvements that have been carried out: diagonal bracing, reinforced knees, sheathing . . .'

'You speak quite passionately, my dear: protectively, as if I had said something disagreeable about your wife.'

'That is because I do in fact feel passionate and protective. I have known this ship so many years, man and boy, that I do not like to hear her blackguarded.'

'Jack, when I said *aged* I referred only to the generations, or ages, of filth that have accumulated below; I did not mean to blackguard her any more than I should blackguard dear Sophie, God forbid.'

'Well,' said Jack, 'I am sorry I flew out. I am sorry I spoke so chuff. My tongue took the bit between its teeth, so I was laid by the lee again; which is very absurd, because I had meant to be particularly winning and agreeable. I had meant to say that yes, there was a hundred tons of shingle ballast down there that should have been changed long ago;

and after having admitted so much and said that we intended to open the sweetening-cock and pump her cleaner, I was to go on and ask whether you would consider selling her to me. It would give me so much pleasure.'

Stephen was chewing a large, rebellious piece of cheese. As it went down at last he said indistinctly, 'Very well, Jack.' And covertly looking at the decently-restrained delight on his friend's face he wondered, 'How, physically speaking, do his eyes assume this much intenser blue?'

They shook hands on it, and Jack said, 'We have not talked about her price: do you choose to name it now, or had you rather reflect?'

'You shall give me what I gave,' said Stephen. 'How much it was I do not at present recall, but Tom Pullings will tell us. He bid for me.'

Jack nodded. 'We will ask him in the morning: he is dead-beat now.' And raising his voice, 'Killick!'

'Sir?' answered Killick, appearing within the second.

'Bring the Doctor the best punch-bowl and everything necessary; then clear away his 'cello and my fiddle in the great cabin, and place the music-stands.'

'Punch-bowl it is, sir; and the kettle is already on the boil,' said Killick, almost laughing as he spoke.

'And Killick,' said Stephen, 'instead of the lemons, pray bring up the smaller keg from my cabin: you may take it from its sailcloth jacket.'

The bowl appeared, together with its handsome ladle; then a long pause before Killick could be heard stumping along the half-deck. From the peevish oaths it was clear that one of his mates was giving him a hand, but he came in alone clasping the keg to his belly. 'Put it on the locker, Killick,' said Stephen.

'Which I never knew you had it,' said Killick with an odd mixture of admiration and resentment as he stood away from the barrel, oak with polished copper bands and on its head the stamp *Bronte XXX* with an engraved plate below *To that eminent physician Dr Stephen Maturin, whose abilities are surpassed only by the gratitude of those who have benefited from them: Clarence.*

'Bronte!' cried Jack. 'Can it be . . . ?'

'It can indeed. This is triple-refined Sicilian juice from his own estate, a present from Prince William. I had meant to keep it for Trafalgar Day, but seeing this is a special occasion perhaps we may draw off an ounce or so and drink the immortal memory tonight.'

The steaming bowl, the melted sugar, the heady smell of arrack; and as Stephen stirred in his concentrated lemon-juice he said, 'I must tell you that there may possibly be some hint of scurvy aboard your ship. It was Martin that noticed it first, to my shame, the valuable man.'

'Certainly. All hands say how lucky we are to have him.'

'He suggested, and I heartily concur, that we should steer for some fruitful island. There is no urgent necessity, with what I have brought with me; but from the medical point of view we should certainly have a relief at some half way stage, if ever you can find one in the limitless ocean.'

Chapter Eight

It was from the mizzentop that they first saw this island, or rather the little isolated flat cloud that marked its presence. So many leagues, so many degrees of longitude had passed under the *Surprise*'s keel, that now, patiently taught by Bonden, the medicos came up by the futtock-shrouds like Christians; and for the last fortnight they had done so without attendance, without lifelines or anything to break a headlong fall, although reaching the top in this, the seaman's, way entailed climbing what was in effect a rope ladder inclined some fifty-five degrees from the vertical, fifty-five degrees backwards, so that one hung, like a sloth, gazing at the sky. Their movements were not unlike those of a sloth, either; but both confessed that this was a far more compendious method, and far more agreeable than their former writhing through the tightly-clustered rigging; and they were not displeased at hearing Pullings say, in the course of a dinner at which the gun-room was entertaining the Captain, that the *Surprise* was the only ship he had ever known in which both the doctors went aloft without using the lubber's hole.

Yet though they had made such progress, and though the ship had advanced so far eastwards, they had not yet exhausted Martin's South American observations – he was still engaged with his particular part of the Amazonian forest, with its extraordinary floor of dead vegetation, huge fallen trees lying across one another, so that in some places there was a great depth of rotting wood and a man had to choose the most recent (hardly discernible sometimes because of the dense clothing of lianas) and soundest trunk in order not to fall twenty and even thirty feet into a chaos of decay: twilight at noonday in those deeper parts and almost devoid of mammals, birds – all high, high above in the sunlit tops – and even reptiles, but oh Maturin what a wealth of beetles! Nor had they done more than touch upon some aspects of Java, with Pulo Prabang still to come (though the bird-skins and the deeply interesting foot-bones of *Tapirus indicus* had been shown), when they heard the cry of 'Land ho!' from the lookout, high above them on the maintopmast crosstrees. 'Land one point on the larboard bow.'

The cry cut their conversation short. It also cut short many a quiet natter in the waist or on the forecastle, for this was during the afternoon watch of a make-and-mend day: and many of the younger, more ardent Surprises flung down their needles, thread, thimbles and ditty-bags. They ran eagerly aloft, crowding the upper yards and shrouds: they made way for Oakes however, since as the lightest and nimblest of those who walked the quarterdeck he had been sent up to the jack itself with a telescope.

'I have it, sir,' he called down. 'I have it on the top of the rise: green with a broad rim of white. About five leagues, almost exactly to leeward, just under that little cloud.'

Jack and Tom Pullings smiled at one another. This was as pretty a landfall as could be wished, and although each had independently fixed the ship's position by several excellent lunars these last few days as well as by the ship's two chronometers neither had supposed that they could reach Sweeting's Island without altering course by more than half a point and that within two or three hours of the predicted time.

'The sails are in the way,' said Martin, 'and we are too low down. Do not you think that by climbing higher still, say to the mizzen crosstrees, above this frustrating topsail, we might get a better view?'

'I do not,' said Stephen. 'And even if we did, would a wise, prudent man with a duty towards his patients creep to that dizzy height for a nearer view of an island that we shall walk upon, with the blessing, tomorrow itself or even this very evening? An island that promises little to the natural philosopher; for you are to consider that these very small, very remote little islands do not possess the superficies for anything considerable in the way of flora or fauna peculiar to themselves. Do but think of the shocking paucity of land birds in Tahiti, so very much greater in mass. Banks remarked upon it with sorrow, almost with reprehension. No, sir. As I understand it, Sweeting's Island is of value to the medical man in search of antiscorbutics rather than to the philosopher; and you will allow me to say, that I wonder at your impatience.'

'It arises from a humbler cause altogether, though in passing I may observe that St Kilda has a wren of its own and the Orkneys a vole-mouse. The fact of the matter is that I am not so truly amphibious a creature as you or Captain Aubrey. Though few people would believe it, I am essentially a landsman, descended no doubt from Antaeus, and I long to set foot on land again – to draw new strength from it to withstand the next few months of oceanic life. I long to walk upon a surface that is not in perpetual motion, rolling, pitching, liable to catch me unawares with a lee-lurch and fling me into the scuppers while my friends call out "butcher" and the sailors hide their mirth. Do not think I am discontented with my lot, Maturin, I beg. I am passionately fond of long sea-voyages and all the charming possibilities that may ensue – the flame-tree on the banks of the São Francisco, the vampires at Penedo itself! But from time to time I long to sit on my native element the earth, from which I rise like a giant refreshed, ready to face a close-reefed topsail blow or the sickening reek of the orlop in the damp oppressive heat of the doldrums with no breath of air and the ship rolling her masts out. It seems to me an age since I sat in a chair that could be trusted; for although we passed many and many an island in our crossing of this enormous expanse of ocean, we did most emphatically *pass* them. Contrary winds and vexing currents had made us late for our various rendezvous: the only hope was this last one, and

Captain Pullings drove the ship in a most pitiless manner – harsh words, peremptory orders, no longer the modest, amiable young man we knew but a sea-going Bajazet – and of course with no thought of stopping, even if sulphur-crested cassowaries had been seen on shore. But tell me, Maturin, is Sweeting's Island indeed so very poor and barren? I have never even heard of it.'

'Nor, Heaven knows, had I until Captain Aubrey spoke its name. It was a cousin on his mother's side discovered it, Admiral Carteret, who sailed round the world with Byron and then again with Wallis, but this time as captain of the *Swallow*, a rather small ship that became separated from Wallis in thick weather off Tierra del Fuego, not I believe without a certain glee on the part of Carteret, since it allowed him to discover countries of his own, including this island, which he named after the midshipman who first sighted it. It was no Golconda, nor even a Tahiti, being inhabited by a surly, burly, ill-favoured set of naked black men with deep-set eyes, filed teeth, receding chins and a great mop of coarse frizzled black hair dyed more or less successfully light brown or yellow. They spoke no recognizable dialect of the Polynesian language, and it was thought they were more nearly related to the Papuans . . .'

'We are never to see the shores of Papua, it appears,' said Martin with a sigh. 'But I beg pardon: I interrupt.'

'Nor we are. As I understand it the Captain's intention, for reasons to do with wind and current and tortuous navigation in the Torres Strait, was to leave New Guinea far on the right hand, strike away into the main ocean as far as this Sweeting's Island, there refresh, and then turn down to bring us to the region of the south-east trades, and so, sailing on a bowline, in which the *Surprise* excels all other ships, slant down to Sydney Cove, blue-water sailing almost all the way, which he loves beyond anything. Nor does he mean to touch at the Solomons, still less to go inside the Great Barrier Reef, or anywhere near it.' They both shook their heads sadly, and Stephen went on, 'From what Sir Joseph told me of New Guinea, it is no great loss. He and Cook went ashore, wading through a vast extent of mud to an indifferent strand, where, without a word, the natives instantly set upon them, firing off what appeared to be crackers, calling out in the most offensive way, and throwing spears. He only had time to collect three and twenty plants, none of them really interesting. And as for the Barrier Reef, I do not wonder at our shunning it, after Cook's dreadful experiences: that is not to say I do not regret the necessity. It wounds my heart.'

'Perhaps the wind may drop, so that we can reach some part of the Barrier by boat.'

'I hope so indeed, particularly at that island from the top of which Cook and Banks surveyed a vast expanse of the reef and on which Banks collected some of the many lizards. But to return to Sweeting's Island – and now I believe I can make out a slight nick on the horizon – Captain Carteret found no gold-dust, no precious stones and no very amiable inhabitants, but he did find a considerable wealth of coconuts, yams, taro, and fruit of various kinds. There was only one village, for although there is reasonably fertile land inshore the people make the greater part of their living from the sea and they congregate in the island's single cove: all its other sides are more or less sheer-to and I imagine it is an ancient volcanic upheaval, or conceivably a sunken, degraded crater. In any event, disagreeable though the people looked, and uninviting, they were induced to trade and Captain Carteret came away with stores that kept his people in health until the Straits of Macassar. He fixed its position with the utmost care and took soundings; but it is very far from being a well-known island and although Captain Aubrey tells me that far-ranging South Sea whalers sometimes call, I do not remember to have seen it on any map.'

'Perhaps it is inhabited by sirens,' said Martin.

'My dear Martin,' said Stephen, who could be as obtuse as ten upon occasion, 'a moment's reflexion will tell you that all the sirenia require shallow water and great beds of seaweed; and that the only members of that inoffensive tribe found in the Pacific are Steller's Sea-Cow in the far north and the dugong in the more favoured parts of New Holland and the South China Sea. I have no hopes of anything but greenstuff and fresh fruit: which reminds me – will you sup with us tonight? We are to eat a mango preserve.'

Again Martin excused himself; and late that evening, when the mango preserve was finished and they were sitting down to their music Stephen said, 'Jack, I ask this perhaps impertinent question only to save myself from uttering unwelcome invitations: is there disharmony between you and Martin?'

'Heavens, no! What makes you imagine such a thing?'

'I have sometimes asked him to sup with us, and he has always declined. He will soon be out of plausible excuses.'

'Oh,' said Jack, laying down his bow and considering. 'It is true I cannot forget he is a parson, so I have to take care what I say; and then again I hardly know what to say in any case. I have a great respect for Martin, of course, and so have the people, but I find him hard to talk to and I may seem a little reserved. I cannot rattle away to a learned man as I can to you and Tom Pullings – that is to say, I do not mean you are not as learned as Job, far from it upon my word and honour, but we have known one another so long. No. Martin and I have never had a cross word. Which is just as well, because it is very unpleasant to be shut up for an indefinite period with someone you dislike – much worse in the gun-room of course where you have to see his goddam face every single day, but quite bad enough in the cabin too; though some captains do not seem to mind. Perhaps he feels I have neglected him. I shall ask him to dinner tomorrow.'

Tomorrow, and the *Surprise* stood in for Sweeting's Island with the breeze two points abaft the beam. She had lain to all through the middle and much of the morning watch, for although Jack Aubrey had his cousin's chart and soundings clear in his mind, conditions might have changed since 1768 and he wanted clear light for the passage into the lagoon. He had it now as he sat there, comfortably filled with breakfast, conning the ship from the foretopsail yard. The sun had climbed forty-five degrees into the perfect eastern sky and it was sending its light well down into the clear water, so clear that he saw the flash of a turning fish far below, perhaps fifty fathoms. There was nothing else to see, no hint of bottom; and according to Admiral Carteret's chart there would be none until they were within musket-shot of the reef, the shore being so very steep-to.

The ship was standing in for a typical passage through the reef with a typical lagoon beyond; this was slack-water, the breeze was steady, the ship had plenty of steerage-way under foretopsail alone, she was pointing just so, with an allowance for her trifling leeway, and he had plenty of time to survey reef (broad and thickly set with coconut-palms), lagoon and island. Not one of those slightly domed islands made of coral sand that he had seen often enough in the eastern South Sea but a more rocky affair altogether, with a mass of trees and undergrowth, a variegated and often vivid green, rising in a steep semi-circle immediately behind the village on its crescent above high-water mark, and both sending back the brilliant morning light. A fairly typical village, with canoes ranged on the sand; but most of the space was taken up by one very long house built on stilts, of a kind that he had not seen before.

He also had time to survey the frigate's decks. They were even more beautifully clean than usual and had been since sunset; and everything was in the most exact order, with all falls flemished and what brass she possessed outshining gold, for it was possible that the king of this island might be asked aboard. Yet even so a good many foremast jacks, and not only young ones either, had found leisure to put on their shore-going rig: broad-brimmed sennit hats with *Surprise* on the flowing band, embroidered shirts, snowy duck trousers with ribbons sewn along their outer seams, and small shining pumps with bows; for the *Surprise*, manned solely by volunteers, was extraordinarily generous with liberty. Most of them had already arranged little bags full of nails, bottles and pieces of looking-glass, since everyone knew how presents of this kind had pleased the young women of Tahiti; and this too was a South Sea island. They had been in the Great South Sea, as sailors reckoned it, ever since they crossed the hundred and sixtieth degree of eastern longitude, and whatever the Doctor might say all hands (apart from a few miserable old buggers like Flood, the cook, whose brother had been eaten in the Solomons) confidently expected sirens. And there on the forecastle stood the two medicos, Stephen looking as eagerly at the island as Martin, although he had cried down its potentialities.

Yet there was something not quite right about the village. No movement at all, apart from the gentle waving of the palms. The canoes were all beached: none on the lagoon, none to be seen offshore.

The sound of the breakers, the moderate breakers, on the reef grew louder: Jack called down to the men in the chains, 'Hooper, carry on: Crook, carry on.'

'Aye aye, sir,' came the two voices, starboard very hoarse and deep, larboard shrill. A pause, then the splashes well out and ahead, and the alternating voices: 'No bottom with this line. No bottom with this line. No bottom . . .'

The entrance was clear ahead and the water turned more green than blue. 'Come up the sheet a fathom,' called Jack. 'Port half a spoke. Steady, steady thus.'

'Steady it is, sir.'

'By the mark, eighteen,' came from the starboard chains.

'By the deep, nineteen,' from larboard.

'Port a spoke,' said Jack, seeing a pallor ahead.

'Port a spoke it is, sir.'

Now they were well into the passage with the reef and its palm-trees high on either hand; the breeze was now on the beam and abruptly the sound of the sea breaking on the outer side and the answering sigh of its long withdrawal was cut off.

The ship moved on in silence, the leads going on either side, the occasional slight changes of course: apart from these calls and the cry of a tern, nothing; a silence on deck until she was well into the lagoon, when she came up into the wind and dropped anchor. No sound from the shore.

'Are you coming, Doctor?' asked Jack: both medicos had run along the gangway the moment the boat was lowered, and they were standing there hung about with collecting-cases, boxes, nets.

'If you please, sir,' said Dr Maturin. 'It is our clear duty to look for antiscorbutics at once.'

Jack nodded, and while muskets, presents and the usual trade-goods were handing down the side he said in a low voice, 'Does not this island seem strangely quiet to you?'

'It does: and almost uninhabited. Yet three sharp-eyed men have separately assured us that they have seen people moving on the fringe of greenery, young women in grass skirts.'

'Perhaps they are assembled in the grove for some religious ceremony,' said Martin. 'Nothing more numinous than a grove, as the ancient Hebrews knew.'

'Bonden, cover those muskets with the stern-sheets apron,' called Jack, and turning aft, 'Mr West, carry out a kedge and keep her broadside-on: two guns to be drawn and fired blank if there are signs of trouble. Ball wide of us if I hold up my hand. Grape if they pursue the boat in their canoes. Carry on, Mr Reade.'

By this time Reade had become wonderfully adept at getting about with only one arm, but there was a nest of anxious hands stretched out below to catch him if he fell; a nest that remained, almost as kind and far more reasonable, when the medical men made their descent, followed by the Captain.

'Shove off. Give way,' piped Reade. 'All together now, if you can manage it: and Davis, you row dry for once.'

These were the last words as they pulled across the lagoon, the officers looking thoughtfully at the silent shore. 'Rowed of all,' cried Reade at last, and the bargemen tossed their oars into the boat, Navy-fashion. A moment's glide and the bows ground up into the sand; bow-oar jumped out to lay the gang-plank and Jack and the officers stepped ashore.

'Heave her about, stern-on, just afloat to a grapnel,' said Jack. 'Wilkinson, James and Parfitt to be boat-keepers this tide – the muskets out of sight. The rest come up the beach with me. No straggling until I give the word.'

Up the white sand, their eyes half-closed against the glare but still looking expectantly right and left at the canoes, the woods, and the long, long house. And in spite of orders Reade, somewhat behind the main group, went skipping away to the canoes.

Some moments later, as a hog rushed from behind the nearest canoe and into the trees, he came running back. He looked pale yellow under his tan and he said to Stephen, 'There is something horrible there. A woman, I think.' The party stopped and looked at him. In a faltering voice he added, 'Dead.'

'Will you wait for me here, sir, without going on,' said Stephen: and there they stood, uneasy, while he walked away, followed by Martin. In this brilliant light the silence was all the more oppressive: all round the group they turned their questioning faces to one another, but never a word, not even in an undertone, until the Doctor, coming back, called from a distance, 'Sir, all the men who have not had the smallpox should return to the boat at once.' And coming up he asked, 'Mr Reade, have you had the smallpox?'

'No, sir.'

'Then take off your clothes: go bathe in the sea, wet your hair through and through and sit by yourself in the front of the boat. Touch no one. Who has a tinder-box?'

'Here, sir,' said Bonden.

'Then pray strike a light and burn Mr Reade's clothes. You have had the disease, sir, as I recall?'

'Yes, when I was a child,' said Jack: and to the men who were standing somewhat apart, 'Johnson, Davis and Hedges, you go back to the boat.' They turned, touching their fore-heads, and walked down the slope, their faces disappointed but above all troubled; and a charnel-house eddy followed them as far as the sea.

'And all the rest of you?' asked Stephen. 'Make sure, now, for this is the wicked and confluent kind.' Another man fell out, muttering something and hanging a shameful head. 'Now, sir, I shall look into the long house; and then perhaps we can search for our antiscorbutics. The hands had better stay here for a while. Do you choose to come, sir?'

Jack walked deliberately after Stephen and Martin, hating each step. He expected something very unpleasant, repulsive; but what he saw and what he breathed as he followed them up the ladder and into the buzzing twilight of the long house was far, far worse. Almost the entire village had died there.

'It is no good we can do here,' said Stephen, having walked up and down the whole length twice with the closest attention; and when they were outside, on the raised platform with its pyramid of ancestral skulls, the lower tiers moss-green, he observed, 'You were in the right of it, Mr Martin, when you spoke of a religious ceremony; and these' – pointing at two hatchets, new but for a little rust, lying on what had recently been a bed of flowers – 'these, I believe, were the sacrifice offered up to preserve the tribe, poor souls.'

Again Jack followed them as they went along, talking of the nature of the disease and of how badly it affected nations and communities that had never known it in the past – how mortal it was to Eskimos, for example, and how this particular infection must have been brought by a whaler, its visit proved by the axes. He felt a certain indignation against them, a resentment for his own unshared horror, and when Stephen turned to him as they joined the others and said, 'I believe we may take coconuts here, and fruit and greenstuff, robbing no man,' he only answered with a sullen look and a formal inclination of his head.

Stephen seized his mood and that of the waiting hands –

the turning wind had told them all they had not learnt from their Captain's face, bowed shoulders, heavy walk – and he went on, 'May I suggest that you should take the nuts, particularly the very young milky nuts, from the palms on the reef, while Mr Martin and I look for our plants inland? Above all, do not stand about in this mephitic atmosphere. But first I beg that Mr Reade may be taken back to the ship and that the loblolly-boy should be told to rub him all over with vinegar and cut off his hair before he goes aboard, where he must be kept in quarantine?'

'Very well,' said Jack. 'I shall send the boat back for you whenever you wish.'

'Not this boat, sir, if you will allow me. This too must be scrubbed with vinegar by men who can show their pock-marks. Another boat entirely, if you please, and it rowed only by hands that run no risk.'

A path led inland from the village: very rough steep ground strewn with boulders to begin with, covered with bushes and creepers; and under the bushes a few dead islanders, almost skeleton by now, with the limbs scattered. Then came a flat place, clear among the trees, its high dry-stone wall proof against the swine that could be heard rooting and grunting in the undergrowth no great way off. In this considerable enclosure grew yams, bananas of different kinds, various vegetables, standing together in no kind of order but evidently planted there – the turned earth could still be seen beneath the springing weeds.

'That must be a colocasia,' observed Martin, leaning on the wall.

'So it is. The taro itself, I believe. Yes, certainly the taro. Its leaves, though bitter, improve on boiling; and it is a famous antiscorbutic.'

They moved on, and always up, the bare rock of the path often polished by generations of feet: three more enclosures, the last with a tall boar reared against the wall, trying to get in. By this time they were far beyond the pestilential smell, and Martin picked up a few molluscs, examining them closely before dropping them into a padded box, while Stephen pointed out an orchid fairly pouring out its cascade of white gold-tipped flowers from the crutch of a tree.

'I was prepared for the lack of land-birds, mammals and reptiles, the more so as hogs have been turned out,' said Martin, 'but not for the wealth of plants. On the right hand of this path from the last taro-patch . . . do you hear that sound, not unlike a woodpecker?' They stood, their ears inclined. The path they were following rose steeply between palms and sandalwood to an abrupt rock-face with a little platform before it, covered with a sweet-smelling terrestrial orchid. The sound, which had seemed to be coming from here, stopped. '. . . I have seen no less than eighteen members of the Rubiaceae.'

Up and up in silence. Stephen, two paces ahead, with his eyes now on the level of the platform, slowly crouched down, and turning he whispered, 'Ape. A small blue-black ape.'

The weak hammering started again and they crept on, Stephen very cautiously making room for Martin, who after a moment murmured, 'Glabrous,' in his ear.

A second of the same kind appeared from behind a palm, and she being upright and clear of the haze of orchids at eye-level could be seen to be a small thin black girl, also holding a nut. She joined the first, squatting and beating her nut on the broad flat stone that obviously covered a well or spring. They looked very poorly and Stephen straightened, coughing as he did so. The little girls clasped one another without a word, but did not run. 'Let us sit here, looking away from them,' said Stephen, 'taking little notice or none at all. They are well over the disease: the first to take it, no doubt; but they are in a sad way.'

'How old would they be?'

'Who can tell? My practice has never lain among children, though I have of course dissected a good many. Say five or six, poor sad ill-favoured little things. They cannot break their coconut.' And half-turned, he stretched out his hand and said, 'Will I have a try?'

215

Their minds were stunned not so much by terror or grief but more by utter bewilderment and incomprehension; and to this was added extreme thirst – no rain these many days past. But there was still sense enough to understand the tone and gesture and the first child handed her nut. Stephen pierced the soft eye with his lancet and she drank with extraordinary application. Martin did the same for the second child.

They could speak now, and they said the same word over and over again, pointing to the great stone and pulling them by the hand. With the slab removed they plunged their faces right in and drank immoderately, their hollow bellies swelling like melons.

'As far as I can see,' said Stephen as he watched them eating the now-broken coconut with dreadful avidity, 'we must take them back to the ship, feed them and put them to bed. While the yams, taro and bananas are gathering a party can search the island for other survivors.'

'Clearly, we cannot leave them here to starve,' said Martin. 'But Lord, Maturin, if only they had been our nondescript apes, how we should have amazed London, Paris, Petersburg . . . Come, child.'

Down the path quite peaceably, hand in hand; but when they came to the highest enclosure the little girls set up a roaring and had to be lifted over the wall. They ran straight to a familiar banana and ate all within their reach. The same happened at the second, but by the third both were too tired and weak to go on and Stephen and Martin reached the edge of the sea carrying them, fast asleep.

'We cannot hail the boat without waking them,' observed Martin.

'Oh what a quandary,' said Stephen, whose child was infested with parasites. 'Perhaps I can put it down.' But at his first attempt the black fingers clung to his shirt with such force that he stood up again, abandoning the notion altogether.

There was no need to hail the boat, however. A far less

keen-sighted man than Jack Aubrey could tell from half a mile that they were carrying not antiscorbutics but some such creature as a sloth or a wombat; yet even he looked a little blank when he saw them close and heard what was to be done.

'Well, pass them over,' he said. 'Pollack, lay them on the sacks by the mast-thwart.'

'But that will wake them,' said Martin. 'Let me walk gently in by the gang-plank.'

'Nonsense,' said Jack. 'Anyone can see you are not a father, Mr Martin.' He took the child, passed it over, its head lolling, and Pollack eased it down on to the sacks in a competent, husbandlike manner. 'When they are as sleepy as that, when they drool and hang loose,' said Jack in a more kindly tone, 'you can tie them in knots without they wake or complain.'

This was eminently true. The children were handed up the side as limp as rag dolls; nor did they stir when they were put down on a paunch-mat by the break of the forecastle.

'Pass the word for Jemmy Ducks,' said Jack Aubrey.

'Sir?' said Jemmy Ducks, whose name was John Thurlow and whose office was the care of the ship's poultry, a term sometimes held to include rabbits and even larger animals.

'Jemmy Ducks, you are a family man, I believe?' At the Captain's wholly unusual ingratiating tone and smile Jemmy Ducks' eyes narrowed and his face took on a reserved, suspicious expression; but after some hesitation he admitted that he had seven or eight of the little buggers over to Flicken, south by east of Shelmerston.

'Are any of them girls?'

'Three, sir. No, I tell a lie. Four.'

'Then I dare say you are used to their ways?'

'Well you may say so, sir. Howling and screeching, teething and croup, thrush, red-gum, measles and the belly-ache, and poor old Thurlow walking up and down rocking them in his arms all night and wondering dare he toss 'em out of window ... Chamber-pots, pap-boats, swaddling clouts drying in the kitchen . . . That's why I signed on for a long, long voyage, sir.'

'In that case I am sorry to inflict this task upon you. Look at the paunch in the shade of the starboard gangway: those are two children brought back from the island. They are asleep. A party is going to look for any other survivors, but in the meantime they are to be washed all over with warm water and soap as soon as they wake up, and when they are dry the loblolly-boy will rub them over with an ointment the Doctor is preparing.'

'Lousy as well as poxed and filthy, sir?'

'Of course. And I dare say he will have their hair off too. When that is done you will feed them in a seamanlike manner and stow them where the lambs were: you may ask Chips or the bosun for anything you need. Carry on, Jemmy Ducks.'

'Aye aye, sir.'

'And if it lasts, you shall have a mate, watch and watch.'

'Thank you kindly, sir: just like by land. Well, they say no man can escape his fate.'

'And if there are no survivors, you shall have two shillings a month hardship money.'

There were no survivors. The *Surprise* sailed away, sailed away, in search of the south-east trades; but they were elusive, far south of the line this year, and to reach them at all she had to contend both with the equatorial current and with faint, sometimes contrary breezes, so that half a degree of southing between noon and noon was something to celebrate.

It was pleasant sailing, however, with blue skies, a darker sea, occasional squalls of warm rain that freshened the air, and the water cool enough to be refreshing when Jack bathed in the morning, diving from the mizen-chains; the ship was still well supplied with bosun's, carpenter's and gunner's stores from her first lavish fitting-out; the hint of scurvy had receded – Wilkins' arm had knit, Brampton's spirits had risen – and she was stocked with long-keeping fresh food.

Long-keeping, which was just as well, since the weeks span out before they found the south-east trades, and even then the languid capricious breezes scarcely deserved their name, still less their reputation for undeviating regularity. She sailed gently on, almost always on an even keel, and the weeks established a steady pattern of her people's life. In the morning they pumped the ship clear of the eighteen inches of sea-water that had been let in through the sweetening-cock, a task in which Stephen and Martin shared, taking their places at the breaks from an obscure feeling that they were responsible for the standing order – a task that was at first looked upon with strong disapproval by the morning watch, but that was carried on out of habit, without thought of complaint, even now that the *Surprise* was as sweet as the *Nutmeg*. Then in the forenoon, their few patients having been dealt with, they returned to the gun-room; and the long even swell from the south-east being so easy and predictable, they did not scruple to lay out even their most fragile specimens on the dining-table. That part of the afternoon watch which was not taken up with dining they usually spent in the mizentop, relating their experiences and observations in turn: Stephen had reached that part of his voyage in which he had walked up the side of an immense extinct volcano whose crater contained an isolated Paradise in which the animals, protected by religion (Buddhist monks lived there), piety, superstition and plain remoteness, had never been hunted or killed or in any way molested, so that a man could walk about among them, exciting no more than a mild curiosity – a country where he had pushed his way through grazing herds of deer and had sat with orang-utangs. Martin had no such glories to offer in the cold bare Patagonian steppes to which his narrative had brought the *Surprise*, but he did his best with the three-toed American ostrich, the long-tailed green parakeet, seen flying as far south as the entrance of the dreadful Strait itself – flying, to the utter confusion of all accepted notions, over tight-packed bands of penguins lining that grim shore – the austral humming-bird, an eagle-owl exactly like the one they had seen in the Sinai desert, and the flightless duck of Tierra del Fuego, whose nest he alone of all Western ornithologists had discovered under a tangle of snow-covered wintergreen not far from Port Famine.

His matter was less, but his delivery was far better, he being used to public speaking; and as he was a tall, deep-chested man his voice carried much farther than meagre Stephen's. When he was speaking of these wonderful eggs it carried right through the open skylight of the great cabin, in which Jack Aubrey was writing home. 'As I said, we had intended to pass between the Solomons and the Queen Charlotte Islands, but we may have to put in at one group or the other in the hope of buying some hogs, our progress has been so slow.' He paused, and having chewed the end of his pen for a while (a quill from one of the smaller alba-trosses) he went on, 'I know you do not like it when I speak ill of any man, but I shall just say that there are moments when I wish Mr Martin at the Devil. It is not that he is not the most obliging gentlemanly fellow, as you know very well, but he does take up so much of Stephen's time that I scarcely see anything of him. I should have liked to run through the score of this evening's piece with him, but they are gnatter-ing away in the mizentop twenty to the dozen and I do not like to break in. To be sure, it is the usual fate of the captain of a man-of-war to live in solitary splendour, relieved only by some more or less obligatory and formal entertainment on one side or the other; but I have grown so used to the luxury of having a particular friend aboard these many com-missions past that I feel quite bereft when it is taken from me.'

The ship's progress was slow, and although her bottom had been cleaned in Callao, in these warm seas it was grow-ing dirty again in spite of her copper, so dirty that it cut half a knot from her speed in light airs. The little girls' progress in learning English, on the other hand, was extra-ordinarily rapid, and would have been even more so if some of the hands had not talked to them in the jargon used on the west coast of Africa.

They were called Sarah and Emily, Stephen having set his face against Thursday and Behemoth; and since he had discovered them and brought them down to the shore he was unquestionably their owner, with a right to name them. He usually spent some time with them every day. When they first came aboard they were amazed and bewildered, and they clung to one another almost in silence in their dim and sheltered quarters; but presently, dressed in the simplest of poldavy shifts, they were to be seen running about on the forecastle, particularly during the afternoon watch, sometimes chanting in an odd guttural way as they hopped from plank to plank, never touching the seams, sometimes imitating the songs the seamen sang. They were good little girls, upon the whole, though rather stupid; and Emily could sometimes be both stubborn and passionate. They remained skinny however much they ate; and they had no claims to beauty. Jemmy Ducks had little difficulty in teaching them cleanliness. They were naturally given to washing when they were in health and their lousiness arose from the nature of their hair, which was coarse and crinkled and stood straight out for six inches from their heads until the ship's barber clipped them bald, and from the fact that in those parts the comb had not yet been invented. And he had not much more in teaching them punctuality, for they quite soon grasped the meaning of the ship's bells. They had obviously acquired a sense of the holy long before they came aboard, and when Jemmy Ducks led them aft, clean and brushed, they looked grave and fell silent as soon as they set foot on the quarter-deck, while at divisions they stood at his side like images for the whole length of the ceremony.

Once communication was established they seemed uneasy if they were asked about their former existence; it was as though the whole of it had been a dream, and that they had now awoken from the dream to natural life, which consisted of sailing for ever, always south-west by south, to the

221

unchanging rhythm of bells, wearing poldavy shifts washed twice a week, speaking a sort of English, drinking the thin milkless porridge called skillygallee for breakfast (cocoa was considered too rich for little girls), eating lobscouse or sea-pie and ship's biscuit (in which they delighted) for dinner, and more biscuit and broth for supper. So much was this the case, so much was this their life, that they were exceedingly distressed when at length a canoe full of Solomon islanders came alongside. '*Black* boogers,' they cried in horror and ran below, although they never showed any signs of disliking the *Surprise*'s Negroes, indeed rather the reverse. And when they were brought on deck, Stephen holding Emily by the hand and Jemmy Ducks Sarah, to see whether they could understand the chief of a village that visibly possessed hogs, they protested that they could not make out a word, would not, and sobbed so bitterly that they were obliged to be led away.

'You may say they are stupid,' said Martin, at dinner in the cabin, 'but have you observed that already they speak with a broad West-Country burr on the forecastle and in quite another English on the quarterdeck?'

'Certainly there is an uncommon linguistic ability,' said Stephen. 'And I have the strong impression that in their own island they used one language or at least vocabulary to their family, another to adults outside the family, and a third for sacred places or beings: perhaps only variations of the same speech, but very strongly marked variations for sure.'

'It seems to me that they are forgetting their own language,' said Jack. 'You never hear them hallooing to one another in foreign as they used.'

'Could you ever forget your own language?' asked Pullings. 'Languages you have learnt, like Latin and Greek, yes; but your own? Though I speak under correction, sir. A post-captain knows more than a commander, in the nature of things.'

Stephen drank wine. At one time he had very nearly forgotten his native Irish, the first language he ever spoke, he being fostered in the County Clare; and although it had surged up from the depths these last years when he spoke it with Padeen, his almost monoglot servant, there were still words, and quite commonplace ones too, whose sounds were perfectly familiar but whose meaning escaped him entirely.

Padeen Colman, wholly illiterate, incapable of innocently giving away any information he might have picked up, for not only did he know very little English but that little was barely comprehensible even to friends because of a defect in his speech, was a perfect servant for one so deeply engaged in political and naval intelligence as Stephen: yet he was much more than that, a kind, gentle, deeply affectionate man to whom Stephen was much attached and whom he intended to find in New South Wales, in the penal settlement to which he had been transported, and to do whatever could be done.

He became aware of a silence round the table, and looking up he saw that they were all smiling at him. 'I ask your pardon,' he cried. 'My mind was far away, a-gathering wool, merino wool: forgive me, I beg. Did anyone ask me a question?'

'Not at all,' said Jack, filling his glass. 'I was just telling Tom that now the time was come to reduce sail; and when the deck is less like the side of a house, you and Mr Martin might like to take off your fine coats and carry your glasses up. These reefs, rocks and islands often have birds for fifty miles around them. Norfolk Island had some prodigious curious birds that made burrows, flying home at night.'

It was not until a little before the *Surprise* crossed the tropic of Capricorn that the trade-wind had really started to blow, but since then, close-hauled or with the wind one point free, she had been showing what she could really do, with topgallants over reefed topsails and a glorious series of jibs and staysails, white and sometimes green water sweeping over her weather-bow, the little girls, soaked through and through and shrieking with delight, her lively deck at an angle that made it impossible to fix a bird in one's glass unless one were lashed to a solid support, when one might well have one's valuable achromatic telescope of more than extra power smothered in foam. She reeled off her twelve and even thirteen knots throughout the sunlit hours and seven or eight by night, with the topgallantsails taken in and in spite of her foul bottom; and all this through a hugely rolling sea that varied from the deepest indigo to pale aquamarine but that always (apart from the broken water) remained glass-clear, as though it had been created yesterday. Her pace slackened only at sunrise and sunset, when Jack and Mr Adams, who dearly loved statistics, took their readings of the temperature at various depths, the salinity, and the atmospheric pressure.

But these were also days during which high white clouds passed in flocks across the sky, while others, higher still by far, moved in the opposite direction on the anti-trade, an interesting phenomenon and one rarely seen to such perfection; yet it had the disadvantage of shutting out the stars and even, for fine observation, the sun; and as Jack did not choose to rely on dead reckoning, above all in these waters, he had decided to proceed at a moderate pace that afternoon, so that his lookouts might catch sight of one of the notorious reefs in these latitudes, the Angerich Shoal, which with rollers of this kind showed as a white boil even at spring tides, and was used by many commanders as a sea-mark.

Jack called for coffee. It came in an elegant silver pot protected by white manila fenders, beautifully plaited by Bonden in the form of robands; and as they drank it the sail came off the ship, the rushing sound of the water along her side diminished, and they no longer sat braced in their chairs.

'When you come on deck,' said Jack, 'do not scruple to walk the windward side. That is where my reef should be if it has any sense of what is right,' and he pushed civility so far as to ask Mr Martin to sup in the cabin that evening and play music, although his execution was indifferent, his sense of pitch and time imperfect, and he always played rather sharp.

They stood by the windward rail of the quarterdeck, discreetly aft; and a fine waste of blue water did they command, an unending series of wide-spaced rounded crests, sometimes topped with white, all crossed with a transverse ripple from the local current. They leant there in their shirtsleeves, spattered by spindrift on occasion, but comfortable in the sun, warm though veiled. 'You met Macmillan, my assistant in the *Nutmeg*, I believe?' said Stephen.

'Just for a moment. A tall thin young Scotchman, very much concerned at being left in charge.'

'An amiable youth, diligent, conscientious, but necessarily inexperienced. I remember telling him of the miseries of human life, particularly as they affect medical men. I spoke of that continual, insistent demand for sympathy and personal concern that exhausts all but the most saintly man's supply before the end of the day, leaving him openly hard in a hospital or a poor practice, secretly hard in a rich one, and ashamed of his hardness in either case until he comes to what terms he can with the situation. But I omitted another aspect, trifling in itself, yet one that can become disproportionately irritating: there is a good example,' – glancing forward to where Awkward Davis was packing a mended shirt into his bag. The massive, lowering creature was sometimes possessed by an elfin gaiety, and now he seized Emily, hoisted her on to the back of his neck, bade her 'clap on tight, now,' and raced up the foremast shrouds, over the top-rim and right up to the crosstrees, the child hooting with joy all the way. – 'That great hulking fellow, for whom I may say I have a real liking, is as you know very well growing madder, and I give him a weekly draught of hellebore to prevent him doing any of his shipmates an injury: he is irascible and exceedingly strong. And every single time he presents himself for his dose with a poor face, a mincing, shuffling gait, a pursed mouth, his great head inclined to one side, and answers my questions in a weak, gasping tone like an old ewe. I should kick him if I dared.'

'Shoal, ho!' from the masthead.

The usual question, the bearing as usual, the usual hurrying up and down; and in time the unmistakable turmoil of white water could be seen from the deck, broad on the larboard beam.

'It is very well,' said Martin when he had looked at it for some time through his telescope. 'And I should be ungrateful to repine: but I could wish that Captain Aubrey had given us as clear a view of the Great Barrier Reef.'

'I had hoped above all for that Lizard Island from which Cook and Sir Joseph surveyed the passages. Yet I can well understand the Captain's reluctance. The *Endeavour* at last got outside the reef by means of these passages, but then the breeze failed them, as it will close to the land, and the huge swell heaved them in, slowly, inevitably, and they helpless, towards the great wall of coral and the mountainous surf. At the very last moment a hint of breeze moved them just far enough for the making tide to sweep them through a channel to the inner side of the reef. I remember Sir Joseph telling us of it, and the horror of those last heaves before apparent destruction were with him still. It was much the same with us in the *Diane*, off Tristan, as I have told you: I was below at the time, but she was within ten yards of the cliff, the precipitous cliff of the island Inaccessible, before just such a providential waft of air edged her aside. And the Captain is absolutely determined not to call upon Providence in that way again: he has nothing whatsoever to say to any reef, coral or otherwise.'

Martin digested this for some time, and then said in a low voice, 'The little girls have quite a family of pet rats now.'

'Indeed? I knew they had one apiece, but not several.'

'Half a dozen at least,' said Martin. 'Do you think that might be a Norfolk Island petrel?'

'It might be, too. There is a group of them somewhat to the east. No, my dear Martin: the east is to the right.'

'Surely not in the southern hemisphere?'

'We will ask Captain Aubrey. He will probably know. But to the right, for all love. Ah, they are vanished and gone.'

They returned to the rats, how mild in temper they were,

and placid, and how they were to be seen wandering about in the day, well above the hold and even the cable-tier: the hands put it down to the unnatural cleanliness of the ballast, flooded every night and pumped clear every day. It was known that rats fattened on the smell; and now, with the barky tossed about so that her ballast was fairly scoured, as clean as Deal beach, there was no smell.

'Sail ho!' cried the masthead, and this time in answer to Jack's 'Where away?' the lookout answered, 'Right ahead, sir. As right ahead as ever could be. Square rigged, but ship or brig I cannot tell.'

The *Surprise* had been making sail methodically ever since she had obtained her fix with the Angerich Shoal, and now she was making a good ten knots. The sail ahead was travelling faster, and presently Oakes at the jack called down that she was 'certainly a ship, weather studdingsails aloft and alow'.

Then later, 'Man-of-war pennant, sir.' And later still, when she was hull-up on the rise, 'Two-decker, sir.'

'Ha, ha,' said Jack to Pullings, 'she must be the old *Tromp*, fifty-four. Billy Holroyd has her now. Did you ever meet Captain Holroyd, Tom?'

'I don't think so, sir. I know him by name, of course.'

'We were shipmates in the *Sylph* when we were boys.' Then louder, 'Pass the word for Killick.'

'Sir?' cried Killick, appearing like a jack-in-the-box.

'Turn over my pantry and see what we can manage in the way of a feast.'

'She has thrown out the private signal, sir,' said Reade to Mr Davidge, the officer of the watch. Davidge repeated the news to Pullings, now serving as first lieutenant again, and Pullings told Jack, who ordered the usual reply, to be followed immediately by *Heave to and come to supper*, while at the same time the *Surprise* bore up to make the signal more perfectly legible and Jack called, 'Stand by to reduce sail and heave to.'

The *Tromp*'s response could not be made out for some

moments, she being head-on with the wind two points on the quarter, but then Reade, who had grown wonderfully adroit at managing a telescope with the far end on some support in the rigging, reported, 'It is *Charged with dispatches*, sir.'

'He cannot stop,' said Stephen to Martin. 'I doubt he would be allowed to pause even if we were beset by ravening sharks, rather than by ravening curiosity.'

Nor did he stop; but he modified the strict rule by easing his sheets as his ship, a slab-sided, Dutch-built vessel on her way to India by tje Torres Strait, swept past the stationary, wallowing *Surprise* within twenty yards, both captains standing on the hammock-netting.

'How do you do, Billy?' called Jack, waving his hat.

'Jack, how do you do?' replied Billy.

'What news?'

'In India they say Boney has done it again, somewhere in Germany – Silesia, I think. Two hundred and twenty guns taken, the Prussian right wing cut to pieces.'

'What news from home?'

'None when I left Sydney Cove. *Amelia* four months overdue and no . . .'

The rest of his words were lost, the strong wind sweeping them along with the ship. All the *Surprise*'s people had been listening openly, without shame: all faces showed the same disappointment; and when Jack gave the order, 'Brace up and haul aft,' they carried it out with less than their usual zest and spring.

'I am so sorry you will not see Captain Holroyd this bout,' said Jack as they gathered for supper. 'You would like him, I am sure. He has a very pure sweet voice, a true tenor, which is a rare thing in a service that requires you to roar like a bull in a basin. But still, I hope we shall profit from Killick's thorough search of the pantry. There may be some Java delicacies that Mrs Raffles was so kind as to put up for us.'

By this time the watch had been set, topgallants taken in

long since and topsails double-reefed; and when three bells in the first watch struck they could be heard in the great cabin, remote but clear, the last note hanging up unpaired. Automatically Jack glanced at the dining-cabin door, which ordinarily opened as regularly as that of a cuckoo-clock, with Killick in the place of the bird saying, 'Supper is on table, sir, if you please,' or 'Wittles is up,' according to the company.

It did not open, though there appeared to be a scrabbling behind it, and Jack poured more madeira. 'But now I come to think of it, Mr Martin,' he said, 'I believe you prefer sherry as a whet. Pray forgive me . . .' He reached for the other decanter.

'Not at all, sir, not at all,' cried Martin. 'I had far rather drink madeira. I should not change this madeira for any kind of sherry. It is dry but full of body; it has given me the appetite of a lion.'

Stephen walked over to his 'cello and sitting on the stern-window locker he played over the 'Rakes of Kerry' in pizzicato. 'You should hear that at some far grassy crossroads on a fine Beltane night with the fire on the hill and the pipes playing and five fiddles and the young men dancing as though they were possessed and the young women as demure as mice but never missing a step.'

'Pray play it again,' said Jack. He did; then again with variations and even some thoughts of his own. At length the door opened and Killick stood there in the opening, pale and apparently demented. 'Is supper ready?' asked Jack.

'Well, the soup part of it is, sir,' said Killick hesitantly. 'Sort of. But sir,' he burst out, 'the rats has ate the smoked tongues, ate the preserves, ate the potted char . . . ate the last of the Java pickles . . . And they are walking about there, paying no heed . . . staring . . . saucy . . . I turned everything over, sir; everything. It took me hours.'

'Well, at least they cannot have got at the wine. Put that on the table, serve the soup and tell my cook to do what he can. Bear a hand, bear a hand, there.'

*   *   *

'A Barmecide feast, sir, I am afraid,' said Jack.

'Not at all, sir,' said Martin. 'There is nothing I prefer to . . .' He hesitated, trying to find a name for salt beef, eighteen months in the cask, partly de-salted, cut up very small and fried with crushed ship's biscuits and a great deal of pepper: '. . . to a fricassee.'

'Still,' said Jack, 'I am sure the Doctor's divertimento in C major will . . .' He almost said 'divert our minds' but in fact ended with 'prove a compensation'.

It was some days later, after a violent blow that was said, and rightly said, to foretell a calm, when they were no more than a couple of hundred miles from Sydney, that Stephen, finding his bedside box of coca-leaves empty, went down to the store-room he shared with Jack to bring up a new supply. The leaves were packed tight in soft leather sausages sewn over with a neat surgical stitch, each in a double oiled-skin envelope against the damp. He had almost exactly calculated the duration of each and, apart from the current, already-opened pouch, there were easily enough of the comfortable little parcels to last till he should reach Callao; for it was from Peru that the coca-leaves came.

The pouches were in a particularly massive and elegant ironwood chest with intricate Javanese brasswork over its top and sides and although he had heard and seen much of the strange confident behaviour of the rats he had no fear of them in this particular instance: apart from anything else this store-room was used for wine, cold-weather clothes, books – it had nothing to do with the pantry. Yet he was not the first sailor to be deceived by a rat. They had gnawed their way up through the very plank, up through the bottom of the chest itself. There was nothing left but rat-dung. Nothing. They had eaten all the leaves and all the leather impregnated with the scent of the leaves and they were clearly eager to get at the chest again, a group of them standing just outside the lit circle of his lantern, waiting impatiently to gnaw at the wood on which the pouches had lain.

'I must take care of our herbs and the portable soup,' he reflected, and he walked into the sick-berth, where Martin was taking stock of the medicine-chest in the hope of replenishing it at Sydney. 'Listen, colleague,' he said, 'those infernal rats have eaten my coca-leaves – those leaves, you recall, that I chew from time to time.'

'I remember them well. You gave me some off the Horn, when we were so very cold and hungry, but I am afraid I disappointed you by complaining that the ensuing numbness or insensibility of my palate – indeed of my whole mouth – made what little food we had miserably insipid, and that I felt no good effect at all.'

'Sure it differs according to idiosyncrasy. For me and I think most Peruvians it induces a mild euphory, an absence of untimely sleepiness and hunger, a tranquillity of mind and perhaps enhanced powers of reflexion. And it is plain that rats feel this even more strongly. I remember now when last I was at that chest, filling my bedside box from an opened pouch perhaps a fortnight ago, I spilt some on the floor; and in the insolence of my wealth I did not gather it all up but left the smaller pieces and the dust. This they must have found and eaten; and they were so pleased with the result that they tried by all means to get at the rest, eventually gnawing a hole through the bottom. So I think we should put all our herbs and the like into metal-lined boxes. The animals having derived such satisfaction from the coca, and having finished it to the last leaf, are now no doubt eagerly, fearlessly searching for more.'

'That would account for the devastation in the Captain's pantry, never attacked before.'

'It would also account for this whole change in behaviour that we have observed: their mildness, their confident wandering about the ship and contemplating the passers-by – this when they had had their leaves. And their eagerness to get more. They stood about me as I gazed at the ruins of my store – my only indulgence, Martin – gibbering, barely able to contain themselves.'

231

'I am afraid it must be a sad vexation to have had your whole supply destroyed,' said Martin. 'But I hope it is not as serious as the loss of tobacco to a smoker.'

'Oh no: it does not cause a vehement addiction, as tobacco sometimes does; though curiously enough some of its effects are not unlike; and it quite does away with the need to smoke. I still enjoy my occasional cigar after a good dinner; but if I have had my little ball of lime-sprinkled leaves in the morning I am perfectly content without it.'

The next day both Emily and Sarah were bitten by their tame rats. They wept; and they wept still more when Stephen cauterized the wounds. In the afternoon the rats disappeared from those parts of the ship where they had caused most astonishment, but they could be heard fighting on the cable-tier and in the hold. Yet there were few people to hear the furious scuffling fore and aft, the death-shriek and the screams of rage, for in this flat calm turtles, green turtles, had been seen basking on the surface, and the *Surprise*'s boats, lowered down with the greatest caution and paddled rather than pulled, caught four, all female and all quite stout, none less than a hundredweight. There was also the killing of the last Solomon pig, as Jack Aubrey insisted upon giving Martin an edible dinner to wipe out the disgrace of supper: a high ceremony for all those brought up with pigs about the house, which was the case with most of the Surprises, and one followed by black puddings and many another delight.

On the evening after this first dinner Stephen retired to his alternative lower cabin, where he could write in unobserved solitude; thrust balls of wax into his ears so that he could do so in something like silence, trimmed his green-shaded lamp, poised his cigar on a pewter dish, and wrote, 'It is whimsical enough, my dearest soul, to think that on this, almost the last day of our voyage, all hands should have eaten like aldermen; yet such is the case, and such will be the case tomorrow, when the gun-room invites Jack and the two midshipmen to what will probably be the last dinner before we enter Sydney Cove, for the wind has revived and through my wax I hear the measured impact of the swell against the frigate's bow. Fresh pork and green turtle! They are good in themselves and after our very short commons they were of course better by far. I ate voraciously and now I am smoking like a voluptuous Turk; which brings me to the curious incident of the other day — I went below to fill the empty bedside box of coca-leaves and found that rats had eaten all my store. It had all gone, even to the oiled-silk outer cases. For some time the behaviour of the ship's rats (a numerous crew) had excited comment, and it is now clear to me that they had become slaves to the coca. Now that they have eaten it all, now that they are deprived of it, all their mildness, lack of fear and what might even be called their complaisance is gone. They are rats and worse than rats: they fight, they kill one another, and were I to unblock my ears I should hear their harsh strident screams. So far I have killed no one, nor have I desired to do so; but in other ways I too feel my lack: I eat exorbitantly, my eyes starting from my head (whereas coca imposes moderation); I smoke and relish it extremely (whereas coca does away with tobacco); sleep is near to closing my stupid eyes (whereas coca keeps one contentedly awake until the middle watch). I hope we shall see Sydney the day after tomorrow, primo, secundo, tertio and so to infinity because in spite of the dismal words "no news from home" I may hear from you, hear from you by some earlier ship. And then, not to be mentioned on the same page, because some apothecary or medical man may renew my stock as it was renewed in Stockholm. I should be sorry to be reduced to the state of the two animals I see but do not hear in the corner by my stool — do not hear, so that their frenzied, tight-locked battle has a horror of its own — yet man (or at all events this particular man) is so weak that if an innocent leaf can protect him even a little then hey for the innocent leaf.'

The gun-room's feast for the Captain was if anything more copious than that of the day before: it was less gorgeous, seeing that in the *Surprise*'s present unlisted state as 'HM's hired vessel' the gun-room did not rise above pewter except for its forks and spoons, but the gun-room cook, by means known to himself alone, had conserved the makings of a superb suet pudding of the kind called boiled baby in the service, known to be Jack Aubrey's favourite form of food, and it came in on a scrubbed scuttle-cover to the sound of cheering. Another difference between the old HMS *Surprise* and HM Hired Vessel *Surprise* was that there were no lines of servants, one behind each officer's chair. For one thing she carried no Marines or boys, the main source of supply, and for another it would have been quite out of tune with her present ship's company's state of mind. There was not so much glory; the sequence of dishes was slower; but the conversation was far less restrained, and when even Killick and the gun-room steward retired Jack, a fine purple with satiety, gazed round the table smiling at his hosts and said, 'I do not know whether any of you gentlemen have touched at Sydney before?'

No, they said, they had not.

'The Doctor and I were there some years ago, when I had the *Leopard*. It was at that uneasy time when the soldiers and Governor Bligh had been at cross purposes, so we did no more than take in what trifling stores the military men would let us have and sailed on. But I was ashore long enough to get a general impression, and a very nasty general impression it was. The place was run by soldiers, and although some time later those who had deposed the Governor were put to stand in the corner for a while, I hear that things are much the same, so I will tell you what I found and what I dare say you will still find when you go ashore. I say nothing about Admiral Bligh and his disagreements with the army; but I will say that quite apart from those quarrels I never met a soldier that did not dislike a sailor. I found them an overdressed, underbred, inhospitable, quarrelsome set of men. I know the army is not very particular about the people who buy a commission in new-raised, out-of-the-way regiments, but even so I was astonished. They had pretty well monopolized trade, forming a ring that did away with all competition; they had taken up all the good land, which they farmed with free convict-labour; they were exploiting the place for all they were worth. But infinitely worse than all that, worse than their corrupt selling to Government at starvation prices, was their treatment of the wretched prisoners. I have been aboard more than one hell-afloat, and they make a man's heart sick, but I have never seen anything to touch the cruelty in New South Wales. Floggings of five hundred lashes, five hundred lashes, were commonplace, and even in the short time I was there two men were whipped to death. I tell you this because these fellows know damned well that people fresh to the place are shocked and look upon them as blackguards; they are very touchy about it, very apt to take offence, and you may easily find yourself called out for a trifling observation. So it seems to me that distant civility is the thing: official invitations, no more. There is no one here who could possibly be accused of want of conduct, but a quarrel with a blackguard is like a court-case with a pauper: the whole thing is a toss-up – there is no justice in either – and while you have nothing to win, he has nothing to lose.'

'Did you say a court-case, sir?' asked West.

'Yes, I did,' said Jack. 'What I really meant was that a blackguard can point a pistol as well as a decent man, and that it is much better to avoid the possibility of such an encounter. There was a jumped-up fellow here called Macarthur who put a bullet in Colonel Paterson's shoulder, though Paterson was all an officer should be and the other was a scoundrel.'

'I met Macarthur in London,' said Stephen. 'He was there for his court-martial – acquitted, of course – and Southdown Kemsley, with whom he had been in correspondence on sheep, brought him to dinner at the Royal Society Club. Loud, positive and overbearing: at first extremely formal, then extremely familiar, full of lewd anecdotes. He wanted to buy some of the King's merinos, and he proposed calling on Sir Joseph Banks, who supervised the flock; but Sir Joseph, who was in close touch with the colony, had had such reports of his undesirability that he declined receiving him. His regiment was universally known as the Rum Corps, because rum was its first basis of trade, wealth, power, influence and corruption. I believe that there are changes now that Governor Macquarie has come out with the Seventy-Third regiment, but the old Rum Corps officers are still here, in the administration or sitting on great stretches of good land granted to themselves by themselves and more or less running the country, alas.'

The dinner did not end on this solemn note; indeed it ended in very cheerful song. But the next day's breakfast was a gloomy affair, although the coast of New South Wales was clear all along the western horizon and the pilot was already aboard. There was a most unaccustomed silence on either side of the coffee-pot, and Jack for one looked yellow, puffy, liverish; he had not taken his morning swim and his eyes, usually bright blue, were now dull, oyster-like, with discoloured bags below them. His breath was foul.

'The Doctor was not drunk too, was he?' asked Bonden in the cuddy where Killick was grinding beans for a second pot.

'Drunk, no,' said Killick. 'I wish he had been. It would make his crabbedness more natural. I don't know what has come over him, such a mild-spoken cove.'

'He slapped Sarah and Emily till they howled again; and he checked Joe Plaice something cruel for walking backwards into him on the forecastle: "Can't you see where you are a-coming to, God damn your eyes and limbs, you fat-arsed bugger of a longshoreman?" Or words to that effect.'

'I tell you what it is, Stephen,' said Jack after a prolonged silence. 'I do not think the gun-room's turtle was quite wholesome.'

'Nonsense,' said Stephen. 'Never was such a healthy, clean-run reptile. The trouble is, you ate too much, as you did the day before, and as you do habitually whenever it is there to eat. I have told you again and again that you are digging your grave with your teeth. You are at present suffering from a plethory, a common plethory. I can deal with the symptoms of this plethory; but the self-indulgence that lies behind them is beyond my reach.'

'Pray do deal with them, Stephen,' said Jack. 'We shall drop anchor this afternoon unless the breeze fails us. The Governor is sure to ask us to dinner tomorrow, and I could not face a laid table as I feel now.'

'You will have to take physic, of course; and it will confine you to the seat of ease for most of the day and perhaps part of the night. You obese subjects are often slow-working, where the colon is concerned.'

'I shall take whatever you order,' said Jack. 'To clean and refit a ship properly and without loss of time, you have to be tolerably well with the authorities, and to be tolerably well with the authorities you have to eat their food hearty and drink up their wine as though you enjoyed it. At present the thought of anything but bare biscuit' – holding up a piece – 'and thin black coffee makes my gorge rise.'

'I shall fetch what is required,' said Stephen, returning some minutes later with a pill-box, a bottle and a measuring-glass. 'Swallow this,' he said, passing a pill, 'and wash it down with that,' passing the half-filled glass.

'Are you sure it is enough?' asked Jack. 'I am not one of your light-weights, you know, not one of your borrel shrimps; and it is a very small pill.'

'Rest easy while you may,' said Stephen. 'You may be the biggest born of earth, but black draught and blue pill will search your entrails and stir your torpid liver; it will sort you out finely, so it will.' He put the cork back into the bottle with a thump and walked off, reflecting upon exasperation, an emotion aroused by some persons and some situations in an eminent degree.

Having edged three dead rats out of the sick-berth he did some work on his records: then he rolled a little paper cigar and climbed to the quarterdeck to smoke it. There had been some candid remarks about tobacco below, and he was obliged to admit that the cold stale smell of several dead cigars that seeped from his lower cabin into the gun-room did make it more like a low pot-house at dawn than was altogether agreeable.

Martin had already been on deck for some time, watching the magnificent harbour opening before them. 'Here is Sydney Cove at last,' he said, with a somewhat irritating enthusiasm.

'It grieves me to contradict you,' said Stephen, 'but this is Port Jackson. Sydney Cove is only a little small bay, about five miles down on the left.'

'Good Heavens! Do you tell me that they are the same? I had no idea.'

'Sure, I have not mentioned it above a hundred times.'

'So this is the home of the Port Jackson shark,' cried Martin, looking eagerly over the side.

'Ha, ha,' said Stephen, to whom the thought had occurred many and many a time before, but not today. 'Let us see if we can fish one up.' He picked his way through a party of men on their knees, improving the look of the quarterdeck seams, and reached for the mizentopsail halliards, to which the shark-hooks and their chains were made fast. But before he could seize them Tom Pullings was there. 'No, sir,' he said very firmly. 'Not today, if you please. There can be no shark-fishing today. We have been preddying the decks ever since two bells in the morning watch. Surely, sir, you would not want *Surprise* to look paltry in Sydney Cove?'

Stephen might have advanced that it was only a small inoffensive shark, not above four feet long, that it had a unique arrangement of flat grinding teeth of the first interest, and that the inconvenience would be trifling; but Tom Pullings' immovable gravity, the immovable gravity of all the Surprises on deck, who had stopped work to look at him, and even of the pilot, a man-of-war's man himself, checked the words in his throat.

'We will fish up a couple for you the day after tomorrow,' said Pullings.

'Half a dozen,' said the bosun.

'Oh if you please, sir,' cried Jemmy Ducks, coming aft at a run, 'Sarah has swallowed a pin.'

The medical men had more trouble, spent more time with this one pin than with the results of many a brisk action, with splinter-wounds, fractures and even the minor amputations; and when at last it was recovered and the exhausted, emptied child had been put to bed they found they had missed the entire approach to Sydney, the shores and the stratified cliffs of Port Jackson and the various branches of the harbour, of which Martin had heard great things. They had also missed the boarding of the ship by an officer from the shore and their dinner itself; but they cared little for either, and Stephen, observing that Captain Aubrey would certainly be indisposed by now, remained below, eating scraps with Martin. He then found himself overcome with sleep, in spite of the gun-room steward's idea of coffee, and retired to his cabin.

It was in this same cabin that he sat next day, in white breeches, silk stockings, gleaming buckled shoes, a newly-shaved face and a newly-clipped poll: his best uniform coat and his newly-curled, newly-powdered wig hung close at hand, not to be touched until the barge was lowered down.

To try his pen, a new-cut quill, he wrote 'Exasperation' six times and then returned to his letter: 'No news, of course: Jack sent as soon as we were moored, but there was no news from home. Official papers, by way of India, yes; but all that matters is still between here and the Cape, somewhere in the southern ocean. I comfort myself by reflecting that it may come while we are still here. And I need comfort. I have told you many times I am sure that the common seaman believes that *more is better* and has to be watched to prevent him swallowing whole vials of physic. In this Jack is as common as any of them, and more dangerous to himself in that he has the habit of command. Late yesterday he formed

239

the opinion that my black draught and blue pill were not working briskly enough, and while I was asleep he practised upon Martin and by means that do him no credit he obtained a second dose: now of course he cannot stir from the quarter-gallery. He is quite incapable of accepting the invitation to Government House this afternoon, and Tom Pullings and I are to go without him. It is not a dinner I look forward to with any pleasure. This morning I was ashore, looking in vain for an apothecary, merchant or medical man who might have the leaves of coca, and I found the miserable place much as I left it – squalid, dirty, formless, with ram-shackle wooden huts placed without regard to anything but temporary convenience twenty years ago, dust, apathetic ragged convicts, all filthy, some in chains – the sound of chains everywhere. And turning into an unpaved, uneven kind of a square I came full upon those vile triangles and a flogging in progress, the man hanging from the apex. Flog-ging I have seen only too often in the Navy, but rarely more than a dozen lashes, and those laid on with a relative decency: a bystander told me that this man had already received one hundred and eighty five out of his two hundred; yet still the burly executioner stepped well back and made a double skip each time to bring his whip down with the greater force, taking off flesh at every blow. The ground was soaked with fresh blood, and there was a red darkness at the foot of the other triangles. To my astonishment the man was able to stand when he was untied: his face showed not so much suffering as utter despair. His friends led him away, and as he went the blood welled from his shoes at every step.

'A little farther on I came to some more of these gaunt barracks and to a street being laid out by a chain-gang, and the beginning of what the men told me was to be a hospital, built at the orders of the new Governor, Colonel Macquarie: I shall be sorry not to see him, but he is away in . . .'

'Boat's alongside, sir, if you please,' said Killick, that for-giving soul, as he took up the precious coat. 'Right arm first. Now let me ship the wig and square it just so. Hold up, and don't you ever move your head, or you will get powder on the collar. And here' – with a transparently false casualness – 'is your gold-headed cane.'

'Your soul to the Devil, Killick,' said Stephen. 'Do you think I am going to walk into a company of officers with a cane, like a grass-combing civilian?'

'Then let me borrow the Captain's Patriotic Fund sword,' said Killick. 'Yourn has such a shabby old hilt.'

'Buckle it on and bear away,' said Stephen. 'How has the Captain come along since I came below?'

'Which he has taken a ninety-year lease of the quarter-gallery: all you can hear is groaning and gushing. He ain't been out since you was there.'

Stephen was carefully handed down the side and sat in the stern-sheets; he was followed by Pullings, shining with gold lace but smelling of mould, and the boat shoved off.

'Another dinner-table,' reflected Stephen, sitting down and spreading his napkin over his knee. 'May it be for a blessing.' The afternoon had begun pleasantly, with Mrs Macquarie and the Governor's deputy, Colonel MacPherson, receiving the guests, mostly officers of the former New South Wales Corps, now substantial landowners, of the Seventy-Third, and of the Navy. Mrs Macquarie, the most important woman in the colony, did not top it the gracious lady, but made them feel truly welcome: Stephen liked her at once, and they talked for a while. Colonel MacPherson had served for many years in India and it was clear that his head had been too long exposed to the sun, but he was amiable enough in his muffled way and he took pleasure in urging the men to drink – the men, for Mrs Macquarie was not to attend the dinner itself, and no other ladies had been invited. 'I am so sorry that Her Excellency has abandoned us,' he said to Mr Hamlyn, a surgeon, who sat on his left. 'She seemed to me particularly sympathetic, and I should have liked to ask her advice. We picked up two children, the only survivors of a small tribe wiped out by smallpox;

and I dread taking them by the icy Horn to a hardly more hospitable England, and they born under the equator itself.'

'She would certainly have told you what to do,' said Hamlyn. 'She is spending this very afternoon at the orphanage. We have a great many little bastards here, you know, begotten by the Lord knows who during the voyage and often abandoned. And as you say, she is the most amiable of ladies: we passed the chief of the morning discussing plans for the hospital.' Stephen and the surgeon did the same until it was time for each to talk to his other neighbour. Hamlyn was at once engaged in a close and even passionate argument about some horses that were to race presently; but on Stephen's right hand the penal secretary, whom he thought of as Mealy-Mouth but whose name was in fact Firkins, was already taken up with a four- or five-handed conversation about convicts, the irredeemable wickedness, sloth, immorality of convicts, the assignment of convicts, their dangerous nature; and for some time he was able to survey the table. Mealy-Mouth, he observed, was a water-drinker; but Stephen, having taken a sip of the local wine, could hardly blame him for that. Immediately opposite was a big, dark-faced man, as big as Jack Aubrey or even bigger; he wore regimentals that Stephen did not recognize, presumably those of the Rum Corps. His very large face had a look of stupidity and settled ill-temper; he wore a surprising number of rings. To this man's right sat the clergyman who had said grace, and he too looked thoroughly discontented. His face was unusually round; it was red, and growing steadily redder. From the confusion of voices and the unfamiliarity of their topics it was not easy for Stephen to make out more than the general drift at first, but that was clear enough from the often-repeated 'United Irishmen' and 'Defenders' – prisoners who had been transported in large numbers, particularly after the 1798 rising in Ireland. He noticed that the Scottish officers of the Seventy-Third did not take part, but they were in the minority and the general feeling was well summed up by the clergyman, who said, 'The Irish do not deserve the appellation of men. And if I needed an authority for the statement I should bring forward Governor Collins of Van Diemen's Land. Those are his very words: in the second volume of his book, I believe. But no authority is needed for what is evident to the meanest understanding. And now to crown all, priests are allowed them. A cunning priest can make them do anything; and there is nothing but anarchy to be foreseen.'

'Who is that gentleman?' asked Stephen in a low voice, Hamlyn having finished with horse-racing for the moment.

'His name is Marsden,' said Hamlyn. 'A wealthy sheep-farmer and a magistrate at Parramatta: and once he is on to the poor old Pope and popery he never leaves off.'

How true. Stephen saw Tom Pullings' bored face, fixed in a dutiful smile, near the head of the table, on Colonel MacPherson's right; and at the same time Tom looked at him – a very anxious look.

'I beg your pardon,' said the penal secretary. 'I am shamefully remiss: allow me to help you to a little of this dish. It is kangaroo, our local venison.'

'You are very good, sir,' said Stephen, looking at it with some interest. 'Can you tell me . . .'

But Firkins was already away on a hobbyhorse of his own, the poverty of Ireland and its inevitability. His words were mostly addressed to the other side of the table, though when he had finished his account he turned to Stephen and said, 'They are not unlike our Aborigines, sir, the most feckless people in the world. If you give them sheep they will not wait for them to breed and grow into a flock: they eat them at once. Poverty, dirt and ignorance must necessarily attend them.'

'Did you ever read in Bede, sir?' asked Stephen.

'Bede? I do not think I know the name. Was he a legal writer?'

'I believe he is chiefly known for his ecclesiastical history of the English nation.'

'Ah, then Mr Marsden will know him. Mr Marsden,' – raising his voice – 'do you know of a Mr Bede, that wrote an ecclesiastical history?'

'Bede? Bede?' said Marsden, breaking off his conversation with his neighbour. 'Never heard of him.' Then resuming it, 'He was a mere boy, so we only gave him a hundred lashes on the back, and the rest on his bottom and legs.'

'Bede lived in the County Durham,' said Stephen in a momentary pause. 'Little do I or other naturalists know of the northern parts of England; but it is to be hoped that some future faunist, a person of a thinking turn of mind, a man of fortune, will undertake the tour, accompanied by a botanist and a draughtsman, and will give us an account of his journey. The manners of the wild Aborigines, their superstitions, their prejudices, their sordid way of life, will extort from him many useful reflexions. And his draughtsman will portray the ruins of the great monasteries of Wearmouth and Jarrow, the home of the most learned man in England a thousand years ago, famous throughout the Christian world and now forgotten. Such a work would be well received.'

Perhaps: the remark, however, was received in disapproving silence, with puzzled, suspicious looks; and eventually the big man opposite Stephen said, 'There ain't any Aborigines in Durham.' While the learned explained to him what might be meant by the word, Stephen said inwardly, 'Let me not be a fool. God preserve me from choler,' and a flow of talk from the upper end of the table swept the incident into the past.

'I am so sorry,' he said, suddenly aware that Hamlyn was speaking to him. 'I was wool-gathering again. I was contemplating on sheep.'

'And I was talking to you about sheep, how droll,' said Hamlyn. 'I was telling you that your vis-à-vis, Captain Lowe, has imported some of the Saxony merinos to make a new cross.'

'Has he a great many sheep?'

'Probably more than anyone else. It is said he is the richest man in the colony.'

The Flogging Parson, his face redder still, had begun savaging the Pope again, and to shut him out Stephen replied in a louder voice, 'Curiously enough it was merinos that I was thinking of, the King's merinos; they are of the Spanish breed, however.'

'Are you talking about merinos?' asked Captain Lowe.

'Yes,' said Hamlyn. 'Dr Maturin here has seen the King's flock.'

'Sir Joseph Banks was good enough to show them to me,' said Stephen.

Lowe looked at him with contempt, and after some thought replied, 'I don't give a . . . a button for Sir Joseph Banks.'

'I am sure he would be grieved to hear it.'

'Why did he try to prevent Captain Macarthur getting any of the King's sheep? Because Macarthur was from the colony, I suppose.'

'Surely not. Sir Joseph has always had the interests of the colony very much at heart. It was largely his influence that brought it into being, you will recall.'

'Then why did he refuse to receive Macarthur?'

'I cannot suppose that he thought a man with Captain Macarthur's antecedents a desirable acquaintance,' said Stephen in a silence broken only by Colonel MacPherson's long-continuing, even-toned account of the Nawab of Oudh. 'Furthermore, Sir Joseph strongly objects to duels, on moral grounds; and Captain Macarthur was in London to be court-martialled for engaging in one.'

Lowe did not seem to hear the later words. At the first he flushed a dull red and he said no more until the end of the meal, only muttering, 'Undesirable acquaintance,' from time to time, much as Stephen muttered within himself, 'God give me patience. Dear Mother of God give me patience,' for the railing about Irish prisoners had begun again, as tedious as the railing of European women about domestic servants but infinitely more malignant.

245

By the time they retired for tea and coffee Stephen had, in spite of his deliberate abstraction, heard as much as he could bear; there was a pressure of contained anger that made his hand tremble so that the coffee spilt into its saucer. Yet now came a pleasant interlude: he walked on the drawing-room terrace smoking a cigar and talking to two well-bred, interesting, Gaelic-speaking Hebridean officers of the Seventy-Third, and the tension diminished somewhat.

He and Pullings took their leave of Colonel MacPherson, and while the Colonel kept Pullings back to tell him that he was sorry Captain Aubrey had not been able to come, that although he had official letters for him they could not be given into any hands but his own, and that he would be well advised to take a couple of pints of rice-water, just luke-warm, Stephen walked into the narrow room where the officers put on their swords. There were few left, Tom's regulation lion-headed affair, three with basket-hilts belonging to the Highlanders, and his own. He buckled it on and walked down the steps into pleasant freshness; and standing there on the gravel he saw Captain Lowe, who said to him, 'I don't give a bugger for Joe Banks; and I don't give a bugger for you either, you half-baked sod of a ship's surgeon.' He spoke very loud and hoarse and two or three officers turned.

Stephen looked at him attentively. The man was in a choking rage but he was perfectly steady on his feet; he was not drunk. 'Will you answer for that, sir?' he asked.

'There's my answer,' said the big man, with a blow that knocked Stephen's wig from his head.

Stephen leapt back, whipped out his sword and cried, 'Draw, man, draw, or I shall stick you like a hog.'

Lowe unsheathed his sabre: little good did it do him. In two hissing passes his right thigh was ploughed up. At the third Stephen's sword was through his shoulder. And at the issue of a confused struggle at close quarters he was flat on his back, Stephen's foot on his chest, Stephen's sword-point at his throat and the cold voice saying above him, 'Ask my pardon or you are a dead man. Ask my pardon, I say, or you are a dead man, a dead man.'

'I ask your pardon,' said Lowe, and his eyes filled with blood.

Chapter Nine

'If it's blood, I must put it in cold water this directly minute,' said Killick, who knew perfectly well that it was blood; the news that the Doctor had run a soldier through, had left him weltering in his gore, ruining the Governor's Bath-stoned steps, ruining the drawing-room carpet, worth a hundred guineas, causing his lady to faint away, had reached the *Surprise* before the barge, and it accounted for the particular consideration, esteem and gentleness with which he was handed up the side. But Killick liked to have it confirmed, to hear the very words.

'I suppose it is,' said Stephen, glancing at the skirt of his coat, upon which he had unconsciously wiped his sword, much as he wiped his instruments when operating. 'How is the Captain?'

'Which he gave over half an hour ago, as empty as a shaken cask, ha, ha, ha! Lord, he was at it all night – never a moment's peace, ha, ha, ha!' said Killick; and still smiling he added, 'He has turned in now, and is snoring as loud as ever he . . .' But feeling that his comparison was not quite genteel he went on, 'I will bring you your old nankeen jacket.'

'Do not trouble now,' said Stephen. 'I believe I shall follow the Captain's example and lie down for a while.'

'Not in them breeches you won't, sir,' cried Killick. 'Nor in them silk stockings.'

Stephen lay in an old patched shirt, so often washed that it was diaphanous in places and wonderfully soft all over. The tension had gone and his body was wholly relaxed; the ship moved beneath him, just enough to show that she was afloat and alive; he fell farther and farther down through the layers of doze, dreaming confusion, sleep, deep sleep, still deeper sleep almost to a coma.

A sleep so profound that he had to climb out of it by stages, reconstructing the events of yesterday, the boredom and the pain of dinner at Government House, the rare violence of its outcome, over in seconds, the obliging discretion of the Highland officers, one of whom picked up his wig, Tom Pullings' mute dismay.

The light increased very slightly and he saw an eye peering through the crack of the opened door. 'What time is it?' he asked.

'Just on four bells, sir.'

'In what watch?'

'Oh, only the forenoon,' said Killick in a comforting tone. 'But Mr Martin was afraid you might be in a lethargy. Shall I bring hot water, sir?'

'Hot water by all means. How is the Captain?'

'Slept all night and now gone ashore, sir, pale and thin.'

'Very good. Now be so good as to prepare a pot of coffee: I shall drink it upstairs. And if Mr Martin should be at leisure, tell him with my compliments that I should be happy to share it with him.'

Martin came into the great cabin, his face lively with pleasure, his one eye shining more than usual; but clearly he was somewhat embarrassed. Stephen said, 'My dear Martin, I know your views on the matter, and to ease your mind to some degree I will let you know straight away that this quarrel was forced upon me by gross physical insult, that I took pains to do no more than disable the man, and that if he is kept on a low diet he will be about in a fortnight.'

'How kind of you to tell me, Maturin. Galley-rumour, with unconcealed delight, had represented you as Attila come again. Though to be sure, I do not know how my principles would stand up to gross insult.'

'I hope your afternoon was more agreeable than mine?'

'Oh yes, I thank you,' cried Martin. 'It was very agreeable

indeed. I was trying to make my way out of this dispiriting, sadly dirty – what shall I call it? – settlement, perhaps. And I was approaching the windmill when I heard someone call my name, and there was Paulton! You have heard me speak of John Paulton, I am sure?'

'The gentleman who played the violin so well, and who wrote of love in such feeling verse?'

'Yes, yes. Anguish Paulton we used to call him; and alas it proved all too true. We were great friends at school, and we were on the same staircase at the university. We should never have lost touch but for his wretched marriage and of course my wanderings. I knew he had a cousin in New South Wales and I intended to find him out, in case he could give me news of John. And there he was! I mean there was John. We were so happy. He had had a sad time of it, poor fellow, for having become a Catholic as I think I told you he could have no fellowship, though he was a capital scholar and very well liked in the college, nor any military employment; and once this woman and her lover had squandered his fortune, such as it was, he was reduced, as I was reduced, to journalism, translation, correcting the press.'

'I hope he is happier in New South Wales?'

'He has enough to eat and an assured roof over his head, but I am afraid he is ungrateful enough to pine for more. His cousin has a considerable tract of land, some hundreds or even thousands of acres, I believe, along the coast to the north, at the mouth of a stream whose name escapes me: each looks after it in turn; and John finds the loneliness very trying. He had thought silence and solitude would be ideal for writing; but no such thing – melancholy rises on every hand.'

'Are the flora and fauna no solace, and they the strangest in the world?'

'None whatsoever. He has never been able to tell one bird from another nor lad's love from heart's-ease, and he does not care. His only delight is books and good company and this country for him is a desert.'

'But his time away from it?'

'For John Sydney too is a desert, with the addition of cruelty, squalor and crime. There are political divisions here, and John's cousin belongs to the minority. John knows few people, and the talk of those few is all of wethers and tegs. A scholarly man, who drinks little wine, who dislikes hunting, for whom books and music are all-important, has little to say to them. How his face lit up when I spoke of you! He desires his best compliments, and begs you will allow me to take you to his house this evening. He pins all his hopes of a return to the land of the living on a novel, of which he has completed three volumes, and he feels that even a very little civilized conversation will enable him to bring the fourth to an end, which at present he is quite unable to do.'

'I should be very happy,' said Stephen, and turning, he called, 'Killick, pray stop scrabbling at the door in that uneasy manner. Come right in or go clean away, will you now?'

Killick came right in and said, 'Which it is Slade, sir: begs the favour of a word when you are at liberty.'

Stephen was at liberty, but Slade, the Sethian elder, found it extremely difficult to bring his word out. After a discourse on the long-established and universally-practised custom of free trading in Shelmerston and the wanton brutality of the preventive men, it appeared that a Sethian, Harry Fell, had been sent to Botany Bay for beating a Customs officer. And not only Harry, but also William, George, Mordecai and Aunt Smailes, the last for harbouring uncustomed goods. The Sethians would like to visit their friends if they could, but they did not know where to find them or how to set about getting permission: they hoped the Doctor might be so good . . . 'Certainly,' said Stephen. 'I am going to the government offices in any case.' He wrote down the names and dates of conviction, and listened to an account of the preventive men's criminal ways of obtaining a conviction, their violence to prisoners and perjury in court.

Bonden, who came when Slade had gone away at last, had

a simpler approach: the names in his list were relations of shipmates, of Surprises; and if the Doctor was going to see about poor Padeen they would take it very kindly if he enquired after them too. No moral justification; the word *shipmates* was enough – shipmates' friends were to be enquired after whether they had committed murder, rape or riotous assembly.

'I must be away,' said Stephen. 'I hope not to be late for dinner, but if I am, pray ask the Captain to pay no attention and never to wait in compliment to me.'

He was late, and the Captain had waited; though scarcely, it seemed, by way of compliment. 'Well, Stephen,' he said with an angry glare, 'here's a pretty cock you have made of things, upon my honour. In one short afternoon you have contrived to guarantee official and unofficial ill-will – ill-will from all quarters. I felt the effect of it at every visit I made. God knows when we shall get the ship cleaned and ready for sea.'

'So did I. The penal secretary's smiles were all gone. He put me off with one miserable excuse after another – enquiries had to be made on stamped paper and backed by a commissioned officer or a justice of the peace – there was no stamped paper available at present.'

'Firkins is cousin to Lowe and he is connected with the whole Macarthur tribe. What in Heaven's name possessed you to run the fellow through the body?'

'I did not run him through the body. I pierced his sword-arm, little more; which was moderate enough I believe. After all he had knocked my wig off.'

'But surely he did not just walk up to you and do so without there had been some words beforehand, some quarrel?'

'I only told him during the course of that dismal feast that Banks did not choose to be acquainted with a man like Macarthur. He brooded over that for the rest of the meal and attacked me as I walked down the steps.'

'It was most irregular. If you had killed him without calling him out in due form, without seconds, there would have been the devil to pay.'

'If it had been a regular encounter I could scarcely have closed and dashed my hilt in his face, which brought him up with a round hitch. Besides a formal meeting would have made much more noise – would have done the lout too much honour. But I do admit that it was a sorry performance: I am very sorry for it, Jack, and I ask your pardon.'

Dinner had been on the table in the dining-cabin for some time, but Killick was too eager to hear what was said to announce it: his long acquaintance with Captain Aubrey told him that it was now useless to expect furious reproaches or foul oaths, so he opened the door and said, 'Wittles is up at last, sir, if you please.'

'This is an uncommon good fish, though luke-warm,' said Jack after a while.

'A kind of snapper, I believe; the best I have ever eaten. Several things are at their most charming when tepid: new potatoes, for example; dried cod beaten up with cream.'

It was indeed an excellent dish; so was the capon that followed it, and the short, thick pudding; but even when dinner was over and they were sitting in the great cabin again Stephen was aware that Jack was not entirely mollified: far from it. This official obstruction (so difficult to deal with under a comparatively new and unknown Governor) was deeply frustrating, and he felt that Stephen had brought it about.

Nevertheless, when they had drunk their brandy Jack stood up and took a packet from the rack that held his telescopes, and before opening it he said, 'Since Firkins chooses to be disobliging about your enquiries I shall go and speak to the Governor's deputy in my character as a senior naval officer and member for Milport. That will produce the information. They do so hate a question in Parliament or a letter to the ministry.'

'That would be very kind of you. And there are also several of our people who have relations here; I should have asked for their whereabouts too, had it been politic. Here are the

253

lists. And if you could put Padeen among them, well down, that might be best. Colman is his name, Patrick Colman. But Jack, pray hold your hand for a day or two.'

'Very well,' said Jack, taking the slips of paper. 'I shall get Adams to copy them out. Now here' – holding up the packet – 'here are the official papers that came by way of Madras. My instructions are merely to proceed with the utmost dispatch according to the orders already delivered to me by their Lordships' directions and according to the advice of the counsellor named therein; I was also to hand you this letter. And here is a note from Mrs Macquarie. A charming woman, I thought.'

'Is she not?' said Stephen. 'Forgive me if I go and deal with this black-sealed affair.'

He sat in his cabin with the lead-covered code-book at his side; but before opening it he read the note, which brought Mrs Macquarie's compliments and the scent of lavender. Mr Hamlyn had told her that Dr Maturin would like to advise with her about some little orphan girls; she would be at home between five and six, and if Dr Maturin was not otherwise engaged she would be happy to offer what little information she possessed. Her Excellency's dashing hand reminded him of Diana's; so did her spelling and her evident good nature. He laid it by, smiling, and took up the black-sealed affair. Deciphered, it gave the names of several more men in Chile and Peru who were in favour of independence and opposed to slavery with whom Dr Maturin might profitably enter into discreet contact; among them, Stephen observed with the keenest pleasure, was the Bishop of Lima. Within this letter lay another, a personal letter from Sir Joseph Blaine, the head of naval intelligence, that required no decoding and that put his heart into the strangest flutter:

My dear Stephen (since you honour me with this friendly use of your Christian name alone),

It was with some emotion that I received your letter, dated from Portsmouth, with its most flattering of all marks of confidence, since it was in effect a power of attorney enabling me to remove all the sums standing to your credit with your unsatisfactory bankers and to place them in the hands of Messrs Smith and Clowes.

And it is with still more emotion that I am to tell you that I was unable to carry out your wishes, for the letter, though impeccably phrased, was signed Stephen, no more. 'I remain, my dear Sir Joseph, your affect. humble servt. Stephen'.

The purport of the document was abundantly clear: the senior partner admitted this, but he said the bank could not act. I took advice, and both lawyers concurred in saying that the bank's position was unassailable.

It angered me extremely. Yet no great time had passed before my anger was sensibly diminished by the news that Smith and Clowes had ceased payment. Shortly after this they were made bankrupt, like many other country firms, alas; and their creditors cannot hope for sixpence in the pound. However in spite of all their many faults, your unsatisfactory people were much more substantial and long-established; they had the confidence of the City and they have emerged stronger and if anything wealthier from the crisis; so that your fortune, though rudely and uncivilly kept, lies in their vaults intact: it may even, who knows, have bred. And I can assure you that your orders about annuities, subscriptions and the like will from now on be most scrupulously observed. Of this I give you joy; and remain, my dear Stephen,

Your affectionate (though disobedient) humble servant,
Joseph

Should you happen to stroll in a mangrove-swamp, and should a specimen (however indifferent) of Eupator ingens happen to pass within easy reach, pray think of me.

It was some time before he could make out what he felt, what was the prevailing emotion amid the turmoil of so many. There was pleasure of course, but also a strong rebellion against it and against the unsettling of a mind that had grown quite composed; and anger at the trembling of his hand. He reflected for a while on the different levels of belief and disbelief. This inherited fortune, which he had always thought disproportionate and somehow discreditable, was after all tolerably abstract and intangible: a dim, remote set of figures in a book in Sydney's Antipodes. How much had its coming or going affected more than the surface of his mind? Yet when the various tides had settled not indeed to a calm but at least to an even swell it appeared to him that upon the whole, whatever the potential disadvantages, it was better to be rich than poor; but privately rich, like that absurd person in Goldsmith. He was about to add 'and probably better to be healthy than sick, whatever Pascal may say' when it occurred to him that the strong emotions of yesterday and today had done away with the exasperation that had been so powerfully with him, as well as the sleepiness and the desire to smoke tobacco.

'Still and all, I shall indulge in a cigar as I walk up to Government House,' he said, as he put on his second-best coat.

'Diffused pleasure, or even joy: no feverish exaltation,' he reflected on his way up from the quay, a fragrant cloud wafting before him: but during the time it took to pass three iron-gangs, many unchained figures in coarse, broad-arrowed clothes, and some pitiful whores, all in this short walk, joy was scarcely apparent. Although on the other hand the explanation of Sir Joseph's letter, the strange though not unpleasant familiarity of Sir Joseph's letter, presented itself all of a piece, with startling clarity, as he paused for a moment looking out over Port Jackson, where an outward-bound local brig of about two hundred tons was lying to with several boats close by to windward and smoke pouring out of her ports amidst a general indifference. The explanation was that in the tedium of copying the lawyer's power of attorney his mind had wandered to an almost finished note to Diana. He had certainly signed hers *S. Maturin*, reserving the *Stephen* for Sir Joseph.

There was one of the smaller kangaroos on the lawn of Government House and Stephen contemplated it from the steps until ten minutes past five, when he sent up his name and was shown into a waiting-room. Here again Mrs Macquarie showed a certain likeness to Diana: she too was unpunctual. Fortunately the windows looked on to the lawn, the kangaroo and several flights of very small long-tailed blue-green parrots, and Stephen sat, peaceful and content, watching them in the extraordinarily brilliant light. 'At least part of the brilliance arises from the fact that so many of the trees hold their dull leaves straight up, so that there is little shade,' he said. 'It gives a certain air of desolation to the land, if not to the sky itself.'

The door opened, but instead of a footman Mrs Macquarie herself hurried in, her hair somewhat disordered. Stephen rose, bowed and smiled, yet with a certain reserve: he did not know whether she had been told about his encounter with Lowe before she wrote to him. Her amiable smile and her apology for being late reassured him, and a moment's reflexion told him that she (again like Diana) had spent many years in India, where white officers, overfed, too hot, too absolute, fought so often that a mere wound was scarcely noticed.

She listened attentively to what he had to say and then asked, 'Are they pretty?'

'Not at all, ma'am,' said Stephen. 'They are small-eyed, dull black, thin and graceless. But on the other hand they seem to me quite good-hearted children, attached to one another and to their friends, and remarkably gifted linguists at least. They already speak a most creditable English, one version for before the mast, another for the quarterdeck.'

'And you do not think of taking them home?'

'They were born almost on the equator itself, and I can

257

hardly find it in my heart to carry them by way of the Horn to islands so damp and cold and foggy as ours. If I could find them a home here, I should happily maintain and endow them.'

'Perhaps if I could see them it would be easier for us to find a solution. Would you have time to bring them tomorrow afternoon?'

'Certainly, ma'am,' said Stephen, rising, 'and I am infinitely obliged to you for your kindness.'

He walked down the lawn to the gate and the kangaroo came across at its awkward four-legged pace, sat up, looked into his face and uttered a very faint bleat. But Stephen had nothing for it and as the kangaroo declined his caress they parted company, the animal watching him until he reached the gate.

He asked the rigid sentry the way to Riley's hotel: no reply but increased rigidity and an uneasy look, until the lodge-keeper came out and said, 'If he was to answer, sir, if he was to answer any but a soldier-officer, he would have a bloody shirt tomorrow: ain't that right, Jock?' Jock closed one eye, never moving his head, still less his person, and the lodge-keeper went on, 'Riley's hotel, sir? Straight on, bear left, and it is just before the first brick house you come to.'

Stephen thanked him now and blessed him later, for his direction was exact; and although the walk had been sad enough, with its many convicts in their dirty prison clothes, some looking vacant, others wicked, others deep in settled melancholy, and its many soldiers, also in a state of harsh servitude but at least with the power of kicking the still more unfortunate, it was somewhat lightened by the friendly greeting of Colonel MacPherson and another officer of the Seventy-Third as they passed by, and much more so by the sight of Martin at their meeting-place, which could have been taken for a crossroads shebeen in the Bog of Allen but for the absence of rain or mud and the presence of three sorts of wild parrot on its sagging thatched roof and a large selection of tame ones in cages or on stands within doors. Martin was still standing by the funereal cockatoo, wrapping the finger it had bit with his handkerchief. 'You buy your experience at a terrible price, I find,' said Stephen, watching the blood soak through.

'I should never have taken my hand away so quick,' said Martin. 'I startled him, poor bird.' The poor bird ran its dry black tongue across the cutting edge of its bill and looked at him with a malignant eye, gauging the distance: another lunge was very nearly possible. 'Shall we go?' he asked, looking at his watch. 'It is almost time.'

'We must take something for the good of the house,' said Stephen, sitting down by a tray of objects designed for visiting sailors: beautiful deep-green pitted emu's eggs, Aboriginal stone axes, spears against the wall, and a flat, angled piece of wood like an indifferent circumflex accent some two feet across. 'House,' he called. 'House, there. House. D'ye hear me now?'

House came, wiping his hands on his apron. 'Was there never a young woman to serve you, gentlemen?' he cried, and when they shook their heads, 'Upstairs with her soldier, for a thousand pound. What may I have the pleasure of bringing your honours?'

'What have you that is long and cool?' asked Stephen.

'Well, Mister, there is the Parramatta river, long and cool in that canvas bucket by the cross-draught; and I am after drawing off a gallon of my own whiskey, a delicate drink if ever there was one. At this time of day the two mixed just so would make a long cool drink equal to the best champagne.'

'Then be so good as to give us a pint of the one and a noggin of the other,' said Stephen. 'But before you go, pray tell me the use of this wooden implement, something between a scimitar and a sickle.'

'That, sir, is an Aborigine's . . . toy, as you might say, since they only use them for play. They hold one end and throw it spinning like a Catherine-wheel and when it has gone fifty yards or so it rises up, curves and comes back to hand. There was an old Aboriginal that used to show it for a tot of rum, and that was his undoing.'

'You throw it from you, and it comes back without rebounding?' asked Martin, who could not easily follow the broad Munster accent.

'You find it hard to believe, sir, I am sure; and so it is too if you have not seen it: but reflect, sir, you are in the Antipodes – you are standing upside down like a fly on the ceiling – we are all standing upside down; which is much stranger than black swans or sticks that fly back to your hand.'

When they had drunk their whiskey they walked on, and Martin said, 'He was quite right. In many ways this is the opposite of our world. I should say as different as Hades from Earth if it were not for the penetrating light. Do you not find the perpetual sound of chains, the omnipresence of ragged, dirty, cheerless men whom we must suppose criminal deeply depressing?'

'I do: and if it were not for the prospect of getting out into the open country I should either paddle about this vast harbour in my skiff or stay aboard, classifying my collections and examining yours with a closer eye. But I think it is the eager cruelty of the oppressors that saddens me even more.'

They paused before crossing the rutted, dusty road to let two iron-gangs go by, one up, the other down, and as they stood a drunk young woman lurched into them, her hair wild, her bosom bare; a handsome young woman, in spite of her blotched face. 'Could they not see where they were going, the awkward buggers? God rot their . . .' The convicts passed; they crossed the street; her abuse followed them, fouler than anything heard on the forecastle.

They walked in silence for some time and then Martin said, 'Here is Paulton's house.'

Paulton himself it was who opened the door and made them welcome, a tall bony man with spectacles, small steel-rimmed thick spectacles, that did not appear to suit him, seeing that sometimes he peered through them, sometimes over the top. Very often he took them off and polished them with his handkerchief, a nervous gesture, one of many; indeed he was a nervous man entirely. But a sensible one, thought Stephen, and amiable.

'May I offer you some tea?' he asked after the ordinary preliminaries. 'In this parching dusty weather I find that hot tea answers better than anything else.'

They made grateful murmurs, and presently an aged woman brought the tray. 'How kind of you to come, sir,' said Paulton, pouring him a cup. 'Martin tells me you have written many a book.'

'Only on medicine, sir, and a few aspects of natural philosophy.'

'And may I ask, sir, whether you can compose at sea, or whether you wait for the peace and calm of a country retreat?'

'I have written a good deal at sea,' said Stephen, 'but unless the weather is tolerably steady, so that the ink may be relied upon to stay in its well, I usually wait until I am ashore for any long, considered treatise or paper – for the peace and calm of a country retreat, as you say. Yet on the other hand I do not find that the turmoil of a ship prevents me reading: with a good clear candle in my lantern and balls of wax in my ears, I read with the utmost delight. The confinement of my cabin, the motion of my hanging cot, the distantly-heard orders and replies, the working of the ship – all these enhance my enjoyment.'

'I have tried your wax balls,' said Martin, 'but they make me apprehensive. I am afraid that there will be the cry, "She sinks, she sinks! All is lost. She cannot swim," and I shall not hear.'

'You were always rather apprehensive, Nathaniel,' said Paulton, taking off his spectacles and looking at him kindly with his myopic gaze. 'I remember terrifying you as a little boy by asserting that I was really a corpse inhabited by a grey and hairy ghost. But I imagine, sir,' – to Stephen – 'that you read books on medicine, natural philosophy, perhaps history – that you do not read novels or plays.'

'Sir,' said Stephen, 'I read novels with the utmost pertinacity. I look upon them – I look upon good novels – as a very valuable part of literature, conveying more exact and finely-distinguished knowledge of the human heart and mind than almost any other, with greater breadth and depth and fewer constraints. Had I not read Madame de Lafayette, the Abbé Prévost, and the man who wrote *Clarissa*, that extraordinary feat, I should be very much poorer than I am; and a moment's reflexion would add many more.'

Martin and Paulton instantly added many more; and Paulton, who had hitherto been somewhat shy and nervous, shook Stephen's hand, saying, 'Sir, I honour your judgment. But when you spoke of *Clarissa*, did the name of Richardson slip your mind?'

'It did not. I am aware that Samuel Richardson's name appears on the title-page. Yet before ever I read *Clarissa Harlowe* I read *Grandison*, to which is appended a low grasping ignoble whining outcry against the Irish booksellers for invading the copyright. It is written by a tradesman in the true spirit of the counting-house; and since there can be no doubt that it was written by Richardson, I for my part have no doubt that *Clarissa*, with its wonderful delicacy, was written by another hand. The man who wrote the letter could not have written the book. Richardson as of course you know was intimately acquainted with the other printers and booksellers of his time; and it is my conviction that some one of their dependents, a man of singular genius, wrote the book, perhaps in the Fleet, perhaps in the Marshalsea.'

They both nodded their heads: they had both lodged in Grub Street. 'After all,' said Martin, 'statesmen do not write their own speeches.'

After a rather solemn pause Paulton called for more tea, and while they were drinking it their talk ran on about the novel, the process of writing a novel, the lively fruitful fluent pen and its sudden inexplicable sterility. 'I was sure, last time I was in Sydney,' said Paulton, 'that I should finish my fourth volume as soon as I was back at Woolloo-Woolloo

– for my cousin and I take turns at overseeing the overseer, you know – but the weeks went by, and never a word that I did not strike out next morning.'

'The country did not suit, I collect?'

'No, sir. Not at all. Yet I had set great store by it when I was in London, distracted by a hundred trifles and by daily cares, with hardly two hours I could call my own until late in the evening, when I was good for nothing; and it seemed to me that nowhere could country peace and quiet reach a higher point than in New South Wales, a remote settlement in New South Wales, with no post, no newspapers, no untimely visitors.'

'But is not this the case at Woolloo-Woolloo?'

'There are no letters, no papers, no visitors, to be sure; but there is no country either. No country as I had conceived it and as I believe most people conceive it – nothing that one could call rural. Imagine riding from Sydney over a dun-coloured plain: shallow stony soil with coarse rank grass, deep bush, and here and there some melancholy trees. I never knew a tree could be ugly until I saw a blue-gum: others of the same kind too, with dull, leathery, discouraged leaves and their bark hanging down in great strips, a vegetable leprosy. You leave what settlements there are, what sheep-walks, and the track grows narrower, entering the bush, a grey-green sombre dusty vegetation, never fresh and green, with vast stretches that have been burnt black and bald by the Aborigines. And I should have stated that it was always the same: these trees never lose their leaves, but they never seem to have new ones either. On and on, skirting several dismal lagoons, where the mosquitoes are even worse, and then at last you climb a slope through lower scrub and there you see a river before you, sometimes a continuous stream, more often pools here and there in the valley. Beyond it stands Woolloo-Woolloo, a stark house set down in the wilderness; to the left the stockade where the convicts live, with the overseer's house beside it; and far inland you can just make out Wilkins' place, the only neighbour within reach. It is true that the convicts have cleared the farther bank for wheat, but it is nothing like a field, only a kind of industrial scar; and in any case it hardly affects the huge featureless expanse of colourless monotonous inhuman primeval waste that stretches away and away before you and on your left hand. The river has a long Aboriginal name: I call it the Styx.'

'That is a sad approach to a country retreat,' said Stephen. 'And the Styx has dismal associations.'

'None too dismal for Woolloo-Woolloo, sir, I do assure you. Indeed they are scarcely dismal enough. In Hades there was no triangle permanently installed as there is in the square at Woolloo-Woolloo and Wilkins' place; for though no man can flog his own assigned servants, both my cousin and Wilkins are magistrates, and each can do so for the other. And in Hades there was at least some company, however faded, some conversation: at Woolloo-Woolloo there is none. The overseer is a gross man, with no thoughts apart from the profit of the land, the acres of bush to be cleared, the harvest that Stanley's brig is to take down to Sydney; and he says I must not talk to the convicts except to give them orders. And although the black men I sometimes meet on our beach or walking by the stream are affable enough – one gave me a piece of ochre, and they have quite often painted my arms and face with the oil that exudes from dead fishes, to keep the mosquitoes away: they use it all over their bodies – our exchange is limited to a few score words. So, do you see, I have no conversation. My rural retreat is not unlike Bentham's solitary confinement: and although no doubt there are men who can bring a novel to a splendid resounding close in solitary confinement, I am not one of them. Though Heaven knows I am sadly in need of an end.'

'You paint a sombre picture of New Holland, sir. Are there no compensations, no birds, beasts and flowers?'

'I am told that ours is an exceptionally unfavoured part of the country, sir, with little game and that little poached by a band of escaped convicts who have somehow contrived to make friends with Aborigines living beyond our northern bush. Little game . . . I have, it is true, been told that emus were crossing our path, but I never saw them; nor, being so short-sighted, have I seen the cockatoos and parrots except as a vague blur. Indeed, Nature's beauties are wasted on me, though her shortcomings are not – I hear the dread-fully raucous voices of the birds, and I feel the innumerable mosquitoes that plague us, particularly after the rains.'

'As for an end,' said Martin, 'are endings really so very important? Sterne did quite well without one; and often an unfinished picture is all the more interesting for the bare canvas. I remember Bourville's definition of a novel as a work in which life flows in abundance, swirling without a pause: or as you might say without an end, an organized end. And there is at least one Mozart quartet that stops without the slightest ceremony: most satisfying when you get used to it.'

Stephen said, 'There is another Frenchman whose name escapes me but who is even more to the point: *La bêtise c'est de vouloir conclure*. The conventional ending, with virtue rewarded and loose ends tied up is often sadly chilling; and its platitude and falsity tend to infect what has gone before, however excellent. Many books would be far better without their last chapter: or at least with no more than a brief, cool, unemotional statement of the outcome.'

'Do you really think so?' asked Paulton, looking from one to the other. 'I am very willing to believe you, particularly as the tale has reached a point where . . . Nathaniel, may I beg you to read it? If it really will do without any beating of drums, or if you could suggest the first notes of the true closing passage, how happy I should be! I could escape from this cruel, desolate, corrupt and corrupting place.'

'I should like to read it very much,' said Martin. 'I have always liked your pieces.'

'The manuscript – you know my wretched scrawl, Nathaniel – is now being fine-copied by a government clerk. Corruption has its uses, though I cry out against it.'

'Is he not allowed to copy, then?'

'Certainly not to the extent he is copying for me. He is the best pen in the colony, always employed for government grants and leases, but until my manuscript is done not a single one will be presented for the seal. He was a forger in real life, and when he is sober he can make you the most convincing Bank of England note imaginable, if only the paper is right.'

'Is there a great deal of corruption in the colony?'

'Apart from the present Governor and the officers who came out with him, I should say that in one form or another it is almost universal. In the lower branches of the administration for example nearly all the clerks are convicts, often quite highly-educated men; and so long as you are reasonably discreet they will do anything you wish.'

'Ah,' said Stephen with some satisfaction. 'I asked because several of our people in the *Surprise* have friends who were transported. I waited on the penal secretary to enquire after them, but it was clear that he did not intend to give me any information; and although Captain Aubrey with his much greater authority could probably oblige him to do so, I fear the intervention might rebound upon the prisoners.'

'With such a fellow as Firkins I am sure it would. The simple, quite harmless way is to apply to one of the clerks who keep the register. Painter would be the best, a quick, intelligent man. He has had two or three shepherds and some real farm labourers, ploughmen, put in the place of others and assigned to us – rare birds in a population mostly made up of more or less sinful townsmen, and highly valued.'

'How can he be approached?'

'As he is a ticket-of-leave man, it is not difficult. A word left at Riley's hotel would bring him to a discreet meeting-place. It might be wiser for you not to go yourself, however; there are so many informers about, and your encounter with Lowe has set the whole Camden faction so very much against you, that it might have some ill effect. If you have nobody suitable aboard, I will go myself.'

'You are very kind, sir, very kind indeed, but I think I have the right man. If I am mistaken, may I come and see you again? I should like to do so in any case, whenever you are at leisure.'

'One of the many things I like about your friend,' said Stephen, peering out over the dark waters of Sydney Cove, 'is that he is not holier than thou, or at least than me. Although he is clearly a virtuous man he is not horrified by moderate sin. Can you make out where the landing-place is? I shall try a hail. The boat, ahoy! Halloo! Show a glim there, you wicked dogs.'

'If we keep steadily down, as near the shore as possible, I think we must come to it in time; but I wish we had not resisted Paulton's offer of accompanying us with a lantern.'

The theory was sound, but the night being singularly thick – no stars, still less any hint of a moon – their practice was slow, hesitant and anxious until they were overtaken by a cheerful, reasonably sober body of the frigate's liberty-men, carrying links.

'There she lays, sir,' they cried. 'Right up against the wharf, warped in this last tide. Didn't you recognize her, sir? The Doctor did not recognize the barky.' The news passed back and a distant voice said, 'Both the doctors are so pissed they did not recognize the barky, ha, ha, ha!'

'To think that I should not recognize my own ship,' thought Stephen, standing there on the gangway; and then with a slight twinge of regret he remembered that the *Surprise* was not his own ship. 'But what of it, for all love?' he reflected. 'The kinds of happiness are not to be compared,' and walking into the cabin he stood for a moment, blinking in the light.

Jack, at his desk with several heaps of papers before him, did not look particularly happy, but he raised his head, smiled, and said, 'There you are, Stephen.'

'You have a worn and aged look, brother,' said Stephen.

'Put out your tongue.' He examined it and said, 'You are not yet recovered from your plethory.'

'It is a plethory of bloody-minded officials that I am suffering from,' said Jack. 'Obstruction at every goddam turn. No one knows when Governor Macquarie will be back and most unhappily his deputy served under my father. Where I should be without Adams I cannot tell; but he can only deal with the smaller repairs and shortages, and I want much more than that – want it with the utmost dispatch, as my orders say.'

'Adams was wonderfully successful in Java,' observed Stephen, 'and with your permission I should like to ask him to carry out some corruption for me too, at a modest level. We went to see a friend of Martin's, an amiable man who has lived here for some time, and he assured me that there is a universal venality among the government clerks. He told me the name of one to whom we should apply for news of Padeen and the men and women in the lists I gave you; and it appears to me that Adams is the man to make the application.'

Adams, consulted after breakfast the next day, was of the same opinion. 'With all modesty, sir,' said he, 'I do not think there is any class of men in the service better suited for making a friendly arrangement or mutual accommodation as one might say than the older captain's clerks. They have seen all the colours of the rainbow, they do not have to top it the nob, and they are not easily done even a very light brown. How much were you thinking of giving for these men's whereabouts, sir? Their places of assignment, as the regulations call it.'

'There, Mr Adams, you fairly pose me. Would a johannes do?'

'God bless you, sir, a joe passes for £4 here. No. From what I have seen I should say a gallon of rum or what they call rum poor souls would be about the going price. We do not want to spoil the market, flashing gold about.'

'I am sure you are right, Mr Adams. But on the other hand pray be so open-handed that Painter does not spare his time in getting information about Colman. He was loblolly-boy, as I think I told you, and I take a particular interest in him.'

'Very well, Doctor. I shall do my best. May I go beyond two gallon if a good deal of trouble is required, if Painter has to call in other clerks, for example?'

'Certainly. Drown him in rum if need be; but first I must fetch you some money for it, and a broad piece or two in case of need; for I do assure you, Mr Adams, that I should not grudge a hatful of broad pieces in this case.'

On the half-deck he met Reade and he said, 'Oh Mr Reade, my dear, tell me, is Bonden away with the Captain?'

'No, sir,' said Reade. 'He is helping Jemmy Ducks make Sarah's clothes. Shall I fetch him?'

'Never in life,' said Stephen. 'I should like to see how they are coming along.'

They were coming along pretty well. Bonden was the best hand at sewing in the ship, and with his mouth full of pins he was trying a roughed-out nankeen frock, fit for Government House, on a rigid, stock-still Sarah, while Jemmy Ducks, his superior in deportment and worldly knowledge, was teaching Emily to curtsy. 'Do not mind me,' he said as he entered their dim retreat. 'Carry on by all means. But Bonden, when you are free I should like a hand in the Captain's store-room.'

'Aye aye, sir,' said Bonden indistinctly; and the little girls gave him a wan, apprehensive smile.

The Captain's store-room had a wealth of those geometrically impossible corners so usual at sea, and in one of these, guarded by a massive iron-bound chest made fast to eyebolts, lay Stephen's tangible wealth, a certain amount of gold, much more silver and some Bank of England notes, in a smaller chest, also iron-bound, also provided with locks, but also made of wood; and as he stood there waiting for Bonden it occurred to him for the first time that the rats, in their frenzy of deprivation, might have pierced this box too.

'They will have spared the gold and silver, I dare say,' he

reflected. 'But a poor simple creature I shall look if I open the inner drawer and find a comfortable nest of paper chewed small with little pink sucklings in it. This happened at Ballynahinch, as I well remember; but that was only laundry lists.'

'Now, sir,' said Bonden, 'if you will lay aft just a trifle, I'll cast off – no, sir: aft, if you please.'

All was well. The rats had scorned the treasure-chest, and by some happy atmospheric chance the elegant Bank of England notes, 'the only paper money that looks worth twopence', he thought, had retained or regained their pristine crispness. He was counting it with a certain voluptuous glee (the ghost of former poverty) when Oakes came below to say that 'there was a gentleman for him on the quarterdeck, if you please, sir'.

'A civilian or a soldier, Mr Oakes?'

'Oh, only a civilian, sir.'

It was Mr Paulton, come to return their visit. Stephen took him into the cabin, sent to tell Martin, and they all three sat drinking madeira until Jack returned, worn, dusty, and very willing to eat his dinner. He at once invited Paulton. 'We keep strangely unfashionable hours in the Navy, sir, but I should be very happy if you would honour us.'

'Pray do,' said Stephen. 'It being Friday we have laid in a noble haul of fish.'

'They have asked the shabby gent,' said Killick to his mate. 'Go and tell the cook.'

Paulton was troubled – had he known the ways of the service he would never have called at such an hour – he had had no intention whatsoever of imposing himself.

His scruples were overcome in time, however, and a very pleasant dinner they had of it. With so much shore-leave there were no other guests, and they talked quite freely about music, discovering a shared devotion to the string quartets of Haydn, Mozart and Dittersdorf, and about New South Wales, which Paulton obviously knew much better than any of them. 'It may well be a country with a great future,' he said, 'but it is one with no present, apart from squalor, crime, and corruption. It may have a future for people like the Macarthurs and those infinitely hardy pioneers who can withstand loneliness, drought, flood and a generally ungrateful soil; but for most of today's inhabitants it is a desolate wilderness: they take refuge in drink and in being cruel to one another. There is more drunkenness here than in Seven Dials, and as for the flogging . . .' Feeling that perhaps he had been talking too long he fell silent for a while, but when the plates had been changed and they asked him about Woolloo-Woolloo he described it in some detail: 'At the moment,' he said, 'it is at the limit of free settlement along the coast northwards, and the uncleared part shows the country as the wretched First Fleet of convicts saw it. No one could possibly take it for Eden, but in certain lights it has an austere beauty; it is not without interest, and I should very much like to show it to you when I go back to take charge at the end of the month. Although the journey is quite long on horseback, because one has to skirt a number of lagoons, it is no great way by sea: the brig that comes up for our wool and corn takes no more than three or four hours, with a good south-east breeze. If I may show you on the chart there on the window-seat you will see that the entrance to our harbour is quite clear. Here, marked by a cairn and a flagpole, is the channel through which the tide flows in and out of our particular lagoon, bringing the brig with it; and here is the mouth of our stream, which flows into the lagoon through the lamb pastures. There are often kangaroos among the lambs, and I believe I could point out the water-mole, which is thought very curious. And no doubt there are countless nondescript plants. It would give me the greatest pleasure.'

'I should like it of all things,' said Jack, to whom these words were chiefly directed, 'if we do not sail before the end of the month and if the ship can spare me: but even if she cannot, I am sure the Doctor and Mr Martin would like to go. They could have one of the cutters at any time.'

As soon as they had drunk their coffee, two bells struck and he excused himself – he was obliged to go up to the Parramatta river with his carpenter to look at some spars, but he begged Mr Paulton not to stir; and it was clear to Stephen that Jack, in spite of his worn, somewhat bilious face, thought Paulton an agreeable acquaintance.

After he had gone Paulton became more confidential. He was ashamed not to ask them before the end of the month, but he did not think it would be the happiest of visits. His cousin Matthews had many virtues: although he was a severe master he was a just one, and he never punished for trifles or from ill-nature as his neighbour Wilkins did; and he was on good terms with the Aborigines, although they sometimes took a sheep and although a related tribe along the coast harboured a group of escaped convicts; but he never entertained and he allowed nothing but water or at the most weak green tea to be drunk in his house. He had many virtues, Paulton repeated, but his enemies might call him a little rigid and unsociable.

'Is the gentleman married?' asked Martin.

'Oh no,' said Paulton, amused.

'I dare say there are a great many waders on the shore of your lagoon,' said Stephen, after a moment's silence.

'I am sure there are,' said Paulton, standing up. 'I often see clouds of birds rise when I go down there to play my fiddle, and they may well have been wading. But now, with my best thanks for a delightful afternoon, I must bid you good day. Oh, and just one last word,' he added in a low voice, 'is it usual to give vails in the Navy?'

'No, no, not at all,' they both replied; and this being nearly the time for Stephen to take Sarah and Emily to be shown to Mrs Macquarie, Martin alone walked back with their guest.

The little girls were quite stiff in their new frocks, and they looked very grave: plainer, poor dears, and even blacker than usual, thought Stephen. 'We are going to see a most amiable lady, at Government House. She is both good and kind,' he said with a somewhat exaggerated cheerfulness.

The four of them made their way up the hill in something near silence, Stephen holding Sarah's hand and Jemmy Ducks Emily's. As ill-luck would have it they passed two iron-gangs. 'Why are those men chained?' asked Sarah as the first clanked slowly by. 'Because they have behaved ill,' said Stephen. In the second a man had fallen and a soldier was beating him. Because of the frigate's peculiar status and her unusual ship's company the little girls had never seen a flogging aboard the *Surprise* nor yet a starting with bosun's cane or rope's end. They shrank away, and their grasp tightened, but they said nothing. Stephen hoped that the carriages (which made them stare), the horses, the people passing by, particularly the redcoats, and the buildings would distract their minds; and he pointed out the kangaroo on the lawn. They said, 'Yes,' but neither smiled nor followed it with their gaze.

Mrs Macquarie received them at once. 'How glad I am to see you, my dears,' she said, kissing each as each made her curtsy. 'What pretty frocks!'

A servant brought in fruit-juice and little cakes, and Stephen saw with relief that they were growing less tense. They ate and drank; and when Mrs Macquarie had talked to Dr Maturin about their hope of a ship from Madras quite soon and about the Governor's journey she turned to them and told them about the orphanage. There were many little girls of their age in one part of it, and they played games, running about in a park with trees. They looked quite pleased, accepted more fruit-juice, more cakes, both saying, 'Thank you, ma'am,' and Sarah asked, 'Have they pretty dresses?'

'Not prettier than yours,' said Mrs Macquarie. 'Come with me and I will show you.'

She walked them round to the stables, where her carriage was waiting, and they seemed reasonably happy until Stephen, standing by the step, said, 'Jemmy Ducks or I will come to see you tomorrow. Be good girls, now, till then. God bless.'

'Ain't we coming back to the barky?' asked Emily, and the wild look returned.

'Not today, mates: you got to see the orphanage,' said Jemmy Ducks; and as the carriage moved off both little girls stood up, looking at him with faces of alarm, distress and woe until it turned the corner.

The walk down was as silent as the walk up, with only Jemmy's involuntary exclamation, 'And in such a country as this, God love us.' At a corner Stephen paused, took his bearings, and said, 'Jemmy Ducks, here is a shilling. Go along that way for a couple of hundred yards and you will find a tavern, a decent house where you may have a drink.'

He went on alone, pacing slowly, mechanically noting the differences between the sea-birds over the water on his left hand and repeating the eminently sound reasons for his action. At the third repetition two figures crossed the road, laughing, and there were Davidge and West standing before him, dressed in their good shore-going clothes. 'Why, Doctor,' said West, 'I believe we have broke in upon your thoughts.'

'Not at all,' said Stephen. 'Tell me, is the Captain back yet?'

'No, not yet,' they said together, and Davidge went on, 'But Adams came aboard just as we were leaving, and he asked after you.'

And indeed Stephen had not been sitting in the cabin five minutes before there was Adams at the door. 'Well, sir,' he said, 'I have carried out your commission. I came away from Mr Painter not ten minutes ago, and on my way down I saw poor Jemmy Ducks, his face running with tears. I hope nothing dreadful has happened, Doctor?'

'We took the girls to the orphanage.'

'What, in a country like this? Well,' – recollecting himself – 'I am sure you know best, sir. Excuse me, if you please. So as I was saying, I saw Mr Painter, as you told me, and he was most obliging; he found me nearly all the present assignments, records and particulars directly. But I am afraid you will not be best pleased with some of what I have to report.' He brought out the lists, each pinned to a sheaf of papers, and laid them on the table. 'Now as for Slade's friends,' he said, 'all is tolerably well. Mrs Smailes was assigned to a man who had served his time, an emancipist as they say here, and who had settled on reasonable good land near the Hawkesbury river; and he married her. Three of the others are on ticket of leave, and work in fishing-boats. Only one, Harry Fell, absconded and joined the whalers. Here are the directions of the others.' He handed Stephen a neat clerkly sheet, names and addresses underlined with red ink, and turned to the next. 'As for Bonden's list, I fear the news is not so good. Two never arrived, having died on the voyage; one died here of natural causes; one absconded and either died of want in the bush or was speared by the Aborigines; and two were sent to Norfolk Island.'

'Where is that?'

'Far out in the ocean, a thousand miles, I believe. A penal station that was meant to terrify the convicts here into submission. They were so ill-used that they are not in their right minds any more. For the rest, some are still assigned servants and some are ticket-of-leave men. Here are their particulars. But as for Colman, sir, I am sorry to say he has had a very bad time of it. He would keep trying to escape. Last time it was with three other Irishmen: one of them had heard that if you walked north far enough you came to a river, neither very wide nor very deep, and the other side there was China, where the people were kind and where you could find an Indiaman to take you home. They were taken by Aborigines, almost dead from hunger and thirst, and brought back for a reward. One of them died from his flogging. Colman survived his – two hundred lashes at twice – and he was to have been sent to a penal colony only Dr Redfern intervened – said it would be his death – and he is to be assigned to an estate along the Parramatta together with half a dozen more. Mr Painter tells me it is reckoned a little better than a penal colony but not much, since the station belongs to a Mr Marsden, a clergyman they call Parson Rapine, who loves having his people flogged, particularly Irish papists. Mr Painter did not think he would last out a year.'

'Where is Colman now?'

'In the hospital at Dawes Point, sir, the northern arm of this cove here.'

'When is he to be assigned?'

'Oh, any time this next few weeks. The clerks see to it as they have leisure.'

'Who is Dr Redfern?'

'Why, sir, our Dr Redfern. Dr Redfern of the Nore. But you would not remember, sir, being, if you will allow me, too young in the service. The Captain would remember him.'

'I know there was a mutiny at the Nore in ninety-seven, following the trouble at Spithead.'

'Yes. Well, Dr Redfern told the mutineers to stick closer together, to be more united; and for that the court-martial sentenced him to hang. But after a while he was sent here, and presently he was given a free pardon: Captain King that was. I served under him in *Achilles*. They like him here – has the best practice in Sydney – but most of all the convicts. He always has a kind word for a sick convict; always spends much of his day at the hospital.'

'Thank you, Mr Adams. I am very much obliged to you for taking so much trouble, and I am sure no one else could have taken it to such effect. These are delicate negotiations, and a false note may prove fatal.' Adams smiled and bowed, but he did not deny it, and Stephen went on, 'And I am heartily glad that there is such a man as Dr Redfern here. Have you ever seen such a place?'

'No, sir, I have not; nor ever expect to, this side Hell. Now here, sir, is an account of my disbursements, and here . . .'

'Pray put it up, Mr Adams, and add this' – passing a johannes – 'to whatever may be left, so that if you do not find it disagreeable you may treat Painter and his more

276

respectable colleagues to the best dinner Sydney can afford. Such allies are not to be neglected.'

When Martin came back to the ship that evening he was carrying a wrapper that held John Paulton's hope if not of fame and fortune then at least of escape, a passage home to a world he knew and freedom to swim in the full tide of human existence.

'Has the Captain returned?' he asked.

'He has not. He sent to tell me he was sleeping at Parramatta. Come below and sit down; and presently we will have supper together. There is no one in the gun-room. That is your friend's book, I make no doubt?'

'Well, these are the first three volumes – I must not dirty them or crumple the pages for my life – and all but the last chapter of the fourth. Poor fellow, he is in such pains for his ending, and I fear he will never bring it off without some encouragement. His cousin thinks all fiction immoral. And really, you know, Maturin, this cousin is not quite the thing. Not only is all fiction disapproved, as being false, tantamount to a pack of lies, but neither pepper nor salt is permitted in the kitchen or on the table, as exciting the senses. And poor John is obliged to carry his fiddle out of earshot before he even tunes the strings. Furthermore, the cousin allows him no actual money – but I am being indiscreet. He invites us to dine on Sunday and suggests that we might play some piece familiar to us all, such as the Mozart D minor quartet we were talking about. I pass this invitation on with no small diffidence, since I know my playing is at the best indifferent.'

'Not at all, not at all. We are none of us Tartinis. Your sense of time is quite admirable; and if you have a fault, which I do not assert, it is that you might sometimes tune a quarter of a tone or less on the sharp side. But my ear is far from perfect: a pitch-pipe or a tuning-fork would have infinitely more authority.'

'How I hope it is good,' said Martin, looking anxiously at the novel. 'False commendation can never have the weight of heartfelt praise. I do not dislike the first page. May I read it to you?'

'If you please.'

> *'Marriage has many virtues,' said Edmund, 'and one not often remarked upon by bachelors is that it helps to persuade a man that he is neither omniscient nor even infallible. A husband has but to utter a wish for it to be denied, countered, crossed, contradicted; or to hear the word* But, *followed by a pause, a very short pause in general, while the reasons that this wish should not be observed are marshalled – it is misconceived, contrary to his best interests, contrary to his real desires.'*
>
> *'So I have very often heard you say, Mr Vernon,' said his wife. 'But you do not consider that a wife is commonly less well educated, usually poorer and always physically weaker than her husband; and that without she assert her existence she is in danger of being wholly engulfed.'*

'If he does not object,' said Stephen, 'I should very much like to read it, when my mind is at rest. But Martin, my mind is not at rest. You know my concern for Padeen.'

'Of course I do, and I share it. I was there, you recall, when first he came aboard, poor dear fellow, and I have liked him ever since. You have news of him?'

'I have. Adams went to the man John Paulton told us about, and this is the record he was given.' He handed the paper. It looked something like a business account, with amounts carried forward from one column to another, but the numbers were those of lashes, days of close confinement in the black hole, the weight of punishment-irons and their duration.

'Oh my God,' said Martin, grasping its full significance. 'Two hundred lashes . . . it is utterly inhuman.'

'This is an utterly inhuman place. The social contract is destroyed; and the damage that must do to people much under the rank of saint is incalculable,' said Stephen. 'But listen, Martin, he is soon to be assigned to the flogging parson I met at Government House, and the clerk, an old experienced hand, a ticket-of-leave man, says he will not survive that regimen above a year. Now my impression is that Mr Paulton told us that the clerks could change an assignment – that Painter himself had sent valuable farm servants rather than ignorant townspeople to Woolloo-Woolloo, presumably for a douceur.'

'That is my impression too.'

'He was quite right about information. Painter was obliging, quick and efficient. So what I very earnestly beg you will do is to go back to Mr Paulton tomorrow, put Padeen's case candidly before him and ask first whether Painter is indeed capable of changing the assignment and secondly whether he – your friend – would agree to receive Padeen at Woolloo-Woolloo when he returns to take charge.'

'Of course: I shall go as soon as he is likely to be up. Do you mean to see Padeen?'

'I am turning the question in my mind. Inclination says yes, obviously: caution says no, for fear of an outbreak on his part, for fear of attracting attention to what must pass unnoticed. But caution I know is an old woman at times; and I am still undecided.'

He lay undecided much of the night, sometimes reading Paulton's MS, sometimes reflecting on the wisest course, so that he was still watching the flame of his candle, guttering now, when there was something of a hullabaloo on deck: scuffling, running feet, a confusion of voices and then Mr Bulkeley's distinct cry, far forward, 'Come out of that, you goddam sods.'

But the ship in port, with her standing rigging being replaced, a variety of repairs in course and her decks all ahoo, was relaxed in appearance and in discipline, and a noise of this kind did not disturb his mind; he continued to watch the flame until it expired. Sleep, faintly pierced by the sound of bells.

'Good morning, Tom,' he said, coming out of his cabin at the accustomed number.

'Good morning, Doctor,' said Pullings, the only man at table. 'Did you hear the roaring in the middle watch?'

'Fairly well. A bloodless frolic, I trust?'

'Only by the grace of God. It was your little girls: they came running aboard and startled the harbour-watch about three bells. They called out for Jemmy Ducks, but he being dead drunk and insensible they whipped up into the foretop and when Oakes and the rest of the watch tried to catch them they flung down the top-maul, which very nearly did him in, together with anything else they could lay their hands on. And they kept roaring out that they would not leave the ship.'

'I did hear the bosun call them goddam sods, but it never occurred to me that he could mean Sarah and Emily.'

'Then they threw off their white frocks and drawers and went up to the crosstrees, where you could not see them in the dark night, they being so very black. They are still there, like kittens that have climbed a tree and cannot tell how to get down again. We have spread a splinter-netting to catch them in case they fall.'

Stephen digested this, drank his gun-room coffee – nothing like as good as Killick's – and asked, 'Has Mr Martin gone ashore?'

'Yes. He went very early, I believe: Davidge heard him singing out for hot water as soon as it was light.'

'Steward,' called Stephen. 'Pray bring more toast. Softtack is a delight, do you not find?'

'Oh Lord, yes. When you have been five months on ship's bread you can hardly have enough of it. But Doctor, what about your little girls?'

'What about them indeed? The marmalade, if you please.'

'Since Jemmy Ducks is still unsteady and not much of a topman at the best of times, do you think Bonden should jump up to the crosstrees? He is a rare one for going aloft, and they know him very well.'

'Oh, as for that, hunger and thirst will bring them down. I am certainly not going to scale ladders trembling in the wind, as I have done in my youth, only to see the little cat skip down of its own accord when I was within hand's reach at last. Let no one take any notice of them, nor look up.'

In the event it was neither hunger nor thirst that brought them down but a mounting urgency. Through the earlier part of the forenoon watch they often cried out that they would not come down, that they would stay in the ship for ever, and that the girls in the orphanage were an ill-looking pack of swabs. But after a while they fell silent. They had been very strictly trained to cleanliness aboard; their lively sense of the sacred and perhaps of taboo was concerned; and it was with a voice of great earnestness that Emily called, 'On deck, there. I want to go to the head. So does Sal. We can't wait.'

The ship's company looked at Stephen, who replied, 'Come down, then. And when you have been to the head, you are to go straight to your hammocks. We shall not turn you ashore.'

Shortly after this Martin returned, and since there were people busy all over the after part of the ship Stephen suggested that they should walk to Dawes Point and view the hospital. 'I found John at home,' said Martin as soon as they were on the wharf, 'and I laid the matter before him, clearly and I think fairly. I said that Padeen was your sick-berth attendant; that because of very severe pain he had been treated with laudanum; that because of inadvertence he had access to the bottle and that without any great moral obliquity he dosed himself, became a confirmed opium-eater; that when you were away in the Baltic, or rather when the ship was on her way back, he was deprived of his supply, and being unable to explain himself, with his defect of speech and rudimentary English, he robbed a Scotch apothecary's shop, for which he was condemned to death, transportation being substituted for the gallows at Captain Aubrey's instance. I added that I had always found him a good and unusually gentle man, very much devoted to you; and I said that as an Irish Catholic he was likely to suffer extremely in the hands of such a man as Marsden. John listened with close attention and he emphatically agreed with my last point. I then asked your other questions. Oh, as for the change, said he, that was only a matter of half a guinea in the right place, and that he for his part was more than willing to make Padeen's life less horrible. "But," he went on, "this poor fellow has been repeatedly punished for absconding. Has Dr Maturin reflected that if he should escape from here, my position for the next year would be intolerable?"'

'The next year?' asked Stephen.

'Yes, since in his present condition John cannot afford to take ship and carry the manuscript back to London himself. He is obliged to send it; and as the voyage takes four or five months each way, while he still has to finish the book and the publisher must be allowed some time to read it and arrange terms with the friend who acts for John, a year seems quite a modest estimate. So he asked whether you would guarantee that Padeen does not escape for that period.'

Stephen reflected for a hundred yards, sometimes gazing at the shabby, disgraceful building on the point, though his mind did not stray from its search for what might lie behind Paulton's words and Martin's presentation of them. *Abscond* was the word almost always used in New South Wales: here it was *escape*. But where one had to proceed by half-tone and nuance, where one wished to reach a tacit agreement, it was folly to call for exact definition.

'No,' he said, coming to a halt outside the hospital gates, 'I cannot guarantee that Padeen will not escape any more than I can guarantee that the wind will not blow. But I will place the cost of a passage home in Mr Paulton's hands, which I conceive deals with the eventuality of an escape. And I will propose a – what is the word? acknowledgment, perhaps: in any case a present, a gratification – if he will dedicate this book, which is more a disquisition on the status of women in an ideal society and a discussion of the currently accepted contract between the sexes than what is ordinarily called a novel or tale – if he will dedicate this book to Lavoisier, who was kind to me when I was young: Diana and I are much attached to his widow, and I am sure it would give her great pleasure. Martin, you understand the present state of these matters far better than I do, being so much more at home with men of letters, so I beg you will advise me on the nature of this acknowledgment, bearing in mind that I am not alone in wishing to honour Lavoisier's memory – I can draw on at least a dozen Fellows of our society.'

The hospital gates opened and a black-coated man in a physical wig rode out on a stout cob. He gave Stephen, who was in uniform, a sharp look, checked his horse, but then rode on. 'I presume that is Dr Redfern,' said Stephen, and his mind was so taken up with reasons for and against calling on him that he scarcely heard any part of Martin's observations on the market in dedications except for his hesitant naming of a sum.

'You are hardly generous to your friend or to Lavoisier's memory,' he said. 'But it so happens that I have something in that order of magnitude with me, in Bank of England notes; which is so much better than promises or a draught on a distant bank. May I trespass still farther on your kindness and beg you to put these propositions to your friend? You will feel any reticence, the first shade of reluctance or offence, before I should do so: you will not mistake the formal for the real. Let us go back to the ship, and I shall put these notes in a cover, so that you may have them with you. I must go back in any case, to shave and put on buckled shoes for Government House. Did I tell you that those wicked creatures escaped from their orphanage and came back to the *Surprise* in the middle watch, declaring that they should never leave her again?'

'Heavens, no! Do you mean to take them back?'

'I do not. On my part the move was one of those reasonable, wise, profoundly mistaken actions, influenced to some extent by my esteem for Mrs Macquarie. I must now go and present my excuses with what face I can put on it, and she having been so kind.'

'What did the little girls object to?'

'Everything, but particularly the fact that some of the other children were black.'

Although Stephen's sallow face was almost pink with close shaving and although his wig was powdered, Her Excellency was not at home. He had been fully prepared for the interview, with excuses, explanations, thanks all to hand; and now, feeling oddly put out, he walked down the drive, only slightly encouraged by the sight of a cockatoo new to him landing in a gum-tree and raising a crest like his own familiar hoopoe. 'Shall I ever, at any time, get out of this sink of iniquity and travel inland with a fowling-piece and a collecting-case?' he asked the kangaroo. Only a little way below Government House the ugly crowds of convicts and soldiers reappeared, enlivened, but only a little, by Surprises ashore. He made his way slowly through them to Riley's hotel and called for a tint of whiskey. It was the man of the house who brought it and on seeing Stephen he cried, 'Why, it is your honour again, and a very good day to you, sir. How well your honour is looking.'

'Tell me, Mr Riley,' said Stephen, 'is there ever an honest horse-coper in this town? Or at least one that merits Purgatory rather than Hell? I saw a yard called Wilkins Brothers with some animals in it, but they did not look quite wholesome to me.'

'Sure they are only purple dromedaries, sir.'

'Ah? They looked quite like horses to me: but miserable screws I will admit.'

'I meant the Wilkins brothers, sir. I take it your honour is not in the penal line?'

'Faith, no. I am the surgeon of that frigate down there.'

'And an elegant ship I am sure she is. But here in the colony by purple dromedaries we mean little small bungling pickpockets, jackeens that get transported for robbing the poor-box or a blind man's tray. You was thinking of hiring, I do suppose?'

'We are here for something like a month, so buying and selling again might be the more easy.'

'Oh more easy by far, with the creature always under your hand, and she used to you.'

'Why do you say she?'

'Because I have three beautiful mares behind the gable of the house itself, and any one of them would carry you fifty Irish miles a day for your month on end.'

They were all three long past mark of mouth, but Stephen settled for a flea-bitten grey with an amiable face and a comfortable walk, the pace she was most likely to travel at, and a somewhat more ancient but very steady bay for Martin, who was no great horseman.

On the grey he rode towards Parramatta; but scarcely was he clear of the houses, barracks and hovels than he met Jack Aubrey and the carpenter. He turned back with them, and learnt that their voyage could hardly be called a success: the spars were there, and remarkable timber too, said the carpenter; but as they were government property it appeared that authority would have to be sought from a number of sources, and Mr Jenks, whose consent had to be obtained first, was not in the way. 'Obstruction at every infernal step,' said Jack. 'How I hate an official.' But his face cleared when Stephen told him of the little girls' escape and asked whether he disliked having them aboard.

'Never in life,' he said. 'I quite like to see them skipping about. They are far better than wombats. Last time we touched here, you bought a wombat, you remember, and it ate my hat. That was in the *Leopard*: Lord, the horrible old *Leopard*, how she griped!' He laughed at the memory, but Stephen saw that he was not his old self: there was an underlying resentment, and he looked yellowish, far from well.

As they were parting to leave their horses at different stables, Jack said, 'Surely it is a very shocking thing for both Governor and Lieutenant-Governor to be away at the same time. I cannot get any sense out of Colonel MacPherson. How I wish I knew when Macquarie was coming back.'

'I mean to wait on Mrs Macquarie again tomorrow, and perhaps she will tell me,' said Stephen.

In the morning, trim once more, but this time with a face not only smooth but with a look of unusual satisfaction, or contained hopefulness, because Martin had come back with a most gratifying account of his interview: John Paulton wholly accepted both proposals – was infinitely touched that Dr Maturin should think his book the proper vehicle for a tribute to M. de Lavoisier, whose death he too had deplored – would welcome Padeen and put him to some gentle task such as watching the lambs – and he sent a graceful note with a postscript reminding Stephen of their engagement for Sunday, which he looked forward to with the keenest delight. More than this, within three-quarters of an hour of leaving the ship, Adams returned with word that the change of assignment had been made. There was no difficulty about it at all; and any other request on the part of the gentleman would receive the promptest attention.

He greeted the lodge-keeper and the saluting sentry (for he was in uniform, his best) and walked up the drive. Beyond the kangaroo he saw Dr Redfern walking down it, and when they were at a proper distance he took off his hat, saying, 'Dr Redfern, I believe? My name is Maturin, surgeon of the *Surprise*.'

'How do you do, sir?' said Redfern, his stern face breaking into a smile as he returned the salute. 'Your name is familiar to me from your writings, and I am very happy to meet you. May I be of any service to you in this remote corner of the world? I have a fair experience of its ways and its diseases.'

'Dear colleague, you are very good, and in fact there is a kindness you could do me. I should very much like to see my former loblolly-boy, Patrick Colman: he was transported, and now it seems he is in your hospital. If you would leave word at the gate that I am to be admitted, I should be most grateful.'

'An Irishman, with a complex dysphony and little English, an absconder?'

'The same.'

'If you will come with me, I will take you there myself: I am on my way. But no doubt you were going to Government House?'

'I have to call on Her Excellency.'

'I am afraid it would be a call in vain: I have just been to see her, and she must keep her bed some days longer.'

They walked down together, Dr Redfern greeted on every hand, and they talked with barely a pause. At one point Stephen said, 'What you say about liver is particularly interesting. I do not like my captain's at all, and should be glad of your opinion,' and at another he said, 'There is another of those vessels emitting smoke. Is it a fumigation against pests, against disease?'

'It is sulphur burning to bring out hidden convicts or choke them to death. Many of the poor devils try to stow away. Every ship leaving is smoked and every boat is stopped by the party at South Head.' But most of the time they spoke about such matters as the thin-thread ligature of arteries, Abernethy's triumphs, and the *Proceedings of the Royal Society*.

When they came nearer Dawes Point Redfern's cheerfulness declined and he said, 'I am ashamed to display this hospital in all its squalid nakedness. Happily Governor and Mrs Macquarie are engaged on a new building.' As they walked in he said, 'Colman is in the small ward on the right. His back is healing, but there is a dejection of spirits and an utter neglect of food that makes me anxious: I hope your visit may comfort him.'

'Do you happen to know whether there are any other Irishmen in the ward?'

'Not now. We lost both others a week ago, and since then he has had almost no company. His dysphony increases in English, what little English he has.'

'Certainly. On a good day he is positively fluent in Irish, and he sings it without a check.'

'You speak the language, sir, I collect?'

'Indifferently; it is a child's knowledge, no more. But he understands me.'

'I shall leave you together while I look at the other men with my attendants: you will feel no constraint, I trust.'

There was a gathering in the hall and then they went in, Redfern accompanied by his dresser and two nurses. Padeen was on the right hand, at the end of a row of quite wide-spaced beds, by the window. He was lying on his belly, so nearly asleep that he did not move when Redfern drew back the sheet covering him. 'As you see,' said Redfern, 'the skin is healing – little inflammation: bone almost entirely covered. Earlier floggings had rendered it coriaceous. We treat with tepid sponging and wool-fat. Mr Herold' – to the dresser – 'we will leave Colman for the moment and see to the amputations.'

It was not the half-flayed back that wounded Stephen, who like any naval surgeon had seen the results of many a flogging, though never on such a monstrous scale, so much as the extreme emaciation. Padeen had been a fine upstanding fellow, thirteen or fourteen stone, perhaps: now his ribs stood out under the scars and he would barely weigh eight. Padeen's face was turned towards him on the pillow: eyes closed, head skull-like.

Stephen laid a firm, authoritative medical hand on his back and said low in his ear, 'Never stir now. God and Mary be with you, Padeen.'

'God and Mary and Patrick be with you, Doctor,' came the slow, almost dreaming reply: the eye opened, a singularly sweet smile lit that famine-time face and he said, 'I knew you would come.' He held Stephen's hand. 'Quiet, now, Padeen,' said Stephen: he waited until the convulsive trembling had stopped and went on, 'Listen, Padeen, my dear. Say nothing to any man at all, nothing. But you are going to a place where you will be more kindly treated, and there I shall see you again. There I shall see you again. Till then you must eat all you can, do you hear me now, Padeen. And till then God be with you, God and Mary be with you.'

Stephen walked out, more moved than he had believed possible; and still, as he walked back to the ship after a particularly interesting conversation with Dr Redfern, he found that his mind was not as cool and steady as he could have wished. A lorikeet, or what he took for a lorikeet, flying from a clump of banksia changed its current for a moment. So did the sound of music in the cabin, which he heard well before he crossed the brow.

It was Jack and Martin, studying particular passages of the D minor quartet: Stephen observed that the viola's sound was mellower than usual, and at the same time he remembered their engagement to dine with John Paulton. Fortunately he was already dressed.

'I have just seen Padeen in the hospital,' he said; and in answer to their enquiries, 'He is in very good hands. Dr Redfern is an admirable man. He told me a great deal about the local diseases, many brought about it appears by the dust, and about the convicts' state of mind. In spite of their failings they are always kind and tender to one of their fellows that has been flogged, and ease his sufferings as much as they can.'

'I remember when I was disrated and turned before the mast when I was a boy,' said Jack, 'that when a man had had a dozen at the gangway his messmates were invariably very good to him – grog, sweet-oil for his back, anything they could think of.'

'Dr Redfern also gave me directions for our projected journey,' said Stephen, taking out his 'cello, 'and will send me letters to some of the respectable or at least intelligent settlers.'

'You did mention a journey before we crossed Capricorn,' said Jack, 'but I have forgotten just what you had in mind.'

'Since the ship is likely to be here for about a month,' said Stephen, 'I thought that with your leave we should travel inland towards the Blue Mountains and back in a southern sweep to Botany Bay for perhaps a fortnight, come aboard to see whether our services are needed, and then make a northern tour, passing by Paulton's place, until she is ready to sail.'

'With all my heart,' said Jack. 'And I hope you will find a phoenix on her nest.'

Chapter Ten

'We seem to have been living this life of wandering tinkers for ever,' said Stephen, 'and I must confess it suits me very well – no peevish bells, no responsibilities, no care for the morrow, wholly dependent on the benevolence of others or of Providence.'

'So long that I have almost come to like this starve-acre landscape,' said Martin, looking over plain, covered, where it was covered at all, with thin coarse grass and low bushes, with gum-trees of various kinds standing here and there, the whole, in spite of the tracts of bare sandstone rubble, giving a general impression of a dull silvery grey-green, hot, dry and brilliantly lit. It seemed completely empty at first, but far over to the south-east a keen eye, or better a small spy-glass, could make out a group of kangaroos of the largest kind, while troups of white cockatoos moved among the taller, more distant trees. 'I sound ungrateful,' Martin went on, 'for not only has it fed me very well – such quails, such chops! – but it is a naturalist's treasure-house, and Heaven knows how many unknown plants that worthy ass is carrying, to say nothing of bird-skins. I only mean that it is wanting in wild romantic prospects or indeed anything that makes a countryside worth looking at, apart from its flora and fauna.'

'Blaxland assured me that there were wild romantic prospects farther into the Blue Mountains,' said Stephen. And for a while they ate steadily: they were dining on grilled wombat (all their meals were necessarily grilled or roasted) and it ate like tender lamb. 'There they go!' he cried. 'And the dingoes after them.' The kangaroos vanished in a fold of the plain half a mile away, moving at a prodigious speed, and the dingoes, which had presumably relied on surprise, gave up the hopeless chase. 'Well you may say starve-acre,' said Stephen, looking east and west. 'I remember Banks telling me that when first they saw New Holland and sailed along its shore the country made him think of a lean cow, with bare scraggy protuding hip-bones. Now you know very well what affection and esteem I have for Sir Joseph; and I have the utmost respect for Captain Cook too, that intrepid scientific mariner. But what possessed them to recommend this part of the world to Government as a colony I cannot tell – Cook, who was brought up on a farm; Banks, who was a landowner; both of them able men and both of them having seen great stretches of its desolation. What infatuation, what wilful . . .' He broke off, and Martin said, 'Perhaps it seemed more promising after so many thousand miles of sea.'

After a silence Stephen reverted to their wandering life. 'What a time it seems!' he said. 'Our faces – forgive me, Martin – have already assumed something of that raw brick-red so usual in New South Wales; and I think we have seen everything our predecessors have seen . . .'

'The emu! The echidna!' cried Martin.

'. . . except the platypus. Blaxland assured me it was not to be found in his neighbourhood, but that it was not uncommon in the streams nearer the coast. He had never seen it, and indeed knew no more than I: it is strange that so remarkable an animal should be so little known in Europe. I have only seen Banks's dried specimen – no dissection possible – and read Home's superficial paper in the *Transactions*, together with Shaw's description, neither based on a living animal. Conceivably our next river – our last, alas – will yield one.'

'How kind Mr Blaxland was, and what a splendid dinner he gave us,' said Martin. 'I know I speak like a man whose god is his belly, but this riding and walking and searching for specimens after so many months at sea gives one the appetite of an ogre.'

'He was indeed,' said Stephen, 'and where we should have been without him I cannot tell: this is no country to lose one's way in. After one day of wandering in the worst kind of bush, we should have ridden tamely home, if we had survived at all.'

Mr Blaxland, a fellow-member of the Royal Society with a large holding inland from Sydney, had made them heartily welcome, and had warned them of the danger of getting lost. Just to the south of his land there were great stretches of a kind of scrub where the leaves joined overhead, where sense of direction was easily lost, and where the parched ground was littered with the bones of absconders. He had lent them an ass to carry their already overflowing collections and Ben, a morose bearded middle-aged Aboriginal, who showed them a hundred edible plants, led them within shot of their dinner as though the desolate featureless plain were marked with signposts, pointed out a whole sparsely-inhabited and to their eyes almost invisible zoological garden, made fire, and sometimes, when they were to wait for some nocturnal serpent, lizard, opossum, koala, wombat, he built them huts from the great sheets of bark that hung from the gum-trees or lay at their feet.

For reasons that did not appear he was much attached to Mr Blaxland; but he was not attached to Stephen or Martin and he was often impatient at their stupidity. He had picked up some Newgate English from the convicts, and as they stared at what seemed to them an undisturbed patch of shale and dead grass he would say, 'Buggers can't see fucking track. Blind, no-see sods.'

'And certainly,' said Stephen, reverting to Blaxland, 'it was a noble dinner. But of all the dinners we have eaten during this journey the one I enjoyed most took place before ever we set out. For a dinner to be more than usually successful it seems to me that the host must be more than usually cheerful, and Mr Paulton was in as fine a flow of spirits as could be imagined. And how well he played! He and Aubrey dashed away as if they were inventing the music by common accord;

it was a delight to hear.' He smiled at the recollection, and then added, 'You did have the impression, did you not, that he was happy to know nothing about Padeen's evasion?'

'More than that: he told me privately that managed with discretion it would be thought he had gone to join his friends in the bush, living with the blacks.'

'You rejoice my heart,' said Stephen. 'And speaking of blacks, it occurs to me that some of our difficulty in communicating with this one,' – nodding towards Ben, who sat at some distance with his back turned – 'quite apart from language, is the fact that he and his people have no notion of property. Each tribe has its frontiers, to be sure, but within that territory everything is common; and seeing that they have no herds, no fields, but walk about all the time for their living, any possessions other than their spears and throwing-sticks would be a useless burden. To us property, real or symbolical, is fundamental; its absence is known to be misery, its presence is thought to be happiness. The language of our minds is wholly different.'

Ben said, 'Shut up. Get on horse.'

They saddled their patient old mares – Ben had nothing to say to straps and buckles: he was a guide and protector of fools for Blaxland's sake, in no way a servant. Indeed, his world did not include the man-and-master relation at all; and nothing that they could give him did he want. Mounting, they rode slowly on towards their last river.

Their last river offered neither water nor platypus; they walked across dryshod. But the monotonous plain had been sloping gently down for some hours and now there were many more trees, and better grown, so that the landscape could without very much exaggeration be said to resemble a park, a dull, ill-tended park. Not altogether without cheer however, for in one of the taller trees Ben showed them a truly enormous lizard clinging motionless to the trunk, convinced it could not be seen: he would not let them shoot it, nor would he use one of the half-dozen spears he carried. He appeared to say that the reptile was his aunt, though this may have been an error of interpretation; in any event the lizard, having been stared at for twenty minutes, suddenly lost its head, rushed up the tree, fell together with a long strip of loose bark, stood open-mouthed, defying them for a moment, and then raced away over the grass, high on its short legs.

'He was a pleurodont,' said Martin.

'So he was. And he had a forked tongue too: one of the monitory kind, for sure.'

This kept them cheerful for the rest of the afternoon, and the next day, having looked at Banks's Botany Bay, they rode into Sydney. The horses made straight for their stable, the ass with them; and in the more squalid outskirts Ben met a group of fellow-tribesmen, some wearing clothes. They walked with him to the hotel, talking away at a great rate; and once there Stephen said, 'Mr Riley, Ben here, from Mr Blaxland's, has been with us these ten days: pray give him whatever is right.'

'Rum,' said Ben in a loud harsh voice.

'Do not let him do himself too much harm, Mr Riley,' said Stephen, and taking the ass's bridle he went on, 'This is Mr Blaxland's ass: I shall send him back by a sailor, to be collected when one of his waggons comes down.'

'Good evening, Mr Davidge,' he said as he stepped aboard and saluted the quarterdeck. 'Would you be so good as to have these bundles carried below with the utmost care? Mr Martin, may I beg you to see that the skins, particularly the emus' skins, are laid very gently in the Captain's store-room? The smell will soon go off; he will not mind it. I must go and report our return. And then, Mr Davidge, may I trouble you for a sober, steady, reliable hand – Plaice, for example – to lead this ass back to Riley's?'

'Well, Doctor, I dare say I can find somebody in his right wits, but Plaice is lashed into his hammock for the moment, having been pumped over – you can hear him singing 'Greensleeves' if you bend your ear forward.'

Stephen could also hear the strong authoritative voice of Captain Aubrey addressing someone in the cabin in formal terms, someone who certainly did not belong to the ship. At the same time he also became aware of the nervous tension aboard – anxious looks, furtive whispering, and the whole ship's company or very nearly so gathered at the stations they would occupy if the frigate were to get under way.

'Tell the gentleman who sent you that this note is improperly addressed, improperly phrased, and cannot be received. Good day to you, sir,' said Captain Aubrey, clear in the still air. Doors opened and closed. An army officer, his face as red as his coat, came out, made an unsmiling return to Davidge's salute and crossed the brow. The moment he touched the land Stephen's ass began a heartbroken shuddering bray and all the Shelmerstonians and some of the less respectful man-of-war's men burst into a rare cackle of laughter, stumping about and clawing one another on the back.

Tom Pullings shot up on deck like a jack-in-the-box and roared out, 'Silence fore and aft. Silence, there: d'ye hear me?' with such extreme vehemence and indignation that the cackle stopped dead; and in the silence Stephen made his way to the cabin.

Jack was sitting behind the piles of papers usual in port for a captain who was also his own purser, but his stern expression changed to a smile when the door opened and he said, 'Why, there you are, Stephen. How glad I am to see you: we had not looked for you until tomorrow. I hope you had a pleasant trip?'

'Very pleasant, I thank you: Blaxland did everything that was kind and hospitable – he desires his best compliments, by the way – and we saw the emu, various kinds of kangaroo, the echidna – good Lord, the echidna! – the small fat grey animal that sleeps high up in gum-trees and that very absurdly claims to be a bear, a great many of the parrot tribe, a nameless monitory lizard, all that we had hoped to see and more, except for the platypus.'

'An agreeable countryside, however, upon the whole?'

'Why, as for that, it is of the first interest to the botanist, and its animals fill one with joy and amazement: the economy of the echidna is scarcely to be believed. But as for countryside, I do not think I have seen anything so dismal or more like my idea of the plains of Purgatory. Perhaps it may improve with rain: at present everything is parched. Even the stream between Botany Bay and here was dry. But Jack, you look angerly.'

'I am angerly. I am in fact so exceedingly out of temper that I can scarcely command my mind and keep it steady to its paper-work,' said Jack, and Stephen, with a sinking heart, saw that he was if anything understating the case. 'When Tom and I were away looking at some timber with Chips a party of soldiers came down with two officers: they said there was an escaped convict aboard and they insisted on looking for him at once, without waiting for my return. They had a magistrate's warrant. Most of our people were on shore-leave or away in the boats, bringing stores: the party was strong, and headed by a captain. West, who was in charge, no longer holds a commission as you know, so what with that and with the likelihood of our being made to look ridiculous if we resisted, he confined himself to making the strongest possible protest, uttered before witnesses, and walked off the ship. They searched her. They had some old Sydney Cove hands with them and they found the man almost at once: they marched him away, sobbing fit to break your heart, said little Reade, who met them as he was coming down from the town. You could recognize the man by the raw bloody places about his ankles, where the irons had been.'

'Was he a friend of some of our people?'

'I am sure he was, but of which there is no telling. No one is going to get himself or his shipmates into trouble, and if you ask questions you will only get that "Don't know, sir" with a glassy look to one side of your head I have heard aboard every ship I ever served in. But think of it, Stephen

297

– to search a King's ship without her captain's permission: it is monstrous!'

'It is indeed extraordinarily offensive.'

'And then they tried to justify themselves by some miserable quibbling over the *Surprise*'s status; but I told them that they were as ignorant of naval law as they were of good manners, that a ship hired by His Majesty and commanded by one of his officers had all the rights of a man-of-war on the establishment, and I named the instances of *Ariadne, Beaver, Hecate* and *Fly*, which clapped a stopper over all.'

'Jack, I hope and trust you did not commit yourself?'

'No. Like King Charles, I do not want to go on my travels again – Lord, they were bitter travels, Stephen – and I kept as cool as a judge. Or as cool as a judge ought to be,' he said, remembering a malignant rambling red-faced ranting old fool at Guildhall in a judge's wig and gown.

'When you say *they*, do you mean the soldiers?'

'No. It is the civilians, the people who have been in the colony a long while and who are well entrenched, together with their allies. They are called the Macarthur clan, and they can make Colonel MacPherson sign any paper they put in front of him. The young fellow I sent away just now brought a note saying that to prevent any further unfortunate incident the authorities intended placing sentries at the brows – a note MacPherson had had to put his name to and the unfortunate lieutenant had to bring. This is one of the reasons we are about to cast off fore and aft and warp out into the cove again. I am damned if I walk in and out of my own ship between a couple of redcoats. But there is another reason too,' he went on in a lower tone. 'That young fool Hopkins, maintopman, starboard watch, smuggled a girl aboard last night, a ticket-of-leave barmaid. By a great stroke of luck West happened to hear her giggling in the cable-tier and we smuggled her ashore again in double-quick time, unseen. Hopkins is in irons, and I shall have the hide off him as soon as we are warped out.'

'Oh no, Jack; no more flogging in this horrible place, I beseech you.'

'Eh? Well, no; perhaps not: I see what you mean. Come in,' he cried.

Reade, very grave, said, 'Captain Pullings' duty, sir, and all is laid along.'

'Thank you, Mr Reade,' said Jack. 'My compliments to Captain Pullings, and I desire he will carry on.'

A moment later nautical cries broke out on the quarter-deck with the due responses fore and aft, the whole interspersed with the sound of bosun's calls, now sharp and cutting, now an eerie wail: the complex process of getting a ship under way, with all its rituals. Jack's attention was fixed on the sequence of events and during this time Stephen considered his face: the whites of his eyes were yellowish; his stern expression had not softened at all at the sight of Reade, as it usually did; and although he had spoken with a good deal of anger it was clear that there was a great deal more as yet unexpressed. Even more than most sailors Jack resented any hint of disrespect to the service: this had been very gross, and it came in an atmosphere of evident ill-will.

The bars of the capstan had been shipped long since, and now it began turning, but with no great exertion, no fife or fiddle, only the sound of bare feet. The wharf slid gently aft, dwindling in size; the view from the scuttle opposite Stephen increased until Government House was within its frame; then the frigate turned eight points to starboard and there was Government House once more, together with much of the settlement, in the broad sweep of the stern-window.

'I shall be glad to be out in the cove,' said Jack. 'It makes much more work, carrying and fetching, but even so . . . Stephen, you would not believe how stupid, reckless and wanton seamen can be. Here is Hopkins with his wench immediately after that wretched business with the soldiers, when a moment's reflexion would have told him that in the first place it was criminal on his part to bring her aboard at all and secondly that it would put us all in the wrong. And I have little doubt that if we had stayed tied up to the side some other young fool would have been at it again. Or half a dozen fools, young or old. You would not believe it.'

None of this was news to Stephen. He knew the consequences of a stay in port rather better than Jack and the extraordinary lengths to which men would go to satisfy their desires. He knew that this urge was concentrated by months at sea and perhaps by the injudicious diet – six pounds of meat a week, however indifferently preserved, was far too much – and even on the quarterdeck, where some degree of education might be expected to soften manners and inculcate restraint he had known officers risk a truly happy marriage in stupid, reckless and wanton fornication. This was no time to impart his knowledge to Jack, however: it was not even a time to ask him to put out his tongue and give an account of his entrails.

After a while he said, 'By the way, how are the little girls? I hope they have given you no trouble.'

'They are very well indeed, I believe; and no trouble at all. I have seen nothing of them, almost. They never come on deck until after dark for fear of being seized, but I hear them singing down below.'

'And what of Paulton? Did you have any news of him while we were away?'

'Oh yes,' said Jack, his face brightening somewhat. 'He called to take his leave some days ago: he has to go back to his cousin's place along the coast, not far from Bird Island. He hoped we would come to see him by boat, or if that were impossible, that you would look in on him during your northern trip. What a very agreeable evening we had with him, upon my word! Such a jovial companion, and such a hand with his violin. How glad I was I insisted upon playing second fiddle: even so, he put me to the blush.'

News that the ship was moored came below, and presently Stephen said, 'Jack, tomorrow I must wait on Mrs Macquarie and try to make my excuses at last. But before that, before breakfast indeed, I should like to examine you to find whether your plethory is wholly digested, and prescribe physic if it is not.'

'Very well. But I tell you what it is, Stephen: we sail on the twenty-fourth. Even if the Governor is back by then, which I think very likely, and even if everything then goes more smoothly, which I think possible, I have decided to renounce some of the repairs and to sail with the change of the moon: I am sorry if it cuts your journey short or interferes with your plans.'

'Not at all. I shall start a little earlier, tomorrow itself, perhaps; and unless we are devoured by some nondescript wild beast or get lost in the worst kind of bush, to which the Labyrinth is child's play and the maze at Hampton Court an inconsiderable toy, we shall be back on the twenty-third. I shall tell Padeen when we pass by Paulton's place.'

'What now?' called Jack, turning to the door.

'Here's a damned thing, sir,' cried Pullings. 'The guards at South Point insisted on examining the blue cutter – tried to stop it – Oakes who was in charge said he would blow out the brains of the first man that laid a hand on the gunwale.'

'Quite right too. The boat was wearing a jack?'

'Yes, sir.'

'That makes it more monstrous still. I shall report it to the Admiralty; I shall raise it in the House. Hell and death, they will be opening my letters and dispatches next, and sleeping in my cot.'

Once more Stephen, brushed, dressed, shaved and powdered to the height of Killick's lofty standards, sent in his card, and this time, although Her Excellency was engaged, he was particularly desired to wait: she would be free in five minutes. The five minutes stretched out to ten and the hall door opened to admit his cousin James Fitzgerald, a somewhat worldly priest, nominally a member of the Fathers of the Faith, a Portuguese order. They looked at one another with a cat-like determination not to show surprise but their greeting and their embrace was affectionate: they had after all spent many a happy day running about the Galtee Mountains together from the house of a grand-uncle common to both. They now exchanged some family news, worked out just when they had last met, which was also in an ante-room, that of the Patriarch of Lisbon, and then James said, 'Stephen, forgive me if I am indiscreet, but I hear you may be going northward, by way of Woolloo-Woolloo, presently.'

'Do you, Coz?'

'And if that should be so, may I advise you to take great care? There is a band of absconders, United Irishmen, hard men, living between there and Newcastle, and some of them think you may have changed sides since ninety-eight. You were seen on the deck of an English ship that chased Gough into the Solway Firth: and after he had been hanged some of his friends were transported.'

'They cannot be men who ever knew me. I was always totally opposed to violence in Ireland, and I deplored the rising. I begged Cousin Edward not to use force. And even now Catholic emancipation and the dissolution of the union – acts of parliament, no more – would deal with the situation. But Buonaparte's tyranny is something new in its kind – far, far more thorough and intelligent – and in this case force is the only remedy. I am willing to help anyone to bring him down; and so, as I know very well, are you and your order. His success would be the ruin of Europe; his help fatal to Ireland. Yet never, never, never in my life have I played the informer.'

Before Father Fitzgerald could reply, a footman came in and said, 'Dr Maturin, sir, if you please.'

'Dr Maturin,' said Mrs Macquarie, 'I am so very sorry to have kept you waiting. Poor Colonel MacPherson was with me in such a state of anxiety.' She looked as though she were going to say more, but changing her mind she asked Maturin to sit down and went on, 'Well, and so you have been travelling about in the bush. I hope you liked it.'

'It was an exceedingly interesting experience, ma'am; we

survived, thanks to an intelligent black, and we brought back an ass-load of specimens that will keep us busy for the next twelvemonth and more. But before I say anything else, allow me to make my most humble apologies for the behaviour of those wicked little girls. It was a truly wretched return for your kindness, and I blush at the recollection.'

'It did not altogether surprise me, I must confess. They were as wild as young hawks, poor little things: and even before they lost their heads, bit the matron, broke the window and climbed down the outside of the house – how they managed not to break their legs as well I cannot tell – they said they did not like the company of girls; they far preferred being with men. Should you like to try again, perhaps?'

'No, ma'am, though I thank you very heartily. I do not think it would answer; and in any case the ship's company would rise upon me. My solution, since I cannot restore them to their native island, now deserted, is to wrap them in wool and keep them below in the high southern latitudes, and in London to confide them to the care of an excellent motherly woman I have known these many years, who keeps an inn in the Liberties of the Savoy, and who keeps it delightfully warm.'

They spoke of Mrs Broad's qualities and of the numbers of tropical blacks who became acclimatized to London; and then Mrs Macquarie said, 'Dr Maturin, may I speak to you quite unofficially about this present unhappy state of affairs? My husband will be back at last in a few days and it would distress him even more than it distresses me: I should so like to make relations just a little better before he returns, if I possibly can. I am aware there has always been rivalry between the army and the navy here – you know the reasons better than I, since you were here in Admiral Bligh's time – but poor Colonel MacPherson is a newcomer, a stranger to it all, and is much concerned at having his letters returned as improperly addressed. As for the contents, he leaves that to the civilians; but he is a great stickler for forms, and it was with tears in his eyes that he showed me this cover, begging me to tell him if I could see the least impropriety in the direction.'

Stephen cocked his eye at the cover and said, 'Well, ma'am, I believe it is usual to add MP to the address of an officer who is also a member, to say nothing of FRS for one who belongs to the Royal Society and JP if he is also a magistrate. But Captain Aubrey is not in the least punctilious and he would never have taken the slightest notice of the omissions if he had not been incensed by what looks very like ill-will, deliberate delay and frustration on the part of certain officials. He met it before, when his ship put in just after Governor Bligh's disagreement with Mr Macarthur and his friends.'

'Is Captain Aubrey a member of parliament?' cried Mrs Macquarie, startled into foolishness. Then recovering herself she uttered a low gurgling laugh and said, 'Oh, oh: there will be some red ears among the civilians: they dread a question in Parliament worse than damnation.'

When Stephen rose to take his leave she asked him whether he would dine informally tomorrow – Dr Redfern would be there and both he and she would like Mr Maturin's opinion of their projected hospital.

'Alas, ma'am,' said Stephen, 'at crack of dawn I am engaged to ride away towards the forests of the Hunter river, the home, I am told, of the carpet snake, and many a curious bird.'

'Pray take great care not to get lost,' she said, giving him her hand. 'Almost everybody goes there by sea. And do let us know when you are back: I should like you to meet my husband, who is a great naturalist.'

In spite of Mrs Macquarie's warning they got lost on their first afternoon. The fairly broad track – for they were not yet beyond the range of scattered settlements – having led over an almost bare sandstone rise which gave them a view of lagoons, a complexity of lagoons, sloped gently down through scrub and scattered trees; and on the right hand they heard a full-throated liquid note of what could only be a lyre-bird, a fairly distant lyre-bird.

'Do you know,' said Stephen, 'that no competent anatomist has ever examined one?'

'I know it well,' said Martin, his eye gleaming.

They left the track and rode gently through the brush towards the often-repeated note until they came to an acacia, where they nodded, silently dismounted, tethered the horses and the ass – they had brought him too, their journey being advanced – and walked as quietly as they could into the bush, Stephen carrying the fowling-piece, for Martin, with only one eye and an unduly tender heart, was not a reliable shot. As quietly as they could: but the bush was close-set, dry, littered with dead horny leaves, twigs, branches; and it grew deeper. They were within fifty yards of the voice when it stopped in mid-phrase; they waited, poised, a good ten minutes, and they were turning disappointed resigned faces to one another when two other birds began. To approach the nearest they had to creep, for not only had the brush changed to yet another kind of eucalypt, but the ground had also grown rocky. Still, they were experienced bird-creepers, and now, with infinite pains and accompanied (they being in the shade) by innumerable mosquitoes, they did get close enough to the bird to hear him chuckling to himself between his calls, and scratching the ground. And when at last they came out into the little bald place with a mound in the middle where he had been doing so they found his marks and his droppings. This was their nearest approach to success; and after the seventh bird they decided that so late in the day it was folly to go farther from their horses. They would return to the acacia where they were tethered.

'But surely this is not the way?' cried Martin. 'We had the great lagoon directly before us when we left the road.'

'I have the compass,' said Stephen. 'The compass cannot lie.'

After a while the compass, or their interpretation of it,

led them through a prickly shrub they had never seen before and whose botanical nature they could not determine: they were following what seemed to be a path made by the repeated passage of some animal when Martin stopped abruptly: turning he said, 'Here is a dead man.'

He was an escaping convict, and he had been speared a week or ten days before. At least they laid a symbolic branch over him before they walked on, forced to make some detours because of stretches of impenetrable bush, but still rising and hoping for more open country.

It was when the sun was as low as their hearts and they stood there in doubt with lyre-birds calling on either hand that they heard the ass's howl not a quarter of a mile behind them. In their agitation they had managed to cross the track without seeing it, and once they were on it again the whole landscape fell into place, direction was obvious, and the great lagoon lay where it ought to lie in relation to the rest.

They woke to the sweetest dawn – day in the east, still night in the west and a sky between them varying by imperceptible degrees from violet to the purest aquamarine. Dew had fallen and the still air was full of scents unknown to the rest of the world. The horses moved companionably about, smelling gently of horse; the ass was still asleep.

Smoke rising straight: the smell of coffee. 'Have you ever known a more blessed day?' asked Martin.

'I have not,' said Stephen. 'Even this uninviting landscape is transfigured.'

A lyre-bird called on the hillside within twenty yards and while their cups were still poised it flew right over their heads, a long-tailed pheasant-like creature, and pitched in the brush beyond. The horses brought their ears to bear. The ass woke up.

'Should you like to pursue him?' asked Stephen.

'No,' said Martin. 'We have seen one now, and if we want to dissect one, Paulton will I am sure oblige us with a specimen. They send dogs in to flush them and shoot them as they rise. I am of opinion that we should never deviate from the track and devote all our time to the waders. There must be hosts of them on the lagoons, together with what ducks the country can afford; and as Paulton said, the track skirts the whole series.'

There were indeed hosts of waders on the shore, long-legged birds stalking about in the water, short-legged ones racing about on the mud, formations a thousand strong wheeling all together with a flash of wings, and everywhere those fluting marsh- and shore-bird cries, often the same as those they had both heard in their boyhood and uttered by birds if not of quite the very species then wonderfully like – greenshanks, stilts, avocets, plovers of every kind. 'And there is an oystercatcher,' said Martin. 'I cannot tell you, Maturin, how happy I am to be lying here on the saltwort in the sun, watching that oystercatcher through my glass.'

'He is so like ours that I am puzzled to say just where the difference lies,' said Stephen. 'But he is certainly not quite our bird.'

'Why,' said Martin, 'he has no white on his primaries.'

'Of course,' said Stephen. 'And his bill is surely longer by an inch.'

'Yet I believe it is not the difference that makes me so happy; but rather the similarity!'

This happiness, which inhabited both of them, received something of a check when the path, which had run by three successive bodies of water without ambiguity, divided into two equally faint arms on the grassy slope of a hill that separated the third body from the fourth, a grassy slope with a spring. They dismounted to let the horses drink and graze, and to consider the interminable complexity of shining water that stretched away and away before them under the vast bowl of sky, with clouds sailing across it on the south-east trade. They could come to no satisfactory conclusion: giving the horses their heads in the hope that instinct would succeed where reason failed did not answer – the horses gazed at them with patient, stupid faces and waited to be told where to go: the ass remained perfectly indifferent – so it was decided by the toss of a coin that they should take the right-hand arm. And after all, they said, even if it should die away, as paths so often did, so long as they kept down to the water's edge they could not get lost in the dreadful bush, since there was no bush down there; and so long as they kept generally northward, along the coast, they must necessarily come to Woolloo-Woolloo. Eased in their minds, they gathered several of the more unusual plants (the habitat was in itself most exceptional), some beetles and the almost perfect skeleton of a bandicoot, and rode on, startling a group of kangaroos when they came round the shoulder of the slope.

The theory on which they proceeded was sound, but it did not make quite enough allowance for the winding of the shores along which they travelled nor for the fact that many of the lagoons were not lagoons at all but deep and many-branched inlets of the sea. The path of course disappeared on an outcrop of bare sandstone, never to be found again – 'Could it have been made by kangaroos?' they wondered – but they carried on happily enough, plagued by mosquitoes early and late but enchanted by the birds, until both food and time began to run out.

An incautious kangaroo, up-wind in a misty dawn, an ancient tall grey kangaroo, perhaps senile, provided food of a sort; but nothing could provide them with time and when at last they found Woolloo-Woolloo, which they did from the seaward side of the lagoon, recognizing it with immense relief (their theory justified – ignominious death averted) by the cairn and flagpost that Paulton had described, and Bird Island just showing in the north, they could not stay more than that night with him in spite of his pleas, still less press on to the forests of the Hunter valley.

'My dear sir,' said Stephen, 'you are very good, but we have almost outstayed our leave. I have promised Captain Aubrey to be back on the twenty-third, and with our horses in their present state and the ass so slow we must start very early tomorrow. If you would do me a kindness, you would see us on our way until even a very stupid fellow cannot miss the track.'

'Of course I will,' said Paulton, and he went on, 'Your cattle are being rubbed down and pampered at this moment by two dealers from Newmarket itself, great hands at preparing a horse.'

Observing his discretion, Stephen said, 'May I ask you to show me the fruit-trees you have in front of the house?'

In the orchard, where some apple-trees were growing in a strange left-handed fashion, filled with incongruous cicadas and still bewildered by the reversal of the seasons, Paulton said, 'I wish I were capable of expressing my sense of your kindness in this matter of my tale: it means freedom for me.'

'You expressed yourself very handsomely in your letter,' said Stephen, 'far more handsomely indeed than ever could be looked for: and I beg you will say no more, but rather tell me of Padeen Colman.'

'I think you will be pleased with him,' said Paulton with a smile. 'He came skin and bone, though that good man Redfern had almost healed his back – he came, by the way, labelled Patrick Walsh, which is I take it the registry clerks' way of covering their traces and confusing the issues to a hopeless degree – and he has been eating ever since. I have let it be known that he is infectious and I have put him by himself in the lamb-pasture hut. If you had come up the stream from the lagoon you would have seen it. May I lead you there now?'

'If you please.'

The meadow was true meadow, the largest stretch of grass that Stephen had seen in New South Wales; it was scattered with thick lambs, some of whom still gambolled heavily, and in the middle stood a cabin built of sods and thatched with reeds, the roof held down against the wind by stone-weighted lines. The reeds came from the beds at the far end of the meadow, where the stream ran into the lagoon, forming the little bay where the settlement's produce was shipped to Sydney. In front of the cabin sat Padeen, singing about Conn Céad Cathach to two young Aborigines, standing there tall and thin before him.

'I dare say you would like to speak to him,' said Paulton. 'I shall go back and stir up the cook.'

'It will not take me five minutes,' said Stephen. 'I shall say no more than that I may be at the mouth of the stream in a boat on the twenty-fourth or two or three days later in case of bad weather; but never before noon. Brief I shall be: I do not wish to disturb his spirits; they have been so sadly racked.'

It did not take him so long; but in that time it was clear to his companions that his own spirits too had been much affected. 'Those black youths,' he said sternly as they sat down to their infinitely welcome meal, 'those black youths that ran away when I came near, do they belong to the place at all?'

'Oh no,' said Paulton. 'They come and go as they choose, in their wandering way of life; but there are nearly always a few of them in the neighbourhood. My cousin will not have them ill-used or their women debauched; he has a kindness for them, and sometimes gives them a sheep, or what they very much prefer, a cauldron of sweetened rice. He is trying to compile a vocabulary of their language, but since they appear to possess at least ten synonyms for everything, all of many syllables, while he has a most indifferent ear, the list makes little progress.'

They talked at random about the remarkable butterflies they had seen all the way, particularly along the last lagoon, and their lack of a net, left behind at Riley's; about the curved throwing-stick seen at the same place; about the Aborigines, and at one point Paulton said, 'Do you really think them intelligent?'

'If intelligence can be defined as an ability to solve problems, they are intelligent,' said Stephen. 'For surely the very first problem is to keep alive; and in such a disinherited country as this the problem is enormous. Yet they have solved it. I could not.'

'Nor I,' said Paulton. 'But would your definition bear close inspection?'

'Perhaps not; in any case I am far too stupid to defend it.'

'Oh dear,' cried Paulton. 'You must both be dropping with weariness. May I recommend a warm bath before you retire? The coppers will be on the boil by now; and as far as my experience goes there is nothing more relaxing for body or for mind.'

'I am afraid we were but dismal guests,' said Stephen, turning in his saddle to wave across the scrub to the disappearing Paulton, who chose this same moment to look back and wave before disappearing down the slope and into the tall bush, 'and even this morning I was somewhat chuff: I particularly wished to prevent him committing himself, so that he could always assert that he was not a party to my actions.'

'Morally he could not possibly do so. He knows perfectly well what we are about.'

'I mean legally. In the foolish rigour of the foolish law I wish him to be able to put his name to an affidavit that says "Maturin never said this to me" and "I never said the other to Maturin". Do you think that could conceivably be a peregrine?'

'I believe so,' said Martin, shading his eye. 'A tiercel. Lewin says they occur in New Holland.'

'That bird,' said Stephen, watching the falcon out of sight, 'is as great a comfort to me as your oystercatcher was to you.' Then returning to Paulton, 'What a good-natured man he is, to be sure; it is a pleasure to be in his company. I only wish his sight would allow him to distinguish a bird from a bat. Perhaps if he were given a microscope, a good compound microscope with a variety of eyepieces and an ample stage, he might take great pleasure in some of the smaller forms, the rhizopods, the rotifera, the parasites of lice themselves . . . I knew an old gentleman, an Anglican parson, who delighted in mites.'

Now that their wisdom was wholly superfluous, the track

being almost a carriage-road, the mares looked quite intelligent, stepping out with a confident pace for their distant
stable, so briskly that in spite of several stops for botanizing
and shooting odd parrots and bush-birds, they reached New-
berry's, an inn on a drovers' road some way north of the
Woolloo-Woolloo track, with daylight and to spare. It was
in this daylight that Stephen saw the boomerang at last. A
dissolute black, wrecked by his contact with the whites but
still retaining his skill, threw it for a tot of rum. The boomerang did all that Riley had said of it and more: at one point,
having returned, it rose and floated above the Aboriginal's
head in a slow circle before descending into his hand.
Stephen and Martin gazed at the object in astonishment,
turning it over and over in their hands.

'I cannot understand the principle at all,' said Stephen.
'I should very much like to show it to Captain Aubrey, who
is so very well versed in the mathematics and dynamics of
sailing. Landlord, pray ask him whether he is willing to part
with the instrument.'

'Not on your fucking life,' said the Aboriginal, snatching
the boomerang and clasping it to his bosom.

'He says he does not choose to dispose of it, your honour,'
said the landlord. 'But never fret. I have a dozen behind the
bar that I sell to ingenious travellers for half a guinea. Choose
any one that takes your fancy, sir, and Bennelong will throw
it to prove it comes back, a true homing pigeon, as we say.
Won't you?' This much louder, in the black man's ear.

'Won't I what?'

'Throw it for the gentleman.'

'Give um dram.'

'Sir, he says he will be happy to throw it for you; and
hopes you will encourage him with a tot of rum.'

In the clear morning, much refreshed, they rode on,
Stephen with a genuine homing pigeon across his saddle-
bow, Martin with a variety of cloth bags full of specimens
attached to his, for the ass was already overloaded.

As they dropped down towards Port Jackson the number and variety of parrots, and their discordant noise, increased: cockatoos in flocks, cockateels, lories, and clouds of budgerigars. And when they first looked down into Sydney Cove they saw no frigate moored there, where they had left her. 'This is the twenty-third, is it not?' asked Stephen.

'I believe so,' said Martin. 'I am almost sure that yesterday was the twenty-second.'

They both knew Captain Aubrey's iron rigour where the time of sailing was concerned, and it was with a more than usual anxiety that they gazed at the empty cove. 'But there goes our launch, passing South Point,' said Stephen, his spy-glass to his eye. 'I can see it has a flag in front.'

'And there, ha, ha, ha, is the ship, tied up against the side where we used to be,' cried Martin, joy and relief overflowing. 'And there is another one tied up just behind it: an even larger vessel.'

'I have a feeling it may be the long-foretold ship from Madras,' said Stephen.

This impression was much strengthened as they came into the town, where tight-turbaned Lascars could be seen contemplating the iron-gangs with satisfaction, and where strange uniforms walked about the streets, staring as newcomers stare. They rode straight to Riley's now crowded tavern, and while Stephen prepared to settle accounts with the landlord Martin went down to the ship with two blackguard boys, wheeling a hand-cart loaded with their specimens.

Riley, who knew everything, told Stephen that the *Waverly* had indeed come from Madras, but that she brought no official packages from India, still less any overland civilian mail; but this was no real disappointment, since she had never been expected to do so. She had however brought out a number of officers, and Stephen sat in the parlour, more or less filled with them, until Riley should be free to deal with the horses.

As he sat there, gazing at the tavern's boomerang and

trying to find some plausible reason for its behaviour, he became aware that one of the officers, a Royal Marine near the doorway, was looking at him with more than ordinary attention. He reflected upon the perception of eyes focused upon one – the gaze felt even when the gazer was outside one's field of vision – the uneasiness it caused – an uneasiness felt by many creatures – the importance of not looking directly at one's quarry – the exchange of glances between the sexes, its infinite variety of meanings; and he was still reflecting when the officer came over and said, 'Dr Maturin, I believe?'

'Yes, sir,' said Stephen, reserved, but not repulsively so.

'You will not remember me, sir, being so busy at the time, but you was good enough to save my leg after Saumarez' action in the Gut. My name is Hastings.'

'Certainly: a patella. I remember perfectly. Sir William Hastings, is it not? May I roll up your trouser leg? Yes, yes: beautifully knit. And that scoundrelly charlatan would have had it off. To be sure, a neat amputation is always a pleasure, but even so . . . And now you have a perfectly sound limb rather than a peg. Very good,' – patting its calf gently – 'I give you joy of it.'

'And I give you joy too, Doctor.'

'You are very good, Sir William. Do you allude to the patella?'

'No, sir. To your daughter. But perhaps you do not think that a subject for congratulation. I am aware that there is a prejudice against daughters: portions, wedding breakfasts, vapours and so on. I beg your pardon.'

'I have not the pleasure of following you, sir,' said Stephen, looking at him with his head on one side, but his heart beginning to beat faster.

'Well, no doubt I mistake. But when I was in Madras, *Andromache* came in. One of her officers lent me a *Naval Chronicle*, and running through the promotions, births, deaths and marriages, my eye caught what I took to be your name: though perhaps it was another gentleman altogether.'

'Sir William, what was the month, and what did it say?'

'As far as I recall it was last April: and it said, "At Ashgrove Cottage, near Portsmouth, the Lady of Dr Maturin, of the Navy, of a daughter."'

'Sweet Sir William,' said Stephen, shaking his hand, 'you could not have brought me kinder, more welcome news. Riley! Riley, there, d'ye hear me now? Bring us the finest bottle that ever you have in the house.'

Riley's finest bottle had no effect on Stephen: joy alone brought him skipping across the brow to the frigate's deck – a care-worn deck with what looked like the whole ship's company busy upon it, though this could not have been the case, seeing that a great many hands were banging away far aft amidst the sound of echoing orders. While he was gazing about at the decorations, the bunting, the meticulous coiling of ropes, Captain Aubrey appeared, accompanied by Reade with a tape-measure in his only hand. Jack was looking thinner, yellower and worried, but he smiled and said, 'Are you back, Doctor? Mr Martin tells me you had a splendid time.'

'So we did too,' said Stephen, 'but Jack, I cannot tell you with what eagerness I look forward to going home.'

'Aye. I dare say you do. So do I. Mr Oakes,' – directing his powerful voice at the foretopgallantmast – 'is that garland to be shipped this watch, or should you like your hammock sent aloft? Now, Doctor, we are about to give the Governor and his people a farewell dinner: that is the cause of all this merriment. You will have time to change, but I am afraid Killick will not be able to give you a hand. He is busier than any hive of bees. Mr Reade, hold the tape exactly there, and do not stir until I give you a hail.' With this he hurried aft, where all three cabins were being thrown into one, and the harassed carpenter was fitting still another leaf to the table.

Although at this moment his wits were not at their sharpest, Stephen grasped the situation – the unnatural cleanliness of all hands, the more than ordinary brilliance of everything that sand or brick-dust could induce to shine, the widespread and deep anxiety that was usual before naval entertainments on a grand scale, which in his experience were prepared as though all the guests were old experienced seamen, censorious, hostile admirals, likely to inspect the blacking of the highest yards and look for dust under the carronade-slides. He went to his cabin below, his mind still somewhat confused by happiness, and found that in spite of everything Killick had laid out all the clothes that were proper for him to wear. He slowly dressed, taking particular care of the set of his coat, and came out into the gun-room, where he found Pullings, sitting carefully in the gold-laced splendour of a commander.

'Why, Doctor,' he said, his face brightening, 'how happy I am to see you back. You look as gay as a popinjay, as cheerful as if you had found a five-pound note: I hope you brought the poor old barky some good luck at last. God love us, what a week!'

'You look as if you had been through a fleet-action, Tom.'

'I may smile again when we sail tomorrow afternoon and when we have sunk the land: but not before. You would think the hands conspired to put us in the wrong, and to give the *Surprise* a bad name. Drunken seamen, paralytic, brought out by lobsters with kind advice on how to keep them in order. Awkward Bloody Davis locked up for beating two sentries into a jelly and throwing their muskets into the sea – they had tried to stop him taking a girl out in a boat. And Jack Nastyface *did* bring a girl out: being so thick with the cook he brought her aboard in broad daylight wrapped up like a side of bacon. He kept her in the forepeak and fed her like a fighting-cock through the scuttle; and when he was found he said she was not an ordinary young woman at all – he wanted to marry her, which would make her free, and would the Captain be so kind? By all means says the Captain and then you can take your wages and go ashore with her: the ship don't carry wives. So Jack Nastyface thought better of his bargain: she went ashore alone, and

316

now all the people despise him. And there was another poor devil swam out . . . several other things. Lord, how I prayed for a party of Marines! The bloody-minded officials had eased off before the Governor came back, but by then the foremast jacks had pretty well destroyed our case and reputation; and although things are smoothed over now and we are tied up alongside again I do not think there is much love lost between ship and shore. I have never known the Captain more worn, nor more apt to grow – well, testy, you might say.' Four bells. 'Now, Doctor,' Pullings went on, 'it is time for me to throw an eye over all; and perhaps for you to put on your breeches.'

'God save you, Tom,' cried Stephen, looking with concern at his pale bony knees, 'I am so glad you noticed it. My mind must have wandered. I should have got the ship a worse name still.'

When Stephen was breeched he sat at his folding desk and wrote to Diana, his pen scratching away at an extraordinary speed, the sheets of paper mounting on his cot.

'If you please, sir,' said Reade at the door, 'the Captain thinks you might like to know that our guests are under way from Government House.'

'Thank you, Mr Reade,' said Stephen. 'I shall be with you as soon as I have finished this paragraph.'

He was on deck just before the first gun of the Governor's salute and he observed with gratification but not much surprise that the half-fledged anxious ship he had last seen was now a serene man-of-war, confident that her yards were squared by lifts and braces to within an eighth of an inch, and that her guests could eat off any part of any one of her decks.

In fact they ate off the full extent of Jack Aubrey's silver, the baize-lined chests being empty but for a pair of broken sugar-tongs; and from behind the Captain's chair Killick surveyed his triumph with whole-hearted delight, a look that sat strangely on a face set in shrewish discontent.

The guests filed in, and Stephen found that he was to sit

between Dr Redfern and Firkins, the penal secretary. 'How very glad I am that we are neighbours,' he said to Redfern. 'I was afraid that after our few words on the quarterdeck we should be torn apart.'

'So am I,' said Redfern. 'And when you consider this table, we could easily have been out of earshot. Heavens, I have never seen such magnificence in a frigate, nor such a sweep of cloth.'

'Nor have I,' said Firkins, and in a low tone to Stephen, 'Surely, Captain Aubrey must be a gentleman of very considerable estate?'

'Oh, very considerable indeed,' said Stephen. 'And he also commands I know not how many votes in both the Commons and the Lords: he is much caressed by the ministry.' He added a few more details to sadden Firkins, but only a few, since his heart was aswim with joy; and he spent most of his meal and nearly all the prolonged port and then coffee drinking in conversation with Redfern. The surgeon was no great naturalist: asked, for example, whether he had seen the platypus he looked doubtful. 'The more modern name is ornithorhynchus,' said Stephen. 'Yes, yes, I know the animal,' said Redfern. 'I have often heard it spoken of – it is not uncommon – and I was trying to remember whether in fact I had seen it or not. Probably not. Here, by the way, it is called the water-mole: the learned names would not be understood.' Yet on the other hand he could tell Stephen a great deal about the behaviour of men to one another in New South Wales and the still more dreadful Norfolk Island, where he had spent some time: the usual but not invariable response to absolute power and the absence of public opinion. So taken up was Stephen with his conversation and with his inner happiness that he scarcely noticed how the party was going; but when he returned from seeing Dr Redfern back to the hospital and giving his opinion on a hydrocele he said to Jack, sitting alone in the reconstituted great cabin and drinking a tankard of barley-water, 'How very well that went off – a most successful dinner.'

'I am glad you think so. I found it devilish heavy going – worked like a horse – and I was afraid other people thought so too.'

'Not at all, at all: never in life, my dear. Jack, before coming aboard today I met a man from the Madras ship, ha, ha, ha! Oh, but before I forget, is this south-east breeze to be relied on?'

'Lord, yes. It has been blowing these ten days together, and the glass has never moved.'

'Then please may I have a cutter early in the morning, and may I be picked up off Bird Island?'

'Of course,' said Jack, waving his empty tankard. 'And should you like some of this? Barley-water.'

'If you please,' said Stephen.

'Killick. Killick, there,' called Jack, and when he came, 'Two more cans of barley-water, Killick; and let Bonden know the Doctor wants the blue cutter at three bells in the morning watch.'

'Two cans and three bells it is, sir,' said Killick, aiming for the door. 'Two cans, three bells.' He struck the jamb a shrewd blow – he was usually drunk after a dinner-party – but he got through upright.

'What do you expect to find on Bird Island?'

'No doubt there are petrels; but I do not think of landing there, alas, with so little time to spare.'

'Then what are you going for?'

'Am I not to pick up Padeen?'

'Of course you are not to pick up Padeen.'

'But Jack, I told you I should warn him. I told you before Martin and I set off, when you said we were to sail on the twenty-fourth. I *have* warned him, and he will be waiting there on the strand.'

'I certainly did not understand anything of the kind. Stephen, I have had endless trouble with convicts trying to escape. The officials have harassed and badgered me for that reason among others and have stinted my stores, supplies and repairs, and to avoid anything really ugly I had to warp

319

out into the bay, which delayed everything still farther. When the Governor came back I went to see him and stated the case as fairly as I could: he admitted that searching the ship without my consent was improper and asked whether I desired an apology. I said no, but that if he would give me an undertaking that nothing of the kind would happen again, I for my part should undertake that no convict would leave Sydney Cove in my ship, and so leave the matter there. He agreed, and we warped in.'

'We are speaking of a shipmate, Jack. I am committed.'

'So am I. In any case, how can you ask the captain of a King's ship to do such a thing? I will make every possible representation in Padeen's favour, but I will not countenance a convict's escape. I have turned several away already.'

'Is that what I am to say to Padeen?'

'My hands are tied. I have given the Governor my word. It would be said that I was abusing my authority as a post-captain and my immunity as a member.'

Stephen looked at him for some time, weighing the value of any reply: the look conveyed or was thought to convey something of pity and contempt and it stung Jack extremely. He said, 'You have brought this on yourself.' Stephen turned, and seeing Killick with the tankards he took one, said, 'Thankee, Killick,' and carried it below.

Davidge was sitting in the gun-room; he told him that Martin was down among the specimens, putting the bird-skins into the brine-tub, and he went on, 'What a wretched dinner that was, upon my word. I am sure that Jack Nastyface, being so disgruntled, poured salt in by the ladle; and any gate the civilians were like a set of funeral mutes. I tried as hard as I could, but they would not be pleased. I dare say it was the same at your end of the table. No wonder you look hipped.'

'Martin,' said Stephen when he reached the store-room and the smell of feathers, 'it appears that there has been a misunderstanding and that I may not take Padeen aboard. I am not quite sure what I shall do. However, the boat will be ready at three bells in the morning watch. Would you care to come with me? I ask, because at dinner Dr Redfern told me that the colonial name for the platypus is water-mole, which I did not know when your friend Paulton told us that water-moles lived in the Woolloo-Woolloo stream. This might be your last chance of seeing one.'

'Thank you very much,' said Martin, looking into his face by the lantern-light and quickly turning away. 'I shall be ready at three bells.'

Stephen asked for a hand to get at his chest, took out a fair sum in gold and notes, locked it again, gave Martin the key and said, 'If I should not return to the ship tomorrow will you be so good as to have this sent to my wife?'

'Of course,' said Martin.

'I do not think I have ever felt such strong and conflicting emotions in my life,' he reflected, walking out of Sydney on the Parramatta road. His intention was to diminish their force by walking far and fast: physical weariness, he had found before, could do away with subsidiary aspects, such as in this case mere exasperation, and after some hours the right course of action would appear. Yet in the hours he walked now nothing of the kind took place. His mind per-petually dropped the problem and flew back to his happi-ness, his present and future happiness. He walked a great way in the darkness, and that part of his mind which was free to be astonished was astonished by the number of nocturnal animals he heard and occasionally saw in the faint moonlight, and they so near the settlement: phalangers, bandicoots, a koala, wombats. 'As for Jack,' he said, 'his hero Nelson would not have acted so: but Nelson was not a righteous man; he had no sudden rush of virtue to the head. Middle age has come upon Jack Aubrey at last, the creature. I never thought it would.' He said this without rancour, as one stat-ing a fact; but he also said, 'One of the great advantages of wealth is that you are not obliged to eat toads. You can do what you think right.'

The question of what he thought right in these circumstances was not solved by the time the moon set and he
turned back. His consideration of the problem was often
interrupted by actions of grace, one of which, a plain-chant
thanksgiving he had often heard at Montserrat before the
French sacked, desecrated and destroyed the monastery,
took him a mile and a half to sing. It was not solved by the
time he reached the ship, footsore and wet from a shower
out of the south-east; nor yet when after a troubled waking
night he heard Bonden's discreet voice in his ear, telling
him the cutter was alongside.

Joy revived, and sorrow with it. He dressed, tiptoed into
the gun-room not to wake the other officers, murmured a
good morning to Martin, and drank a cup of coffee.

The cutter's masts were already stepped; and as he made
his way down into it Stephen noticed with satisfaction that
the crew were all old shipmates, man-of-war's men. Bonden,
who had no notion of the Doctor's common sense, whatever
his book-learning might be, nor of Mr Martin's, had provided boat-cloaks against the keen night air; and he said,
'Now where away, sir, if you please?'

'Do you know Bird Island?'

'Yes, sir: saw it as we were coming in, and Captain Pullings took a fix on it.'

'Well now, before that island there is a point, two or three
miles to the south; and south again of that point, on the flat
coast there is the entrance to a lagoon, marked by a flagstaff
and a cairn. That is where we must go. How long do you
think it will take?'

'With this breeze on the quarter, sir, we should be there
by noon, easy. Shove off afore, Joe.'

By the time they had sailed down the long harbour, dawn
was just beginning to break, a dawn so pure and exquisite
that even Joe Plaice, who had seen ten thousand of them at
sea, looked at it with mild approval, and Martin clasped his
hands. Stephen saw nothing of it: he was asleep, wrapped
in the boat-cloak. The cutter passed the headlands, met the

wide-spaced waves of the open sea, made a little offing close-hauled and then steered north-east, which changed the boat's motion to a corkscrew roll of the kind that may make even hardened seamen uneasy if they have been ashore for some while. Stephen slept on: he slept on when the surface ripple caused by the changing tide brought spray sweeping diagonally across. Martin arranged the cloak to cover Stephen's head, and seeing that he was not easily to be woken said to Bonden in a low tone, 'We are going at a fine pace.'

'Yes, sir,' said Bonden. 'We shall have time and to spare, and I should stand off the shore to keep the Doctor a little drier, only I am afraid of missing the flagstaff.'

'Do you think we are near?' asked Stephen, suddenly awake.

'Well, sir, I reckon we can't be a great way off.'

'Then as soon as we raise Bird Island I shall watch the shore with my glass; and as for getting wet, the sun will soon dry us. It is much higher than I had expected, and exceptionally warm.'

So they sailed on, the hands forward talking quietly, the boat all alive with the breeze, the sun climbing until cool spray was welcome and cloaks were laid aside.

'There is your island, sir,' said Bonden; and on the rise Stephen saw it clear, nicking the horizon beyond the point.

'So it is,' he said, and both he and Martin took out their telescopes. Steadily the low sandy coast filed by; and presently they agreed that this part or that might be familiar. Yet from the sea one dune or even one clump of stunted trees looks very like another and there was no certainty until once again, and with something of the same relief, they saw the flagstaff and its cairn.

'And it is not yet eleven o'clock,' said Stephen. 'I am afraid I have roused you men from your hammocks too early.'

'Never you mind us, sir,' said Plaice with a chuckle. 'We should have been swabbing decks else. This is more like a picnic, as they say.'

Bonden steered for the opening. To his surprise Stephen was able to tell him that there was a fathom of water over the bar at the lowest tide, and a deeper passage with the cairn and the flagstaff in a line, bearing due east. Bonden took the cutter through the moderate flurry of breaking waves, along the entrance, into the quiet waters of the lagoon, and so to the stage where the Woolloo-Woolloo harvest was brought down to the brig.

'Now, Bonden,' said Stephen, 'make a fire – you have brought your dinners, sure?'

'Yes, sir; and Killick put up this parcel of sandwiches for you and Mr Martin.'

'Very good. Make a fire, then, eat your dinner, and go to sleep in the sun if you like. The ship is to pick us up off Bird Island this evening. I may not come down, but Mr Martin will, not later than two or half past. And let nobody stray. There may be venomous creatures in these reeds.'

There were certainly butterflies, some of the same kinds that they had seen before, others larger and still more spectacular; and as they walked up along the stream through the reeds and bushes they netted several. But the extreme contradiction of spirit was still as strong on Stephen as ever, the ebullient joy and the wound; and his heart was not in it. Nor was Martin's: Stephen, though never loquacious, was rarely as silent as this – the mood was catching.

They passed through the reed-bed to the firm ground and the open air, the vast sky, of the meadow. The stream was on their left hand, whereas on their first visit it had been on their right and they had crossed it much higher up. 'We are in a new part of the pasture,' observed Stephen. 'I can just make out the cabin, a good half-mile farther off than I had expected.' Lambs; a flight of whiter cockatoos; far over a drift of smoke. 'We might walk a furlong or so along the stream,' he went on. 'We are much too early.'

In time of flood the stream was clearly ten or fifteen yards in breadth, with deep-cut banks; but there had been no flood for some years and now they were covered with a fair number of bushes and tall soft grass growing between them, while the stream itself, winding through the meadow, was no more than a stride across, a rivulet connecting a series of pools. The first of these pools had some interesting plants, which they collected, and a millepede; at the second Martin, who was ahead on the path, whispered, 'Oh my God!', stopped, stepped cautiously back. 'There they are,' he whispered in Stephen's ear.

They crept along the top of the bank foot by foot, bent, so that when they raised their heads and peered through the fringe of leaves and reed-plumes they could just command the surface of the pool. The platypuses took no notice: they had been swimming round and round when first Martin saw them. They went on swimming round and round, one after the other, in a broad ring, lost and absorbed in their ritual. They both swam low, surprisingly low, in the water, but the light struck the surface at such an angle that for the watchers there was no reflexion: they could see everything below, from that scarcely believable duck's bill to the broad flattened tail, with the four webbed feet between them.

Presently Stephen whispered, 'I believe we can creep nearer still.' Martin nodded, and with infinite caution they edged slanting down the side, Stephen steadying himself with the handle of the net. It was inch by inch now, each bush, each young tree, each tuft of grass very carefully negotiated. At water-level the going was easier and they carried on their serpentine approach to the soft damp mud of the pool-shore itself, each behind a clump of rushes, peering through the shaded gap between them. As he had done when he was a boy, reaching a point within hand's touch of a cock capercaillie calling and displaying in the spring, Stephen closed his mouth, so that the sound of his heart, loud in his throat like a hoarse old clock, should not be heard.

He might have left it open. The platypuses were wholly given over to their dance. Stephen and Martin sat there, easy on the yielding ground, watching, noting, comparing; and still the platypuses turned. Their ring took them far out over to the other side, where the sun showed their fine brown perfectly, and it brought them in towards the shadow, quite close to the rushes.

A laughing-jackass called, and under the din Stephen said, 'I am going to try to catch one.' Slowly, slowly he sank the net when they were at their farthest turn; slowly, slowly he edged it out into the pool, under their invariable path. Twice he let them pass over it: the third time he raised the leading edge just in front of the second, the pursuing animal. It dived instantly: but into the net. He stepped through the rushes waist-deep into the pool, trusting neither the handle nor the stuff with so much weight; and with great strides he waded to the bank, his shining face turned to Martin and his gentle hand feeling into the purse. Warm, soft, wet fur and a strongly beating heart: 'I mean you no harm, my dear,' he said and instantly he felt a piercing stab. A shocking pain ran up his arm. He scrambled to the bank, dropped the net, sat down, looked at his arm – bare shirtsleeved arm – and saw a puncture with a livid swollen line already running up from wrist to elbow. 'Take care, Martin,' he said. 'Put it back. Knife – handkerchief.'

He cut deep and twisted the tourniquet hard, but already there was a stiffness in his throat and his voice was growing thick. He lay back in the mud and explained that he had known similar idiosyncratic cases – a bee-sting, a scorpion, even a large spider – several cases – some survived, some did not – over in a day, one way or the other – but there hanging over him was Padeen's anguished face, and Paulton was saying, 'Oh dear oh dear, Martin, I thought a naturalist would know the male has a poisonous spur: oh dear oh dear, he is swelling – he is turning blue.'

'A poisonous spur?' asked Stephen through his pain, hoarse, unrecognizable. 'The male alone? In all the whole class of mallamia, mammalia . . .'

The more or less coherent, rational hurry of words stopped, because the power of speech left him, and presently the power of sight. Yet he was still present, though at a great distance, and not in darkness though he could see nothing but rather in a deep violet world that reminded him of a previous state when, surprised by grief and an involuntary overdose of laudanum, he had plunged right down the inside of a lofty tower in Sweden: in this state too he could hear the remote voices of his friends, but now the hallucinations were absent or benign.

The voice he particularly heard was Paulton's, who seemed oppressed by guilt and who explained again and again that everyone at Woolloo-Woolloo knew that you had to take great care of the water-mole – by warning cries and vivid signs the black men had said, 'Touch him not' – he had seen an Euro-pean dog die within minutes – he blamed himself extremely for not having mentioned the danger – had supposed it was common knowledge. 'How can you speak so, John?' said Martin. 'No more than two or three dried, shrivelled, imper-fect specimens were ever seen in London, and those only female.' 'How I regret it,' said Paulton. 'How bitterly I regret it.'

There were gaps not so much in Stephen's consciousness as in his perception of things; and after one such blank or pause it was Bonden he heard, telling Padeen 'to lift his head easy, mate, and lay it on my shoulder: never mind the blood'.

A strong voice said, 'We must get him back to the ship,' and now no doubt he was being carried; but that part of his mind which was not taken up with the burning pain and the unearthly violet in which he had his being observed that the seamen took Padeen's presence for granted and that they comforted him in his distress.

Now there was the easy motion of the boat, the creak of thole-pins, the sea-air on his stiff, tumid, sightless face; and now among the perceptions that failed him were those of pain and of time, so that although he heard both Jack's deeply anxious voice saying to Padeen, 'Lay him in my cot, Colman, and then jump down to the gun-room for his leather cushion: you know where it is,' and the often-repeated expla-nations at the ship's side, he could not set them in order;

nor had order any significance in this immeasurably deep violet well.

Then his concern at the loss of sequence disappeared; and with the eventual return of light and a confused sense of time his recollection of the loss faded. Time started again quite far back, with the strong voice saying they must return to the ship; and the events leading to those words and the reason for his present inner happiness fell into place, though not without a lingering dreamlike imprecision as he lay there at his ease, contemplating.

'Back to the ship': and indeed here was the old familiar rise and heave, the creak of his hanging cot, the attenuated smell of sea and tar. But it was not quite right either, for now here again was Padeen's face hanging over him: which was nearer delirium or dream than reality. Yet at all hazards he wished the face a good day, and Padeen, straightening with a great smile on his solid factual face said, 'And God and Mary and Patrick be with your honour,' then in English, 'Captain, sir, he . . . he . . . he has spoken in his . . . his . . . senses.'

'Dear God, I am so happy to hear it,' said Jack, and very gently, 'Stephen, how do you do?'

'I have survived, I find,' said Stephen, taking his hand. 'Jack, I cannot tell you how ardently, how very ardently, I look forward to going home.'

P.S.

Ideas,
interviews
& features ...

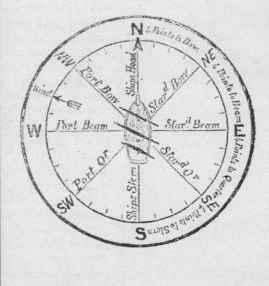

THE NAVAL WORLD OF
JACK AUBREY
N. A. M. Rodger

The period which Patrick O'Brian has made his own, the Great Wars against France, is at once the least and the best known part of all British naval history. It is often referred to as the 'classical' age of naval history, and it is almost always the period to which both academic historians and common readers refer when they think of the history of the Royal Navy under sail. The reasons for this have to do both with scholarship and literature. Among serious historians of the Navy, this was almost the first period to be thoroughly treated. The scholars of what might be called the first great age of British naval history (say from 1890 to 1914), looked back on the Great Wars as the last, and also the longest and fiercest, real naval war, the culmination of centuries of experience, the reference point by which the Navy's development both before and after might be judged.

To their labours we are indebted for a mass of detailed analysis of how and why the wars were fought at sea which is still unequalled for any other period with the possible exception of Queen Elizabeth's reign. Of the forty-eight volumes published by the Navy Records Society between its foundation in 1893 and the outbreak of the First World War, twenty-two dealt wholly or partly with the Revolutionary and Napoleonic Wars. At the same time this was the first period of British history when the Navy and its activities attracted detailed interest from the public at large, and when the Service itself generated a substantial professional literature. This is the era of the first naval periodicals and annuals, of Steel's *Navy List*, of the *Naval Chronicle*, of the biographical dictionaries of

Charnock and Marshall.[1] It is the era in which newspaper coverage of naval affairs increased enormously, and about which many officers and not a few ratings subsequently wrote memoirs. Moreover this was the period depicted in fiction by the naval historical novelists, of which Patrick O'Brian is the latest, and the first was probably John Davis, the anonymous author of *The Post-Captain*, or *The Wooden Walls Well-Manned* of 1805. The first great age of the naval historical novel was in the 1820s and 1830s, when the three Captains, William Glascock of *The Naval Sketch Book*, Frederick Marryat of *Peter Simple* and *Midshipman Easy*, and Frederick Charmier of *The Life of a Sailor* and *Ben Brace* were writing lightly fictionalised accounts of their own services, for the entertainment, in many cases, of men of their own generation.[2] Marryat had served as a midshipman under Lord Cochrane, and incidents from the spectacular career of that most theatrical and flamboyant of officers appears both in Marryat's novels and in Patrick O'Brian's.[3]

From fiction, contemporary journalism and subsequent scholarship, therefore, a mass of material is available for the novelist seeking to reconstruct a vanished world. The historian's problem is that in spite, even in some cases because of this wealth of evidence, we still know far too little about the daily life of the officers and men of Jack Aubrey's day. In default of documentary research, scholars must draw on the same materials as the novelist, and there are few who can do so with the imaginative power of Patrick O'Brian. Moreover there are particular dangers in drawing on much of this material to describe relations between officers and men, for many of the memoir-writers and novelists (including Marryat) were explicitly or implicitly participating in a debate on the reform of naval discipline which was taking place in and after

1. John Charnock, *Biographia Navalis*, 6 vols (London: R. Faulder, 1794–98); John Marshall, *Royal Naval Biography*, 8 vols (London: [n. pub.], 1823–35).
2. This subject is studied generally in C. N. Robinson, *The British Tar in Fact and Fiction* (London: Harper, 1909);
C. N. Parkinson, *Portsmouth Point, The Navy in Fiction 1793–1815* (London: University Press of Liverpool, 1948) is a convenient anthology.
3. For Marryat see: Christopher Lloyd, *Captain Marryat and the Old Navy* (London: Longmans, 1939). Much of *Master and Commander* is drawn from Cochrane's command of the ill-named sloop *Speedy*, with which in 1801 he captured the Spanish frigate *El Gamo*.

the 1830s. Part of their object was to demonstrate how bad things had been,[4] which makes them unreliable witnesses to what things had really been like – but no more unreliable than extrapolation from research on the Navy of fifty years before, which is the best the historian can offer at present.

It needs to be emphasised that we are dealing with an era of social change, especially in the 1790s. In any other area of British history it would seem absurd to stress something so obvious, but naval history is still technically rather backward, and many standard works still submerge the developments of periods as long as two centuries under some bland generalisations about the age of sail. The half century from 1750 to 1800 may seem a short time, well within the careers of individual officers and men, and yet it is clear, even in our present state of ignorance, that the social life of the Navy changed greatly during that time. These changes may be divided into the material and the psychological.

It has been calculated that the total number of seafarers employed in British ships was nearly 130,000 at the height of the Seven Years' War, and over 150,000 during the American War.[5] At the height of the Seven Years' War the Navy mustered nearly 85,000 officers and men, and during the American War the figure rose to nearly 110,000; by 1800 the Navy required about 125,000; and in 1810 the figure attained 145,000.[6] In principle the Navy needed most if not all the seafarers who were in peacetime employed in the merchant service – but merchant shipping contracted little if at all in wartime, and the inevitable result was an acute shortage overall. The gap between peacetime supply and the wartime demand of the Navy and merchant service combined was made up by dilution of skills, with a large recruitment of landmen into the Navy, and by widespread employment of foreigners in merchantmen, among other expedients.[7] The manpower situation had undoubtedly worsened over fifty years. An analysis of the musters of ships commissioning at Plymouth between 1770 and 1779 shows that 62% of the ratings were petty officers, able seamen or idlers against 38% ordinary seamen, landmen or servants.

4. For Marryat see: Lloyd, *Captain Marryat*, pp. 237 & 256. The later stages of the naval reform movement are dealt with by Eugene L. Rasor, *Reform in the Royal Navy: A Social History of the Lower Deck 1850 to 1880* (Hamden, Conn.: Archon Books, 1976).
5. David J. Starkey, 'War and the Market for Seafarers in Britain, 1736–1792', in *Shipping and Trade, 1750–1950: Essays in International Maritime Economic History*, ed. by Lewis R. Fischer and Helge W. Nordvik (Pontefract: Lofthouse, 1990), pp. 25–42, App. I. These figures are better than those given in N. A. M. Rodger, *The Wooden World: An Anatomy of the Georgian Navy* (London: Collins, 1986), p. 149.
6. Christopher Lloyd, *The British Seaman, 1200–1860: A Social Survey* (London: Paladin, 1970), pp. 288–289.
7. Rodger, *The Wooden World*, pp. 155–158;
Ralph Davis, *The Rise of the English Shipping Industry in the Seventeenth and Eighteenth Centuries* (London: Macmillan, 1962), pp. 326–327.

Only 6% had been pressed, 94% had volunteered, not many had been recruited by the Impress Service and virtually none were turned over from other ships. The majority (63%) were Englishmen, with 20% born in Ireland, and only 2% outside the British dominions.[8] A similar analysis of Plymouth ships commissioning in 1805 reveals a very different picture. So large a number of the crews had been turned over from other ships that it is not possible to make a direct comparison of the proportion of volunteers and pressed men, but it is clear that it had changed very much for the worse. Almost all the new recruits came from the Impress Service via the guard-ship, rather than entering for a particular ship. The ratio of skilled to unskilled had virtually reversed: only 35% were rated petty officers, able seamen or idlers, but 65% were ordinary seamen or landmen. Only 47% were English, and only 58% British, while the Irish (four fifths of them unskilled) had risen to 29%, and foreigners to 6%.[9] These figures are strong evidence that the Navy's manpower situation was much worse during the 'Great War' against France than it had been in the American War twenty-five years before. Another sample, of men serving on the Leeward Islands station between 1784 and 1812 (but mostly during the Great War) shows 55% English and 30% Irish.[10] Since Ireland was, from the point of view of naval manning, largely a reservoir of unskilled men, this also points to an increasing shortage of seamen. The result was that nightmare of manning with which Jack Aubrey and all officers were familiar, a situation in which the Sophies might be described as 'a very fair crew. A score or two of prime seamen, and a good half of the people real man-of-war's men, which is more than you can say for most line of battle ships nowadays'.[11]

One category of recruit which the Navy had always been reluctant to accept was criminals. An act of 1744 had allowed magistrates to send the Service 'rogues and vagabonds', together with 'idle and disorderly persons', but in practice at that date the Navy was extremely reluctant to take any class of prisoner except smugglers and debtors. To some extent this reluctance was overcome by the pressure of necessity during the American War, and another act of 1795 widened the scope of those who might lawfully be sentenced to naval service to smugglers, embezzlers of

8. N. A. M. Rodger, 'Devon Men and the Navy, 1688–1815', in *The New Maritime History of Devon*, 2 vols ed. by Michael Duffy and others (London: Conway Maritime, 1993), I, 209–215, Table 6.
9. Ibid., Table 10.
To preserve the comparison, Americans have not been included as foreigners in 1805, but in that year a further 5% had been born in the Americas (including Canada and the West Indies).
10. John D. Byrn, *Crime and Punishment in the Royal Navy: Discipline on the Leeward Islands Station 1784–1812* (Aldershot: Scolar, 1989), p. 76, n. 2.
11. Patrick O'Brian, *Master and Commander* (London: Collins, 1970), pp. 23–24.

naval stores and men with no lawful trade.[12] Magistrates in some, though not all, counties made a practice of sending thieves and petty criminals to the Navy, but it is not clear how many of them were actually accepted, and in the present state of our knowledge we should be cautious in accepting at face value contemporary officers' rhetoric about the 'dregs of the jails'.[13] The same comment applies to the imprisonment of landmen, which was illegal and virtually unknown in the 1750s, but is often said to have been widespread by the end of the century.[14] The evidence certainly exists to prove or disprove the statement, but until it has been investigated there is not much we can usefully say.

A worsening manpower situation was bound to affect life on the lower deck in many ways, mostly adversely. For the professional seafarer, landmen were troublesome messmates and meant more work for the men who knew their business.[15] A general shortage made it much more likely that men would be turned over from one ship to another without being granted leave. Lack of leave was one of the complaints of the mutineers in 1797,[16] but again we lack hard evidence with which to analyse the situation. Leave was certainly given often in the 1750s, and a recent study concludes that some, though not all captains were still giving regular leave at the end of the century,[17] but it seems probable that the complaints of lack of shore leave, and in particular of turning-over crews without leave when ships paid off, will be found to be justified. One probable cause of the lack of leave is the coppering of the ships of the Navy during the American War.[18] From the military point of view this was an enormous advantage, making ships faster and allowing them to stay out of dock for years at a time. It was certainly one of the reasons why the Navy was able to hold its own during the American War against a coalition of enemies which was greatly superior in numbers. But the necessity of docking several times a year had provided the opportunity for regular leave, and it seems likely that coppering, in a desperate war which called for every effort, had the effect of reducing the opportunities for leave by increasing the 'availability' of the ships.

12. N. A. M. Rodger, *The Insatiable Earl: A Life of John Montagu, 4th Earl of Sandwich* (London: HarperCollins, 1993), pp. 202–203.
13. Rodger, *The Wooden World*, pp. 170–171;
Clive Emsley, 'The Recruitment of Petty Offenders during the French Wars 1793–1815', *Mariner's Mirror*, LXVI (1980), 200–205;
Lloyd, *The British Seaman*, p. 137.
14. Lloyd, *The British Seaman*, p. 127.
15. Rodger, *The Wooden World*, pp. 115 & 228.
16. Conrad Gill, *The Naval Mutinies of 1797* (Manchester: [n.pub.], 1913), pp. 138 & 284.
17. Rodger, *The Wooden World*, pp. 137–144;
Byrn, *Crime and Punishment*, pp. 160–161.
18. R. J. B. Knight, 'The Introduction of Copper Sheathing into the Royal Navy, 1779–1786', *Mariner's Mirror*, LIX (1973), 299–309.

The bad effects of 'turning-over' men was not simply that it denied them leave, for if the people were divided among several ships in need of men, as usually happened, it broke up the natural social unit of a ship's company. It is clear that, however they had been recruited and whatever their initial feelings, men could and generally did become contented members of a ship's company after a while – specifically after not more than twelve or eighteen months' service.[19] Taking men from a settled ship's company and distributing them wherever they were wanted might meet a short-term need, but it acted powerfully to destroy men's loyalty to their ship and their officers. This was always to some extent a necessity of wartime operations, but it seems to have become a serious problem during the American War. As early as 1776 Lord Sandwich observed that:

it is to be wished that every ship should form a regular ship's company, which will be much broken into if we go on borrowing and lending;[20]

and in 1783 Nelson complained that:

the disgust of the Seamen of the Navy is all owing to the infernal plan of turning them over from Ship to Ship, so that Men cannot be attached to their officers, or the officers care two-pence about them.[21]

His friend Collingwood thought exactly the same:

There is one thing in the use of those [men] we have which I think is ill judged, the frequent shifting of them from ship to ship, and change of officers so that people do not feel themselves permanently established. To make the best use of all the powers of a body of men it is necessary the officers shou'd know the characters and abilities of their people, and that the people shou'd feel an attachment to their officers, which can only exist when they have served some time together.[22]

The worse the shortage of men, the more difficult it was to avoid this experiment, but it gravely damaged men's loyalty and morale, and was a powerful incentive to desertion.[23] It made it much harder for men to join or rejoin the officers of their choice, for not all possessed the talent, or luck, of Barret Bonden:

19. Rodger, *The Wooden World*, pp. 194–197 & App. IV.
20. Rodger, *The Wooden World*, p. 152.
21. Sir N. H. Nicolas, *The Despatches and Letters of Vice Admiral Lord Viscount Nelson*, 7 vols (London: [n. pub.], 1844–46), I, 76.
22. C. Collingwood to Dr. A. Carlyle, 20 Mar 1795, in *The Private Correspondence of Admiral Lord Collingwood*, ed. by Edward Hughes, Navy Records Society Vol. 98, (1957), 66.
23. Rodger, *The Wooden World*, pp. 195–197.

How did he come to be at liberty at such a time, and how had he managed to traverse the great man-hungry port without being pressed? It would be useless to ask him; he would only answer with a pack of lies.[24]

Tactless as well as useless, for many men deserted from one warship to join another whose officers they preferred.[25]

Perhaps the gravest material decline in seamen's conditions between 1750 and 1800 was caused by inflation. The seaman's wage (an able seaman received 22s. 6d. a lunar month net of fixed deductions) had been established as long ago as 1653, but it seems to have remained more or less competitive with peacetime wages in merchant ships for at least a century. In wartime wages rose to levels which the Navy could never match directly, but it had the means to establish loyal cadres of long-serving men who could form the nucleus of wartime expansion. From the 1760s, however, wages in the merchant service rose steadily, and by the outbreak of war in 1793 the Navy had fallen well behind. How far is difficult to say with precision, for wages in merchantmen varied from trade to trade, port to port and season to season. Recent work suggests that in the first half of the eighteenth century wages averaged about 29s. a calendar month in peacetime and 42s. in wartime.[26] The Seamen of the London River (where wages were generally higher than at other ports) successfully struck for 40s. a month in 1768.[27] In 1792 a seamen in the Baltic trade might earn 30s. a month, but during the war this rose to as much as five guineas.[28] By 1815 merchant seamen's wages in various trades ranged from 35s. to 60s; though in all cases they were subject to heavier and more arbitrary deductions than in the Navy.[29] Probably Captain Pakenham was exaggerating when he told the Admiralty in 1796 that seamen could get four times as much money in the merchant service, but undoubtedly the naval wage by then was much less than merchantmen paid even in peacetime.[30] This, together with the operation of the bounty system which often had the effects of rewarding landmen more highly than seamen, was the

24. Patrick O'Brian, *Post Captain* (London: Collins, 1972), p. 176.
25. Rodger, *The Wooden World*, pp. 193–195.
26. Marcus Rediker, *Between the Devil and the Deep Blue Sea: Merchant Seamen, Pirates and the Anglo-American Maritime World 1700–1750* (Cambridge: Cambridge University Press, 1987), pp. 304–305. These averages must conceal wide variations and it is not clear how representative the sample is.
27. Public Record Office, ADM 7/299 No. 40.
28. Simon Ville, 'Wages, Prices and Profitability in the Shipping Industry during the Napoleonic Wars: A Case Study', *Journal of Transport History*, 3rd Series II, (1981), No. 1, 48–51.
29. Jon Press, 'Wages in the Merchant Navy, 1815–54', *Journal of Transport History*, 3rd Series II, (1981), No. 2, 48.
30. *Private Papers of George, Second Earl Spencer*, ed. by Julian S. Corbett, 2 vols Navy Records Society, Vol. 48 (1914), 105–107.

principal grievance of the Spithead mutineers in 1797.[31] They secured an increase to 28s. a month net for an able seamen, and in 1806 this was again raised to 32s. net.[32]

By the late 1790s there were therefore several material disadvantages to life in the Navy which had grown up, or at least grown much worse, since the 1750s. It may be, however, that they were not the only or even the most serious social problems of the Service. It has been argued that the Navy in Anson's day was a product of its times, largely innocent of the tensions of class-consciousness, held together by internal bonds of mutual dependence between patrons and followers which threw officers and their men into close contact. In such a world the distant, and almost feeble authority of the Admiralty counted for much less than the officers' powers to reward, and their need of reliable followers.[33] As a social system it offered strong incentives to mutual accommodation, and both officers and men were reluctant to push disputes to extremes. If the men had occasion to complain, they generally found senior officers who took them seriously. If complaints were not met, the resulting mutinies invariably conformed to established rules which confined them to the status of a sort of formal demonstration. Only mutinies openly led or covertly incited by officers broke the rules, and only then did authority react with severity. Respectable mutinies conducted in accordance with Service tradition, in pursuit of proper objectives such as the payment of overdue wages or the ejection of intolerable officers, could expect to get what they demanded, and with no question of punishing the mutineers.[34]

It is clear that this solidarity, almost intimacy between officers and men was breaking down by the 1790s, and was largely destroyed by the effects of the French Revolution. It is perilous to generalise about changing attitudes, especially on the basis of anecdotal evidence, but there can be little doubt that this was a period of growing class-consciousness and tension between officers and men. It shows in an increasing intolerance of complaint, and a notably harsher attitude to mutinies. As early as 1780 a mutiny at Spithead, on grounds completely justified both by tradition and the letter of the law, was treated with considerable severity, though the incapacity of the admiral commanding may have been a factor in this case.[35] By the early 1790s even successful mutinies had become extremely

31. Gill, *The Naval Mutinies*, p. 264.
32. Gill, *The Naval Mutinies*, p. 35;
G. E. Manwaring & Bonamy Dobrée, *The Floating Republic* (London: Geoffrey Bles, 1935), p. 257.
33. Rodger, *The Wooden World*, pp. 119–124 & 205–206.
34. Ibid., pp. 237–244.
35. *The Private Papers of John, Earl of Sandwich*, ed. by G. R. Barnes & J. H. Owen, Navy Records Society, Vols. 69, 71, 75 & 78, (1932–38), III, 246–247;
Rodger, *The Wooden World*, p. 125.

risky affairs,[36] and the course of the French Revolution confirmed officers in the idea that any complaint, or even a hint of independent thought, called for harsh repression. Of the 1797 Spithead mutiny, conducted with great moderation and good sense for entirely traditional objectives, one captain remarked,

> . . . the character of the present mutiny is perfectly French. The singularity of it consists in the great secrecy and patience with which they waited for a thorough union before it broke out, and the immediate establishment of *a system of terror.*[37]

Sir William Hotham thought the concession of cheap postage to the ratings had been a fatal move, since encouraging men to read and write letters was bound to tempt them to think for themselves,[38] while Collingwood for the same reason deprecated even allowing ships' companies to subscribe to patriotic collections.[39] Significantly, it is at this period that officers came to think of the Marines as 'men which we look to in general for protection' in the event of mutiny,[40] something quite foreign to the objects of the corps as established in 1755. By 1797 the Admiralty no longer felt that officers' promises to their men needed to be kept if it were inconvenient to do so.[41]

In parallel with the widening gulf between officers and men came a growing snobbery among the officers.[42] In 1794 the Admiralty signalled its distaste for levelling principles by replacing the old ratings indiscriminately, with three classes of boy, distinguished on a class basis.[43] The coming of peace in 1815 allowed the process to be taken further, with a widespread sifting of the commissioned officers ironically known as 'passing for a gentleman'.[44] In all this the Service simply reflected the

36. Jonathan Neale, *The Cutlass and the Lash: Mutiny and Discipline in Nelson's Navy* (London: Pluto, 1985), pp. 5–7 & 87–91.
Some allowance has to be made for this author's anachronistic preconceptions, but his evidence is eloquent.
37. *Spencer Papers*, II, 112.
38. A. M. W. Stirling, *Pages & Portraits from the Past, being the Private Papers of Admiral Sir William Hotham, G. C. B. Admiral of the Red*, 2 vols (London: Jenkins, 1919), II, 119.
39. Oliver Warner, *The Life and Letters of Vice-Admiral Lord Collingwood* (London: Oxford University Press, 1968), p. 85.
40. *Spencer Papers*, II, 119.
41. *Spencer Papers*, II, 143.
42. Michael Lewis, *A Social History of the Navy 1793–1815* (London: Allen & Unwin, 1960), pp. 42–43, 159 & 269.
See also: N. A. M. Rodger, 'Officers, Gentlemen and their Education, 1793–1860', in *Les Empires en Guerre et Paix, 1793–1860*, ed. by Edward Freeman (Vincennes: Service historique de al marine, 1990), pp. 139–151.
43. Lewis, *Social History of the Navy*, pp. 89–90 & 152–153.
44. David Hannay, *Naval Courts Martial* (Cambridge: Cambridge University Press, 1914), p. 44;
N. A. M. Rodger, 'Officers, Gentlemen and their Education', pp. 139–151.

changing climate of opinion in British society ashore, and the ratings generally shared their officers' values. Many of their complaints were directed at low-born officers,[45] and it is striking to hear the words of the mutineers in one ship at the Nor in 1797, sending two of their officers ashore:

> The first Lieutenant, they said, was a *blackguard* and *no* gentleman, and by no means fit for being an officer. That the Master was like him; both of them a *disgrace* to His Majesty's Service.[46]

The most zealous defender of the privileges of birth could hardly have put it better, and the officer who tells this anecdote remarks that 'we all had proofs enough of the correctness of their observations'.

With growing class-consciousness and mutual suspicion between quarterdeck and lower deck went a steady rise in the severity of punishments both formal and informal, and a growing tendency to indiscriminate brutality. Although we have little systematic research, it is certain that court martial sentences increased as the century went on, and probable that the same was true of flogging at captains' discretion.[47] In principle no captain might award more than twelve lashes without a court martial, but in practice two or three dozen was common, and as many as 63 or 72 are recorded.[48] This in itself was not usually a grievance, for the cat remained, as it had always been, the good man's defence against his idle, troublesome or thieving shipmate; it was the growth of casual and indiscriminate brutality which aroused so much resentment. As one ship's company put it to Lord Howe in 1797:

> My Lord, we do not wish you to understand that we have the least intention of encroaching on the punishments necessary for the preservation of good order and discipline necessary to be preserved in H.M. navy, but to crush the spirit of tyranny and oppression so much practised and delighted in, contrary to the spirit or intent of any laws of our country.[49]

45. For example: *The Adventures of John Wetherell*, ed. by C. S. Forester (London: Michael Joseph, 1954), p. 15.
46. 'Peter Cullen's Journal', ed. by H. G. Thursfield, in *Five Naval Journals, 1789–1817*, Navy Records Society, Vol. 91, (1951).
47. PRO, ADM 12/22;
Hannay, *Naval Courts Martial*, p. 68;
Peter Kemp, *The British Sailor: A Social History of the Lower Deck* (London: Dent, 1970), pp. 112–113 & 185;
N. A. M. Rodger, 'The Inner Life of the Navy, 1750–1800: Change or Decay?', in *Guerres et Paix 1660–1815* (Vincennes: Service historique de la marine, 1987), p. 173.
48. Neale, *The Cutlass and the Lash*, p. 31.
49. Gill, *The Naval Mutinies*, p. 278.

Or, in Dr Maturin's words:

> The world in general, and even more your briney world, accepts flogging. It is
> this perpetual arbitrary harassing, bullying, hitting, brow-beating, starting
> these capricious torments, spreadeagling, gagging – this general atmosphere
> of oppression.[50]

It would be tedious to recite the many examples to be found in both reliable and unreliable sources, but two, not extreme, cases may be cited. Captain James Burney reported serving in a ship in which the maintop-men were flogged because another ship had swayed up her yards faster,[51] while in 1794 a petty officer was court martialled and flogged for refusing to 'thrash the men up' from below.[52] In both cases what was shocking to lower deck opinion was not simply the brutality but the fact that the sufferers were prime seamen, as it shocked Jack Aubrey to hear that his coxswain Bonden had been flogged by Captain Corbett.[53] The ignorant landmen had always been herded about their work with blows, but that smart topmen should suffer likewise offended every seaman's idea of natural justice and the social order within a ship's company. Resentment at such abuse of authority led the mutineers of 1797 to put ashore large numbers of their officers. At Spithead 114 officers were removed, including four captains and Vice-Admiral Colpoys.[54]

It is possible that part of the problem was the many inexperienced or simply bad officers brought in by rapid wartime expansion. This was certainly the opinion of some contemporaries; Collingwood condemned captains who, 'endeavouring to conceal, by great severity, their own unskilfulness and want of attention, beat the men into a state of insubordination.'[55]

No doubt this was part of the problem, but it was certainly not the whole. Behind the growth in class-consciousness and mutual suspicion between officers and men lay another secular trend which affected the Navy along with the rest of society: the growth of state power and centralisation. In the 1750s the authority of the Admiralty still largely relied on co-operation with senior officers whose patronage represented much of the real power within the Navy. By the 1790s the Admiralty was in

50. O'Brian, *Post Captain*, p. 203.
51. Kemp, *The British Sailor*, p. 179.
52. Hannay, *Naval Courts Martial*, p. 66.
53. Patrick O'Brian, *The Mauritius Command* (London: Collins, 1977), p. 67.
54. Gill, *The Naval Mutinies*, pp. 79 & 269–276.
55. G. I. Newnham Collingwood, *A Selection from the Public and Private Correspondence of Vice-Admiral Lord Collingwood: Interspersed with Memoirs of his Life*, 4th edn (London: James Ridgway, 1829), p. 58;
See also: Warner, *Lord Collingwood*, p. 97.

process of taking much of that power into its own hands. A succession of gifted and arrogant administrative reformers, notably Sir Charles Middleton, Lord St. Vincent and General Bentham, attempted to improve the discipline of the Navy, and the efficiency of the Navy Board and the dockyards, by the method traditional among reformers in every age: centralisation in their own hands.[56] This was only one example of the way that the growing complexity of society and the pressures of a desperate war forced, or permitted, the British government to become more efficient, more centralised and more powerful.[57] One of the effects of this development in the Navy was to weaken the old personal bonds of mutual obligation between officers and their followers which had been one of the major cohesive forces of the Service in earlier years, and replace them with an artificial discipline. Where officers' powers to reward had weakened, their powers to punish had to grow to compensate. When officers and men were less and less known and beholden to one another as individuals, they needed an impersonal authority to regulate their relations.

An illustration of this trend is the Admiralty's attitude to captains' personal followings. In Anson's day captains and admirals were almost always allowed to take at least their particular followers with them from ship to ship, and they were strongly encouraged, indeed compelled, to use their local influence to recruit men in their home districts.[58] During the American War Sandwich favoured the same methods, and publicly praised officers who recruited their own ship's companies from among their followers:

Such a mode of procuring men creates a confidence between the commanding officer and the seaman. The former is in some measure bound to act humanely to the man who gives him a preference of serving under him; and the latter will find his interest and duty unite, in behaving well under a person from whom he is taught to expect every present reasonable indulgence, and future favour. These, and other instances of a similar nature which have come to my knowledge, have enabled me to point out one thing that might, in my opinion, be the means of furthering the naval service; that is, trusting less to the assistance of the Admiralty board, and giving every possible encouragement to the captains appointed to the command of ships to complete their own crews.[59]

56. Rodger, 'Inner Life of the Navy', pp. 176–177.
57. Clive Emsley, *British Society and the French Wars, 1793–1815*, (London: Macmillan, 1979), p. 179.
58. Rodger, *The Wooden World*, pp. 155–157.
59. William Cobett, *The Parliamentary History of England*, 36 vols (London: R. Bagshaw, 1806–20), XVIII, 1261. Sandwich was referring specifically to Captains Philemon Pownoll and John McBride.

It seems that during the American War about 230,000 men were raised for the Navy, of which the shore-based Impress Service raised 116,357 or about half. These in turn can be divided into 72,658 who were paid bounty as volunteers, leaving 43,699 pressed men. Recruiting by men-of-war or their tenders stopping merchantmen at sea, and direct recruitment by ships of volunteers ashore, accounted for the other half. In all cases these figures refer to individual instances of recruitment; the Navy lost so many men by desertion and otherwise that it had to recruit two men for every one borne on a ship's books, and it must be that in many cases the same men were recruited more than once.[60] It is not possible to say exactly what proportion of these figures represent men volunteering to serve with particular officers, but it must certainly represent a considerable part of the volunteers both ashore and afloat. It is certain that captains were individually responsible, for raising half the men in the Navy, and consequently that their influence was bound to be felt in every aspect of recruiting. As Commodore Rowley wrote to Lord Sandwich in November 1778,

Most of the *Monarch*'s men have been of my own getting and have been tried, and many of the men would not have come into the Navy if it had not been to sail with me.[61]

In such cases, the captain was not only supplying the Navy's need of manpower, but acquiring a great deal of independent authority in the process. He and his men were personally linked, while the Admiralty was beholden to him for his efforts.

By the end of the century this had completely changed. Naval recruitment was almost entirely in the hands of a centralised organisation, the Impress Service, and individual captains were not encouraged to raise their own men. A particularly favoured officer like Captain Sir Edward Pellew, the darling of Lord Chatham, was still allowed to take men of his own raising from ship to ship in the early years of the Revolutionary War,[62] but by then this was an exceptional indulgence, not permitted to other captains, or even admirals.[63] Though the Navy was desperately short of

60. R. G. Usher, 'Royal Navy Impressment during the American Revolution', in *Mississippi Valley Historical Review*, XXXVII (1951), 673–688, (677–682).

61. National Maritime Museum, SAN/F/17/8.

62. C. Northcote Parkinson, *Edward Pellew, Viscount Exmouth, Admiral of the Red* (London: Methuen, 1934), pp. 96, 115 & 213;

N. A. M. Rodger, '"A Little Navy of your own making". Admiral Boscawen and the Cornish Connection in the Royal Navy', in *Parameters of British Naval Power 1650–1850*, ed. by Michael Duffy (Exeter: University of Exeter, 1992), pp. 82–92, (pp. 89–90).

63. P. S. Graeme, *Orkney and the Last Great War, Being Excerpts from the Correspondence of Admiral Alexander Graeme of Graemeshall, 1788–1815* (Kirkwall: W. Peace, 1915), pp. 19–26;

G. Cornwallis-West, *The Life and Letters of Admiral Cornwallis* (London: Holden, 1927), p. 263.

men, the Admiralty was prepared to forbid captains raising men by private arrangement,[64] and the reason seems to have been that the process would establish links of mutual obligation independent of Admiralty authority. What had been the real cement of the Navy fifty years before, the 'immemorial custom of the service' to which Aubrey appealed when Admiral Drury tried to deprive him of his followers, had become subversive of the new discipline.[65]

All the trends we have been considering tended to make the life of the ordinary rating worse in 1800 than it had been fifty years before. Commanded by officers to whom he was an entire stranger, cut off from them by a gulf of mutual incomprehension and suspicion, subject to harsh discipline (and in some ships to capricious brutality), forbidden leave for years at a time, his lot was undoubtedly worse than his predecessor's in the Navy of Anson's time. Against all these trends, however, we must set another which was beginning to work in the opposite direction. By 1800 there were a considerable number of officers in the Navy, most of them Evangelists or influenced by evangelical piety, who brought to their ships that high-minded conception of duty and moral obligation which we consider typically Victorian. It is at this period that church services – a marked eccentricity in the Navy of the 1750s – began to be common-place aboard ship. Of Dr Byrn's sample of ships serving in the Leeward Islands between 1784 and 1812, 40% held divine services; moreover 18% received scriptures distributed (on request) by the Naval and Military Bible Society, which is an indicator of officers with evangelical convictions. Collingwood is a good example of this new type of officer: his social and political ideas were rigidly conservative, he was a firm disciplinarian, and had a horror of the least sign of independence from his men. But he attended to their material and spiritual wants with scrupulous care, he condemned excessive flogging as 'big with the most dangerous con-sequences, and subversive of all real discipline', and he insisted that his officers address their men with courtesy:

> If you do not know a man's name, call him sailor, and not you-sir, and such other appellations; they are offensive and improper.[66]

In return he received the devotion of all who served under him:

> A better seaman – a better friend to seamen – a great lover and more zealous defender of his country's rights and honour, never trod a quarter-deck. He

64. Rodger, 'Inner Life of the Navy' pp. 177–178.
65. Patrick O'Brian, *The Fortune of War* (London: Collins, 1979), p. 18.
66. Warner, *Lord Collingwood*, pp. 110–111;
Collingwood, *Collingwood Correspondence*, pp. 51–54.

and his favourite dog Bounce – were well known to every member of the crew.
How attentive he was to the health and comfort and happiness of his crew! a
man who could not be happy under him, could have been happy no where; a
look of displeasure from him was as a bad as a dozen at the gangway from
another man.[67]

Collingwood was an exceptional officer, but by no means unique, and the
sort of approach to discipline which he exemplified began to be more
influential in the Navy in the early years of the new century. Aubrey for
one, an officer of rather different upbringing, agreed entirely,

> that none but a fool started, struck, beat or abused hands for not knowing
> their duty when those hands could not conceivably know it, having only just
> gone to sea; that any officerlike man knew the names of all the people in his
> watch; that it was quite as easy to call out Herapath as You, sir.[68]

The new edition in 1806 of the Regulations and Instructions removed the
limit of twelve lashes which a captain might award at his own discretion,
and which had long been a dead letter, but only four months later the
Admiralty forbade running the gauntlet, in 1809 it forbade 'starting' (the
common practice of officers and petty officers of 'encouraging' the men
with sticks or rope's ends), and in 1811 it instituted quarterly punishment
returns. These were scrutinised, for in the following year Admiral Laforey
in the West Indies was ordered to check the excessive flogging in his
squadron.[69] It was some time before all these orders were properly
observed, and a long time before the new attitudes permeated the Service
(if only because it was an extremely long time before the officers bred up
during the Napoleonic War retired from service), but they represented
the visible trend in 1800. Not everyone welcomed it; in that year a
disgruntled surgeon was dismissed the Service at court martial for
complaining that the captains of the Navy had turned republican and
favoured the men over their officers.[70] That certainly never happened, and
in the Victorian Navy relations between quarterdeck and lower deck were
if possible even more distant and class-ridden, but they were considerably
more humane.

It is instructive to draw a contrast in leadership between generations.
Officers like Collingwood looked after their men from a deep sense of
moral, and more particularly religious, duty; the image of paternal care,

67. *Landsman Hay: The Memoirs of Robert Hay, 1789–1847*, ed. by M. D. Hay (London:
Rupert Hart-Davis, 1953), p. 66.
68. Patrick O'Brian, *Desolation Island* (London: Collins, 1978), p. 93.
69. Byrn, *Crime and Punishment*, pp. 19–20.
70. Hannay, *Naval Courts Martial*, p. 66.

and the Biblical resonance which it aroused, were never far from their minds.[71] Fifty years before an equally outstanding captain of ships and of men, Augustus Hervey, had aroused the loyalty of his people without the aid of any detectable moral or religious feelings. For his generation good followers were a professional necessity, and the officer who did not look after his men could not expect loyalty, obedience, or success in a demanding and dangerous career.[72] By Collingwood's day a system of discipline had been established which could and did support an officer in his authority even if he did nothing to deserve respect, even if he was known to be cruel and tyrannical. Captain Robert Corbett was infamous throughout the Navy for his mindless brutality; he aroused complaint, mutiny and reprimands by court martial, but was repeatedly rewarded with new commands until eventually he was killed in action, possibly by his own men.[73] The Admiralty of fifty years before certainly did what it could to support captains' authority, but the fates of Captain William Hervey or Captain Penhallow Cuming show that it would not countenance brutality.[74]

On the graph which might be drawn connecting Augustus Hervey in the 1750s with Cuthbert Collingwood half a century later, Jack Aubrey, though younger than Collingwood, represents an older style of command, one which still retained something of the rough intimacy of the old Navy. Definitely no Evangelist, nor one whose contacts with men like Mr Ellis could be said to have been fruitful,[75] he nevertheless represents the new world in his sense of obligation towards his men, as distinct from a mere understanding that it was in his interest to treat them well. There were other, probably many other captains in the Navy like him, under whom good men were happy to serve:

I like this ship much better than any other the Capt. whose name is Moorson is of very amiable disposition the officers all merit esteem and the ship is of great force . . . a man of war is much better in wartime than an indiaman for we laught at and seek the danger they have so much reason to dread and avoid I find it the very reverse of what was represented to me to be for when we have done our duty we may go to the fire to sleep or read or write or anything.[76]

71. Byrn, *Crime and Punishment*, p. 102;
Warner, *Lord Collingwood*, p. 82.
72. *Augustus Hervey's Journal*, ed. by David Erskine, 2nd edn (London: Kimber, 1954).
73. Lloyd, *The British Seaman*, pp. 243–245. O'Brian, *The Mauritiu Command*, p. 223.
74. Rodger, *The Wooden World*, pp. 211–212, 214 & 235.
75. O'Brian, *Master and Commander*, p. 231.
76. J. Powell, topman of the *Revenge*, to his mother, 12 Jun 1805 (original spelling) in *British Naval Documents 1204–1960*, ed. by John B. Hattendorf and others, Navy Records Society, Vol. 131 (1993), No. 330.

We must beware of exaggerating the degree to which relations between officers and men had changed for the worse. Ill-treatment attracts notice, and was already attracting notice at the time, out of proportion to its frequency. Yet change was undoubtedly happening, in parallel with the changes which British society was undergoing. The old social order with its rough informality and its strong sense of solidarity in the shared dangers of the seafaring life could not possibly have survived the growth of class and political consciousness ashore. The French Revolution, in particular, poisoned the relations between officers and men for generations, perhaps for ever. Moreover some of the changes within the Navy paralleled those taking place in working lives ashore. A seaman's work, skilled, varied and independent as it was, never resembled that of a factory hand, but the new discipline moved as far in that direction as it could. In place of the irregular, almost anarchic ways of the old Navy, officers began to adopt the image of the ship as a machine, her men reduced to so many mechanical components.[77] At the same time the rise of the idea of duty, undoubtedly influenced by the evangelical temperament, was in time to lead to material improvements in the life of the common seaman analogous to those produced ashore by the Factory Acts. Even now, however, nearly two centuries later, when the conditions of service of the naval rating have changed totally and the concept of duty towards subordinates is a commonplace of command, discipline remains more formal, artificial and perhaps uneasy than it was in the 1750s. It is arguable that by 1800 the crucial transition to a 'modern' social structure, and attitudes to command and authority to match it, was already well under way if not completed. Our existing knowledge, however, which is rich but fragmentary, calls for imagination even more than learning to interpret it. How far the modern naval officer stands from the world of Jack Aubrey and Stephen Maturin no one can say with more authority than Patrick O'Brian.

The author is indebted to the Association of North Sea Societies and the Stavanger Maritime Museum for permission to draw on material used in the author's essay 'Shipboard Life in the Georgian Navy, 1750–1800; the Decline of the Old Order?', which appeared in *The North Sea: Twelve Essays on Social History of Maritime Labour*, ed by Lewis R. Fischer and others (Stavanger: 1992), pp. 29–39.

This essay is taken from
Patrick O'Brian, Critical Appreciations and a Bibliography,
edited by A. E. Cunningham, and is reprinted here
by kind permission of the British Library

77. Lewis, *Social History of the Navy*, pp. 275–276.

A MISERABLE SET OF CONVICTS

Secret Instructions to Lieutenant Cook, 30 June 1768

Whereas the making Discoverys of Countries hitherto unknown . . . will redound greatly to the Honour of this Nation . . . and may tend greatly to the advancement of the Trade and Navigation thereof; and Whereas there is reason to imagine that a Continent or Land of great extent, may be found to the Southward of the Tract lately made by Captⁿ Wallis . . . You are therefore in Pursuance of His Majesty's Pleasure hereby requir'd and directed to put to Sea with the Bark you Command so soon as the Observation of the Transit of the Planet Venus shall be finished and observe the following Instructions.

Two years after he received secret instructions to sail in anticipated discovery of a 'Land of great extent' near the recently discovered New Zealand, Lieutenant James Cook arrived in what would soon be named Botany Bay in New South Wales at the helm of the *Endeavour*. On board were the naturalists Joseph Banks and Daniel Solander, who over the course of Cook's epic voyage had employed themselves busily collecting specimen samples of the flora and fauna of the extraordinary new worlds in which they found themselves. The remarkable samples that they collected, accounting for about 110 new genera and 1,300 new species, gave Botany Bay its name, and would go on to form the core of the collection of the British Natural History Museum. Many of the samples are still preserved there today, some in their original collection trays, others carefully pressed between the pages of specimen books and beautifully illustrated by Sydney Parkinson.

You are to employ yourself diligently in exploring as great an Extent of the Coast as you can ... You are also carefully to observe the Nature of the Soil, and the Products thereof; the Beasts and Fowls that inhabit or frequent it, the Fishes that are to be found ... and in Case you find any Mines, Minerals, or valuable Stones you are to bring home Specimens of each, as also such Specimens of the Seeds of the Trees, Fruits and Grains as you may be able to collect.

When, in 1775, the American Revolutionary War cut off Britain's access to the vast open reaches of North America that it had hitherto put to happy use as a destination for sentenced criminals, it was Joseph Banks who first suggested the new colony of Australia as an alternative destination for Britain's unwanted and overcrowded convicts. Twenty years after British sailors first set foot on Australia, 11 ships landed in Botany Bay with a cargo of over 700 convicts, who were promptly put to work to build the colony that would be their home.

Conditions in the new colony were tough – but so were the convicts. They had to be in order to survive the rigours of their journey south, as Watkin Tench – a marine who sailed with the first convict fleet – recounted in his *Narrative of the Expedition to Botany Bay*:

> After a passage of exactly thirty-six weeks from Portsmouth, we happily effected our arduous undertaking, with such a train of unexampled blessings as hardly ever attended a fleet in a like predicament. Of two hundred and twelve marines we lost only one; and of seven hundred and seventy-five convicts, put on board in England, but twenty-four perished in our route . . . [When] the reader is told, that some of the necessary articles allowed to ships on a common passage to West Indies, were withheld from us; that portable

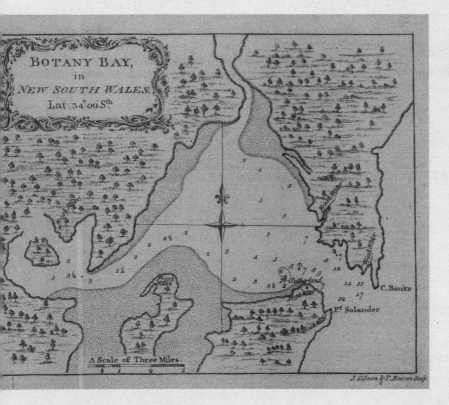

soup, wheat, and pickled vegetables were not allowed; and that an inadequate quantity of essence of malt was the only antiscorbutic supplied, his surprise will redouble at the result of the voyage. For it must be remembered, that the people thus sent out were not a ship's company starting with every advantage of health and good living, which a state of freedom produces; but the major part a miserable set of convicts, emaciated from confinement, and in want of cloaths, and almost every convenience to render so long a passage tolerable.

On land, the convicts were worked hard and severely punished for any misdemeanours. Death was often the sentence for crimes ranging from petty theft to attempts to escape, and was meted out regardless of class, education or background, as the following extract from Tench's account illustrates:

Samuel Peyton, convict, for having on the evening of the King's birth-day broke open an officer's marquee, with an intent to commit robbery, of which he was fully convicted, had sentence of death passed on him at the same time . . . [He] was but twenty years of age, the greatest part of which had been invariably passed in the commission of crimes, that at length terminated in his ignominious end.

The following letter, written by a fellow convict to the sufferer's unhappy mother, I shall make no apology for presenting to the reader; it affords a melancholy proof, that not the ignorant and untaught only have provoked the justice of their country to banish them to this remote region.

Sydney Cove, Port Jackson,
New South Wales, 24th June, 1788

My dear and honoured mother!

. . . My dear mother! with what agony of soul do I dedicate the few last moments of my life, to bid you an eternal adieu! my doom being irrevocably fixed, and ere this hour to-morrow I shall have quitted this vale of wretchedness, to enter into an unknown and endless eternity. I will not distress your tender maternal feelings by any long comment on the cause of my present misfortune. Let it therefore suffice to say, that impelled by that strong propensity to evil, which neither the virtuous precepts nor example of the best of parents could eradicate, I have at length fallen an unhappy, though just, victim to my own follies.

. . . The affliction which this will cost you, I hope the Almighty will enable you to bear. Banish from your memory all my former indiscretions, and let the cheering hope of a happy meeting hereafter, console you for my loss. Sincerely penitent for my sins; sensible of the justice of my conviction and sentence, and firmly relying on the merits of a Blessed Redeemer, I am at perfect peace with all mankind, and trust I shall yet experience that peace, which this world cannot give. Commend my soul to the Divine mercy.

I bid you an eternal farewell.

Your unhappy dying Son,
SAMUEL PEYTON

JACK AND STEPHEN,
THEIR TRAVELS

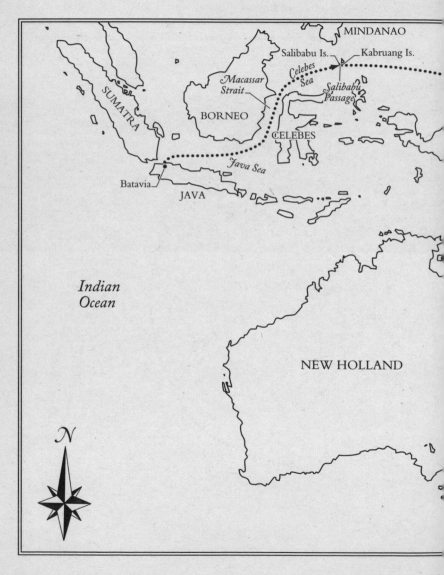

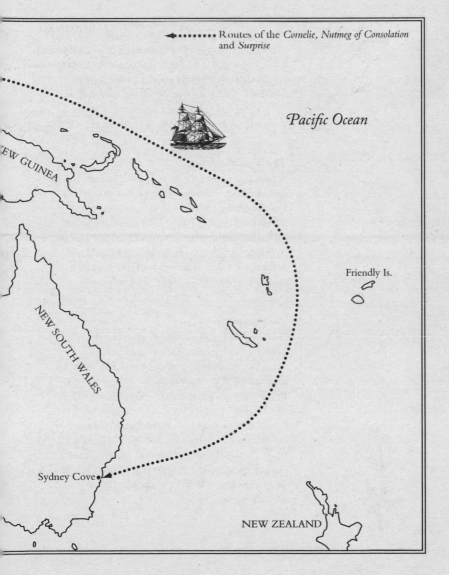

Routes of the *Cornelie, Nutmeg of Consolation*
and *Surprise*

Pacific Ocean

NEW GUINEA

NEW SOUTH WALES

Friendly Is.

Sydney Cove

NEW ZEALAND

HAVE YOU READ?

The next three books in the Aubrey-Maturin series.

READ ON

Clarissa Oakes
Unexpected orders and temperamental winds direct Jack and Stephen towards the Friendly Isles. Friendly they may be, but to whom? As Jack strains to win another island pearl for the Crown, secrets and lies amongst his crew conceal a stowaway who might prove as dangerous as the ferocious battle that follows.

The Wine-Dark Sea
A taut pursuit of an American privateer sends Jack and Stephen speeding from the South Pacific along their mission route to Peru. Their secret objective – to foment insurrection and destabilise Spanish and French interests in South America – is undermined when Stephen's cover is blown and he must flee across the Andes to Chile, and safety.

The Commodore
Back in England at last, Stephen finds himself in the role of single parent and must act quickly to protect those he loves from traitorous agents at the highest levels. Personal concerns are set aside, however, when orders arrive for the friends to set sail for Africa's west coast at the head of a mighty squadron charged with disrupting the slave trade. It is a doughty mission, but one that pales next to their true charge, which all too soon sees them hurtling towards home – and into desperate battle.

FIND OUT MORE

Joseph Banks's collection is still housed at
the Natural History Museum, London
(www.nhm.ac.uk). Many of his papers are
held in the Mitchell and Dixson collections
at the State Library of New South Wales,
in Sydney, Australia. These amount to
approximately 10,000 manuscript pages
and include correspondence – principally
letters received, but also reports, invoices
and accounts – and journals, plus a small
quantity of maps, charts and watercolours.
However, for those unable to travel to
Australia to view the collection, some of
his papers have been digitised, including
his journal from the *Endeavour* voyage, and
can be viewed online or downloaded at
http://www2.sl.nsw.gov.au/banks/.

A Narrative of the Expedition to Botany Bay
by Watkin Tench has been published by
ebooks@Adelaide, and can be downloaded
or read in its entirety at http://ebooks.
adelaide.edu.au/t/tench/watkin/botany/. It
is a fascinating account, which encompasses
the rigours of the sea voyage, the wonder
of the fleet's arrival at Botany Bay, uneasy
interactions with the Aborigines, and the
trial and punishment of convicts.

Many online resources exist for those
interested in tracking the convict history
of Australia, most aimed at users hoping to
trace their genealogy. Ancestry.co.uk allows
database searches for specific names, dates
and ships, and in some cases images of
the original Transportation Registers –
including that listing the 'unhappy dying'
Samuel Peyton.

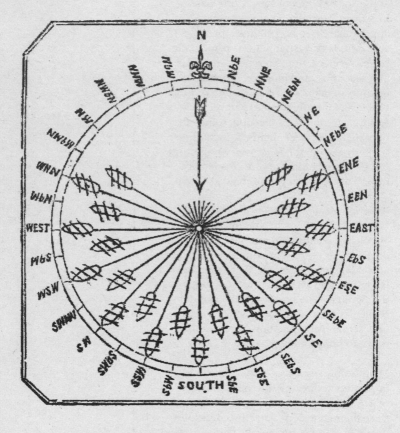